Pulled Into Nazareth

By Connie Kronlokken

The author believes that all quotations in this book have been used under the "commentary and criticism" fair use of copyrighted materials.

Published by

Lightly
Held
Books

DEDICATION

To Don S., Richard, Priscilla, Don E., Rachel, Brad
and to the memory of David B. and David P.

Pulled Into Nazareth

Paul carried his sister's small son Christopher halfway up Nob Hill to where the old Ford station wagon was parked. It was early, the middle of June, and the sun sent shafts of light down through the fog. Paul could feel Christopher's sleepy head, his soft hair against his neck. Crossing an intersection, they saw the painted cable car climbing California Street one block away and heard its clanging bell.

Stopping so that Christopher could watch the cable car, Paul turned around to look at his sisters. Line's face was also sleepy, her eyes big and lazy from a late shift at the hospital the night before. Four years older than Paul, her red-gold hair was piled untidily on her head. Line made faces at her son as she wrapped a shawl tighter around her shoulders. Her sleepiness hadn't stopped her from going out at 6 a.m. to wish Paul farewell.

Marty, a year younger than Line, looked wide awake, though she hadn't combed her fine dark curls. She was up with the sun every day of the week, going to work in an office. Even with thick-rimmed glasses, she was prettier than Paul remembered. She carried the day-pack Paul had stuffed his clothes into, and the army surplus feather sleeping bag Dad had found for Paul before he left home.

I guess we're grownups now, Paul thought as he turned back and headed up a side street. The three siblings had always been close. As a child, Line was the ring-leader; Sparky, Dad called her. Marty and Paul had joined her in everything she did.

A pang of fear shot through Paul, but it felt like adrenaline. He did not want to leave after a week spent tromping around San Francisco with his sisters, but he was also determined. He was headed into his future, to Alaska, where no Mikkelson had gone before. Mother's sister, Aunt Mabel, had been an early missionary there, but of his own family, Paul was the first. Finally ready to strike out on his own, he wanted to get far away from the

1

fishbowl experience of being a pastor's kid in a small town where everyone knew of him, but no one knew who he was.

Marty had been the family pioneer on the West Coast. She lived first in Berkeley and now in San Francisco, acquiring an elusive boyfriend named Erik, whom Paul never did meet, and a job which paid the rent and bought groceries. Line had recently joined Marty in San Francisco, fleeing violence in Chicago and a husband who was caught up in it, bringing her small son Christopher, not quite two.

Paul's heart heaved over when he saw the green Country Sedan station wagon with the Iowa plates. It couldn't be helped. He would have to leave. The car had sat in its parking spot all week, as they didn't need it in San Francisco. Paul was protecting it for the rigors of the long drive ahead. Paul put Christopher down on his sturdy little feet, unlocked the car and Marty handed him the small packs she carried.

Line put her arms around Paul. "I don't know what to say," she said.

"I think we've said it all," said Marty quietly.

"Thank you so much," said Paul. "I'm so glad I came!" It would have been much shorter to go straight to Fairbanks from Iowa, but with both sisters in San Francisco, Paul could not resist. He smiled at their ruddy faces, then picked up Christopher and bussed his soft pink neck.

Christopher giggled and curled up as if he had been tickled. But Line took him from Paul and put him on her hip. Marty gave Paul a hug and then the two girls stood there as Paul got in the car and turned the ignition. He could give them a ride back down the hill, but there was no sense in it. Goodbyes had already gone on long enough. He closed the door and pulled out, leaving the little trio standing on the sidewalk, waving.

Paul pulled into the morning traffic and in a few minutes was crossing the Golden Gate Bridge going north. The huge iron-red stanchions carrying the cables rose above him into the breaking clouds. Patches of light shone on the water. Paul glanced to the right to see the receding collection of white buildings on the hills that made up the city. Driving north, he entered an arched tunnel painted with a rainbow. Steeling his mind, Paul accelerated up the hill, doing what he had told himself, and everyone else, he was going to do.

Silently Paul reviewed what that was. He wanted to get out where nature was both mother and father, to track animals and learn from the native peoples what they knew about living in the north. He wanted to make enough money to be independent, sharing his love of the world with his students. And he wanted to find a home, a place of his own where the seasonal and star patterns were his to watch and he could stay long enough to learn the weather cycles. A place, he hoped, that had not been spoiled by American softness and comfort.

That was it. It was all he wanted. Paul had had polio as a kid. One of his legs was thinner and weaker than the other, though it didn't keep him from canoeing and even skiing. He had no illusions about homesteading in the bush. He didn't want to trap or hunt animals. But he did hope to get out into the wilderness which surrounded every Alaskan town and just be there.

Paul had been reading the *Fairbanks News-Miner* for months. Fairbanks, on the inner plains between mountain ranges, had extreme weather, but probably not much worse than Moorhead, Minnesota, where Paul had gone to college. Fairbanks was the home of the University of Alaska and there was a lot going on there. The population of Alaska was small, but many residents had chosen it. Paul was one of them.

Through applications, recommendations and phone calls, Paul had secured a job teaching biology and chemistry at Lathrop high school. He didn't feel he knew enough chemistry, but he was sure he could keep ahead of the students. He also knew that native Alaskan kids who wanted to go to high school had to leave their villages and go to the Bureau of Indian Affairs high school at Sitka or board in Fairbanks or Anchorage. According to Marcia, the teacher Paul had met when he was in college, it wasn't easy for them.

Long thoughts assailed Paul as he wound through the mountains of northern California, and into the farming flats of Oregon. He camped at night wherever he happened to be, restricting himself to peanut butter sandwiches, campfire potatoes and onions and the occasional hamburger. Most of his money went for gas.

It was summer and easy living. Paul picked up a couple of longhaired, bearded hitchhikers who told him stories of logging and fishing, helping him see the land he passed through. Paul wished he didn't have to keep pushing on. At night he pulled out his guitar and played, sometimes attracting people to his campfire and music. He skirted Portland and Seattle and in a couple of days, crossed the border into Canada.

In British Columbia, Paul headed north through the Fraser River Valley, which cut between the Canadian Rockies and the coastal range. At first the road snaked through amazing mountains, the tops still white with snow, along the river which carved ever deeper into the earth. It left dry canyon walls and benchlands which were now farmed. Paul flowed along the highway, wondering at the eons preceding men, the action of water on the earth.

But then the earth flattened and the road followed the river straight north. The weather was mild and there was little vegetation, infrequent traffic and many miles between the small towns. The sun didn't set until almost 10 p.m. Paul was further north than he'd ever been, but he still had a long ways to go. At this point in June the sun would be up until 9 p.m. at the Mikkelson summer cabin on Lake Michigami in Minnesota he decided.

Dwarfed by the country and aware of his smallness, Paul tried to be patient with the car. He kept the oil and water topped up in the engine and sometimes took off the distributor cap to make sure the points were clean. Old Green was doing pretty well, he thought, anthropomorphizing it into a companion. But he was worried. Could she go the distance?

As day passed into day, Paul was unnerved by the enormity of what he was doing. No one knew where he was. It was a strange feeling. He wondered if he had ever felt it before. He hated to keep moving, wanted to stretch out on the ground and sleep. At night, Paul watched the Milky Way coursing through the summer triangle, Altair, Deneb, Vega, his head sticking out of his sleeping bag on the tailgate of the station wagon before sleep overcame him.

In Prince George, Paul was greeted by a huge man made of wood with a cap and a big painted smile looking down on the highway. He stopped to buy a post card with the picture of the figure on it, but then laughed at himself. Dad and Mother would find it odd if he sent that! Instead he bought a scene of the Canadian Rockies topped with snow.

Writing on it, "The view from here," Paul sent the postcard, though it was really a view from the day before. Mother and Dad were at home in Haroldson, Iowa, with Paul's younger sisters Kristen and Hanna. Haroldson wasn't anywhere either, he thought. Such small points humans were on the globe. No bigger than twinkling lights in the sky.

From Prince George the road angled east through a pass alongside a railroad toward Dawson Creek where the Alcan Highway began. Paul camped beside a small river. According to his calculations the trip was only half over. He still had almost 1,500 miles to go.

At a coffee shop the next day, Paul spread ketchup liberally on his hamburger. More food value, he thought. His beard had become a sandy stubble on his chin. He ran his hand over it as another hairy guy of middling age sat down beside him and hailed the waitress as if he knew her.

"Howya doin' Steve?" asked the sweet-faced waitress as she poured him coffee and placed a piece of pie slathered with whipped cream in front of him.

"Great!" said Steve. "Sun's shining. Still plenty of daylight ahead." He took a huge forkful of pie and turned to Paul. "Where're you headed?"

"Fairbanks," said Paul.

"You got a ways to go," said Steve. "Lots of trucks going back and forth, like me. No railroads from here on in. Everything goes in by truck! All the groceries, tools, mail, furniture, fixtures. I pick up stuff off the railroad and truck it on in. Make a run almost twice a week."

"Wow," said Paul. "Do you have an empty truck coming back?" He listened carefully to how Steve spoke, but it wasn't very different from American speech.

"Not always," said Steve. "Some furs, smoked fish or meat."

"So the route works?" asked Paul. "I've got an old station wagon and I'm hoping for the best!"

"Got the *Milepost*?" asked Steve, pulling a worn red booklet from his jeans pocket. He put it on the counter between them. "Tells you what's going on, every single mile!"

Paul looked hard at the red booklet, but up in the corner he saw that it cost $2.95. Probably worth it, but he had his trusty *Road Atlas*. He would have to get his information from people, he decided. "Kind of expensive for someone like me," said Paul. "Can you tell me what to look out for?"

Steve looked sympathetic. "Good luck!" he said. He stood up and stretched his full height, his plaid shirt struggling out of his pants. "Not much to worry about this time of year. Gravel roads mostly, except for some rough patches past Teslin when you hit the Yukon. It's tundra there. They have a hard time keeping that section drivable. Get gas whenever you come to a station. You'll be fine," he said.

"Thanks!" said Paul. "I'm sure I will." He stood up too. The waitress came by with the checks, but Steve grabbed them both as Paul pulled out his wallet.

"Catch you next time." Steve winked at Paul as he laid some wrinkled Canadian dollars on the table. "Welcome to Canada!"

It was not the first or the last kindness that was done Paul on his trip. By the time he hit the wide concrete and steel bridge on the Peace

River, he had stopped being apprehensive. One mile at a time, he thought. The road was dusty, but Paul rolled up the windows and kept going until late at night.

Much of the Alcan highway skirted lakes or rivers. At Muncho Lake small animals with white rumps and black tails stood in the road. The males had rams' horns. Paul stopped the car and leaned quietly on the hood as the animals moved about. A pickup stopped and the driver and his two young sons piled out to have a look.

"Stone sheep," the father nodded to Paul. "Make good trophies. And good eating! We see them a lot around here."

"Stone sheep!" said Paul. His heart clenched up a little. The man assumed he was a hunter!

"Yup," said the man. "I like a good moose steak best, myself. But these'll do in a pinch." He smiled at his boys. "Huh, boys? Lamb stew? How about it?" Neither of the boys said anything, but they smiled and the younger one kicked at the dirt.

"They're beautiful," said Paul. The animals were ignoring them, moving freely up the highway and into the hills at the side of the lake.

"Muncho Lake!" said the Dad, smirking. "Season starts in August. I saw your Iowa plates. Looks like you're a long ways from home."

"I was expecting caribou, maybe moose," said Paul. "I've never heard of these."

"Caribou are moving around," said the man. "Heading to their calving grounds in northern Alaska. You'll probably see some as you get into the Yukon. Buffalo. Grizzlies are out. Eating berries. I'd stay away from any sows."

"Don't worry!" said Paul.

"Don't miss the hot springs on up the road!" said the man as he and his sons got into the small truck. Paul noted three rifles stacked on the rack in the back of the cab.

A few miles farther on a campground was noted as Liard Hot Springs. It was hours from twilight, but Paul could not resist. He pulled off and parked his car. The smell of sulphur, like rotten eggs, came at him as he walked toward the steam he could see rising in the air in the woods. An actual geothermal pool right next to the highway.

A bushy head stuck out of the water and a little pile of clothes was stacked on a wooden deck beside it, as if the person had just pulled off his clothes and jumped in!

"Come on in, the water's fine!" came a shout. "Doesn't get any better than this!" The man stood up to show Paul that he wasn't wearing any clothes whatsoever.

Paul took the hint and stripped. He waded in, an exclamation escaping his lips. The pool was so hot he couldn't believe it.

"A little cooler over here," said the voice of the guy who was now almost submerged.

Paul moved toward the voice. His skin was beet red where it had been in the water.

"Gets the road dust off," said the voice. "And no mosquitoes!"

"You aren't a-kiddin'," said Paul. "It feels positively tropical!"

"Yep, tropical," said the voice. "There are orchids around here!" He paused as Paul gingerly moved around the pool. "This your first time?" he asked.

"Yeah," said Paul sheepishly.

"Dunk down, get your hair wet. It's okay," said the man. "Good for you!"

Paul lay back in the pool. The hot water felt like heaven.

"Get out after a little bit and cool down," nodded the bushy-haired guy as he pulled himself out of the pool and put on his damp clothes. "It's hotter than your body temperature."

"Sure," said Paul. "I'll do that."

That night Paul pulled his sleeping bag up all around his face with only his nose sticking out. He was hot in the bag, but the mosquitoes were behaving like the Alaska state bird, as Paul had heard them called. Paul slept and early in the morning headed straight for the hot springs to clean off the sweat. The sky had clouded over and a few raindrops began to come down. It felt good to Paul. The rain would settle the dust.

On the road Paul drove slowly through light and sometimes heavy rain in a heightened state. His mind was quiet and he felt he was completely present at each point. How many more wonders did the road ahead hold? More lakes, more mountains stretched out ahead, more wildlife. Paul was afraid he couldn't hold much more.

When he paid for his gas in White Horse, the attendant said something about mid-summer. "What day is it?" asked Paul.

The attendant pointed to a grimy calendar on the wall. "June 21!"

It was the longest day Paul had ever experienced. By evening the rain had stopped. Paul kept going. Driving west into a blaze of pink clouds with aureoles of brightness around them, Paul looked at his watch. It was 11 p.m. and the sun was still up.

In the morning the sun was up at 4:30 a.m. Not Paul. He lay in his sleeping bag, listening to rustlings of trees and birds. "This is the first day of the rest of my life," he thought. He was about to drive into the state of Alaska. He couldn't wait to get to Fairbanks, to be able to do something besides drive, to hear something besides the roaring of tires on gravel.

The road above Kluane Lake was corduroy, built on logs over the permafrost and then covered with sand. Paul slowed on the dusty washboard, trying to be patient. He stayed far behind trucks, so as not to catch their dust. The road angled north, and finally entered Alaska, where all of a sudden it became asphalt! The endless squish of tires on damp gravel stopped and Paul could drive faster.

Paul's anticipation picked up. The country was gorgeous, marsh, lakes and clear, flat rivers meandering through vistas of snow-capped mountains. Piles of cumulus hung over the lakes, reflected in the clear waters. Pulled off the highway by a lake eating peanut butter crackers, Paul watched cranes of some kind flying with their long necks out-stretched. Two of them settled on a small pile of vegetation near the edge of the water. Paul mentally marked the stop. He would definitely come back.

Late in the afternoon, Paul pulled into Fairbanks. It looked like an outpost. Driving down the main street, Paul's heart sank. He did not know how to approach this bleak town he had chosen as his home. Three years before the city had been inundated by a flood, with only the University buildings on the hill undamaged. New flat concrete buildings had been slammed down any old how. Most of them had oil drums, engine parts, tools, abandoned tires and lumber stacked near them.

At the end of the street was a collection of small house trailers and trucks parked in a campground. When Paul pulled in, a woman came right over to him and asked whether he would join her family for food and music. "We're the resident gypsies," she said, her sun-brown face merry and laughing. She led Paul toward several picnic tables slid together. Paul could see seasoned-looking men pulling accordions, violins and guitars from their vehicles.

There wasn't much food left, but it was different from anything Paul had had in a while. He filled a paper plate with baked beans, macaroni and cheese and pickles. It was delicious, and so was the evening music. The day had been warm and people wore light clothes. Kids jigged around at the edges of the group. The people seemed to have an almost European feeling to them, most a little older than Paul.

Paul pulled out his guitar and tried to play along, but the songs were unfamiliar. They sounded like polkas from the Lawrence Welk television show. "Polish songs," said the woman who had pulled Paul into the group. "Ahhh," Paul's face lit up. Interesting! A little while later, dead tired, Paul crawled into his sleeping bag and fell asleep while the music was still playing.

When he woke up, no one was moving. Only a few dogs roamed at the edge of the campground. Paul put on a clean shirt, closed up his car carefully and washed and neatened himself as best he could. He walked into town, looking at everything. The town was spread out, as if people weren't used to being close to each other. The buildings were sterile, utilitarian. But the Chena River looped through town, placid and beautiful in the strong sun. Only a month ago it probably had ice in it.

Paul found the high school and sat in front of it, somewhat disoriented. He needed a place to stay and a way to get money for the summer. His teaching job didn't start until September. He hadn't seen any place that looked like it might be for rent. How did you get a job without a place to live? He noted that the grocery store needed a stocker, but would kids who had seen him stocking groceries respect him as a teacher once school started in the fall?

Every evening that week the "gypsies" at the campground cooked food together and made music. Paul bought hotdogs to contribute. There was talk of jobs. The carpenter's union was hiring, especially if you were Polish! But Paul had no idea what he would need to know to get into a union. There was also talk of men going off to fight forest fires, but Paul knew they wouldn't want him if there was a lot of running and jumping involved.

Trying to keep his panic down, Paul wandered through town on Friday morning. People didn't walk much, he noted. Or maybe there just weren't very many people! He felt strange. He had never thought about the acceptance school and church gave him, the family within which he had always moved. He wanted to get out of town and track animals, but until he had solved some of his problems, he didn't dare.

Guitar music came from a bar on the main street, but Paul didn't have money to spend in bars. Teachers probably didn't go into them either. Paul knew the Lutheran church would welcome him, but he held it in reserve, hoping he wouldn't need to get caught up in that utterly familiar atmosphere. Marty had said he could borrow money, he remembered, and Dad did too.

As Paul wandered by the long, low high school, he saw a car park and a man get out and go toward the building. Paul went up to him as he stood unlocking the door. "Good morning!" he said. "I'm a teacher here this fall. Do you have a moment?"

The man stretched out his hand. "Sure! Glad to meet you. Come on in! I'm Superintendent Smith, Carleton J. Smith."

"Paul Mikkelson," said Paul. "I'll be teaching biology and chemistry."

"Just out of college?" asked Mr. Smith, as they walked down the corridor which could have been in a high school in any town in the United States.

"Yes," said Paul. "Trinity, in Moorhead, Minnesota."

"Hmmmm, Mikkelson. Are you Finnish?" asked Smith.

"No. Norwegian, with a little bit of Dane in there. M-i-k-k-e-l-s-o-n," smiled Paul, already feeling better. "I just drove up the Alcan highway this week!"

Smith looked at him and sighed audibly. Paul understood. The superintendent must have a lot sitting on his shoulders. He did not want to take on Paul's troubles. "Well, look around," said Mr. Smith. "We're proud of our building. Ten years old. Survived the flood," he said. "The science labs are down that corridor. Let yourself out when you're done."

"Thanks!" said Paul. "Good to meet you!"

"Mikkelson, Mikkelson," said Superintendent Smith. "Enough 'k's' in your name to be Finnish." He scribbled a phone number on a piece of paper. "Call up Arvi Kukkonen. He's got his fingers in everything in Fairbanks. He might have time to help you get situated. Tell him I sent you."

Paul looked down at the precious piece of paper. "Thank you so much, Mr. Smith! I look forward to working with you in the fall!"

Late that afternoon Paul entered a driveway winding through trees that reminded him of the road to the Mikkelson cabin at Lake Michigami. It was lined with spruce trees interspersed with birch, poplar and thick undergrowth. He pulled up into a clearing to see a vigorous man in a plaid shirt, who waved Paul into the wooden log house without getting off the bulldozer he was using to clear brush.

Inside, Carol Kukkonen introduced Paul to her kids while she made tea. Two of the daughters were spooning cookie dough onto a sheet. A large window looked out over the ridge, down to the river and across to the mountains. In the yard another kid was talking to a tethered horse and feeding him fresh hay.

"We keep building," said Carol. "Keeping pushing the animals out of their stables and making them into rooms!" she said as a pot whistled on an old iron stove. "This part of the homestead was owned by a trapper. We took it down log by log and moved it to this ridge." Carol kept talking, making Paul feel at ease. "We just got back from a year in Massachusetts, where Arvi was going to school. We could have stayed, but we missed this place! Missed the warmth. Can you imagine?" She giggled like a girl.

Paul could see why. A cheerful chaos showed the Kukkonens' easy-going ways. Dishes of various kinds, candles, lamps cluttered the counters. Books covered the shelves which wrapped around the edges of the room. Ropes and tools and jackets hung along the walls where there were no shelves. Stacks of paper, letters, reports, covered every flat surface. A bunch of steel buttons with slogans on them were stuck into the ceiling over the table. Covered buckets stood on the floor. All sizes of shoes and sandals were piled on small carpets near the entry.

When Arvi came in he sized Paul up and down, probably even taking in the polio Paul usually managed to hide. "Teaching at Lathrop?" he said. "Good for you!"

Carol passed cookies as they sat at the crowded kitchen table. The younger kids reminded Paul of his own brothers and sisters, coming over to politely nod to Paul and take a cookie.

"Lutheran college, I think that is," Arvi said when Paul mentioned Trinity. "They've had some good influence here in Alaska, working in the villages. You'll have some Eskimo and Indian students at Lathrop."

"That's why I wanted to teach high school," said Paul. "I'd like to get to know some of them."

"There's going to be another boom on," said Arvi, "as soon as the Alaskan Federation of Natives gets its claims settled. Oil money's going to come pouring in here. And people! Time to start building high schools in the villages, I hope."

"Sounds like it," said Paul.

"Arvi's the principal of one of the elementary schools," said Carol, looking at him fondly. "We came here in 1952. Things have changed a lot since then!"

"You must have a vehicle, right Paul?" asked Arvi. "We've got a cabin on the place we could rent you."

Paul breathed out. "I sure would like that," he said.

Arvi walked Paul over to a small separate cabin, built of logs with a pitched metal roof. "Rented it to a couple of university students last year," said Arvi. "Course you'll have to haul your water and chop your wood, like we all do. We don't have plumbing out here. That's why we have sauna parties! Every Sunday night. Summer and winter."

"It looks great," said Paul. A wood stove stood just off one wall and the thick logs looked like they were good insulation. Simple furniture was built in except for some chairs. "My folks have a cabin in Minnesota, but we only use it summers. I've got a lot to learn about living in the north!"

"You'll do fine," said Arvi. "You've already got a leg up if you're from Minnesota."

Paul's fears sloughed off him and he stood up as tall as he could. He could not believe his luck at finding these wonderful people and this small, perfect cabin. Perhaps he was, indeed, home.

2

Marty went to Yosemite in Lewis' Volkswagen bus, along with Chloe and Corina. They left on an October Friday, when the light was as clear and blue as an eye. Marty was delighted to get out of the city, watching out the window as the light vehicle toiled along Route 80. Golden grass on the hills looked like the fur of a bear, with sage green trees against them in the valleys. California colors, she thought to herself. She felt free and easy, since she had given up waiting around for Erik.

Chloe, on the front seat next to Lewis, directed the trip. Marty and Corina, on a built-in back seat, were along for the ride. Chloe and Corina, sisters, lived with their mother and her boyfriend, and Lewis, in a lively household near Buena Vista Park. Their mother Linda was always collecting people to make music or food together. She and her daughters were all beautiful, but Chloe was willful and mysterious. Marty didn't know her well, but traveling together changed that!

Lewis, whom they all called Louie, worked in the mailroom at Cardigan Shores. He came almost daily to Marty's department, smiling, his long dark hair bobbing, dropping off mail and packages. He had gone to Antioch College, known for its student activism.

Louie was Chloe's boyfriend, but his actions toward Marty showed some ambiguity in his feelings. Sitting on her couch when he came to dinner by himself, they looked long at each other and played toesies. Louie took Marty on his motorcycle up to Twin Peaks in the dark to have a look. Marty rode with her arms around his waist, pressed into his long back, San Francisco spread below them like strings of colored Christmas lights.

Louie had built the back seat into the Volkswagen. Its cushions folded out into a bed for Lewis and Chloe, while Marty and Corina would spread their sleeping bags out in a tent. Marty was afraid it would be cold at night. She had brought all the woolen clothing she could muster.

Louie pulled into a campground near a creek in the rolling golden foothills. Chloe spread a colorful quilt on the grass and she and Corina lounged on it. Corina, who could not have been more than 19, wore an embroidered Mexican blouse, loose and gathered at the top, showing off her full, round body. Chloe's top was sleeveless, fitted close to her tan, limber body, made of Indian cotton and embroidered with a row of little mirrors sewn into it. Beside them, California girls to be sure, Marty felt uptight in her black cotton turtleneck.

Marty followed Louie over to the creek. It was so beautiful with the light coming through the trees and sparkling where it fell on the placid stream. The sun had settled more into the south and lit red and golden leaves from behind, translucent with color. It made Marty's heart ache. She pulled off a few of the heart-shaped leaves. Poplars? They looked almost like the cottonwoods of her childhood in North Dakota.

Louie skipped flat stones across the deeper part of the creek. Marty tried too. She had always known how to flick a stone using her wrist, but Louie was serious. His stone skipped many more times than Marty's. After a few minutes, Chloe came and plucked at his sleeve. She pulled a wicker picnic basket filled with food from the van.

Hummus, pita bread, cut vegetables and fruits as well as cheese and even stuffed grape leaves emerged from Chloe's basket. Marty took salami, cheese and crackers, along with apples, from her backpack. Louie brought out a bottle of Boone's Farm apple wine and some paper cups.

"Wait!" said Marty, reaching for her boxy camera. She wanted to get a photo before it all became a mess of crumbs. Chloe draped herself artfully upon Louie, her long golden hair blending with his dark curls. Corina knelt appealingly beside them. For once, Marty wished it could be a color photograph with all the light sparkling around them.

"A loaf of bread, a bottle of wine, and thou," said Louie. "Or maybe thee?" he questioned. "What's the plural of thou?"

No one said much as they ate and Marty didn't know how to insert herself into the long-held family atmosphere she observed between the three of them. Louie had been tamed by it, and so was Corina.

Marty knew it was uncool to talk about books. Most of the people she knew in San Francisco did not read very much. It was not like living with the Chertoks in Berkeley, who had stimulated Marty's intellect. The Chertoks told her she would miss the academic atmosphere when she moved to the city, but Marty wanted what the city had to offer. It was an art, the art of living, Marty thought. At last Marty asked, "Did you make the hummus yourself?"

"Yup," said Chloe dismissively. "Linda's recipe, from some friend of hers. But we modified it." Chloe called her mother by her given name which Marty found shocking. But they did live together like a bunch of sisters.

"It's delicious," said Marty. "I like Middle Eastern food."

"We should get going," said Louie. "The sun goes down so early now and it's hard to set up camp in the dark." He stood up and brushed crumbs off his jeans. Chloe lazily followed. Marty admired the grace with which she moved. They packed the food away and shook out the quilt. Warmth would soon go away along with the sun.

The closer you got to the mountains the less you could see them. Woods of many colors closed in on every side. But shortly they drove into a long grassy meadow, the floor of a valley which cut through the mountains. "Half Dome," said Corina when Marty pointed to a dramatic mountain rising to the left, sheared off as if cut with a bread-knife. It dominated the valley.

Louie parked, claiming a picnic table and fire ring. The air was indeed nippy, and Marty put on a woolen shirt.

Corina was proud of the little tent, showing Marty how to put it up. "I've been coming here my whole life," she said. "There used to be a giant tree you could drive through, but it fell down last year." Marty had slept outdoors in the woods near Santa Cruz with Erik, but never camped in a tent. She was impressed by the ingenious little pack with poles which lifted into an airy two-man tent.

The dark came down quickly. Louie started a wood fire and they cooked hot dogs on sticks. A couple of campers were parked in the campground, but not many people were visible. It was quiet and Marty was glad. She warmed her front at the fire, then turned like a hot dog herself to warm her back. The woods rustled and the fire sparked and fizzed.

"We can't leave any food out," said Louie as they packed up after dinner. "Bears will smell it and find it. Even toothpaste. Put your pack in the car. But don't worry if you hear snuffling around the tent. They won't hurt you if there's no food."

Marty did not feel this was reassuring.

Louie put more wood on the fire, and Chloe passed around a joint. Marty took a tiny toke. Herbal smelling smoke joined the smell of the crackling wood. They stood quietly around the fire for a long time, watching the embers glow in the fire pit. Marty felt around in her mind, trying to see if she noticed anything more, but she didn't feel very different than she usually did. Hearing might be intensified. She was not sure this was a good thing out in the wild!

Chloe wrapped herself around Louie and Marty tried to imagine Erik being there. Maybe if he had enough weed to keep him occupied, she thought. But if Erik were there, it would have been his scene, not Chloe's.

The next morning Marty was in exploration mode. She wanted to walk all over the valley and see what there was to see. But by ten a.m. no one had emerged from the camper. Corina too seemed to be fast asleep.

Marty sat at the picnic table with her journal, trying to keep her fingers warm in the frigid air and writing down everything she saw. Two deer wandered through the grass, the low angled sun behind them etching them against the wide golden meadow. Marty wondered what the beautiful tree near the trail was. Its leaves were brilliant colors shading from yellow to orange to red, with a stalk of bright red berries on each branch. She took a few photographs as a sleepy Corina rolled out of the tent in a sweater and headed toward the rest room.

When Chloe and Louie finally emerged, they were lazy. "There's nothing to see," Chloe responded to Marty's eagerness. "Just people. Just be here. It's great to just be here." It was almost what Jack, Marty's city friend who insisted there was nothing much going on out in the world, would have said.

Marty looked at Louie, who seemed to sympathize. "We'll go for a walk after we eat something," he said. "You have to see the Ahwahnee at least," he looked at Chloe to confirm. "One of my favorite spots on earth is the meadow behind the Ahwahnee," he told Marty.

"The Ahwahnee?" asked Marty. She knew it was uncool to be a tourist. But she did not agree that there was nothing to see.

"It's a hotel. Named for the Indians who once lived here. It's huge, with big fireplaces and windows. Just about the kind of house I'd like to live in." Louie laughed. "Not likely. Can't even afford to spend the night there."

"Do you know what this is?" Marty asked Corina, holding out the leaves of the interesting tree.

"Dogwood, I think," said Corina. "Really beautiful in the spring. Some of the leaves turn white, like flowers."

"Oh, dogwood!" said Marty. Dad had planted a dogwood once at his parents' house. But Marty had never seen it in the autumn, or the spring. She tried to calm herself down. She was, after all, traveling with others. It was wonderful to be in Yosemite Valley and she could see what was around her. It was all new and lovely. It was also nice not to be caught in the net of anyone else's desires. She was alone and free, with friends who asked little of her. Marty was happy.

The massive structure of the Ahwahnee nestled below a mountain. Tall stone pillars flanked the entrance to the wood, stone and glass hotel. Marty wandered with Louie, Chloe and Corina along the polished floors, past the wood and leather furniture, admiring the carpets and the huge fireplaces. Candelabras hung from the ceiling with lamps made to mimic candles. They stepped out the back onto a terrace which looked out over a spacious meadow. Marty could hardly imagine a place which felt better in its setting.

Marty saw it through Erik's eyes. He must have been here, she thought. He had grown up in Los Angeles. Perhaps he had even stayed in the hotel, as his parents were rich, if distant. As a tiny baby, Erik's mother had given him to her mother to raise because she wanted to be a movie star. Then she changed her mind and took him back. Marty thought it had marked him.

"We could get married here," Marty heard Chloe saying to Louie as they walked through the brush.

"Many have," he replied noncommittally.

"I was just kidding," Chloe said, punching Louie in the arm and skittering away from him. Louie followed.

The meadow was a large space left wild spread out in back of the rustic hotel. People wandered through it, but no one bothered each other, hidden by small plants, trees and the golden grasses. Marty felt the hush of transcendence hover around her. It was newness as well, the unfamiliarity, the surprise of it all. She wandered off toward a red-leaved tree.

The sun in the middle of the day felt wonderful on Marty's skin, but there was also a hint of crispness, of the mountains around them. Marty could have settled down with a book and spent the afternoon in the meadow, moving in to sit in one of the leather chairs in the hotel when the shadows lengthened. But she could see Chloe and Louie coming toward her through the grass, with Corina trailing behind.

"We're going back to camp," said Louie.

"Okay," said Marty. "I'll just walk around a little and join you soon."

Shops, restaurants, hotels and campgrounds dotted the valley. Yosemite was known the world over. Incomparable paths with the mountains in the background meandered through the woods, the colors rich in radiance. Marty walked slowly, glad to be alone with her thoughts.

Marty wondered whether Chloe and Louie would get married. She was 24 herself, past the age when Mother and Dad had married. Despite the women's liberation movement which echoed around them, Marty very much wanted to be married in the end. She wanted a family of her own, hopefully more secure than the precarious one she observed in her sister, whose husband was in New York. Line hadn't seen him in more than a year.

That evening there was another woods fire, more food and weed to smoke. Marty felt peaceful, but a little lonely. She wondered what the others thought of her. In the morning, after sleeping very late, Louie drove them all back through the richly-colored landscape to San Francisco.

Marty was glad to go over the Bay Bridge and into the white city that evening. It was sad though. The weekend was so short, and there was so much she wanted to do. Tomorrow she would have to go back to work. It was almost as if there hadn't been a weekend!

Line was at their apartment, eating rice and vegetables with Christopher in the tiny kitchen. "Erik came by. He seemed mad that you weren't here," she said casually.

"What did he say?" asked Marty, her heart tightening in her chest as she put down her backpack and sleeping bag.

"Nothing," said Line. "He came to the door and I told him you had gone to Yosemite with some friends, and he just stalked off!"

Marty felt anxious. Line and Erik didn't like each other. But there was nothing she could do about it.

At work on Monday, Marty was at her desk when the word went around the dictation pool: "Janis Joplin is dead." It was heart-stopping. She was hardly any older than Marty. She had died of a drug overdose, like the great guitarist Jimi Hendrix shortly before. Something was definitely over, people said. Marty wasn't sure what.

A pall hung over the day, though it was sunny and warm. "Let's go to South Park," said Betsy at lunchtime, gathering Marty and Joyce to come with her. Before the 1906 earthquake, the park had been the site of homes for San Francisco's wealthy. They had fallen to rubble and burned. Now the park's graceful oval was surrounded by industrial buildings and warehouses.

"Did you ever see Janis perform?" asked Betsy as they walked. She was a jeweler, studying lost wax casting and making intricate rings and beautiful, suggestive pieces to hang on the end of chains around one's neck. She was a little plump with golden skin. Marty loved the hollow in the curve of her clavicle. A California girl and Jewish, she had grown up in San Bernardino.

"Once," said Marty. "At the Carousel. It was so packed I couldn't even see her, but I could hear her!"

"Just our age," lamented Joyce sadly. "Unbelievable." Joyce was half Korean, with long dark hair and a little-girl manner. Like Marty she had grown up in the Midwest. "I've got one of her albums."

"I went to the Monterey Pop Festival," said Betsy. "I'm not sure how I got there, and I had no idea it would be such a big deal. But Janis was amazing. Jimmy Hendrix was there too. Set his guitar on fire. And everyone was so stoned. It was beautiful," she said wistfully.

"When was that?" asked Joyce.

"Two years ago maybe?" said Betsy. "Or more? It was the beginning of the summer of love."

"Wow," said Joyce. "She was famous for less than three years."

Famous, thought Marty. What did it mean? She had arrived in California after the summer of love, but had lived with Joyce and others in a communal apartment near the Haight Ashbury briefly. Now she, Betsy and Joyce, college graduates, typed entries dictated by attorneys for publishing in legal tomes.

At a small corner grocery, a man made sandwiches for the girls. They took the wrapped sandwiches and spread out on the grass, tucking their skirts around their legs. At Cardigan Shores, women were required to wear skirts to work, though other offices now allowed women to wear pants. Marty could see Louie near the playground. She waved and he waved back.

Irrepressible, the girls talked of their plans. "I can't wait for Eileen's lunch," said Betsy, hugging herself.

"Friday," said Joyce. Eileen, a petite, stylish older woman, was retiring and Cardigan Shores, because of her long tenure and the esteem in which she was held, would send the entire typing pool to the Garden Court at the Sheraton-Palace Hotel.

Eileen held court in the large room with its ten desks the whole time Marty worked at Cardigan Shores. Eileen had once been rich, had gone to parties and danced in San Francisco hotels as a young girl. She lost all her money and had to go to work during the war. Eileen's best friend Marge, who moved about in a wheelchair because she had MS, had also been in the typing pool a long time. The two of them regaled the younger girls with stories during coffee break.

Eileen had a wry sense of humor and an aristocratic sense of propriety. Marty was in awe of her. She lived in an apartment on Nob Hill with a parakeet and refused to go out except to work or to mass at Old Saint Mary's. Even if someone asked her to dinner she refused. "I don't go out," she said, giving you the distinct sense that nothing could measure up to the exacting rigors of her expectations. She had lived a life. She was not prepared to let a lesser life obscure her rich memories.

Friday came eventually. Marty wore her best clothes, a brown gabardine skirt with a white blouse and a red sweater vest. The Sheraton-Palace was within walking distance of the Cardigan Shores office, so most of the girls walked. But Eileen was sent in a taxi with Marge.

Marty had never been to the hotel. She entered the gleaming glass door with its polished brass fittings and looked down the long lobby set with ornate chairs to a sunlit door at the end. To the right was a dark bar with, Marty could see, a Maxfield Parish painting of the pied piper hanging over it. The hotel too had been rebuilt after the 1906 earthquake. It was said that the opera star Enrico Caruso, who had been staying there, wandered around the morning after the earthquake clutching a painting and howling that he was never coming back to San Francisco.

Marty followed her friends toward the middle of the long corridor and was entranced by the glass-ceiling of the huge room in which they were to dine. Ornate rounded brasswork held up the clear panes, as if it were a conservatory. Large plants and palms were set about the room, and a long table had been laid for the ten people attending Eileen's lunch. Flowers ran down the middle and gleaming silver lay across heavy white linen napkins on the beautiful tablecloth.

Betsy clutched Marty, drawing her to sit at a place next to her. Eileen sat in the middle of the table where everyone could hear her, and their supervisor, the infamous Gerry, sat at the head. Marty did not feel intimidated. She had spent a year at Oxford University, being an au pair for a professor's family. Nothing in San Francisco was a match for the ancient high culture she had moved within in England.

Nonetheless, Marty did not say much. She murmured to her friends, but kept her eyes on Eileen, who told decorous, self-deprecating jokes, and mocked the whole proceeding. Marty looked at the wonderful sky light falling on her friends through the glass ceiling. Celebrations were odd, she thought. Of course they were honoring Eileen, but the true delight for Marty had been listening to Eileen's enthralling stories day after day. Eileen described herself as a "holy terror" as a young woman, utterly oblivious to poverty or want.

They ordered food from long, ornate menus. After cocktails, the meal was served in courses, salad first. It was silly, Marty thought. Salad obviously should follow the main course as in Europe. The food was good, but not as good as Irene Magnusson's everyday meals, which Marty had eaten in Oxford. Marty ate Chicken Kiev, cutting it carefully into small bites and napping it in its rich creamy sauce.

Marty wondered whether Eileen would still refuse to go out once she had retired and had long days to herself. She knew Eileen liked to read. Because Eileen brought F. Scott Fitzgerald to mind, Marty once asked her if she liked his stories. He had written about people like Eileen. But Eileen would hear none of it. Fitzgerald was anathema. Class and Catholicism had gotten Eileen through life.

Brandies were served after dinner. Marty drank the fiery golden liquid, remembering her first cognac on an Icelandic flight to England when she was 20. Marty would never know what Eileen did with herself. She would miss the touch of elegance that the small figure with her iron-grey curls and well-fitting suits had given to the typing pool. Gerry, who was also older than most of the girls, was no substitute. She was a smoker, a drinker who had divorced her husband. Her stories of cocktail parties and her wayward daughter were not appealing to Marty.

When the party broke up, the girls went back to work but no one got much done. It was Friday after all. After work Marty went to Samantha's house, where Line dropped Christopher on her way to work at the hospital.

Christopher was hiding tiny metal cars in the couch cushions while Sasha, his dark-haired friend, tried to vroom his into Christopher's. "Have you had a busy day?" Marty asked Christopher, who was two and beginning to say a few words.

Samantha smiled. "They're always busy!" She sighed and slouched into a chair. The sweet smell of cooking fruit came from the kitchen where apples from the bushel Samantha and her husband had brought home from Sonoma boiled in a kettle. "Want some applesauce?"

"Sure," said Marty. Samantha's apartment was no bigger than Marty and Line's, but it was full of furniture. Untidy shelves climbed the walls, lamps and bowls and toys littered the tables. A big empty television screen faced its dead eye toward the sofa.

"The applesauce is cooling," Samantha said. "I just put a little cream on it, myself." She had a Russian background, lovely pink skin and full-fleshed arms. "I think it's a little too hot for the boys."

In the tiny kitchen Samantha gave Marty a saucer. Marty spooned applesauce from the kettle and drizzled it with heavy cream from a carton. Laced with cinnamon and cloves, the applesauce was delicious. It reminded Marty of the clove-spiced crabapple pickles her own grandmother made.

Marty breathed with pleasure. "This is so good!" she said. "I just had this elegant lunch at the Sheraton-Palace, a retirement party for one of the people in our department. But none of the food was as good as this."

Samantha smiled. "Real food," she said. "Straight from the orchard!"

"Yeah," Marty said. "I feel absolutely monkish after I've had a meal like that. So much effort spent on how things looked and the dishes and how they were served. I like simple things." Marty paused. "But I did have Chicken Kiev, which I'm sure your family used to make. So rich!"

"Oh yes," said Samantha, a bit ruefully. "Chicken Kiev and coulibiac and all those sinful things."

"We better go home," said Marty, standing up. She collected Christopher's jacket and the little bag Line usually sent with him. "Come on Christy," she said.

At their own apartment a few blocks away, Marty cooked up pasta and vegetables and topped them with cheese. It was more for Christopher than herself. She felt stuffed. When Christopher went to sleep, Marty stalked around the house, wondering whether she would ever hear from Erik again. Where was he, and what was he doing? She glared at the silent black telephone with its long cord trailing through the room.

At last she sat down with a pen and paper, and wrote a letter to Mother and Dad. How could she explain this amazing world, so full of different cultures, places and people, to her folks back in Iowa?

It was easier to write to Paul. He was living in a cabin with a woodstove, snug and warm but far from town. He wrote that he banked the snow, which had already started, against the cabin as insulation. His biggest problem was getting to school, which was seven miles away. It didn't make sense to try to get Old Green started most of the time. He hitched a ride with his landlord, who kept the road open because he too needed to get to school. Paul put his skis in the pickup and skied the last couple of miles, skiing home at night.

"I'm fit as a fiddle, but would like to hear from you!" wrote Paul. Marty felt sad that he was alone. Paul did write about the sauna parties his landlord, a Finn, had every Sunday night. His life too sounded interesting and exotic. She wondered whether he knew that Janis Joplin had died.

"When we were growing up in North Dakota, I could not imagine the world I now live in," wrote Marty to Paul. "A mountain paradise one weekend, and a formal lunch in a grand hotel the next. 'The world is so full of a number of things, I'm sure we should all be as happy as kings,'" Marty quoted from a Robert Louis Stevenson poem in the old book they had in North Dakota. But it made her feel wistful. It was not quite enough. Where was Erik?

3

Line felt suspicious when she returned from work one night to find Marty and Erik attached to each other on the couch, their faces shining. Sadly, she had begun to find that happiness for Marty did not always result in things that helped her.

"Erik has found a place for us," said Marty, oblivious to Line's dismay. Marty was still in her work clothes, black stockings and a skirt. A bottle of wine stood on the floor, and the two of them held glasses.

"A place for us?" asked Line. She spread her wet umbrella to dry in the hall and kicked off her wet shoes.

"A place where we can all live. It's out near the park. You would only need to take one bus to work!" Marty bubbled.

"Oh?" said Line. This was certainly a new development. "How's Christopher?" she asked, sinking down on the day bed. The rain drummed on the concrete below the slightly open window. It was February, and the rain was mild, portending the luxuriance of spring. Rain did make Line happy.

"He's fine," said Marty. "Sleeping." She hopped off the couch. "Do you want a glass of wine, Line? Let's have a toast!" She was half way to the kitchen. The irrepressible Erik, blonde curls framing his face, sat up from where he had been lounging.

But Line's hackles were already up. "Marty," she said. "I'll have to think about this. It isn't that easy for me to just up stakes and move. What about Samantha?"

Marty pursed her lips as she poured a glass of wine for Line. She sighed. "Sorry, Line. I know you'll have to think about it," said Marty. "Will you come and look at it with us tomorrow? It's supposed to have a garden in back."

"A garden?"asked Line. Marty knew how to get to her! She took a sip of wine and nibbled at the crackers and cheese Marty pushed toward her. Her mind was running through all the factors in her life that might affect a move.

Stephen, her husband, was one. He was in New York, staying with his parents as his mother was very ill with cancer. He wanted to get his doctorate and was hoping to do it in Santa Cruz at the new university. It was developing a "history of consciousness" department, and Greg Calvert, one of his SDS friends, thought it was great. Stephen would be in California by August, he told Line, and he hoped she and Christopher would join him.

Line felt this as a pressure. Other than this invitation, Stephen had done nothing whatsoever to convince Line that she and Christopher were important to him. He often said so when he called, but none of his actions showed it. Actions spoke louder than words. Line would trust Stephen when she saw the whites of his eyes. It had been almost two years.

Even then Line wasn't sure that moving back in with Stephen was the best thing for her and Christopher. She had gotten so used to taking care of their son by herself. She was hoping to get into a neo-natal ward at Children's Hospital soon and she loved San Francisco. She was making friends with fascinating people in a Sufi group, from whom she was learning about healing, herbs and massage. She hoped to expand her own skills and ability to take care of others.

Christopher was growing and thriving. Line did not regret running away from Chicago, but she felt bad Christopher did not have his father. Though she trusted Marty completely to take care of Christopher, Marty didn't seem to have much self-control around Erik. And who was Erik? Line couldn't get a handle on him. Utterly charming in some ways, he refused to be pinned down about his whereabouts or his actions. What did it mean that he wanted to live with Marty?

All of this coursed through Line's practical mind that night as she lay down beside her sleeping son. The idea of a garden, however, was a powerful draw. Herbs, thought Line. She could grow her own herbs and experiment with them, test her own curative concoctions. Rain dripped hard on the concrete in the window well. Line fell asleep imagining bees buzzing through the blue flowers of her own lavender, rosemary and borage.

The next morning sun poured through the southern front windows. The sounds of George Harrison's new album rolled through the house, the long chords and choruses of "My Sweet Lord." It had been a Christmas present and they often played it. Erik ran out for the Sunday paper and some sweet rolls while Marty made coffee.

"Alleluia," sang Line along with the record on the cheap, tinny stereo as she made an omelette with Christy standing below her mimicking and jigging. "Krishna, Krishna."

Soon they were all dancing as the guitar music swung through the house. Erik in a slightly soiled buttoned down Oxford shirt, the sleeves rolled up, a hole in the knee of his jeans, danced with Marty whose long dark hair fell down her ample chest across a rose-colored hooded sweatshirt. "Tell me what is my life, tell me who-o am I without you-ou-ou?"

The rhythms were just what Line could get behind, the solid four-beat anthems with philosophical lyrics. Steady, serious. "Isn't is a pity, how we break each other's hearts." They knew the songs well, like hymns. It's like going to church, Line thought.

Erik, a lapsed Catholic, must have had the same thought. "This is much better than going to mass," he said. "I've got the incense," he said, lighting up a joint. The acrid green smoke joined the smell of coffee.

"Sacramental bread and coffee," said Marty, reverently. She poured more boiling water through her precious brown ceramic Melitta pot.

When George Harrison's voice broke into a Dylan song, "If not for you, my sky would fall ... I just wouldn't have a clue," Line watched as Erik, sunny and dancing from one foot to the other, put his arms around Marty, holding her tight. Line turned away, picked up Christopher and danced with him to the cheery music. She was thinking about Stephen, three thousand miles away in a hospital room with his mother.

After the sweet, lazy morning, they all got into Erik's old Plymouth and drove across town. Erik had a key from the real estate agent. The flat was a railroad apartment with a long hall going back to a bathroom and kitchen. Three large rooms opened off the hall. In front, bay windows looked out on the street where a few dejected jade plants were corralled in a cement block fence.

The large empty kitchen had lots of windows and plenty of space for a huge table in the middle of the room. In back, down some stairs, a deep yard reached back toward a fence. Acacia trees were in yellow bloom at the back near the fence but in the foreground there was just scruffy grass and a few shrubs, a low concrete wall.

Line sat on the bottom step, mentally filling in the yard with vegetables and flowers while Christopher chased a black and white cat up the fence. The garden was shared with an upper flat, but obviously no one paid much attention to it.

When Marty and Erik appeared at the top of the steps, Marty asked, "What do you think?"

Line took a deep breath. It felt dangerous. She did not want to live with Marty and Erik and watch them pawing each other all day, or seeing them fight. But of course, she would. "It's great," she said. "I think we should do it."

"See!" crowed Erik. "'And I try my best to make everything succeed.'" It was a line Harrison had sung that morning.

Line sighed. Despite the sweet, sunny morning, it did not feel right to her. She foresaw trouble, but there was no help for it. Until she figured out what was happening with Stephen, she would stick with Marty. Marty was high as a kite, Line could tell. Line resolved to spend all her time in the garden with Christopher. The garden would be safe enough. She would have to find someone else for Christy to stay with while she did her shifts at the hospital.

Line and Marty gave notice at the Larkin Street apartment and moved out to Kirkham Street north of the park in March. It was easy to do. They had no furniture, only a few books and some clothes, the cheap stereo and the sewing machine. Erik provided a double bed and a couch. They found a large wooden table for the kitchen at Busvan Moving and Storage and a mattress for Line. She wanted to get a water bed, as she was sure it would be better for her back. But it needed a frame and Line just couldn't commit to how big and heavy the whole thing was.

Life in the new house seemed to go on as before. Marty and Erik both took the bus downtown to work, leaving Line and Christopher the big, empty house and garden in the mornings. They were so close to Golden Gate Park they could walk to it!

One evening, Line arranged to meet her friend Julia in the arboretum. "I'll find you in the stone circle, in the native plant section," said Julia on the phone.

Line carried Christopher across streets, as he didn't like being cooped up in the stroller any more. He liked to walk by himself. They slipped into the arboretum through the entrance at the back.

The winding, sandy paths at the edge of the arboretum were lined with leggy flowers in all shades of the blue and purple spectrum poking through the thick green cover of plants and shrubs. Some had white centers. "Cineraria," said Line to herself. Even after a year Line was still trying to get used to the plants that grew in the San Francisco climate, said to be like the mild desert climate around the Mediterranean. It was so unlike the lush, humid Midwest.

They passed a pond thick with water plants. They could hear frogs peeping. Christy threw a few stones in the pond to hear the satisfying 'plop' they made, as Line held him tight around the waist to keep him from falling in. All winter the temperature had hardly dipped below freezing and the frequent rains made the place look perfect, as if it needed no care.

They crossed a little stream and entered the circle of stones Julia had mentioned. Different grasses and shrubs surrounded the circle, studded with small golden poppies and other flowers. Small grasses grew in the soft stone beneath their feet. A gorgeous buckeye, perfectly shaped, put out clumps of leaves like little parasols just beyond the circle. It was a good place to keep an eye on Christopher.

At the foot of the buckeye, a gardener in a green park uniform was digging up some plants and leaving others. Line went over to see what was in his wheelbarrow.

"Some of these can be saved," said the gardener. "They're just not in the right place."

"I see," said Line. "How do you know?"

"By whether it's native or not," said the gardener. He began describing what plants had to do to survive in semi-desert climates. The intensely golden yellow California poppies, for instance, used deep taproots to get down deep into the water table. Some plants stored water in their roots, others became deciduous at an odd time to conserve their water.

"I'm trying to learn California plants," said Line. "Like this one." She fingered a blue flowering shrub nearby.

"Ceanothus," said the gardener, who said his name was Bill. "California lilac, some call it."

"Not much smell," Line sniffed. "Not like our lilacs."

"Nope," said Bill lightly. "This one's Jepson Ceanothus. There are many species, and some do have fragrance. Have you visited the fragrance garden yet?"

"Oh, yes," said Line. "Christy likes it," she said, looking over at him. He was trying to climb up on the low stone wall.

"All these stones, and the stones in the fragrance garden, come from a twelfth century Spanish monastery," said Bill. "Some up on the hill too, and some left over by the tea garden."

"I've seen them," said Line. "All jumbled up in heaps. They're a mystery. Why are they there?" The stones were soft, mellow earthy colors, some of them carved as if they had been part of columns.

"Limestone from Spain," said Bill. "Old moneybags, William Randolph Hearst bought them up, shipped them over. He thought he was going to build a mansion in northern California. But he ran out of money and gave them to San Francisco. They were all crated up, numbered and marked. But the crates burnt up in a warehouse fire and now no one knows what's what any more."

"Wow," said Line. "That's quite a story." Marty would enjoy hearing about it.

"We're happy to have them," said Bill.

"The arboretum is a wonderful place," said Line, wistfully. "It must be nice to work here."

Christopher began crowing and pointing, just outside the stone circle. Line went over to him. A pair of brown speckled quail walked slowly by, scratching in the sand. They looked so funny, each with a little topknot of golden feathers wagging as they waddled along. Line put a hand on Christopher so he wouldn't scare them.

"Those are the immature birds," said Bill, coming over to look. "They're coming along though."

Christopher reached up his arms to see whether Bill would pick him up. Bill gave off an ordinary vibe, almost as if he were family. He picked up Christopher in his soiled gardener's hands. "You're a fine one," he said. "Taking care of your mother."

Line saw Julia heading toward them, her full colorful skirts swishing around her. She worked at a laboratory during the day, dressed not at all like her Sufi self. A long shadow followed her and Line noticed all the shadows had grown. Julia greeted Line happily and clucked at Christopher. Bill stuck out his hand.

"Getting to be closing time," said Bill. "Guess I better clean up and go home." The arboretum gates closed at sunset, summer and winter. But Bill did not leave. Line noticed he stood around watching and listening, collecting his tools and his wheelbarrow.

"We missed you on Thursday morning," said Julia to Line. The two of them had met on one of the weekly walks through the park Joe and Guinn Miller, two shining older Theosophists, led. They dispensed wisdom and friendship to those walking with them. After Sufi Sam died in January the walks took on poignancy. Sam, who looked like an Old Testament prophet, had told Joe Miller before his death, "Take care of my disciples." It reminded them all that they were not going to live in these bodies forever.

Line loved the camaraderie, the way this large group of people flowed together, but were also independent. The more often she went out with the group, the more people she knew. Joe, an impish man with a shock of white hair, jutting white eyebrows and goatee, refused to be anyone's guru. But he spoke freely and loudly in a harsh old voice to anyone who would listen.

"Joe was telling us about this Sufi woman Dorothy Maclean who is able to hear what plants say to her. She calls the plant spirits 'devas'. Way in the north of Scotland, they are raising huge vegetables and amazing flowers by doing what the plants want."

"Not very surprising," said Line. She listened to what things told her all the time when there was enough silence around her.

"I'd really like to go there," said Julia. "Findhorn. It sounds so magical."

"Yes," said Line. She took Christopher's hand as they walked slowly on the park paths to a big grassy lawn. Bill was nowhere to be seen. The sun had set and the sky was a clear light bowl above them, pink toward the ocean in the west.

"Joe is always telling us we have the spark inside of us. But if I could just go there, and see it," said Julia. They sat down on the grass. Someone was playing a guitar under a huge tree. Christopher collected the thick pink petals of magnolia blossoms which had dropped off. They were bigger than his hands.

Line sighed. She wasn't going anywhere. "I've put in some potatoes and a rosemary in our garden," she said. "The soil is really sandy. I know this part of town was all sand dunes at one time. It's a wonder anything grows." They wouldn't get rain in the summer, but she could water, and the plants would find moisture deep in the thin soil, she hoped.

Christopher grew restless. The big gates to the arboretum were shut, but the little party walked out the metal turnstile gate. It fascinated Christopher because bars enclosed them as they walked through, turning only one way, not letting them back in.

At home, Marty had arrived from work. Line set a pot of water on the stove to boil for long spaghetti. Marty pulled out a can of Japanese baby clams with a geisha pictured on it. Cooked with lots of chopped parsley and a few green onions, it made a quick sauce. They never knew who would be there for dinner.

That night was quiet with just Julia, Marty, Line and Christopher slurping up the long noodles. Line mopped Christopher's face, which was covered with green sauce.

"I'm thinking of becoming a vegetarian," said Julia. "I don't want to eat anything with eyes."

"Clams have eyes, I think," said Line. "Or something to sense with."

"No!" said Julia, who had a background in science. "They're mostly just a muscle. And anyway, I'm not there yet," she said. "Wali Ali wants me to move near the Mentorgarten and work with him." The Mentorgarten was Sufi Sam's home before he died, where he started his circle dances and walking practices, as well as taught Hindu and Buddhist dharma classes. Wali Ali, his secretary, now planned to make it a continuing place of study. "There's no meat at the Mentorgarten," said Julia.

"Interesting," said Line. "I love the dances and Sufi meditations, but I can't dedicate myself to practice right now."

"You have to feel it within yourself," said Julia. "If you feel it, you'll know."

Yes, thought Line. She did indeed know what was within. She looked surreptitiously at Marty. There were spiritual seekers everywhere, and many were as self-righteous as some of the church members Line had known. Line did not doubt Julia's integrity, but she hadn't known her long. Time would tell.

On the subject of poseurs and seekers, Line and Marty agreed. Though they had quite different interests, they were united in their philosophical ideas. Line respected Marty's hard-headed book knowledge, and knew that Marty looked up to Line's own first-hand physical experience. They were honest with each other and shared a desire to know the reality of life. If Erik wasn't around, Line found it easy to connect with Marty.

At present they were both reading anything they could find about Georges Gurdjieff, who advocated self-knowledge, as rigorous and objective as possible. He had had many students who wrote about the experience. Gurdjieff had his detractors, but Line found his teaching valuable. Spirituality was in the air and she and Marty were both searching.

What Line loved about Sufi Sam and Joe Miller was that they did not think any specific set of doctrines would save you and get you into heaven. Sufi Sam had used an amalgam of wisdom practices from the East to help people along the path. He never pushed it. It was more of an offer. It was up to you.

Line knew people who wanted a guru to follow, but she did not need that. "Be still," Joe Miller said. "Look within." Line wanted to be a good person and help others. She knew she had light within her and she wanted to let it shine.

"Jack and Nathan want us to come over this weekend," said Marty after Julia left. Jack, with his long experience and vicious dissection of society, had been a teacher to them both as well. "They've just moved too, and they want us to see their new digs."

"It's great we can all move around the city and still stay friends," said Line. She did miss Samantha. If Marty was busy when Line did her Saturday shift, Line still took Christopher to Samantha's, not minding the extra buses. For her weekday shifts Line had found an older woman nearby who took in children for the day. Line was pretty sure she just set the kids in front of the television. But there were two other toddlers for Christopher to play with. Line wasn't too worried.

Line did not ask whether Erik would come to Jack and Nathan's with them. Erik was around a lot, but he still came and went as he pleased. Marty just shrugged her shoulders. It seemed to be part of their agreement. Ask no questions and I'll tell you no lies, Line guessed. It still wasn't clear what Erik was up to. He sometimes brought his friends to the house, a very eclectic bunch. Line thought most of them were some variety of stoner, but many of them were interesting, and certainly smart.

A musty smell greeted Line's nose when she and Marty, with Christy by the hand, climbed the ancient carpeted stairs to Jack and Nathan's apartment near Haight Street. The front room was littered with boxes, furniture and wrappings on the floor. The walls and the hardwood floor were bare. The room was artfully lighted, however, by an ancient glass lamp. Jack and Nathan collected things they hoped to re-sell at flea markets. It was their only living, but they seemed to be good at it.

"Nathan has quite an eye," said Jack. "And I'm not so bad at it myself."

Jack ladled out bowls of chili and Nathan poured red wine into mis-matched glasses. They all sat at the kitchen table, Christopher in Line's lap.

"Nathan's movie's about to come out," said Jack. "They're calling it *McCabe and Mrs. Miller*. Gotta see it."

"Nathan's movie?" asked Line. She had forgotten Nathan was in a movie, but Marty hadn't.

"The one where he's in a pioneer town hauling buckets of water to put out a church fire?" Marty said.

"Yup," said Jack. "It's going to be great. It's got Julie Christie in it. The director did *M.A.S.H.*"

"Oh yes," said Marty. "Altman. Where do you get all your information, Jack?"

But Jack just shrugged. "It's in the air!" he said.

31

Line knew about *M.A.S.H.* only through what Jack and Marty told her. It was a hit movie about lackadaisical surgeons in a mobile hospital during the Korean war. It was supposed to be funny as hell, and the surgeons were brilliant. Line didn't get to movies much. It was easier to get out during the day with Christopher.

Nathan, younger than Jack, dark and gorgeous, disappeared into another room and came back with three large hatboxes. Smiling, he opened one and pulled out two bowler hats! He set one rakishly on his dark curls and handed the other to Marty.

"Eh, Charlie Chaplin?" said Jack, looking quizzically at Marty. "Take off your glasses. Some eyebrows, a little mustache." His hand sketched them in.

Jack opened the other boxes and gave Line a stiff, beaver top hat! He put one on his own head. "Abraham Lincoln," he said. "Pleased to meet you." He held out his hand like a politician. It was perfect.

"Now Line," Jack said. "I think you're going to have to be George Sand. Put your hair under your hat. Wait a minute," he said. He went in the other room and brought out the silk sash to a bathrobe. Putting it around Line's neck, he tied it carefully in a Windsor knot. "This is exactly how she looked when she was dressing like a man," he said.

Line laughed. Nathan held a mirror in front of her. At her feet Christy's eyes grew round with confusion. "It's all right, dah-ling," Line said, leaning down to kiss him, the hat tilting on her head.

"Gorgeous," said Jack in a Brooklyn accent. "Give her a cigarette, Steed," he said to Nathan, who stood about with an umbrella like Steed in the *Avengers*.

"I'm thinking Butch Cassidy," said Nathan, copping a slightly different attitude.

"Oh, right!" said Jack. "When they were posing for photographs!"

Line could barely keep up with Jack. He was so fast and funny.

Marty took off her bowler and picked up Christopher who was threatening to cry. "I'm no actress," she sighed. "But I wish I had a camera." She was giggling too.

"They're in perfect condition," said Jack. "Hatboxes and all. Someone will pay handsomely for them."

Line took off the tall beaver hat and smoothed it to feel the nap. It was fun to dress up and great to be with Jack and Nathan. The warmth and ease of the night expanded around them. If only it were all so simple, she thought. At the edge of her consciousness hovered the gardener in the arboretum in his dirty, dark green pants.

4

After getting a wood fire going in the stove on a school morning in April, Paul set an iron skillet on top of it and put in rashers of bacon and three eggs. The sun was already sending low shafts of light through the cabin windows, warming up the colors of the wood, Paul's blankets, the simple shelves of food, the table where Paul worked.

When Paul had planned to live in Fairbanks, he had thought only of the long, dark winters and the intense summers. He had not reckoned on this surprising rush of spring light which turned snow to slush and mud and made the undergrowth alive with budding shrubs and trees, to say nothing of the energy of the excited birds.

Paul cleaned out the warm bacon grease with a piece of bread, but he left an egg in the pan. Stepping outdoors he set it on the ground near the woodpile. The red fox who hung out around the cabin would know that Paul had put it out for him.

Foxes were loners, though they did form family groups. Paul identified with this one deeply. A small reddish male, it had appeared in the fall and denned nearby all winter. Paul often saw its delicate tracks in new snow and sometimes caught its eye as it wandered by, silent and careless in the sun. By this time of year it would find plenty of voles, shrews and small birds, but Paul put food out every once in a while. Arvi, Paul's landlord, thought it was a young male hoping to establish its own territory and mate. It must have felt safe near their homes.

The sky was a blue bowl reaching to infinity, pale at the horizon. Paul sniffed the wind. He wasn't sure whether it was an actual Chinook from the south, but it did carry more of a verdant scent than he had smelled for a long time. In winter, Paul's nose became an entirely different sense organ! He couldn't smell much and had to protect it from the bite of the cold and ice fog. But the vernal equinox was passed, he had come through one winter. He was proud of himself.

Indoors, Paul picked up the chess piece he had been carving the night before and squinted at it. Did it look like a bishop? It didn't matter. Just so it wasn't a rook! The winter had given him lots of time to work on the pieces. It was easy with wood. If he didn't like a piece, he just threw it in the fire and started over! But he had his eye on working in stone once he got the hang of it.

"Do what you've never done before, see what you've never seen," sang Paul to himself. "Get on your bike and do what you like." It was a Donovan song he was learning from an album his friend Brian had.

By 7:45 a.m. when Arvi barged through the door of his homestead, a steaming mug of coffee in his hand, Paul was standing by the door of the pickup. Behind him Paul could see the warm kitchen full of activity as Arvi's kids got ready to board a school bus.

"Great day in the morning!" Arvi said as he swung into the driver's seat.

Paul smiled and got in on the passenger side wearing his mud boots and carrying a rucksack with his school shirt, tie and good shoes in it. Though there was no longer enough snow to ski home at night, Paul still didn't want to rouse Old Green, his station wagon which had spent the winter in hibernation. Temperatures were still below freezing, though they climbed up during the long sunny hours.

"It's a good thing we've got Egan back," Arvi greeted Paul, referring to the current governor of Alaska. "Those boys down in Juneau were just making a mess of things." Arvi was talking about the negotiations over native claims that was going on.

Stewart Udall, interior secretary under Lyndon Johnson, had decreed a freeze of Alaskan land use until native claims could be settled. The Alaskan Federation of Natives was negotiating with the state and the federal Bureau of Land Management to get a settlement. There had been little progress until Egan, Alaska's first state governor, returned. Arvi was optimistic, hoping that the natives would get a fair shake.

Paul didn't have much to add about politics. He was too overwhelmed. What he knew he heard from Arvi. Thick-set and bearded, Arvi superintended an elementary school just outside of Fairbanks and was deeply interested in education. He had a homesteader's independence and a doctorate from Harvard, the perfect combination! His shelves were lined with books and the stable, which was attached to the house, was full of horses.

"How's that science club going?" asked Arvi.

"Not so well," Paul admitted. "Everyone's out for duck and ptarmigan, I think," he said. In the winter it had been basketball. Few of the kids were interested in electronics or the simple lab experiments the school could afford. "I'm not even sure what 'science' means to them. Or to me, any more."

"Well, you've gotten a start," said Arvi. "One guy told me that after Neil Armstrong stepped on the moon the native peoples decided they were behind, that they would never catch up. It hit some young men hard."

"I want to go out for ptarmigan!" said Paul. "Not shoot them, just watch them."

"Yup, if you can't beat 'em, join 'em," said Arvi.

"You've never done that!" said Paul. It was his impression that Arvi always bucked authority and started up ventures as he saw the need. Arvi told him about being dismissed from a teaching position because he let the kids go over to the bookshelves and read when they were finished with their work. The hardliners didn't want this lack of discipline! Luckily things were a little more relaxed now.

"I mean the native people," said Arvi. "There's so much to learn. It's only your first year. Just figuring out where they're coming from and what it means to be Indian or Eskimo, is a good start for your first year."

"Exactly," said Paul. "I'm working on it." The native high school kids he knew had a lot to contend with. "A couple of us are working on a generator," said Paul. "Lots of uses for that."

"Yes indeed!" said Arvi as he dropped Paul on the highway.

"I'll probably stay in town tonight," said Paul as he slammed the pickup door.

Arvi raised his hand in blessing. "Onward!" he said.

Paul started hiking up the road in the chill morning air. Snow lay in damp, dirty swaths between the spruce and bare birches and alders on the sides of the road. He had two miles to go and he liked to arrive at school as early as possible, to have time to compose his thoughts before students piled in and over-ran the classrooms.

No matter how you looked at it, there was a big divide between the white kids, some of whom had been born in Alaska, and the native Athabascans, Yupik, Inupiat and Inuits. The native kids stuck together, their education ruled by the Bureau of Indian Affairs. Most Alaskan villages had no high school, so the kids who wanted an education left their homes and went to boarding schools, or boarded with families in cities. Many of the boarders stayed after school as long as possible as they weren't treated as well as they ought to be.

Among themselves, the native kids stuck with their cultural groups, but stood solidly together against the white kids. It was amazing to see. The Athabascan Indians were bigger kids, while the Eskimos were smaller. Yupiks were mostly from southwest Alaska, while the Inupiats and Inuit were from the north, the Inuit above the Arctic circle. There were a few of each in Fairbanks, but more Athabascans since they lived up and down the Tanana River.

The kids didn't talk about it, of course. And Paul understood from observation, or things older hands said. Paul tried to see each interaction as simply as he could, working with individuals. Paul could well remember being in big hospital wards as a kid, far from his family, struggling to find his place. His polio was obvious to anyone who looked, so Paul didn't feel a need to mention it, conducting himself as if he was perfectly normal.

A highlight of the winter had been Paul's ski runs home to his cabin on clear nights, the aurora borealis shifting green, pink and gold and lighting up the sky. Tracks of moose, snowshoe hare, squirrels, fox, vole and shrew had been visible when the snow was new. Paul had sharp eyes that easily adjusted to any light, and he'd become acutely attuned to the phases of the moon, sometimes timing his trips to it. He had lived in the sky those nights, the cold made bearable by his movement.

But many nights, either a storm or the ice fog kept Paul from going home to Chena Ridge. Those nights he stayed with his friends Brian and Linda. He loved being out alone, but he was careful. Arvi insisted he check in every night like a good neighbor.

Nothing in Alaska was really as he expected, Paul thought. There was so much to learn and sink his teeth into. He hardly had a handle on it and hadn't gotten much chance to do the things he wanted. But, he thought, a thrill of euphoria coursing through his body, he had gotten through the school year. The next one was bound to be easier.

A car pulled up beside Paul and he jumped in. It was the shop teacher, Alf.

"Friday," Alf greeted Paul solemnly from the middle of a brown bushy beard.

Paul smiled. "Yup," he said. Friday meant music, one way or another, though it was not without its hazards. Paul had noticed the young teachers all had the same problem. They wanted to have fun, but they didn't want their students to know how much! It sometimes meant going out to the Howling Dog Saloon in a nearby town, a rompin', stompin' rock and roll bar. "Howling Dog?" he asked.

"Maybe," Alf was noncommittal. "Don't know yet."

"Me neither," said Paul.

"Might be a good night to camp," said Alf.

"Might be," said Paul. Alf was thinking about hunting. Though most game was hunted in the fall, people who lived on the land needed fresh food in the spring after the long winter. They looked for greens in the woods, and shot migrating ducks or bear.

Paul thought about revving up his old station wagon and heading out along one of the rivers. He couldn't afford to get out in the bush, where there were no roads and you had to drop in by small plane. But there were great places to go near Fairbanks. A newly established waterfowl refuge had been set up on an old dairy farm, Creamer's Field north of town. The sandhill cranes would soon be flying in to their nesting grounds. Paul had been amazed by their numbers as they left for warmer climates the previous August.

At school, Alf parked and Paul had time to put on his good shirt, his tie and organize his thoughts before students thronged in. He had been purposely conservative that year, following the textbooks, sticking to the rules and blending into the woodwork while observing the situation.

That morning Paul could tell that the fresh, bright days were getting to the kids too. In a month they would be back in their villages. But first there was the school talent night, concert, proms and graduation to get through.

None of these involved Paul. Over the winter, basketball had been the biggest draw. Paul, as a young single teacher, hung out after school to provide a place for those who weren't in sports, mentoring guitar players, chess and checkers games and learning wood carving, as well as sponsoring the science club.

One young Yupik, Steve, who took his American name from *Hawaii-Five-0*, was interested in mechanics. Paul encouraged him to bring in his snow mobile engine, which was ailing. They took it apart with Alf's help, and Paul learned more than Steve! Now they were working on a generator.

Paul had never done much with mechanics, possibly because Dad hadn't. Dad left that branch of science to others, but Paul realized that in a place like Alaska, he ought to know something about it! The four-stroke engine on Steve's Ski-doo fascinated Paul, though he hated the noise and didn't want one of his own. Intake, compression, power, exhaust. It was so simple! He happily got his hands as greasy as Alf and Steve. There was even an Athabascan girl, Sylvia, who paid close attention as they adjusted the rings to prevent flutter and made sure the valves were opening and closing properly.

Classes bumped along. Paul watched his students for any interest whatsoever. Chemistry that year had taken them quite far into mining as some of the students knew something about it. Paul was more comfortable in biology, but so many of his students had butchered and skinned animals or cleaned fish that it didn't have the impact it did in the Lower 48. The textbooks came from New England and were not very representative of the Boreal environment they were in, but Paul got out to the University library and boned up when he could. His students knew more than he about some of these things, but he was charged with providing an overview and he did the best he could.

At last the day was over. No one stayed after school on Friday night. Paul walked over to Linda and Brian's apartment when he had cleared up his room, packed away microscopes and slides, adjusted the grow-lights and watered the plants in the school's makeshift greenhouse. He puzzled over how to get natural light to the plants, now that it was so abundant, but the science lab faced north.

Outdoors, Paul stretched. The air had warmed up but his wool coat felt good. He stopped to get a six-pack of beer to contribute to the dinner he knew Linda would be making.

Linda, tall and rangy with a colorful apron over her jeans, stood at the stove in the warm kitchen, browning onions and chopped moose meat she had bought at the grocery. Like Mother would have, she threw in cans of tomatoes and beans to make a chili. "Hey, Paul," she said. "I was expecting you."

"I'm grateful," said Paul humbly, taking off coats and sweaters and doffing his boots. "I'm so glad you guys put up with me." Three places had been laid at their small apartment table. Paul handed Linda a beer and put the rest in the fridge.

Paul picked up his guitar, which had ended up at Brian and Linda's because their apartment was drier and had better temperature control than his cabin. He played a few riffs of the Donovan song that was running in his head. "Get on your bike, and do what you like," he sang. "Oh-h-h, get on your bike and do what you like."

Linda and Brian had electricity and a phonograph. Brian loved the same music Paul did, songs with lots of story behind them, and he ordered albums by Bob Dylan, Leonard Cohen, Donovan. Paul and Brian listened to the songs and wrote out the chords and lyrics.

Brian, lean and tall, also with a thick, bushy dark beard, showed up, kicking off his boots before bussing Linda at the stove. Paul was ashamed of his own thin, blonde mustache and goatee, but he couldn't do much about it. "Hey, Paulie," Brian said taking a beer out of the fridge.

Paul nodded and kept playing. He looked out the window at the back yard of the lot across the street. Unlike streets in the small towns Paul had known, houses sat on long skinny lots facing the derelict contents of the opposite home's back yard, old oil drums, machine parts, lumber, tarps, wood. There was no shortage of broken machinery around Fairbanks. No one got rid of anything in case its parts could be re-used.

"So, what say you?" asked Brian. "Upper Limits? A group called Cliff and Janey are playing there tonight I'm told." Brian worked at the university, doing maintenance. Paul had met him last summer when Arvi found Paul work there briefly. Brian was also taking classes and trying to get work for the federal government as a surveyor, figuring there was lots of Alaska to survey!

"Sure," said Paul. He liked the Upper Limits, a teen club started by parents that had music and food on Friday and Saturday nights. It wasn't a place you went to drink and get loose. You were a teacher there as you were every day. Fairbanks had a small town atmosphere as there were few places to go and it was often fun to meet a student's parents.

Shafts of sunshine streaked across the small, oilcloth covered table as they sat down. Linda and Brian looked at each other as if they were brimming with something, a secret from Paul.

"You ask him," said Linda.

"No, you," said Brian, deferring as he cut a piece of Linda's homemade bread and sopped it in the chili. "She's your friend."

Linda turned to Paul. "Do you have plans for the summer, Paul?" she asked conspiratorially.

"Haven't exactly," said Paul. "I guess it's time to think about it!" The moose tasted dark and gamey, delicious. "This is so good, Linda!"

"Thanks," said Linda. "One of my friends knows some people who are proving up a big homestead. They're putting in a lodge and cabins for tourists on a lake a few miles from the railway between Fairbanks and Anchorage. They've done a lot of the heavy work, but they're looking for a jack-of-all-trades to help out this summer."

"We thought of you," said Brian. "I know you haven't gotten out in the bush as much as you'd like. And this is the bush! There's no road yet, but they're working on that this summer. And it's pretty close to the railway line."

Paul sat listening. He had taken the train down to Anchorage once at Christmas, just to see the country. It was a wonderful trip.

"They're nice people, two couples apparently, just getting started," said Linda. "I'm just supposed to put the word out."

"Sounds great," said Paul, musing. He shook his head. He hadn't been able to think about vacation, about being able to choose how he spent his time. Just staying around Fairbanks would be fine, he thought, now that he had a little money.

"We're flying down to Texas," said Brian. "For a month. See the home folks."

"As soon as school gets out!" said Linda. "I'm so excited! Brian's taking a month off, but that's all he can get."

"Back in time for the midnight sun ballgame!" Brian said. "You missed it last year. It's the best!"

"Too muddy for baseball in the spring, isn't it?" asked Paul.

"Yeah, they don't start playing games until the middle of June," said Brian.

Paul had seen a few games in the short season last summer. But he was still overwhelmed, his mind flying back and forth over the territory. He struggled mentally back to the question at hand. "Could I meet these people?" he asked.

"Sure," said Linda. "I'll fix it up one of these days, if you're interested."

"I would be," said Paul. "I'll have to think about it."

"Okay!" said Brian. "Men do the dishes tonight!" he decreed.

Linda smirked. "Not much to do," she said, but she decamped to the couch and turned on the television.

According to the news, there had been another huge march protesting the country's involvement in Vietnam, 500,000 people in Washington alone. "I guess Wally Hickel must be feeling pretty proud," said Brian. The Alaskan Hickel had lost his job as Secretary of the Interior because he criticized Richard Nixon, suggesting Nixon listen to the concerns of his young constituents concerning the war.

"Didn't help to lose Hickel," said Paul. "Turned out he was a good guy!" He had also been good at negotiating with the Alaskan Federation of Natives.

"Yeah, Miller was useless," said Brian. At the end of December, Governor Egan had taken over from former governor Miller, who was stonewalling, insisting the state didn't owe the natives anything.

Brian scrubbed the bottom of the chili pot with a piece of woven metal. "What does Arvi think?"

"He's optimistic," said Paul, lifting the dry dishes into the cupboard. "They're going to get this thing settled. Then he wants the villages to build high schools. It's the obvious solution. They could become community centers!"

"Yeah," said Brian. "Money flowing in. That would help."

"So you care what Arvi thinks too?" asked Paul.

"He's a fixture on the liberal side," said Brian. "Everyone up at the university knows him. The state's kind of stagnant, economically, until this thing gets settled."

Paul thought about how much Arvi had influenced his thinking. Even though he wasn't politically attuned, politics surrounded him. Arvi was a member of a Quaker meeting and had been a homesteader since 1952. When he fired up the sauna on Sunday nights, friends came from all around. The discussion was wild and free-ranging. Nothing was off limits!

This too had been overwhelming to Paul. Naked bodies discussing everything from philosophy to free love. He had come to Alaska to be surrounded by nature, but the people were every bit as interesting. Nothing kept him from Arvi's Sunday night saunas!

Brian put the black iron chili pot on the stove and turned a burner on to dry it. Running water and electric heat were such novelties to Paul that he watched. Of course it cost them. The apartment was tiny and heating bills immense, but there were two of them and they were happy.

"So! Let's get this show on the road," said Brian.

Linda turned off the television. The sun still had not set, would not until 10 p.m. It made the cold air deceptive. It was freezing. They pulled on boots, woolen coats and scarves.

The three of them walked the few blocks to the Upper Limits downtown. The sun, low on the horizon, threw everything into high relief, casting their long shadows on the austere, barren roads. Hot breath coming out of their mouths and noses caught the light.

"You should make up your mind about going out to the bush this summer," said Linda. "You're probably not the only one wanting the job!"

"Yeah," said Paul. "It's just that I haven't thought anything about vacation yet! Of course I'm interested, but I can tell you for certain Monday."

"Sounds good," said Linda. "I won't see my friend until then anyway. You could probably go down on the train and see the place. It's at a flag stop! No station, nothing!"

"Wow," said Paul.

"They got the main buildings up last year," said Linda. "But I guess there's lots to do still. Finish work and hauling stuff, helping with the kids. Probably not much pay beyond your board and a place to sleep. I told them you played the guitar!"

"Sounds great," said Paul. "I'm just not sure whether I should go home or not."

"Home?" asked Linda. "Iowa?"

"Yeah," said Paul.

"Ummmm," said Linda. "I understand. I can't wait to get home, actually."

"But I haven't saved much money," said Paul. "I should probably stay here." His teacher's salary didn't give him much leeway, but he didn't expect much either. His salary was spread out over the summer. If he didn't spend it, it would get saved.

At the Upper Limits, the windows were hung with curtains to keep out the late sun. Paul and Brian got bottles of pop and Linda found a table at the back against the wall with other grownups. The two young sons of the owners ran around, serving pizza and burgers. In front, below the stage was a small place for dancing.

"Now we all know not much good comes out of Anchorage," said the high school student who introduced the band. Everyone laughed. The rivalry between Anchorage and Fairbanks was legendary. "But tonight, we've got the best from Anchorage, Cliff and Janey!"

"Thank you, thank you!" said Cliff. He strummed his 12-string into a dark, powerful, Johnny Cash-sounding riff, a song which even Paul knew. "We got married in a fever, hotter than a pepper sprout ..." sang Janey.

Just to get the kids going, thought Paul. He was surprised to find himself thinking more like a performer than a listener. And indeed, when they finished Cliff said, "Now this song doesn't reflect Janey and my relationship. We just like it!"

They had lots of songs, just what Paul liked. Some they had written themselves and some songs by Dylan, the Beatles. Paul loved the powerful 12-string sound.

Listening, Paul thought about being a Dot, way back in high school. How it took a dynamic, crazy guy like Dennis Dugan to pull a group together. Dennis had come back from his military service, but his partner, Michael, had not. Paul didn't have much contact with the town where he'd gone to high school, but Dad had found out and let Paul know.

As the evening progressed, Cliff and Janey asked a local guitar player to come up and play with them. Brian nudged Paul, "Should have brought your guitar," he said.

But Paul shook his head self-deprecatingly. He hadn't performed in public in Alaska, though Linda was threatening to put him up on the "talent night" list at school. He felt good. Such a big world and he was part of it. As a kid in rehab after painful polio surgeries, he had had no idea he would get to have such a life. He bowed his head, inwardly thanking the Lord, as he knew Him. He couldn't imagine life getting much better.

5

Line felt Christopher's little hand on her shoulder and woke up, late, as usual. All she could see out the window was the grey sky, as thick fog lay banked over the city.

"Good morning Christy," said Line.

"Morning," said Christopher. "Milk," he said simply, standing there in his little cotton shirt and night-time diaper.

Line smiled. "Okay, come on," she said. Christopher was too little to open the refrigerator, though he did try to climb on chairs and get the cereal in the cupboard. Line stretched and wrapped a blanket around her shoulders as she went out to the kitchen. Her bare feet were chilled on the wooden floor.

The presence of sleeping people could be felt all over the house. It was Saturday and, when Line came in from work the night before, Marty,

Erik and their guests were still smoking and drinking, talking, a Bob Dylan record playing in the front room. Christopher was asleep on the mattress in Line's room. In the bathroom Line had smelled a sickly sweet, burnt smell, as if someone had been cooking something.

Two mud-encrusted 10-speed bikes rested along the walls in the hall with pannier bags disheveled and open. Their owners, a brother and sister, had ridden clear across the country from New York State. Line had opened the door to them the day before. She was impressed at how quiet they were, both in body and language. Spent and silent, they introduced themselves as Erik's friends and asked for water.

Line did not even want to ask them questions. All those days of riding, even over the mountains. She left them to spread out in the front room, packed up Christopher and went to work as she normally did.

The big unfurnished house creaked and echoed in the cold July fog. Line sat at the wooden table in the center of the spacious kitchen, drinking coffee and eating toast as Christopher downed bowl after bowl of cereal and milk. She had found a health food store nearby, and Christopher's cereal was mostly oats, raisins and other toasted grains. No sugar in it at all.

Line wondered why rooms felt cold and melancholy when it was foggy, even when they were inhabited. Eerie mumbling and voices preceded Richard and Rosalyn as they entered the kitchen. "Coffee?" Line asked the two athletic, wind and sun-burned people who loomed over her. She stood up and turned on the gas below the teakettle.

In a moment, Marty was there, in thick socks and a long quilted robe, now ragged at the sleeves, threads hanging off it where the quilting was separating. Bright and smiley, she took over making coffee and put slices of wheatberry bread in the toaster for the guests. Line retreated, listening.

"We are going to run out to the coast today," said Rosalyn, smiling. "Sort of finish the ocean to ocean ride."

"It's only a couple of miles away," said Marty.

"I don't want to stop riding," Rosalyn said. "It's like I don't know anything else!"

"There's the concert tomorrow," said Richard. There were free rock concerts every Sunday in Golden Gate Park. Line didn't pay much attention to them.

"Yeah!" Marty appeared to be excited by this, but Line knew she would probably get a headache. Marty got sick migraine headaches so bad she had to retreat to a dark room until they subsided. Marty associated them with sunlight, but there were other reasons too. Line felt apprehensive.

"I'll be working tonight," Line said looking at Marty. She did not have to say what she was thinking.

"Don't worry," said Marty. "I'm not going anywhere today. We'll be fine, won't we Christopher," she said, hugging him. "Other people can go to the grocery store."

"Good," said Line. "Thank you, Marty." She liked some of the people who turned up, but not all of them. Richard and Rosalyn were good people.

Stephen called for Line that morning. "I'm in Santa Cruz!" he said. "Finally!" His mother had died and he was scouting a place to live before beginning his doctoral program at the University that fall.

"Oh?" asked Line.

"Just let me get settled and I'll come and see you."

"Come and see me?" Line shook her head and hung up the phone. When Stephen called back immediately, she did not answer. It was hard to explain even to herself the depth of her unhappiness about the limbo she was in because of Stephen. She both longed for him and had a black anger toward him that she was afraid to bring to the surface. She also thought of Bill, the gardener who had taken a shine to her. She could hardly go to the arboretum any more without him turning up in his green uniform. It was all such a mess.

That night when Line got home from work, she was appalled to find a man sitting at the kitchen table with two large pearl-handled pistols in front of him. Erik sat across from him, lazily slouched in his chair, as if he were very relaxed, the essence of cool. Marty stood to one side under the lamp over the stove, watching, an expression of mixed pride and anxiety on her face. Erik reached up and ran his hands through his thick, blonde hair, calming himself.

"This is Javier," said Marty, who seemed hypnotized. "He came to see Erik." But then she looked guilty and came over to Line. "Christopher's been in bed for an hour," she said low.

The man was attractive, with a thick dark mustache and dark eyebrows in a handsome face. He stood up, gallantly bowing to Line. "I must go," he said in a thick Hispanic accent, wrapping the six-guns in cloth and putting them in a leather shoulder pack. "I came to introduce myself to Senor Erik, whom I've heard about. A fine man."

Erik stood up and followed Javier out the front door.

"He wanted to talk 'business,' he said," whispered Marty to Line.

"I'm not staying here," said Line sharply. "It's no place for a kid." Marty looked guilty, but she did not reply.

Line went down the hall to her bedroom, and there, indeed was Christopher, his little chest rising and falling as he breathed. She put her head down on the pillow beside him and wept.

The next morning she called the phone number in Alaska Paul had given them for emergencies. He didn't have his own phone, but he lived in a cabin near a family who had one.

"Paul's out in the bush, doing carpentry," said the woman who answered the phone. "But we can put your message out on the radio, the bush telegraph." She laughed warmly. "He'll probably come straight home when he hears you're in Fairbanks. His cabin is empty this summer," she said. "I'm Carol. I would love to meet Paul's sister!"

Line was heartened by the lovely, rich voice. "I'll call again when I get my plane ticket," she said. "Thank you so much!"

While everyone else was in the park, singing and dancing, she began packing her few things together. On Monday morning, she left a message for her supervisor at the hospital saying that she had to leave and wasn't sure when she'd be coming back. She took Christopher with her to a travel agent and bought an airplane ticket to Fairbanks.

Erik and Marty drove them to the airport. Marty wore a long face. "I'm sorry, Line," she said, hugging Line goodbye.

"Don't worry, Marty," said Line, looking steadily at her with love. "Nothing works forever. You have helped us so much." She was feeling lighthearted by this time, ready for the new. Christopher's big eyes followed the huge planes moving beyond the glass windows of the airport lounge. "Airplanes," said Line. "We're going to fly in an airplane to see Paul. Remember Paul?"

Erik knelt down, his face next to Christopher. "No hard feelings, little man," he said. "See you soon."

"I'll miss you, Christy," said Marty, gathering him in her arms and lifting him up. "You're getting so heavy!" she said as she handed him to Line, moisture in her eyes.

"Remember how we said goodbye to Paul just a year ago?" asked Line. Christopher was almost too big to put on her hip any more.

"Wow," said Marty. "It doesn't feel that long ago!"

Line carried Christopher toward the exit door and waved to Erik, who touched two fingers to his forehead in salute, and Marty, whose face was as sad as if they were leaving forever.

Line wasn't sad. She was excited. Alaska, the land of the midnight sun. It was probably warmer there than in was in San Francisco.

Line's eyes were glued to the window as she sat with Christopher sleeping in her lap. Far below were islands, the sea, tiny towns. As the plane lowered itself into Fairbanks, Line saw snow-covered mountains. Fairbanks looked tiny, strung out along a wide river. But it was indeed warm when Line and Christopher walked down the steps and across the tarmac to the low, ugly airport.

Line spotted Paul's ruddy face coming toward them. A quizzical smile split his face, embedded in shaggy hair and beard. "What are you doing here?" he asked the mystified little boy, lifting him up.

"I don' know," said Christopher.

Paul laughed. "You will soon! You're putting your foot in it, Christopher, and no mistake!" He chortled.

"Is it okay?" asked Line. She had never been able to speak to Paul. "Is it okay that we came?" She reached up to hug his weathered soul. He had an odd, fragrant smell. But Line was impressed at how confidently he moved.

"Sure!" said Paul. "But we'll put you to work. There's so much to do in the summer, because now there's enough light. I have to get back tomorrow. I left the tractor at the rail stop, and I'm hoping you'll come. There are a couple of kids out there, where I'm working. Five and three. I think Chrisopher will love it."

"Wow!" said Line. "Kids! And I can help?"

"You're not a-kidding," said Paul. "We'll go shopping tonight, stay at my cabin and then take the Peddler out early tomorrow morning. It's a freight train. It was kind of convenient I came in. We needed cement, and I've got a grocery list too."

They waited until Line's poor taped-together suitcase was unloaded from the hold of the plane, and then walked over to where the old green Mikkelson station wagon was parked. Line was amazed. "It still runs?" she asked.

"She was in hibernation all winter," said Paul. "But she does run."

Fairbanks looked flat, spread out and ugly, compared to the packed together tall buildings of San Francisco with its lush parks, hills and ocean views. Paul stopped first at a lumberyard and hefted two 50-pound bags of cement into the back of the station wagon. At the grocery store, Line noticed how expensive everything was. She wished she had thought to bring food. The vegetables looked small and bruised. Paul bought flour, graham crackers, rice, steel cut oats, a bag of onions, raisins and chocolate.

"There's plenty of green stuff in the woods, if you know what you're doing," Paul said. "Little did I know Euell Gibbons would one day serve me in good stead!" he laughed.

Paul moved fast and decisively, while Line felt bewildered. She yawned. According to the clock over the checkout stands, it was 10 p.m. but it looked like late afternoon. "The stores stay open this late?" she asked. There were few people in the store.

"Everything stays open!" said Paul. "Trying to make hay while the sun shines. There's a sense of urgency in the summer. Sheila's getting berry fever, she says! You'll probably have to pick berries for jam and syrup. My friends will be out there, living in their cabins all winter, depending on that syrup!"

"And you'll be here?" asked Line. "Teaching?"

"Yup," said Paul. "How long are you staying?" He lifted Christopher up in his strong arms. "Are you a good berry picker?" he asked. Christopher was all eyes. He appeared to love Paul, patting his beard to see what was under it.

Line looked crestfallen. She had come without a plan. None at all. "I really don't know, Paul," she said. "I don't know what I'm doing. It's crazy at Marty's place, people, drugs, music. It wasn't good for us, though I love San Francisco. I guess I just thought I would hang out for the summer, take a break, see what happens."

"That's fine!" said Paul. "There are so many people our age around. It's exciting! But everyone's short of cash, helping each other out. Maybe you could fish. No one even has time, and we'd love some fish to eat."

"Great," said Line. "It sounds great."

Paul's cabin smelled musty, shut up in the heat and damp of the summer. Line carried Christopher in and laid him on the bed. He was probably hungry, but she didn't want to wake him.

"I wonder how my fox is doing," said Paul. "There's a red fox who hung around all winter. I hope he stays." He started a fire in the wood stove. "I just need to dry the place out," he said, opening all the doors and windows.

It was a small log room with the stove, a table, shelves for a few dishes and books and the single bed against the wall. "You can have the bed," said Paul as he fed sticks into the iron belly. "I'm used to the floor now. I set my tent up on the floor of one of the unfinished cabins in the bush, as a mosquito net! But it is kind of small."

Line gave an anguished sigh. "Paul! I'm completely unprepared! I just didn't think!" She looked out the window at the purple twilight finally settling over the night.

"Don't worry," said Paul. "We'll figure it out. I'll bet Arvi has a tent we can borrow, and sleeping bags. That's all you need. I hope they're still up!"

Paul carried the sleeping Christopher in his arms and they walked over to a neighboring cabin which was much bigger and more spread out.

At a spacious wooden table, kids were eating popcorn and drinking a cool drink Carol had made from wild rose hips, leaves and petals. Line was surprised at how good it tasted. The room was dry and fragrant with the smell of the fruit jam Carol's oldest daughter was cooking.

"The hips we're drinking are from last year," said Carol. "Wild roses are in bloom right now. It's berry time," she said. "Dina's making crowberry jam. The crowberries are the first to come out. They're a little like a blueberry, but they're not good raw, kind of bitter and tannic tasting. Their flavor really comes out when they're cooked!" She turned to Dina. "Give Line a taste." Dina dipped a spoon into the boiling liquid and handed it to Line, who held it out to cool.

"There are some poisonous berries," said Arvi. "Any white berries. If you're going berry picking, make sure someone shows you what to pick! Paul's pretty good. He can spot a mushroom at 50 feet!"

"Also bears," said Carol. "Bears are after berries just like you!"

"Bears?!" said Line. She looked at Christopher, who was stuffing popcorn in his mouth. She licked the hot spoon of jam. The taste was a little like blueberries, but Dina had put cinnamon and honey in the mix.

"Plenty of berries to go around," said Arvi. "You seen any bears in your area, Paul?"

"We do have one, that we know of," said Paul. "I saw him once from a distance." He looked at Line. "Don't worry. They don't see us as food," he said. "They're just like us, wanting to fatten up for the winter. And they do like berries."

In a crowded storage area, Arvi found an army surplus tent for Line and sleeping bags. "Nobody ever throws anything away out here," he said. "It all comes in handy sometime."

"Thank you so much," said Line. Christopher was falling asleep in her arms.

"You're welcome," said Arvi. "One thing we've learned from the Eskimo: Property doesn't mean much. They don't worry about it at all. If someone needs something, it's theirs."

"Some of us are learning that," said Paul, smiling. "I know quite a few people who aren't!" He and Arvi exchanged knowing glances.

The night felt short to Line. In the morning, clouds and fog obscured the mountains. Paul drove the few miles into Fairbanks and stopped to pick up his friend Brian.

"So this is your sister!" said Brian. "Paul's told us a lot about you!" Brian would drive the station wagon to his place and park it until Paul returned.

On the train, they loaded everything Paul had picked up into a box car. Only one railroad car had seats in it for people. Line and Christopher pressed their noses to the glass as the train wound through the misty mountains, the forests, along rivers and through intermittent rain.

Paul was euphoric nevertheless. "I love this run!" he said. "I'd love to be a train man, if I weren't teaching." He was eating a peanut butter sandwich, just as Line had when coming across country from Chicago to San Francisco.

"How's teaching?" asked Line.

"It's getting there," said Paul, evenly. "I think next year will be better than last."

At the flag stop, they loaded everything into a wagon at the back of the tractor, covering it with a dirty blue tarp. "I'm worried about the cement," said Paul. "I don't want it to get wet. You can sit under the tarp if you want to."

Line looked at him as if he were crazy. "What do you think Christy," she asked. "Do you like the rain?"

"Rain, rain!" said Christopher, looking up at the sky. It was just misting, but dark clouds hung around the mountains to the west.

"That's the Alaska Range," said Paul, following their eyes. "Mt. McKinley towers above our lake. It'll be out one of these days, and you'll see it in all of its majesty. Denali, the Athabascans call it. The high one."

"We're fine," said Line. She sat in the wagon on the hump of cement bags, holding her son.

"This is the worst part," said Paul. "There's no road, so we're going to go right through the bush. I have to go slowly. It'll take a few hours, even though we're only going eleven miles."

Line twisted and turned with the load as they wended their way over roots, fallen logs, boggy places. It was like riding a horse. There seemed to be a track Paul was following, but it was hard to tell. The tractor's engine ground along so loud Line couldn't hear much else.

The rain squalled, coming down harder, but it didn't bother Christy. He opened his mouth, trying to catch raindrops and so did Line! When it stopped, their hair was plastered against their heads. Line shivered, but it wasn't terribly cold.

They stopped for a snack in an open meadow. Paul dug up a salami and cut chunks off it. The woods didn't look too different from what Line was used to near Lake Michigami, witchy looking spruces, birch and poplar, but the lower plants were unfamiliar.

"That's your crowberry right there," said Paul pointing to a plant with evergreen-like leaves. "That's fireweed. It changes color all summer. And that's cotton grass. Lots of different kinds."

It was still as they sat. All they could hear was the dripping of water off the leaves. All of a sudden Paul pointed silently. In the misty distance was a large moose, its great flared antlers opened toward them.

"It's a moose," said Paul to Christopher. "Moose."

"That's a lot of antler," said Line, looking at the breadth of the rack on the animal. "How do they sleep with all that on their heads?"

Paul laughed and spoke quietly. "Good question! But, according to observers, they lie on their sides and let one antler touch the ground." The moose was moving along the trees at the edge of the open space. "The antlers drop off every year. Moose need to eat a lot of vegetation!"

Slowly the moose disappeared into trees. "What a majestic animal!" said Line. None of them could take their eyes off it. The moose animated the terrain.

They hadn't seen many animals. Mostly the track wound through thick brush and trees. Line felt drier when they got back in the wagon and Paul started up the engine again.

At last they arrived at a collection of cabins near the edge of a lake. It was late afternoon and the weather was clearing, though the forest dripped with moisture. Line smelled meat cooking as Paul directed her into a large cabin, carrying groceries.

"Hey!" said a woman with warm, enveloping arms. "I can't believe you came all this way," she said. She looked to be about the same age as Line.

Line was sore and happy not to be moving. "I'm so glad to be here!" she said.

"We usually cook together," said Sheila. "It's just more fun when everyone's working so hard. Bonnie and Ed have their own cabin, but tonight I'm cooking for everyone." She stood beside an amazing old wood stove, with painted doors and porcelain handles on the ovens below and cupboards above. Line could imagine it bumping through the bush, lashed to a cart behind the tractor. It was the only way it could have gotten there. The cabin looked cozy, with shelves of canned goods, books, curtains on the windows.

"They have two kids," said Paul. "We have to keep a good eye on them and that's a communal job too. Someone's always the dedicated kid-watcher."

Line laughed a little hysterically. She was tired. "Remember when Mother used to divvy up chores?" she said to Paul. "I can see her handwriting on the paper taped to the refrigerator. Paul – little kids. Line – dishes. Marty – set the table."

"How many kids were there?" asked Sheila. "Did you bring onions, Paul? I sure could use an onion."

"Yep!" said Paul. He fished in the grocery bags and found the bag of onions.

"There were six of us," said Line. "Ellie was way ahead of us. She's married and has two kids now. Then me, Marty and Paul ganged together. And then came 'the little kids,' Kristen and Hanna. They're still at home. They were the ones we had to watch."

"It sounds like a blast," said Sheila. "I grew up in Montana, with a brother and ranch hands all around. Kind of different. My mother was sick a lot, but my grandmother lived with us. She taught me everything I know."

"Which was a lot," said Paul.

"We've been here for a year," said Sheila. "So things are starting to be under control. It was a lot more primitive when we started! Not a thing here!"

"You'll be a guest tonight," Paul said to Line. "But tomorrow!" he threatened teasingly.

"I'll do whatever you need," said Line. "I'm so glad to help."

"Let's go find the others," said Paul, catching Christopher up in his arms and carrying him out the door.

Outdoors the air smelled lush and fragrant. Along the horizon was a piece of blue sky, but the mountain was so large it was already obscuring any sunshine that might slip through. Paul showed Line the lodge, which rose high, two stories, with spaces for windows and doors. The roof was on, but the windows gaped open. "We're waiting for the road," Paul said. "They expect to finish it in September or so. When the road comes, everything will be easy."

Jack and Ed were building a sauna. "The best way to get clean!" said Paul. "Seeing these buildings go up gives me such a sense I could do it myself! Or almost by myself. A great feeling of independence!"

Bonnie and her kids were, yes, picking berries! "Some blueberries," said Bonnie. "And a few raspberries. I'm marking out the areas."

"I'll help tomorrow," said Line. "Or whatever you need me to do."

Little Anita walked right up to Christopher and offered him a handful of blueberries. She had on cotton shirts, shorts and mudboots on her sturdy little legs, but Line could see evidence of bites on her deeply sun-browned skin.

"Mosquitoes?" asked Line.

"Not too bad here," said Bonnie. "We're lucky. And it's getting better. The fall is the best time here. Short but sweet."

"Fall? Already?" asked Line.

"Not quite," said Bonnie. "But we can feel it. It's like a shadow falling, making us all hurry."

In the next few days Line didn't know whether she or Christopher was happier. He did get mosquito bites, which Sheila plastered with herbal lotion. Line stuck with the kids, picking quarts of berries, outdoors most of the day. Sheila and Bonnie boiled them into syrups and jams. The men worked into the evenings, roofing, fitting, chinking, planing. After supper they lay in a row on the floor of Jack and Sheila's cabin, spent, listening to the Northwind, the 'bush telegraph' as people called it.

One night Line sorted through herbal specimens she and Bonnie had collected. They would be dried for tea and various purposes. All of a sudden, they all heard on the radio: "Line Mikkelson Cohen, your husband is in Fairbanks at the Gold Rush Motor Lodge. Please meet him as soon as you can. Line Mikkelson Cohen, your husband Stephen is waiting for you at the Gold Rush Motor Lodge."

Line stood there gaping, herbs in hand. All of a sudden she knew it was why she had come. She had wanted Stephen to come to the ends of the earth to find her. And here he was. He had done it. Wiping away tears, she slipped out into the cool air of the evening with everyone's eyes upon her.

6

Marty paid for a prune Danish and coffee at the counter of the Scandia Bakery and took them to one of the little tables crowded together in the small room. There were the twins, Vivian and Marian, dressed to the nines in leopard-skin coats, red hats perched over their tightly curled bleached-blonde hair, matching handbags over their arms. Exact copies of each other, they were a fixture on the streets of San Francisco. As Marty watched, they each raised their cups and took a drink, their images reflected in a long wall mirror. Four vivid copies!

The delicious smell of baking bread permeated the room, and from the half balcony above that jutted out into the room Marty heard the rolling and pounding of dough. The room was cozy with warmth on the bright cold day. A little sign near the silver coffee urns said that the bakery planned a special breakfast on December 13th, the Swedish Festival of Lights. Marty wondered whether she had it in her to get up early and come on her way to work.

Dosing her coffee with half and half and sugar, Marty threaded her way back between the tables, the cup and saucer jittering. There was the well-dressed older lady Marty often saw, talking to a man in a suit and tie much younger than she. And the intense young Swedish man she sometimes talked to. Marty avoided him. She was afraid he would ask her out.

Marty was thrilled to be downtown, wearing a double-breasted brown suede jacket, a woolen sweater and jeans, on her own, doing as she pleased. She did miss Line. In the two previous years they had done their Christmas shopping together. Last year every item was silver, set with turquoise stones: rings, bracelets, and a tie pin for Dad. They didn't spend a lot of money. It was more about the thought. They were sure they had as much fun wrapping up and sending the presents as the family did opening them.

But Line had reunited with her husband and moved to Santa Cruz, where they lived in a residential assistant apartment while Stephen got his doctorate in history. They were poor, but Line loved the coastal town and the interesting people she was meeting. "It's full of gardens," she told Marty on the phone. Marty had visited once. She hoped Erik would go down with her for a day around Christmas.

Behind her Marty heard a Russian conversation. The bakery was her touchstone in the city, on Powell Street, the busiest, most tourist-infested street in town. It was run by a Swedish family, man, wife and vivacious, dark-haired daughter. The daughter was rarely there, but Marty had once seen the room full of dark gypsy-looking Eastern Europeans joking with her.

Marty tried to eat her pastry slowly. She could never decide between the cherry and the prune. They were each light and utterly fresh, with a dollop of fruit and a light vanilla sugar glaze. The quality was so reliable that Marty didn't try to make pastry herself. Whenever she came downtown, she found herself on Powell Street, walking past the bright, jangled Woolworths, past the wonderful bookstore where she could look at art books as long as she wanted, drawn by the Swedish Bakery. Line must miss it too.

Powell Street was chaotic. People waited in long lines for the cable car, which was put on a turntable at Market Street, and pushed around so it could catch the northern cable up Powell to Fisherman's Wharf. The cable car was a marvel. Marty had seen the huge turbines which pulled the cables under the street. Powell Street was also full of musicians, dancers, drummers, Salvation Army Santas jingling their bells, collecting money. Drunken people and beggars beyond shame interspersed the festivity.

Books, mused Marty. Perhaps she should buy books for Christmas presents this year. The coffee was delicious. Marty refilled her cup with a little coffee, more half and half. She had to admit to herself that her stomach was often upset. She suspected that if she drank less coffee it would settle down. She didn't expect to be less anxious. If she wanted that, she shouldn't live with Erik, in a city far from home! But she loved Erik. And she loved the city, could not get enough of walking, keeping her eyes open, seeing what she could see.

Marty took out a notebook and made a list of people she needed presents for. Dad and Mother liked books about nature. She would find a pictorial reference book for Ellie's family of two little girls. A gardening book for Line, and *Wind in the Willows* for Christopher. He was almost old enough. She wasn't sure about Paul in Alaska, but something would strike her when she looked. Kristen liked animal books and magic Hanna who was not so little any more loved fairy tales.

Marty loved to think about each of them, her immediate family. She would buy something nice for Erik, and perhaps something from San Francisco for Aunt Rose, who had long been her benefactor. But that was it. She didn't try to buy presents for friends, unless she made food or brought wine to a party.

Mats, the Swedish man with a carefully groomed golden beard, a black leather jacket and an air of inner angst, stopped by Marty's table. He was studying at an art academy, and of course he could be found at Scandia Bakery.

Marty was noncommittal. "I'm going Christmas shopping today," she said. "I have so much family, mostly in the Midwest, and I have to get things in the mail. It's getting late!"

"Late indeed!" said Mats gruffly. "Nice to see you. Be well."

Marty watched him go out the glass doors onto the bright street. She looked at herself quickly in the mirror, trying to see what he saw when he looked at her. It didn't matter, she thought. He could think what he liked. She collected her dishes and put them in a tub near the coffee urns, making sure to leave her table free of crumbs.

Blinking, she went out into the frosty sunshine. Christmas in the city was a rush of energy. Try as she might to keep up her own studying and thinking, Marty always got caught up in it. Every store window was filled with intricate, beautiful displays. Christmas carols played and the windows of Macy's were hung with lighted stars. A great tree was brought into the rotunda of the City of Paris and stood under its glass dome. The beautiful round balconies allowed one to see it from above, studded with lights, ornaments, packages, glittering tinsel and ribbons. Marty could not resist walking into the store to have a look.

After shopping, she went home on the streetcar, tired but happy, clutching bags filled with purchases. In the front room, she found Erik working at the sloping drafting table he had installed in the bay window. He was making a rendering, a precisely imagined drawing of the façade of a building.

Marty reached around Erik's neck and kissed him, delighted to see him up and working. She had sewed café-style cotton curtains for the bottom windows, so people on the street couldn't look in, but the top windows were open to a flood of southern light.

"What are you doing?" she asked, looking over his shoulder. The drawing showed a two-story building with a few pine trees half-sketched in. She knew enough not to ask why he was working on Saturday. Architects didn't seem to keep 'banker's hours' as Marty did. She kept any extra time she had for her own literature studies.

"This is the resort James and I are bidding on," he said, hunched over his drawing.

"Where is it?" asked Marty. "It's good!" she said. She had been surprised when she saw how meticulous Erik's drawing was. He was particularly good at renderings, which enabled a client to see what the building might look like, as if in a photograph.

"Arizona," said Erik. "If we get it, we'll have a partnership. If not, c'est la vie."

"Venturi windows," said Marty, noting the arcs of the top floor windows. It was a particular curve often seen at the moment.

"Yeah," said Erik, miffed. "We have to show that we understand today's vernacular." He stood up and stretched. "I need to drive to Lake Tahoe tonight. Want to come with me?"

"Tonight?!" Marty was surprised. It was already late and the light would not last long.

"Yeah," said Erik. "I waited for you because I thought you'd enjoy it."

"Sure," said Marty.

"We'll go up tonight and tomorrow we'll take it slow and enjoy the drive back."

"Wow," said Marty. "It's kind of sudden."

"Well, do you want to go or don't you?" Erik looked impatient.

"I do," said Marty. "I'd love to. I bet it's snowing! I haven't seen snow in ages!"

"That's what I thought," said Erik. "Come on, put a bag together and we'll go. We can stop for dinner on the way."

It was a lovely night, snow falling softly, illuminated by the headlights as they drove into the mountains. Marty wished it were daytime. She could just make out the evergreen trees, piled with snow on either side of the road. Christmas trees.

With his right hand, Erik expertly flipped a Beethoven tape into the cassette player and hit the button. He slid his hand between Marty's legs. "This is the life," he said. "Nice thigh beside me, good music, driving. The best."

"And the snow!" said Marty. "It's magical."

The road climbed gradually, and the music built. It was warm inside the car. Marty began to be sleepy, but she worried that Erik would not be able to stay awake unless she did. She shook the thickness out of her head, tuning herself to the music, as it became an anthem of victory and power.

They found an isolated hotel beside the highway, with a stream rushing noisily along beside it. No one else was there, but the waiter came over and offered them a meal. They sat at a table spread with a red and white checked cloth under a window. The light-colored pine-board walls were full of knots. Light from the room fell on the snow outside and they could hear water falling on rocks as it splashed down the hill.

They ate a lasagna which had probably been made the day before, but was hot and tasty, and went to bed in a cold room under a large pile of blankets.

Marty shivered under the blankets trying to get warm.

"We're 7,000 feet up, it says," said Erik, reading a placard on the wall. "And this place is 70 years old." He turned out the light and got into bed. Marty crawled over toward his warm body. It all felt fresh, so far from their normal habits and lives. Simple.

The symphonic feeling stuck with Marty when she woke. The pinewood bedroom walls were tinged with the pink and gold of sunrise. Marty lay there, warm and peaceful, though she could tell the room was ice cold.

Finally she raised herself up enough to look out the window. The sun had not come through yet but ribbon clouds of all colors were stretched across the east. She could see where the sun was going to come, and then it did, a gold ball behind the bare, snow covered branches. She could also see the stream edged with icicles and a hanging bridge going back into the snowy white woods.

Mornings were the best, Marty thought.

"Whoooo! It's like a knife edge," said Erik when he got out of bed. "Let's get out of here."

Marty dressed quicker than she ever had. They went down to the dining room, where a wood stove crackled. A few other people in thick sweaters were having breakfast.

Marty had pancakes and coffee. She knew it would not do any good to ask Erik where they were going. If she asked him no questions, he would tell her no lies. The only way to know was to keep her eyes open and put things together. She looked out at the stream rushing through the snow and ice.

Marty suspected, for instance, that Erik had a backpack full of cocaine he might be delivering to someone in exchange for a backpack full of money. Javier dealt in cocaine and Erik now went to his house. Erik had told Marty that once he showed up and there was Miles Davis, sitting half asleep at a table. She knew that Erik sometimes used heroin. When Richard, a Stanford physics student who had ridden across the country with his sister that summer, wanted to try heroin, he came to Erik.

Marty's instincts told her these were dangerous games. But she had no experience of them. She did not know what to worry about. Erik did not include her in any of his experiments, except when he had a delectable sheet of acid and wanted to do it with her. He and Marty had had epic acid trips. Once she remembered feeling herself to be Pocahontas having sex with Erik. She felt that her skin was brown and that she lived in some ancient time, an elemental woman. And then it all changed, and changed again, the air full of color and pattern.

Mostly, acid was an opening of the doors, letting in more sense perception than one could normally handle. It had released Marty from the harsh judgments she made of herself. She especially liked coming down slowly in the morning, the certainty that she was alive, that life was important. She did not beg Erik for acid trips, but if one came along, she did not refuse.

They drove through the snow-covered scenery, entering South Lake Tahoe, and then slipping over the line into Nevada. Erik stopped at the Sahara Tahoe, a tall hotel and casino. "Come on," he said to Marty. "It's too cold to stay in the car."

Steel slot machines known as one-armed bandits stood around the lobby and people with vacant-looking faces were putting coins in them. "Just stay right here," said Erik to Marty. "I have to see a man about a horse." As he left he looked over his shoulder. "Want some quarters?"

Marty shook her head. She felt disoriented. She knew places like this existed, but they were hard to imagine. She sat in a big tacky plastic lounge chair and looked around. Ancient cigarette smoke hung in the room, as well as active fumes. Half empty glasses with straws in them, lipstick, ashes and dirt stood on the tables. Perhaps the place was cleaned now and then, but it certainly was heavily used.

The whir and chink of coins and machines was loud. As Marty watched a line of cherries appeared on the face of the machine next to her and a handful of quarters clinked into a metal cup. The older woman playing immediately fed them back into the machine! She was neatly dressed in a blouse and sweater, her hair tightly curled. She could have been any of the women Marty knew who attended church at home. But this woman wasn't dishing up salads for the Ladies Aid.

Marty pulled out her coin purse and found two quarters. She put them into a vacant machine, pulled down the lever and watched as the little pictures of fruit rolled around in front of her. Nothing happened. She lost two quarters and that was the end of that. She sat back down.

At last Erik appeared in the door of the elevator. He looked somewhat elated, with a little smile on his face. He grabbed Marty's hand and they left. Escaped, is more like it, Marty thought. The cold, fresh, clean air felt wonderful.

"That place is what I imagine hell to be," said Marty.

Erik laughed. "You're right! Le Inferno!" He lit up a joint and fished through his collection of tapes as they sat in the parking lot. "It's not so bad, actually," he said. "I like playing blackjack. I like seeing how the people act. But it's all rigged." He hit the buttons and Bob Dylan's voice came over the car's speakers. "You can't win."

Marty was glad he knew this. She was also glad he was more relaxed as the green, acrid smoke filled the car. Erik handed her the joint. "No thank you," she said.

"Lay, lady, lay; lay across my big brass bed," sang Dylan. The car pulled out onto the highway, the snowdrifts blue on either side in the sun. The highway was wet, but not icy. Erik gunned it as they pulled away, spinning down the road, sneaking a look at Marty.

"Why wait any longer for the world to begin. You can have your cake and eat it too," sang Dylan. Marty grinned broadly back at Erik. How often he had nailed her emotional state. They were in it together, escaping down the road.

On the other hand, she wondered, could you really have your cake and eat it too? Would they escape with their lives? She had begun to imagine that their names would be spread across the newspapers, victims of some violent crime or drug bust. She had begun to wish she wasn't a Mikkelson, to fear that she would sully the family name.

But lots of people Marty knew were involved. She had tried cocaine herself at a party. It didn't feel like much, so her natural austerity prevented her from doing more. Coke was expensive. Marty didn't need it. A cup of coffee or a bar of chocolate raised her spirits just as well. Even they were sinful! Marty was losing her concept of sin. Ignorance was worse.

They floated down the mountain, listening to Bob Dylan all the way. Erik had all of his albums on tape. Marty was happy when Erik was. They drove across the valley and then through the big silver trusses of the Bay Bridge, the city shining white beyond. Marty knew she was with Erik to dispel her ignorance. Beauty, ugliness, she saw them all when she was with him.

Nevertheless, Marty felt a sigh of relief when they stood at Line's door in Santa Cruz on the day after Christmas. The place was hard to find, in one of the dormitories at Cowell College were Stephen and Line were resident assistants. The buildings were set in a grove of tall redwoods with a stunning view of Monterey Bay. Marty and Erik had been there once before, in the fall. It was very quiet now, the students home for the holidays.

Marty and Erik stood on the landing outside the apartment door, above a flight of open cement steps. It was cloudy, but not raining. To the west the clouds sat in heavy rolls along the horizon, touching the ocean.

Line opened the door, radiant and laughing, in a long skirt with a loose Indian tunic over it, her red-gold hair falling in big curls below her shoulders. She hugged Marty and then Erik.

"Such a spectacular view," said Marty, indicating the view to the west.

Line nodded. "Yeah, I'm still not used to it. Stephen's not here," she said. "He's always so desperate to study and he doesn't get much time. He's at the library." Beside her stood the little, resolute Christopher, holding a toy car.

Marty knelt down and hugged the little boy. She could not look at him without guiltily thinking about how much he had been through in the last year. Line had told her that Christopher had not cottoned to his father when they all got together. But today he seemed golden and happy.

Erik looked around and realized he could get away. "I'll be back," he said. He had friends nearby. Marty had fully expected him to leave.

"I'll have dinner ready by five," said Line. "You said you wanted an early one, right?"

"Yeah," said Erik. "It's a long way down here."

Line drew Marty into the tiny all purpose room, which had a kitchen counter with refrigerator, sink and a stove on one side, a sofa and a big window looking out on a second floor deck. A little Christmas tree stood in the corner, decked with popcorn and cranberry chains and sugar cookies. Marty knew at a glance that there was more love than money in their celebration.

"Oh, Line," said Marty. "How was your Christmas?"

Line looked at Christopher. "What do you think, Christy?" she asked. "Did you have fun?"

"Christmas!" he said. "Vroooom! Vroooom!" He ran the car across the floor and up to the tree.

"I think he's finally getting it," said Line.

"Does Stephen mind?" asked Marty. Stephen was Jewish.

"No," said Line. "Christmas is for Christopher. That's all. It's American as apple pie. Stephen thinks we can all get along."

"Good," said Marty. "I had fun picking presents for everyone, but I missed doing it with you. We can open yours tonight at dinner."

"Sure," said Line. "Marty," she hissed quietly. "I think I'm pregnant!"

"You are?" Marty noticed her evident glee.

"I think so. Haven't tested for it yet. But I sure feel like it."

"Wow," said Marty. "How does that feel?" But she didn't have to ask.

Line was grinning from ear to ear. "Wonderful," she said. "It feels like we're going to be a family after all!"

"That is great," said Marty. She could not imagine it. With Erik? How would that ever work?! She wanted to hug Line, but there was still a Midwestern reticence between them.

"Would you like some pumpkin bread?" asked Line. "I've been baking."

"Amazing, Line, in this little house?" asked Marty.

Line rummaged in the cupboards and came up with slices of pumpkin bread on plates. "At least it has plumbing!" she said. "After being at Paul's place, I appreciate it so much!"

"That would be especially hard with kids, I think," said Marty.

"Oh Christy didn't mind," said Line. "He was fine. It's just that they were hauling ALL their water. And I kind of like being clean."

"I know what Paul wants," said Marty. "He wants to get closer to wilderness. It's enough for him. He'll put up with a lot to get it."

"Yes, it's definitely wilderness," said Line. "But I like civilization. The people I met in Alaska were really nice. Kind of like North Dakota people. They were anxious to help each other."

"I'm glad he's happy," said Marty. "And I'm glad you're happy!"

"There's this amazing guy here," said Line. "Alan Chadwick. He's making incredible gardens for the university. He's doing French intensive gardening and he teaches interns! He works first on the soil, aerating it and stuffing it with compost. Then the plants that result are full of nutrients and make wonderful food! I've been hanging out with him. He likes me," said Line. "Do you want to walk over and have a look?"

"Sure," said Marty.

They put on jackets, dressed Christopher and wandered over to a hillside near the entrance to campus. The road curved through tall redwoods which obscured the grey sky.

Half way up a steep bank along the road, stood a thin muscular man in white shorts and a sweater with a shock of blonde hair. The bank was lush with interesting greens, bushes and shocks of tall, dying blooms. He appeared to be loosening the soil around a hydrangea, whose drying blossoms had taken on antiqued sepia colors. Marty did not hold hydrangeas high on her hierarchy of flowers, but these were gorgeous. She felt as if she had never looked at them before.

"Good afternoon, Linochka," said the man in what sounded like an Oxford accent. He was very tall when he stood up, his face and limbs very brown. "I hate to cut them, but I suppose I will," he said, indicating the hydrangeas.

"This is my sister Marty. Alan Chadwick," presented Line with a flourish, smiling broadly. "I've been telling her about your work." Line's glow indicated that much was going on beneath the surface. She had always been somewhat nonverbal, trusting faces and actions more than words. Marty could see that Chadwick responded.

"I'm honored," said Mr. Chadwick.

Marty did not know what to say. She certainly had not expected to meet this paragon of a man. "Happy holidays," she said, extending her hand.

"How was that arugula," asked Chadwick. "Did it go well with your chicken?"

"Just delicious!" said Line. "I've never had anything like it!"

"In England they call it rocket," said Chadwick. "The piquant taste sets off fatty meats very well, in my opinion. Well, Ciao!" he said, turning back to his digging.

Marty and Line walked away under the terribly tall redwoods. Marty felt tongue-tied, but curious. Even in Oxford she had hardly met such an aristocratic-looking Englishman. "You do fall into the most interesting situations," she said to Line, low.

"Digging on the day after Christmas," said Line. "The garden is his life. And this one only has flowers. The vegetable garden is much bigger!" She turned to Marty, as if revealing a secret. "He had hollyhocks in that garden this summer! I showed Christopher how we used to make hollyhock dolls. Remember?"

Marty did. "Hollyhocks!" She had not seen them since leaving North Dakota. A rush of memory came over her. "Oh Line! I miss you so much!" she said, looking at Line with all of her longing heart.

The chicken that Line roasted that evening in her tiny oven was delicious with rice and the fragrant arugula leaves Alan Chadwick had given her. Stephen presided and, to Marty's delight, Erik turned up just as they were sitting down to eat in a motley collection of chairs around the small, crowded table. Line tucked Christopher into a tall wooden chair between herself and the window.

Steam rose from the dishes and Line looked pink and flustered. Stephen invoked a blessing upon the food. Erik was mellow and amenable, listening.

64

"I think I've picked my dissertation topic," said Stephen as he spooned up mashed potatoes. "A.J. Muste. Hardly anything has been written about him. Do any of you know who he was?"

"Sorry," said Marty. "I don't."

"That's my point," said Stephen. "He was a socialist, became a Quaker and advocated nonviolence in some of the big textile strikes in the 1920's. In his 70's he helped organize against the Vietnam war and also advised Bayard Rustin, who worked with Dr. King. And Americans don't know anything about him!"

"A worthy topic," said Erik. "Makes me think of the most revolutionary man I know, Christopher Alexander. He taught at Berkeley when I was there, kept trying to get us to make intuitive decisions about design. The university didn't like it one bit!"

Erik jumped up. "For instance! Alexander would take two items, like this jam jar and this pen. Then we would each have to say which one was more a mirror of our selves, our inner selves, our souls! He dared use the word! Usually, most people chose the same item as a mirror of their inner selves." He brandished the two items.

"That's easy," said Line, pointing to the jam jar. The pen was an ordinary Bic pen, made of ugly plastic. The jam jar was a clear glass mason jar into which Line had stuffed rosemary she had gathered to cook with.

"Stephen?" asked Erik. They all looked at Stephen as he screwed up his face.

"I would have said the pen, except the one you chose is so ugly!" he said.

"Exactly," said Erik. "I think we can all agree."

"But on what basis?" asked Stephen.

"That's the point," said Erik. "I don't think anyone knows."

Marty looked at Line, mischievously, proud of Erik. Art could be as radical as politics. It was turning into a wonderful Christmas.

7

Paul set off for the Athabascan village of Minto hunched behind Leon Alexander on a bright yellow Ski-doo on Palm Sunday afternoon, his mitts laced together around Leon's waist. Fairbanks schools took off during

Easter week, partly to give the students a chance to let off spring steam and go duck hunting! Behind them, Leon's father had his son Randy, a freshman at Lathrop High School, on the back of his snow machine.

Muffled so that only his eyes were visible, Paul had plenty of time to look around him as they drove the long miles under a grey sky. The Skidoo made a terrible racket, droning on at 40 mph as the trail followed the long, straight stretches of the Livengood-Dunbar sled road north through the Tolovana River valley. The temperature was below freezing and Paul wished he were poling along on skis, but it was much too far for that.

It looked as though they were heading into nothingness. There was no mark of a road through the bare trees, the spruces loaded with snow, the mountain ridges all around. Paul would have loved the more silent trip behind sled dogs. But mushers spent more time running or walking behind their sleds than riding, to spare the dogs. Paul could not have done it. He would have been nothing more than a package wrapped in a sleeping bag on the sled. It wouldn't be fair.

Minto was 120 miles from Fairbanks by highway, but only about half that taking the sled roads the native Alaskans knew. Paul owed the trip to his friendship with Marcia, who was now teaching in the Athabascan town. He had met Marcia years ago in Minnesota while she recovered from breaking her leg. Paul had come to Alaska partly because of her.

The town of Minto had been moved from its old site recently, which was subject to flooding. New Minto was on a mountain bench, facing the wetlands to the east. Neal Charlie, chief of the village, had prayed for the move and had been strong enough to make it happen. He was highly respected and pushed his relatives to keep their own language and culture high in esteem. The Alexanders were related to the Charlies by marriage.

Marcia chose to teach at the new Minto school because of its reputation. She and Paul wrote letters to each other and met now and then in Fairbanks. Paul sometimes sent Marcia books and supplies she asked for by mail. When her student Randy went to high school in Fairbanks, Marcia asked Paul to keep an eye out for him. Randy fared better than most Athabascan high school students because his father, Bobby Alexander, kept a cabin near town and worked for the railroad.

Mr. Alexander drove a Johnson Skee-horse which belonged to a neighbor, but Leon's Ski-doo belonged to their family. Mr. Alexander bought the Ski-doo to get back and forth from Fairbanks to the village as he didn't want to leave his dogs alone when he did railroad runs. An important dog sled race was to be held during Easter week.

When they turned off the long, flat sled road, Paul knew they were nearing their destination. The sky descended into twilight, but the snow around them reflected any light at all. They were traveling in a half-lit, shadowy world, the boreal forest.

Paul had been warned about the steep bank down to the frozen Tolovana River, but he trusted Leon as they bent below the wind-shield of the bright yellow machine. He leaned with the machine as Leon carved left and then right down the slope, as if on skis, the machine sending up spray behind them. The river was iced over. Paul remembered how fast snow and ice became slush in April the year before and hoped it would still be ice in a week. They climbed the opposite bank.

On the ridge above the river they stopped beside Mr. Alexander and Randy, Leon getting off the noisy machine. Paul stood up and stretched. He was glad for the rest. Leon's handsome face was framed by the fur of his trapper hat with long ear muffs. A dark Asian-looking mustache sat on his upper lip. The Alexanders wore Army surplus white rubber bunny boots which kept one's feet both warm and dry.

Leon didn't say much, but Paul knew that he saw everything. Observation was of primary value in Alaska. Young people watched and learned from their elders. Words were not wasted. It's the same in the Lutheran culture, Paul thought. Words are actions. You are who your actions say you are, and you'd better not do things lightly. You will surely be held to account.

Mr. Alexander pointed. Perched on a hillside were the new buildings of the town under thick pelts of snowy white icing, laid out on two parallel roads. Below was a large slough, laced with bogs and ponds connected by streams.

"Beaver," said Leon, indicating snow-covered piles of logs on a frozen pond. They looked exactly like the lodges Paul had seen near Lake Michigami. "You are staying at the teacher house?" he asked.

"I think so," said Paul.

"I'll drop you off."

In town, Mr. Alexander and Randy wheeled off on the snowy roads, headlight shining in front of them. Leon stopped at a duplex next to a long, low building of new painted boards. He cut the noisy engine and stepped off his machine.

Marcia must have heard them, because she opened the door with a huge smile on her face. Standing in the light, she looked like home to Paul in a Norwegian sweater with bright red threads knit into white and black.

"Come in, come in!" she said. "I made cookies!" But Leon got a wild look on his face and brushed off her greeting. He hopped on his snow machine and gunned it up the street.

Paul entered the new little duplex, shuffling off his boots. It smelled of a pine wood fire, and indeed, there was a whiff of browned sugar.

"You'll probably stay with Abel and Jack next door," Marcia said, her face pink and flushed. "You must know that everyone knows everything here, and wants to know more about the teachers!"

"Are you kidding? I was a pastor's kid in a small town," said Paul, unburdening himself of parka, mufflers, mitts. "I understand perfectly. It's so great to see you in your actual place!" Marcia had almost the same background as he did and it was easy to talk to her, like a sister.

"Someone delivers my water. Usually," said Marcia, showing off her tidy kitchen. "There's propane heat, but wood fires are my friends in the winter." She showed off her little home, indicating the crackling fire in the free-standing iron stove.

"Just like mine," said Paul. "Except I have no heat if I don't chop wood. And I carry my water from Arvi's well."

"Honey bucket?" she asked.

"Oh, yeah," said Paul. "But, you know, it's a little easier for guys!"

"Yeah," sighed Marcia. "The school has a bathroom. I usually go over there."

"Wow," said Paul. "That's amazing!"

"It's a real community center," said Marcia. "Everything happens there." She put a kettle of water on the stove, and pulled out a plate of cookies.

Paul sank his teeth into one of them. "Warmth," he said. "Chocolate chips. Civilization," he breathed. He looked closely at the stove. "Does that have an oven?" he asked. He was remembering helping lug the huge old wood-burning stove, with its painted enamel oven door and lids, out to Jack and Sheila's cabin the summer before.

"Yes," said Marcia. "Everyone likes sweets! Even Leon. Usually I can lure him in here with a plate of cookies."

"Leon?" asked Paul. "Is he about my age?"

"Yeah," said Marcia, softly. "Somewhere around our age." She poured hot water over instant coffee, making a cup for Paul and one for herself. She sat down across from him at the diminutive dining table. "I wanted to come to Minto because the Charlies are such a strong family. They promote education and get the young people to resist alcohol. They're pretty successful. It's much better here than at my last village. The kids all get more school than their parents did. Neal Charlie only went to fourth grade."

"It's so interesting," said Paul. "Such a crossroads of cultures. Randy's a great kid. He sure is headed outward. I think he's college bound."

"Yeah," said Marcia. "He's one of the youngest in that family, so he may get to college."

"But then he doesn't learn the skills his parents have," said Paul. "You can't really do both, can you?"

"He'll never know all the secrets of trapping and hunting, and dog running that his father knows," said Marcia. "But he'll be able to get work. I'm afraid they're all going to disappear pretty soon, once they start building that pipeline. Money talks, everyone listens. Even the Athabascans."

"I've taken my education in a different direction than my parents expected me to," said Paul. "Don't you think everyone does?"

"Yeah," said Marcia. "I do." She looked dreamy-eyed. "Nobody thought I'd stick it in Alaska. But they've got me," she said. "Book worm that I am, I've got an adventuress in there somewhere."

"With me, it's religion," said Paul. "I can no longer accept that Christians are the only ones who know God. My folks thought I'd be a pastor, but I can't distinguish between the sacred and the profane any longer. Either it's all sacred, or it's all profane. Hardly matters," he said. "Living up here, I think it's all sacred."

"Do you still go to church?" asked Marcia.

"No," said Paul. "I've been impressed with Arvi's Quaker meeting. But it isn't as if I'm looking for a group to belong to."

"I can see how it would be painful for your folks," said Marcia.

"I try not to call attention to it," said Paul. "I'm really open. I just don't use all that sin and salvation language any more."

"The Athabascans hold their elders with a lot of respect," said Marcia. "The Charlies are upstanding people, good examples, so they have influence. In some of the villages, the elders aren't as responsible. Those villages suffer." She stood up and went over to the stove. "Another cup, Paul?"

"Yes, thanks," said Paul. It was almost as if he were in Minnesota. "But the interesting thing about education is, if you go beyond your elders, then what?"

"Beyond?" asked Marcia. "Maybe in a different direction. But I don't know about beyond."

"You're right," said Paul. "My dad is the finest man I know. It's just that things are different now. And I'm open to it."

"Paul, do you know what a potlatch is?" asked Marcia. "There's going to be a big potlatch after the dog race. You'll get to see it! I'm so glad you got to come!"

The dog race the next day was a sprint race, not one of the really long ones. People came from villages and homesteads near and far. Marcia introduced people to Paul as they stood near the finish line. Their shadows were long and blue against the crystalline snow in the noon sunshine.

The huskies were beautiful animals, loping through the snow, hitched to light wooden basket sleds. The men came in, running behind their dogs. The first man over the finish line, one of the Charlie brothers, climbed on the short runners which stuck out behind the sled, leaning over, spent. Up close, Paul thought he must be in his fifties, about Dad's age, though his skin was more lined and weathered. Paul's Aunt Mabel, who lived many years in the Arctic, had the most wizened brown skin, criss-crossed with finely-etched wrinkles.

Paul and Marcia approached the beautiful dogs with their light fur and dark ear tips. They were being fed dried fish as a reward. Paul had not been much involved with dogs in Alaska. Arvi and his wife had horses and only one hunting dog. It was hard to keep animals well-fed and housed, though they were extremely important and useful in the bush. Paul looked inquiringly at Mr. Charlie, who nodded. Paul scratched the heads of the huskies, looking in their light-colored, shining eyes.

"The Charlies will give the potlatch," said Marcia later, as they left. "Neal Charlie will spend everything he has on it."

"Everything?"

"Yes," said Marcia. "Everything. The food, the gifts. It's the custom. It shows how much respect and wealth the chief wields."

"And then he has to start all over?" Paul opened the door to the school, and they both left their boots in a pile in the entry.

"Yes," said Marcia. "The families all save up and contribute, but it's so foreign to our concepts of property. I still don't really get it."

"I have noticed this among our kids at the high school. It drives the people they are staying with crazy. It's like if they need something, they feel they're entitled to it. Like communism was meant to be," said Paul. "To each according to his need ..."

"It's taken time for people to accept me here," said Marcia. "But the more I understand them the better. And then there's Leon," she said low.

"Leon?"

"I think I'm falling in love with Leon," she said simply. "Which scares the hell out of me."

Paul looked at her. That explained a lot. He could see why Marcia was concerned. Two cultures. You did need an adventurer's heart for that!

The floor of the school gym was covered with strips of white butcher paper. Against the wall, women arranged food on long tables. As people came in, they filled their plates and settled with their families and friends on the floor, using the clean butcher paper as a 'table.' Marcia had brought plates and cutlery, as had everyone else, to avoid the waste of paper plates. "You must take whatever you are offered," she cautioned Paul. He piled his plate with moose stew, rice, berry sauce, fry bread and salmon.

"Beaver," said one of the women, holding up a spoon of meat. Paul nodded and held out his plate. He had never tasted beaver.

Paul sat down by Abel, the teacher he had stayed with the night before. Marcia walked around, refilling cups of tea. "A potlatch can celebrate the first catch of a child: fish, rabbits, ptarmigan," said Abel. "An older person comes up and passes on his story, so that the child can hold on to that person's luck. The potlatch helps the kid have good luck for the rest of their life."

Paul was stuffed. He didn't dare go near the food tables. After everyone had eaten, the butcher paper was taken up and cleared away with a great deal of energy.

Chief Charlie, a vigorous man in his fifties, began a song, tapping two sticks together. Paul could not understand what he was saying, but he did notice that everyone became still, including the children, listening.

Others got up to speak, while people listened respectfully. A woman began a song, and others took it up. First the men danced and then the women in their colorful cotton dresses. It didn't look difficult. Paul saw one of the younger girls pull Marcia into the line of dancers. Yes, he thought. She was ready for adventure.

"We should be glad it isn't a funeral," said Abel. "A funeral potlatch can last a week! This one seems to be about spring, and about the sled dog race."

"A great village," said Paul.

"I think our 'potluck' comes from the potlatch," said Abel. "Native cultures do it all over the northwest."

The potlatch lasted late into the night. There was no way for Paul to slip out and go to bed. In the end, from a big pile of gifts on a table, Neal Charlie hung a beaded necklace around Paul's neck. "Thank you for taking care of our boys," he said. Very moved, Paul nodded his head and looked the chief in the eye.

Leon was less stiff with Paul on the way back to Fairbanks, understanding now that Paul was more of a friend than a rival. The two snow machines started early and found the ice on the river still solid. Leon dropped Paul off at Chena Ridge early in the afternoon.

In his own cabin at last, Paul was glad for the quiet. The air was freezing and damp. He built a fire in the woodstove, careless about how much wood he used. Spring was coming! Finding the cleanest snow he could, he filled a pan with it and put it on top of the wood stove. As warmth returned, slowly, to the room, he drank his favorite instant Lipton tea flavored with lemon and sugar. It was another kind of home, his own place, his own mind without interruption. He badly needed it after a weekend filled with people.

In truth, Paul's own values were not that far off the Athabascans. His own northern ancestors treated nature and animals as if they were sacred, living in conscious relation to them. And he had thoroughly imbibed Jesus' instruction to "lay not up for yourselves treasures on earth, where moth and dust doth corrupt, and thieves break through and steal." He was not interested in property for its own sake. But he did love his independence and the ability to think as he liked. He tried to imagine how Marcia would fare in the village of Minto. It was like living in a small town in North Dakota. Would he chafe at the need to attend all the native gatherings if he were in Marcia's shoes?

Fairbanks was spread out and full of unusual people and diverse cultures. Some of them were the result of an early rush for gold, some were homesteaders who felt Alaska offered the best place to avoid the crush of civilization in the Lower 48, some were native Eskimo and Indians. The presence of the University brought in scientists and researchers. The weather was like that of the upper Midwest, if set between mountain ranges. Paul was glad he had chosen the town.

But it had been almost two years now since Paul had been home to see his family. He had saved up enough for the airplane flight to Minneapolis, and he hoped that Dad, Mother, Kristen and Hanna would be at Lake Michigami in June. He hoped to spend two or three weeks there, before returning to the bush near Hurricane, where Jack and Sheila were building a resort. He could not wait until school was out!

Paul sat close enough to the stove to feed wood into it. He picked up the book Arvi had pulled off his shelf, saying to Paul: "This sounds like you, Paul. Nessmuk camped and canoed with a minimum of equipment. He got it down to a science. 'Course he was in the Adirondacks, mostly. Little warmer there!" It was a slim little book and detailed the ideas of a man who called himself Nessmuk. It was called *Woodcraft*.

The one thing Paul lusted after was a canoe. There were acres and acres of clear ponds, sloughs and marshes nearby where he could canoe, but the big Grumman, freight-carrying canoes he had seen in Alaska were way beyond his means, and his abilities. He longed to set off in a light canoe, as he had on Lake Michigami so often, with a lunch and a day in front of him. It did not look very likely. Jack had a boat which Paul took out now and then, but in the bush in the summer there was an atmosphere of urgency. Everyone worked. Rather like when Dad came up to the cabin for his brief vacation with a head full of projects!

Nessmuk's book contained a long discussion of wooden canoes, clinker-built with thin cedar boards lapped over each other. "Test it and you will find the lapped halves have gained in strength about twenty per cent," he wrote. Paul was intrigued. Viking boats had been lapped wooden strips. Paul had spent some of his extra hours in the school wood shop that winter. Finish work at the resort also taught him things about wood.

Dad would have had something to say about all this, Paul thought. But it was growing very dark. Paul lit his kerosene lamp and opened a can of mushroom soup. He cooked up some noodles and topped them with the soup and some tuna. It was Sunday night. He could use a wash. He headed out to the Kukkonen's sauna.

Paul slipped into the hot cabin full of steam. Naked bodies large and small ranged along the wooden benches. A large female neighbor sat beside Carol and her daughters with only a curtain of steam between themselves and the men. The sight had grown less disconcerting to Paul over time.

"Eh, Paul!" said Arvi. "Glad you're back!" He stood in the altogether, clean-shaven in the middle of the room, his long brown hair curling around his shoulders. Arvi was chief in his own home, a young chief. He threw a bucket of snow on the hot stones above the fire pit and the steam rose higher in the room.

"Me too," said Paul. He sank down in the space Arvi's son made for him on the men's side.

It turned out they were discussing the environmental impact report regarding the pipeline the oil companies wanted to build across the state which had just been released.

"3,500 pages! Nine volumes!" said one of the neighbors. "And it just tells us what everyone knows! The caribou won't be able to get to their calving grounds if they build a pipeline with a road beside it!" Caribou made long migrations from Canada and central Alaska to get to the edge of the Beaufort Sea for calving every year. The oilfields at Prudhoe Bay were just west of the calving grounds.

"It'll be a disaster, a big, wide scar across the state that will never go away," said another.

"Oil spills," said another. "Any oil that comes out of Alaska will have catastrophic consequences to the wilderness and those who live here. Washington is too far away to be dealing with the oil companies. Those guys need to come up here and see what havoc they're wreaking."

"All we can do is keep raising the issues," said Arvi. "It's taken this long. And they've shot down some bad ideas. Like that tanker sailing through the Northwest Passage with an icebreaker ahead of it. Now that was a good idea for sure!" he said sarcastically. But he seemed to be advocating a moderate path.

"You saw how they made sure the native corporations can't choose from the land in the path of the pipeline, didn't you," said the neighbor.

Paul was glad he was surrounded by people who didn't want the oil companies to come in. The corporate interests were intent on profit and on perpetuating the military and industrial complex, big business. They insisted that America shouldn't be so dependent on foreign oil. Why not be less dependent on oil altogether, Paul wondered.

"They're going to find a way," said Arvi quietly. "It will change this state irrevocably. We can only keep negotiating and hope for the best."

Paul agreed with that too. He could not wrap his life around what the oil companies did or did not do. He must live simply and try to stay out of the clutches of business by needing little. Getting hold of a canoe seemed ever more important!

"How was New Minto?" asked Arvi. He knew how to direct a conversation.

"It's a really fine town," said Paul. "I went to a potlatch." He looked down. All he was wearing was the beaded necklace Chief Charlie had given him. "As you can see!"

"Those Athabascans," said Arvi. "They've got it right. What's good for the group is good for the individual."

"Aw, they've got just as many problems as anyone else," said the large woman. "Maybe more. In-fighting, alcohol. Incest."

"Not in Minto," said Paul, staunchly, knowing he didn't really know what he was talking about.

Arvi laughed. "You got a good introduction, Paul," he said. "The Charlies are a great family. Just amazing how they got that town moved!"

But Paul was still thinking about whether education helped native people or not. Once people got a dose of Westernized life they didn't seem to want to go back. But was that a good thing? He wanted Arvi's opinion.

"Education is value neutral," said Arvi. "It can be used for good or for ill. It's all education, in the end anyway, Athabascan, German, Greek, Roman. We Westerners think we've got it figured out, but we haven't got the last word on anything! It's all a work in process."

"3.8 billion people in the world," said one of the neighbors. "Sure doesn't seem like it up here. But that's what the oil's all about. Resources are finite, but we never seem to be satisfied!"

"Okay, who's first in the Danish plunge? That'll shut us up!" said Arvi. "Come on Paul, last in, first out!"

Paul's inner temperature was very hot by this time. But he hadn't realized that Arvi was now using the icy plunge pool instead of a roll in the snow after a sauna. There was little fresh snow left and what there was was dirty.

Called on, Paul knew there was no way out. He stood up, grabbed the rope and let Arvi lower him into the pool without much more than a loud exhale of breath. "Whoooo-eeeee!" he said.

"Next!" bellowed Arvi as Paul's naked body rose into the steaming room. Paul rushed out into the entry and grabbed his towel, warming himself with its roughness. Very refreshing, **after** he got out! He put on a clean t-shirt and his other woolens. He sighed. He felt terrific.

8

At a pocket of beach near Santa Cruz, Line watched an egg, floating on the wash of water out beyond the surf. Not too far from it was a heavy log, which floated just as gently. It was a striking contrast. The sun was brilliant in the late August afternoon, lighting the breakers as they ambled into the natural bay. She noticed that Christopher, in his little dungarees rolled up at the ankle, had wandered over to the rocks where the tide was washing ever closer to a cliff.

Line looked at Stephen, who lay on his stomach beside her on the cotton rug, his thin body as much a part of the book he was reading as present with her. "Can you go get him," Line asked Stephen. She was hugely pregnant and felt like a whale, lolling on the sand.

Christy's running off had become a pattern, an aggressive act on the part of the little four-year-old. He usually did it when the three of them were together. At first Line had gone after him, trying to placate him. But after months of this, Stephen and Line agreed that Christopher must come to terms with his father.

Stephen smiled at Line, rolling over to look at her and reaching up to stroke her sunny face. He sprung up on long, grasshopper legs. "Be right back," he said. He raced across the curve of sand toward the cliff which abruptly ended the beach. The afternoon tide left swirling pools between the rocks as the lacy breakers came in.

Line watched him go. They preferred this smaller piece of sand to the crowded beach beside the amusement park promenade Santa Cruz was known for. Seabirds covered a piece of rocky cliff, open at its base, now surrounded by the ocean. Inland, in a eucalyptus grove, thousands of Monarch butterflies gathered in the winter, enjoying the mild temperatures. The beach did become crowded once in a while. People who used it came for its wild beauty.

Line watched intently, shading her eyes with her hand. At first she saw Stephen lean down and look in the tidepools with Christopher, not rushing him. But Christy would not take his hand. Eventually, Stephen picked up the lanky little boy and tossed him over his shoulder. Clearly, Christy was as stubborn as his mother!

"What did you see?" asked Line as they came toward the blanket and Stephen set him down.

Christopher scowled at Line and refused to speak. He looked at the sand and began stuffing pebbles in his pockets.

"Look, Christy," said Line, putting her arms around his middle and pointing out the plain white egg. "Do you see the egg?" Of course he did. Christopher had sharp eyes. She pointed to the heavy, water-soaked log. "And the log? One is so big and one is so little, but the water holds them both up!"

Stephen too knelt beside them, anguish on his face.

"How did that egg get there?" Line asked Stephen. Her eyes were merry, trying to tell him not to worry.

Stephen shrugged. "Who knows? Maybe it floated up here from the city pier."

"But it's amazing that they both bob along as if they were nothing! The water is so powerful! And gentle with the egg."

Stephen nodded, musing. "Life is powerful. More than any of us really know."

Christopher said nothing. Line took Stephen's hand and stood up, with some difficulty. "Well," she said, cradling her stomach, "Let's go home and have some supper." It was a stand-off. Line did not know what would break Christopher's long-running snit. She understood he had been her little man for a long time, the poor kid. It was her fault as much as anything Stephen did that Christy was angry with them.

Line awkwardly took the corners of the blanket Stephen handed her, folding it as they went. When they met in Alaska in the sweetest days Line could remember, Stephen had agreed with Line that they spend at least one day a week as a family. Stephen told Line, "I have been in agony without you. Thank you for waiting for me all this time. I will do whatever is necessary for our family, if you will allow me my work." His fervent words had soothed Line ever since.

It had been something of a shock to them both to find that Stephen's first-born son would not be disciplined by him or even willingly listen to him. Neither of them knew that the long separation would affect the little boy so much. But Line could not believe that the rift could not eventually be overcome. Steady, simple family contact was the remedy.

In the evening Line opened every window in the apartment, trying to get air to pass through. Usually it wasn't a problem. The proximity of the ocean cooled the apartment during the night, a moist fog blanketing the area.

Line and Stephen sat with Christopher when he was tucked into bed, reading in the lamplight. Line read a chapter from *Pippi Longstocking*, a book about a girl who lived with her monkey and a horse. Stephen read a Dr. Seuss book called *Green Eggs and Ham* in a number of voices, one for Sam-I-Am and one for the narrator. Line listened with envy. Her own voice was something of a monotone, while Stephen's was full of emphasis and drama.

"All right," said Line. "That's it. We're having green eggs and ham tomorrow morning for breakfast!"

"No-o-o-o-o-o!" said Christopher.

"You'll see," said Line. "They're delicious! Good night! Sleep tight my beautiful boy." She leaned down to kiss him, then stood up and left the room. Only recently had Christy slept the whole night in his own bed. She trusted the memory of the waves on the beach that afternoon to lull him to sleep quickly.

"Good night, Christopher," said Stephen, giving him a kiss and turning out the light.

They left the door open on the small darkened room and went into the big room. "Green eggs?" questioned Stephen. "Where are you going to get those?"

"Spinach," said Line. "But we'll have to find some ham." Tomorrow was Sunday. She hoped Stephen would make an early grocery run.

The two of them curled up together on the couch in the quiet, Stephen's arms curving around the top of Line's big belly. "I'm so glad you picked Santa Cruz," Line told Stephen. "I'm so happy here." It was a frequent theme.

"It's incredible," said Stephen. "A place new enough not to be under the spell of the Establishment. Where things can happen." But then his tone changed. "It's coming though," he said darkly.

Line knew what he meant. Alan Chadwick had been driven away earlier that year. The provost of Crown College, Kenneth Thimann, hated the fact that Alan had grown beautiful gardens without chemical fertilizers of any kind. The university froze Alan out of its new agroecology farm program, causing him to leave.

"Page tried to keep Alan," said Line. "He and Paul Lee." Page Smith, Stephen's mentor and provost of his college, Cowell, was teaching history from the point of view of ordinary people rather than from the study of 'great men.' A sort of 'history-from-below' approach.

"People have been saying Thimann played a part in the development of Agent Orange which they use in Vietnam to deforest and contaminate food supplies," said Stephen. "It's basically dioxin, which causes huge health risks, birth defects and cancers."

"Really?" asked Line. Stephen was often way ahead of others in knowing truth, with his deep political sources. Nevertheless, she tried to stay hopeful. "Everyone was so passionate about that garden. I'm sure some of Chadwick's legacy will remain." Though she wasn't free to become an actual intern, Line had helped in Chadwick's gardens as much as she could. She had been stunned to see how the place changed, how the spirit went out of it when Alan left.

"We've cracked open the Establishment in so many different areas," said Stephen. "We've got to keep that rift open." Stephen could be grateful and stoic too.

Line knew he felt he had landed in a better place than many of his radical New Left friends. Line was proud of him. He had given up managing SDS people and projects to get his doctorate, and concentrate on teaching. American history as it was taught in schools and universities was, from the perspective of a brash, young democracy, proud and sure of itself. Stephen did not see it that way after participating in the turbulent history of the 1960's, which still affected everything. Like Page Smith, he taught from a different point of view.

Line stretched and changed position. "The Birth Center is a crack in the established medical profession," she said. The impending birth of the new baby was never far from her mind.

"You are absolutely right," said Stephen, stroking her tummy. "Do you feel ready?"

"Oh yes," said Line. "Do you?" While looking for classes that would involve Stephen, she had found the Birth Center. All kinds of classes were taught there and, even though it was frowned on, the Birth Center supplied the names of midwives. Line and Stephen had been working with Nina Carpenter, a midwife who thought Line was a good candidate for a home birth.

"I can't wait," said Stephen. "It'll be exciting."

"Could be any day now," said Line.

A breeze wafted through the hot, silent rooms. "I'm falling asleep," Line said. She was thinking of Christy. She did not want him present at the birth. He was just too little to deal with mess, emotion and unexpected consequences. She had arranged with a friend to take Christopher to her house when Line started to feel contractions. She was not so sure about Stephen either, but since it was possible, she wanted the baby to be born at home with him there.

The week was poignant for Line as she made her customary rounds. She lugged a basket of clothes down the steps to the laundry, trailing Christopher as she usually did. He liked helping, pulling wet clothes from the washers and stuffing them in dryers. He ran his little cars over the concrete outside the dark laundry room on the first floor of the college.

Line dragged a chair out into the sun and sat waiting for the clothes to dry. She was happy the place wasn't overrun with students yet. She enjoyed the simplicity of being alone with Christopher. He had been her staunch little man through all her changes, uncomplaining and ready for new things. But it wouldn't be long before there would be two children and Line would have to weigh and prioritize their needs.

"Here Christy," she said. She gave him a piece of chalk so he could draw roads. It would have been nice to hang the clothes out on a clothesline, but that was not allowed. Line dreamed of a house, a free-standing house with a garden of their own. She was deeply grateful that she didn't feel pressured to work. Stephen had enough money from teaching to keep them in food, but a house would have to wait. For now they were the resident grownups in a college full of undergraduates. Line could only hope that an extra child wouldn't make things difficult.

Stephen had gone to the library. He used every spare moment for research, ordering books and taking notes. Line was glad to see him revive their friendship with Bernie and Kay Freeman, who both taught at the University of California in Santa Barbara. They were local activists, taking on whatever needed doing in their city. Line and Stephen had been down to see them that summer. Bernie gave Stephen advice on his research.

Line folded clothes on a table in the dark laundry room. "Come on Christy," she said. "Help me take the clothes home." Christy would certainly have to help her once the baby was born. He stood up manfully and helped Line tug the basket of clothes up the stairs.

After a nap Line wedged herself behind the wheel of the car Stephen had bought and drove herself and Christopher to the Birth Center. It was a small storefront with tables and secondhand furniture, colorful curtains and a relaxed atmosphere. The armchairs were full of women and babies. Line stopped in often to help counsel and discuss birthing. Women shared with each other all the physical and emotional things that related to having children. It was a great hangout.

Christopher was quite at home. In the play area, another little boy was building towers with wooden blocks. Christy seemed confused by the babies all over the room. One day he had asked whether they could take home a baby Line cradled in her lap.

"Not this one," Line said. "This one isn't ours. But soon we'll have a baby of our own."

Line made herself a cup of hot tea and joined a group crowded around a table, listening to a small woman with kinky hair wrapped in a scarf tell about the birth she had just had at home. She carried her new baby in a sling over her shoulder. "Did they have to dig their fingers into me so hard after the birth?" the woman asked.

Line smiled and others laughed. "They're trying to make sure no blood clots get left in you," said Raven Lang. She had started the Birth Center. With her long dark hair and loud voice, she spoke her truth with clear and passionate intensity.

"Well it didn't feel very good," said the woman.

"You wouldn't like the alternative!" said Raven. "How was everything else?"

"It was pretty amazing," the small woman said. "It felt so nice to have Patrick with me. We were really intimate while we were waiting for the second stage of labor. I got so relaxed, and I think he respected me more after the whole thing was over."

"Exactly," said Raven. After a bad birthing experience at Stanford Hospital, she became interested in everything about it. She attended home births and began teaching classes. Originally she advocated going to the hospital to have one's baby, but after she watched the normal pregnancy of a friend she had counseled slowed, and then botched by a doctor, she decided women must take matters into their own hands.

Line had been lucky. She had given birth to Christopher in a large, busy obstetrics ward which served many poverty-stricken women. She was a licensed practical nurse and by the time of Christy's birth had seen enough deliveries to take some charge of herself. Now she hoped to avoid, once again, hospital procedures, which might involve drugging a woman and separating her from her baby to keep conditions "sterile."

Raven and Nina and the other midwives were warned not to continue assisting at home births. It was considered illegal to practice this kind of medicine without a license. The one doctor in the Santa Cruz area who had been willing to attend home births had been forced to stop by the medical community. But midwives continued to quietly assist women who wanted their babies born at home.

"Surely knowing how to properly transport someone to the hospital who is bleeding too much is not practicing medicine," Raven told Line. The midwives did not take money for their services. They were also studying everything about birth, sharing experiences in workshops with people up and down the coast, and keeping statistics about births both at home and in the hospital.

Line found hospitals in Chicago congenial, for the most part, and she hoped to take up nursing again when her children were in school. But she was also deeply thrilled by the work of the people associated with the Birth Center. Why shouldn't women take back their right to the experience of a natural birth?

"Have you got names for your baby picked out?" Nina asked Line as she tightened a blood pressure cuff around her arm.

Line smiled. "I keep thinking of plants," she said. "Maybe Heather if it's a girl. If it's a boy, he's going to get named after some revolutionary, I'm sure. My husband's writing about A.J. Muste for his doctorate."

"Looking good," said Nina. "Normal blood pressure." She put the listening part of the stethoscope she wore around her neck against Line's tummy. "150," she said. "In some people's minds that would be a little girl, and you are carrying rather high." She laughed. "Old wives' tales, I guess."

"Old wives," said Line. "Sounds good to me!"

"50-50 chance in either direction," said Nina. "So is it okay if I bring my friend Annie? I know it's kind of crowded at your place, but she wants to learn."

"Fine," said Line. "I'm going to just put a mattress and plastic sheet on the floor in the middle of the big room," she said.

"I'm looking forward to it," said Nina, humbly. "You seem so sure of yourself in the process. And it will probably go quickly since it's your second."

Line knew Nina had not caught as many babies as Raven, but she liked and trusted her. She could not birth a child by herself. She supposed she was looking forward to it also, though she was a little scared. Mostly about Stephen. He had not been allowed at Christopher's birth. Would he be steady for this one?

The days were warm and still. On the first day of September, Line began to feel that the baby was coming.

"Christy," she said. "Dad's going to take you to Alice's house." She found clothes for him and packed some snacks.

Stephen returned with Nina and Annie. The four of them looked at each other. "I guess it's just us then," said Nina, giggling a little nervously. "How's it going Line?"

"I'm fine," said Line. She was thinking of music. The contractions increased, like a crescendo, peaked and then de-crescendoed. She was riding them. Here it was again.

Nina gave Stephen a big watch with a second hand. "You're the timer," she said. Stephen sat beside Line on the couch, rubbing her back as she arched into the crescendo.

"It's so hot," said Line. She stood up, walking around the small apartment. Sweat dripped down her back. She wanted to rip off the light tent dress she was wearing. And why not?

"I'm glad!" said Nina. "It'll feel good to the baby when it comes out."

Annie made tea, dipping green teabags into cups and handing one to Line. She didn't say much and neither did Stephen.

Nina talked, low and slow, as if she needed to. "In natural birth, the emphasis is on nature," she said. "We're letting it do the work. The midwife is there to watch and assist." Line could see that she was saying this for Annie's benefit.

No one had to tell Line to relax. She had given herself over to the forces of nature. She remembered the egg, floating on the ocean so gently. Gently does it, she thought.

Stephen seemed to have caught her thought. "It's like the ocean," he whispered to Line. "It's like watching the breakers roll in."

Line, spent, smiled at him. "I'm so glad you're here," she breathed. She was glad he was able to sit still without removing himself to a book off in the corner. "I wonder what the tide will bring in," she said dreamily.

"Where do you want me to rub?" asked Stephen. "Your neck? Your head?"

"Your hands feel so good," she said. "Anywhere." She felt hot and sweaty and took off the light dress. What did it matter what anyone saw at this point?

"You know those people who left San Francisco in a big caravan and moved to Tennessee?" asked Nina. "Steve Gaskin's wife Ina Mae delivered all of their kids as they traveled, and later at the Farm, I heard. They called their contractions 'rushes,' I guess to take the emphasis off pain."

To Line it was as if Nina was speaking through a curtain. She watched Nina take things from her cloth bag and show them to Annie. "We need to sterilize these," Nina said, handing Annie scissors, a clamp for the umbilical cord and an ear syringe.

"Okay, Line," said Nina. "Let's have a look." She put on disposable, sterile plastic gloves and measured the dilation. "The baby's looking up," she said. She listened for the baby's heartbeat. "Good and strong," she said, looking at Line and Stephen.

Line knew babies usually looked down as they came out, but it was probably fine. There seemed to be a lull in the proceedings. But then, Line felt things change. "I have to push," she said. "I have to push." She turned over onto her hands and knees and gave in to the need. After the contraction de-crescendoed, Line sank onto her side, feeling Stephen reach around her to hold her.

"You're doing so well, baby," Stephen said.

"I'm going to scrub up now," said Nina. "I don't want to use gloves when I catch the baby. Tell me when it is 15 minutes, Stephen," she said as she stood at the sink, washing her hands for a very long time.

Line could feel Nina's tension, her excitement, but it didn't bother her. She was beyond them. Dimly she was aware of Annie, standing in for Nina. "The cervix is getting bigger," Annie said.

"Great," said Nina, over her shoulder. "Just relax, Line. It's coming on well. You can pant between the contractions." She knelt beside Line on the floor.

After a couple more intense contractions Line heard Nina say, "There we go! The head's almost coming!" Line could smell the coconut oil Nina was rubbing around her cervix, but she didn't feel the fingers. She was too numb.

"Look quick!" Nina called to Annie. "It's turning! Oh, here it comes! Line! Your baby's head is out!"

Line could feel Nina's hands holding the baby, gently keeping it from coming out in a rush and tearing her. "Easy, Line, easy," said Nina. Stephen did not stop massaging Line's shoulders, though Line could feel his excitement too.

With another contraction, Line felt a little body slip out. "You have a little girl!" said Annie. "Hallelujah!"

Line laughed weakly. "Hallelujah!" she said. A rush of blood followed the baby, and then she heard its cry. The cry of her little girl. Heather, she thought. A little purple flower that could grow anywhere.

Nina held the wet little girl carefully. "Lie down, Line," said Nina. "Let's see how this is doing."

Line lifted her leg awkwardly over the umbilical cord and lay down, looking up hungrily at the little girl, who had patchy white vernix still on her skin. Nina put her on Line's chest and Line tried to put the baby's mouth to her breast. She looked up at Stephen just above her. She could feel Nina kneading her stomach, massaging the fundus at the base of her vagina and feeling for the afterbirth. It was painful, but the baby at her breast helped.

"Would you like to cut the chord?" Nina asked Stephen. "It's stopped pulsing." She put a sterile clamp on it and let Stephen cut it with the scissors.

"It's tough!" Stephen said. "And slippery!"

"Little Heather," said Line softly. "Thank you all so much!"

"Thank you, Line," said Nina. "You make it easy."

After a moment Line's uterus began to work again, expelling the placenta into a bowl Nina held for it. Line felt Nina massaging her belly in earnest!

Finally Nina wrapped a blood pressure cuff around Line while Annie did cleanup. She dabbed the baby's skin with a wet cloth, and wrapped a cotton blanket around the little girl and one around Line. Nina and Annie stood in the kitchen, examining the placenta to see if it was all there.

Line could hardly take her eyes off the little girl. Long, delicate eyelashes crept out from her tiny closed eyes. Then she opened them and looked around. "Look Stephen! She's looking around," she said. After a while Line looked up at Stephen and asked, "Is Heather fine with you? We should use your mother's name for her middle name."

Stephen stroked the little girl's head. "Mama would have liked that. Heather Sima Cohen," said Stephen softly. "It's fine. I can't wait to tell Poppa."

"And Christy," said Line.

Annie came with herbal tea. There were more details, Stephen took notes; but Line was done. She could rest. She wanted to be in her own bed when Christy came home. She let Nina and Stephen help her up and sit in the rocking chair while they cleaned up the sheets and put the room to rights.

Stephen prepared to take Nina and Annie home and return with Christopher. "Shall I tell him?" he asked.

"Of course," said Line.

When they arrived, Christopher burst into the apartment and found Line and Heather sleeping in the big bed. Line smiled. "You can touch her," she said. "Do you want to hold her? Go sit on the couch," she said, "And Dad will bring her to you." She held Heather up to Stephen.

Christy ran into the big room and sat obediently on the couch, his little legs straight out in front of him. Stephen put the bundled Heather into his outstretched arms and Line followed, slowly. She sat down beside them and looked up at Stephen.

"We can keep her, right?" said Christy cautiously.

"Yes," said Line. "She's ours."

"Forever?"

"Forever," said Stephen. "She's your new sister."

"My sister." Christopher bent his head down to the tiny red face which opened in a yawn, the little arms jerking with the effort.

Line looked at Stephen. We're going to be a family after all, she thought.

9

Marty entered the flat one evening after work to the usual spill of white envelopes, advertising and bills which had been pushed through the mail slot. It was a warm day in September, the sunlight disappearing fast. Marty was delighted to be home. She fanned through the letters, separating out the ones for Erik (most of them). One was addressed to Line, who had been gone for more than a year.

The flat felt cavernous, white-walled and empty. Marty found, when she tried to put Erik's letters on his drafting table, that it was gone! She hadn't seen him for almost a week and had no idea where he was. She was used to it, she had to admit, but this was too much. She raced into the bedroom. Many of his clothes hung in the makeshift wardrobe as usual, some shoes in a row beneath them.

Marty picked up the receiver on the black phone in the niche in the corridor and dialed the last office number she had for Erik.

It was late for someone to be working, but Erik picked up the phone. "Hey! Don't worry, darling. It's all fine. I just moved my stuff into the office." It was his lazy, charming voice.

"What office?!" asked Marty. Her voice echoed off the hardwood floors and bare walls. The railroad flat had always been a bit plain, but now it felt empty.

"Where I'm working," said Erik. "At the number you are calling." But then the timbre of his voice changed. "Marty," he said urgently. "Take the day off tomorrow. Pack up your stuff and don't answer the phone. I'll stop by and pick you up at 8 a.m. I've rented us a new apartment."

Marty sank down on the floor. "What??" She could not believe what she was hearing.

"Don't worry about the dishes," said Erik. "Just pack things you like, your clothes and books and camera."

"Why?" asked Marty. "What's going on?"

"Nothing," said Erik. "It's just getting a little hot there. We need to move on."

"Move on," said Marty.

"Yeah," said Erik. "I got a really great apartment. This friend built it. He's a stained glass maker."

"It's not making sense," said Marty, her voice rising. "Why didn't you tell me?"

But Erik became haughty in a second. "Marty," he said firmly. "You know. We agreed. I'm not going to tell you everything about my business. Just be ready in the morning. You'll see. It's going to be great."

Marty backed down. "Okay."

"I was going to tell you." Erik's voice changed to conciliatory. "I wanted it to be a surprise."

Marty did not know how much, if any of this were true. It was not the behavior of a partner. Where we live is my business too, she thought. But there was nothing she could do about it. She knew all was not well with Erik, that he was leading hidden lives. She still didn't know exactly why, but she had vowed to love him unconditionally, to try by her own loving kindness to allow space for him to settle down. "Okay," she said. "Couldn't you come home right now?" What he said frightened her.

Erik appeared to consider this. "Can you be ready in two hours?" he asked. "Just take the important stuff."

"Okay," said Marty. "You'll be here?"

"In two hours," said Erik. "I'll have my friend's truck." He paused. "Don't answer the phone," he said. "I love you, darling. I'll be there."

Marty hung up the phone. She was frightened and could feel the adrenalin surging through her. Was Erik just making things into an adventure or was there really some danger? She had no way of knowing. She ran down the street to the nearest liquor store and begged some cardboard boxes.

In an hour Marty had packed her books, photographs and papers into boxes, her clothes into a suitcase. Her portable sewing machine stood beside them in the hall, covered with an armload of things on hangars. She stood disconsolately in the kitchen, making herself a piece of toast with butter. The phone rang and did not quit. Marty took the featherbed off the bed and wrapped it around the phone.

Marty stood at a kitchen counter, cutting one Valencia orange after another in half, squeezing them in the glass juicer and drinking them one at a time. Each of them tasted different, some sweeter, some tangy. Whatever she thought might be driving Erik, she felt the best thing was just to treat whatever he said as if it were the truth, observe and not ask a lot of questions. Things had begun to deteriorate, she thought. She and Erik were happy when they were together, but few people came to the house any more. Marty wasn't sure why.

For Marty, Line's leaving had opened a great hole. Line had just had a second child. Line and Stephen were poor, but Marty envied Line her stability.

Slowly Marty had filled her life with friends and pursuits since Line left. She bought a 35mm SLR Pentax. It was a huge purchase and her favorite possession. She was taking a photography class at the DeYoung

Museum from an interesting Japanese-American. And she was using an employment agency to look for the work she wanted, doing temporary jobs until a permanent job in an architectural office turned up.

The front door slammed. Marty froze, but all of a sudden, there was Erik, putting his arms around her. His very blonde hair was tucked into a rakish Butch Cassidy cap. "Are you ready?" he asked. "Come on. I'm double-parked."

The muffled phone was still ringing in the background. As they left, Marty looked longingly at the blue cotton featherbed. Kate had sent it from Europe and Marty had spent many a foggy evening wrapped in it. Erik said, "Leave it. I've gotten us a better one."

The new apartment turned out to be in the dense area of North Beach where old wooden buildings were jammed right up to the edge of the street. It was dark when they arrived and Marty had only a dim sense of the place. They took steps up from the street, and then another flight of steps.

"David's been renovating this place for a while," said Erik, depositing Marty and her bags at the top of the steps and turning on a light. By this time, he had pulled off his cap and was his old, relaxed self. "I'll go park the truck," he said. "It might take me a while. There's no parking around here for blocks!" he smiled. "Make yourself at home. It's yours, darling!"

Marty felt disoriented. She stood in the middle of the room, looking around dazedly. At her feet was a wonderful carpet, thick tufted, dyed wool, probably authentically Turkish or Afghani. A freestanding Swedish fireplace stood near the wall with two beautifully-designed chairs in front of it, iron and leather. It was not the hippie apartment of a transitory person.

The room was large, with long thin windows looking out on the lights of the city. On a bookshelf were a few books about the architects Erik loved, Luis Barragan, Frank Lloyd Wright, Hundertwasser. The flat was almost empty, but, in a bedroom alcove, there was a large mattress on a platform. In the tiny closet Marty recognized some of Erik's better clothes and shoes. The cabinets in the kitchen were empty. No one had eaten here yet.

Marty did not know what to do. She walked around the apartment, her bags sitting in a heap in the big front room. It was mystifying. But soon Erik returned, carrying two wineglasses. "Want to go out?" he asked her. "There's wonderful food all around us."

"No, thanks," said Marty. "I'm so disoriented," she said.

"Oh, no matter," said Erik. "I'll get you oriented!" He held up the glasses. "I nicked these from Enrico's down the street. Actually they gave them to me." He opened the refrigerator where there was a bottle of white wine.

Handing Marty a glass, Erik pulled her down onto the carpet in the middle of the room. "Let's drink to our new life," he said.

Marty shook her head at him, smiling. Erik was impossible. She melted. Whatever was happening, she decided she would worry about it in the morning.

It was a lovely night. In the morning, Marty called in sick and they went out to breakfast at Mama's, a sweet café at one corner of Washington Square. It was small, but not too full at 10 o'clock in the morning. Finally Erik told her more about what was going on over M'omlettes and French toast.

"I made a lot of money on a deal, but this one guy thinks he should have gotten more of it. So I'm spending it fast," Erik said. "I've been wanting to move anyway, and talking to David about this place. So luckily it was about ready last week. I got the carpet, because it's a good place to invest money. Christopher Alexander has a big carpet collection he's amassed over the years. Seemed like a good idea."

"And what about the old place?" asked Marty.

Erik shrugged. "I'll cut off the phone and the PG&E and call the landlord today. They can take care of it." It was so like him to assume that others would clean up his mess.

"Mail?"

"Write all your friends and tell them your new address," suggested Erik.

Marty sighed. She kept her life very simple. She gave Erik money for rent each month and bought the food they had at home. He took care of his car and took them to restaurants and movies if they went out. "I guess it'll be fine," she said.

"We'll go buy dishes and things to cook in today," said Erik. "I think that's all we need."

"Yes," Marty conceded. "I knew it was time to move. We don't need that big flat any more."

"We won't bring anything into the new place we don't love," said Erik. "And when you get your architecture job, I'll bet you'll be a lot closer to it than we were out by the park."

Marty nodded. She and Erik certainly thought alike about space. "I love the apartment," she said. "But I feel left out when you don't tell me what's going on." Her voice was plaintive.

Erik looked at her as if she should know better. "We're not going over this again," he said. "I've got enough to worry about," he said gruffly. He waved to the waitress and asked for more coffee. "It's a new start. It's going to be great," he said.

In Erik's presence Marty didn't have time to think things through. They went downtown and bought dishes and wonderful cooking pots and brought them home in a taxi. Marty felt like a newly-wed. But she did hope Erik would take himself off soon, so she could think. She hardly knew what street the apartment was on, and what was around them. She had never spent much time in North Beach.

Erik showed Marty how to get up on the roof, where there was a tiny, glassed-in room. Here were Erik's drafting table and drawings. The sweeping view from the flat roof was of house tops and adobe chimney pots, beyond them the Bay and its bridge. Coit Tower was the highest point. Looking north, Marty could just see the steeples of the St. Peter and Paul church next to Mama's, where they had had breakfast.

Late that afternoon, when the tags and plastic and bags were all in the garbage, Erik said, "So are you okay, then? I need to go by the office."

"Sure," said Marty. "Go ahead!" She ran water in the sink and began washing the new dishes and placing them in the new wire dish drainer.

Erik ran his hands around her waist and up under her shirt. "Nice," he said, kissing her neck. "Please stop worrying. I'll be home later."

By this time Marty knew that Erik was with her because of trust. She knew it mattered more than whether she was beautiful or talented. She had watched Erik fall for people and then lose trust in them. Marty was independent, had few needs and she was in love with Erik. Their bodies matched each other and they were compatible in how they saw the world. Marty was stuck with being Erik's angel.

And what do I need? Marty asked herself as she set her few books on the bookshelves. She loved Erik. He was gorgeous and funny and they had lots of fun together. He didn't seem to be interested in a family, which bothered Marty, and he didn't treat her like a partner. But what I need is to be sat on, thought Marty. I need someone to tie me down and possess me, and keep me from running around. Erik did that. So did his insistence that she be his angel.

This involved being the wife in the household, but it especially meant she couldn't badger Erik about anything he did. Including how much he drank. Erik preferred being stoned, but occasionally he drank more than he should, Marty thought.

The big room felt cozy, the thin windows letting in the low-angled September light from every direction. There was no table to eat on, but Erik said David, their landlord, was making them one. Marty hung her clothes in the small closet. She did not have many. She did not like to swoop around in velveteen and lace, though she had a few peasant dresses. She was more of a beatnik, wearing minimalist black turtlenecks and jeans. Like April, Marty thought, remembering her friend from college.

The bed was lovely, laid with a thick comforter and pillows. Marty needed a chest for some of her things, and lamps. A thin wooden table carved with the Gothic crosses one expected to find in a church stood against the wall. Where had that come from?

I'll get used to it, Marty told herself. It'll be great. She tried to imagine what she would tell Mother and Dad, her friends when she wrote to them.

On Saturday, Marty went to her photography class. She still felt a little disoriented, but the city itself hadn't changed. From the old flat on Kirkham Street she could walk to class, but now she took the familiar N streetcar out to 9th Avenue and walked through the thick greenery of the park. Marty loved the fall, when the fog wasn't so thick and the air was still. The days were shorter and the sun moved south, a sweet reminder to enjoy every single day as the rains were coming.

This is my home, Marty said to herself as she slipped through a side path past the Shakespeare garden and under a muddy cement arch where children always called, hoping to hear an echo. She emerged onto the big open concourse where the DeYoung Museum was set across from the aquarium. An old fashioned band shell at one end and the Japanese tea garden next to the museum were all deeply familiar to Marty. She shared the park with many people, but the time she spent in it made it her own.

The art school was being run out of the museum, with studios for painting, sketching and making pottery, as well as a small darkroom. David Fukuyama, Marty's teacher, had learned photography in the army. He had a large presence which was difficult to pin down in language. There were only a few students. David simply told them to go out and shoot and bring in their results.

For the first time, Marty actually developed the negatives of a film herself in a small plastic container. They worked in black and white, of course, as the chemicals for color were too complicated and introduced too much technical discussion. Art photography was generally black and white. The class was about texture, composition and tone.

Marty photographed what she liked, moved by everyday domestic life. Looking at beautiful dishes carefully placed she thought she saw more than was actually there. At the old house, she had set a pattern of wineglasses in the sun on a coarsely-grained white cloth and photographed the shafts of light that passed through the dark wine and the glasses. She photographed a stand of eucalyptus trunks, her handmade leather sandals on a beautiful Navajo rug and the light passing through a bouquet of lilies.

"I want to show you how to develop a sepia image," said David that morning. "It's just a matter of using different chemicals. But it gives a very different feel to the photograph. Pick an image you want to give that sort of patina and we'll set it up so you can compare black and white to sepia."

"That's interesting," David said, looking at Marty's contact sheet of prints and pointing to the wineglasses. "Why don't you work with that one?"

"I like the one of the sandals on the patterned rug," said Marty.

"The sandals are sliding out of the picture," said David. "If you're going to photograph something, you must get it all in the frame."

"But I think I was trying to get the design in the rug," remonstrated Marty.

David just looked at her. "It doesn't work," he said.

"But why?" asked Marty stubbornly.

"Look at it objectively," said David. "What do you think?"

Marty knew he was right, but she didn't know why. The edge of the sandals did graze the edge of the picture, the Navajo pattern in the rug showed up in shades of grey. The weave of the rug was sharply focused, but perhaps the picture was really about the sandals after all. Marty didn't want to admit it.

They worked in the orange darkness, setting up a negative on the enlarger, focusing it on creamy paper and then putting it in a developer tray, a stop bath and finally a fixer. The chemicals smelled bad, but that was the price for making art. There was always a price.

Different papers affected the image as well as the sepia tones. Sepia images looked good on creamy paper and had an older feel. They were softer than the crisp images on stark white glossy paper. "Shades of darkness and light, framing, textures, contrast," said David. "It's all you've got, but it's enough."

David put a negative of his own in the enlarger tray and focused it, white paper under the glass. In the developer liquid, the image came up crisp, simple, absolutely a picture of reality. It was of a man with a hose in his hands washing down the steps of City Hall with a gush of water. David swished it around with a tongs and pulled it out, squeegeeing off the liquid and hanging it up with a clothespin on a cord. "A picture's got to mean something. I like robust images. I took a series of truck drivers. People working."

Marty did not expect to be a photographer. She was doing it to help herself see. And to document the life that felt so full to her. Somehow framing something, putting it in a little rectangle you could focus on made you see it better. The world was so big, and so seductive. A photograph was like a poem, directing attention. She printed several small copies of the wineglasses on different papers.

"After the army I bought a bike and followed my girlfriend down to Carmel," David told them as they sat around after class, talking. "I had hair down to my waist." Marty could clearly imagine it, the purring motorbike, his thick black hair whipping in the coastal wind. "She was a Norwegian blonde. We're married now, but we wanted something more. We're going to have a baby."

Something more, thought Marty. She did badly want to be married, but she was out beyond her known boundaries. She did not know what was going to happen next. Maybe a new job. She did not think it would be marriage.

After class Marty walked back through the gates of the arboretum, the great garden full of plants and trees. Everywhere she looked she saw images of Line in her bright red-gold hair and long skirts. And little Christopher, a long stick in his hand, his jean pockets full of rocks. They had spent so much time here together. And now Line had a baby girl, Heather. Marty tried to imagine Line with her new baby. In the distance she saw Bill in his forest green uniform, kneeling beside a wheelbarrow full of plants. Bill liked Line and asked Marty about her.

Marty walked across the pond, listening to her footsteps on the wooden bridge. She headed off to the side toward the demonstration gardens. Set among pavilions constructed by *Sunset* magazine, the gardens showed people things they could do in their own gardens. The coolest and quietest was an Asian one, with a lovely Japanese maple throwing the shade of its tiny, hand-like leaves over a small stone lantern and wooden slatted benches. The maple leaves were beginning to turn, golden and red. Marty sat down.

Marty didn't mind being out beyond her boundaries. She expected it, had courted it. But how did she know what was right when she encountered things she had never before imagined? Were the drugs she and Erik used good for mental exploration or exploitative? Should she enjoy the money Erik made selling them? Everyone Marty knew experimented with drugs, and the dealers who provided them were heroes to some. Of course drugs were also trouble and Marty was glad she knew so little about Erik's "business." She was also worried about other things, like whether you could photograph people without invading their privacy. Whether she should be spending money on herself instead of giving it to people who had less than she did.

Reminding herself of her family helped Marty. Line wasn't so far away. Marty could have asked her what she thought about any of these things. She would not ask Mother and Dad, as they lived in an older, traditional world. All Marty was sure of was that this, this city, this garden, this place, was hers. It was where she was meant to be. She must take things as they came, finding her way.

Marty examined the tiny Japanese maple leaves, the color surging through their veins. They were beautiful and the sun was so warm and bountiful, blessing her. She slowly walked through the park toward the streetcar stop. Marty went all the way downtown, getting off in the Financial district and taking the walkways above street level, which angled through the new buildings and down the steps to Walton Park.

Small, long-needled pines lined the edges of Walton Park. Two sides of it were open, level ground leading off toward the Embarcadero, the edge of the city. Marty walked through the park and up Broadway, an ugly street full of sleazy clubs and bars. She climbed the Kearny Street steps, so steep at this point cars weren't allowed. She passed the Basque peasant restaurant she went to with friends, where people were served at long tables and there was only one dish each evening. And now I live here, she thought. How surprising.

At the top of the steps, Marty paused and looked out toward the water, where a small tugboat was pushing a paper barge deep into the bay.

Sun and blue sky over the grey water. Yes, Marty thought, the city is mine. I know it better all the time.

That week, Marty got a call from Candace, the girl she was working with at the agency. "I've got your job," Candace said. "You're going to love it. It's in the programming department of a big architectural firm. They do hospitals mostly, but other things too." She explained where Marty should go for the interview. "Just be yourself," she said. "It's perfect for you. I know you can get it."

Marty usually did well at work. It wasn't creative; she was just doing administrative work. But she was punctual, quick on the keyboards and liked pleasing people. Her need for a job tied her down also. Like Erik it kept her from floating away. And she found friends at every job. Bright people, like her just out of college.

Lipman, Mancuso and Pierson occupied a huge room on the second floor of a building near Fisherman's Wharf. Marty met with Tib Thibodeau, a large, amiable man with graying hair, who ran the programming department. "We're doing master planning for hospitals and other institutions. We need someone to type planning and design documents, correspondence and meeting notes, and keep track of our voluminous paper files! They keep getting bigger!" he said.

"It sounds great!" said Marty. She had only seen the small firms of two or three architects that Erik bounced around in. This one seemed to have a place for her.

"So, it looks like you went to a Wittenberg college? English major? Good grades?" he asked.

"I graduated Magna Cum Laude," said Marty. It had not seemed important at the time, but maybe it showed that she knew her English grammar.

"Architects aren't very good spellers," said Mr. Thibodeau. "And their grammar is poor as well. We would count on you to help us out."

"I can do that," said Marty, enthusiastically. "I'm so interested in architecture!"

On the way home, Marty took her time. Times of transition were stressful, but also gave her more freedom. She had taken an afternoon off for the interview, and now she was able to stop at Malvina's for a sinful, delicious cup of coffee. She bought a loaf of the Italian bread which was made only of flour, salt and water on Green Street. Neither she nor Erik could determine why it was so good.

When Marty came up the steps to the apartment, the phone was ringing. She unlocked the door and picked up the phone. It was Candace calling to tell her she had gotten the job. "They want you to start on Monday," she said.

Marty sighed. It was another change, but "I can't wait," she said. "It's such a big company. They even have an architectural library!"

"I'm sure you'll do well," said Candace. "I'll tell your temp counselor you're not available any more. She'll be sorry to hear it!"

Marty couldn't wait to tell Erik. He would turn up his nose. He liked being his own man, working freelance and being able to do more than just drafting someone else's ideas. But freelance was risky and uncertain. He could afford it. Marty could not. What she needed was a steady flow of money which allowed her to spend her weekends and evenings reading, writing and photographing. And this job was an entry into the exciting world of architecture.

Marty cut a piece off the Italian loaf and spread it with butter. The ever-changing city, she thought. Home.

10

Paul woke up in the middle of the night, knowing the full hunter's moon had risen. The chill was coming up in the cabin and he felt like staying snuggled in his sleeping bag, but no. He had promised himself to get out of bed, go outdoors and have a look. He threw on a parka and his boots. Opening the door, crisp, cold air greeted his nose. The hoots of a northern hawk owl repeated themselves as Paul listened. Passing the stable, where he could hear the horses snuffling, a light sugary snow crunched under his feet. Paul walked toward the clearing below the homestead.

The night sky was utterly clear, transparent. It was easy to feel the sky was infinite in Alaska. Along the northern horizon, shifting curtains of green and pink sent shafts of light into the middle of the sky. The moon was high already, weirdly opalescent behind the curtains of the auroras. Two large white snowshoe hares raced along the edge of the trees below.

Why did people sleep at night, Paul wondered. It was such a great time to be out. He was feeling nostalgic about his cabin on Chena Ridge. In a couple of weeks, he would move into an apartment near the university in Fairbanks. Could the night sky be as beautiful in the new place?

Paul had spent the last two years on Arvi Kukkonen's homestead, seven miles from the high school in Fairbanks where he taught. But it was often hard to get back and forth to school in the thick ice fog and other dangerous winter conditions. Sometimes he could hardly see ahead of his skis. He figured he had tempted fate long enough.

It was Paul's third year teaching high school biology and chemistry, as well as two sections of remedial math. He had settled down a lot by this time, and could look around him and see what, in his own unique self, he was doing with his life. It was a big topic on which Paul mused constantly.

The moon glowed, throwing the witchy shadows of the narrow black spruce on the light, crunchy snow. The auroras came with an accompaniment of Bach in Paul's head. He was singing with his college choral group, watching Oddmar Svendson direct them in the complicated a cappella fugue "All breathing life sing and praise ye the Lord, Alleluia." Paul laughed at himself. His deep Christian overlay was often close to the surface!

It was October. Most of the deciduous trees had lost their flaming leaves, but a few hung on. Yellow birch leaves, red oak leaves. It wasn't hard winter yet. Paul picked a yellow birch leaf off the ground and examined it in the moonlight. Its veins streamed down to the stem like a river, like the Tanana or the Chena, pouring into the Yukon in its unrelenting path into the sea. Or like the veins in people, in all mammals, flowing back and forth to their little pumping hearts. Paul had seen a bear running recently in the woods near Ermine Lake, a fantastic sight. The huge mound of flesh moved, paws outstretched, streaking through the woods. Its powerful movement was dependent on a heart like his own.

The owl had moved into a black spruce near Paul. Its resonant hooting was one of Paul's favorite sounds. Paul went back to his cabin and zipped up his sleeping bag around him. If he put his pillow in the corner of the bed, he could see the cold silver moon shining in the window. It was impossible to sleep. Paul lay half awake, thinking happily of his life.

Teaching young people who had come from the Lower 48 alongside Athabascans and Eskimo was difficult. In chemistry and biology, Paul could depend on some interest from the students. In the remedial math classes he could not. But he found them both interesting. In some of his classes, he had begun to veer off the textbook into his own interests. Music, the natural world, carpentry all helped Paul teach.

Paul had even come to appreciate Dad's interest in communications, radio frequencies, antennas and receivers. He didn't want it to take over his life as Dad's hobby had done. But Paul did help students set up ham radios and get their licenses. His student Randy Alexander loved communicating with his family and neighbors in Minto.

Paul wondered whether any of the Alexanders would be awake that night. The men had a cabin on the other side of Fairbanks when they were not in Minto. Paul had become close to Randy and was learning a lot from Randy's father. Randy was avid about books and learning science but his older brother Leon was more knowledgeable about hunting. Leon also kept asking Paul what he knew about the pipeline oil companies wanted to build between Prudhoe Bay and Valdez. Leon was sure there would be a job on the pipeline for him.

Bobby Alexander, their father, would be intent on getting winter meat at this time of year, a caribou or a moose or two. The meat would freeze and be chopped up for steaks and stews all winter. Mr. Alexander was doing what he had always done. He could read sign better than anyone Paul knew. He could look at scat, tracks, feathers, dens and roosting signs and tell how long they had been there, what directions they took, what the animal was thinking at the time. Paul would never get to that level, no matter how hard he tried. Was what Randy got from his education worth the loss of what his father knew?

Mr. Alexander fostered high school education as a parallel to what he taught his boys about methods of living in the subarctic wild that he learned from his Athabascan ancestors. He also worked for the railroad to supplement his income. Randy had a shot at college. But that probably meant he would not go back to the village. He would end up in a city, doing a professional or managerial job. Alaska needed Athabascans in these jobs, but would it be a better life?

When he didn't feel like going back to sleep, Paul got up and made a small fire in the wood stove. The moon was setting behind the ridge and the cabin was dark at 5 a.m. Using a kerosene lamp for light, Paul heated water and made coffee and then a big breakfast. He made himself sandwiches and headed out.

Dawn was starting to pink the clear sky in the east. Fall in Alaska was short and poignant. In September briefly the woods were awash with color and thousands of birds, sandhill cranes, mallards and Canadian geese, migrated through the area. Now, in the middle of October, most of the color was gone, as were the birds.

Paul headed for the little lake he had found a couple miles north, a wide spot on Cripple Creek. The creek had been dredged and dammed up by gold mining operations and no longer flowed, but Paul liked it in spite of the damage. Stagnant pools and marshy areas remained after mining became unproductive.

Light snow had fallen, making it easier to walk through the woods, but Paul still scrambled over deadfall and picked his way through the hummocks. The new snow was crossed by many animal tracks. A mouse trail ended abruptly, with a set of scuff marks and a hint of claws. An owl had found its prey.

Paul's finely tuned temperature gauge, which responded to how much he was sweating and the number of shirts he was wearing under his parka, told him it was about 20 degrees Fahrenheit. A flock of brown sharp-tailed grouse exploded out of the bushes with a flutter of wings and lighted on top of spruce trees as he approached. A white ptarmigan was less jumpy, merely walking away from Paul.

At the pond, a thin film of ice, patterned like frost, had crystallized on the surface near its edges, around the rushes and weeds. Paul dipped his hand in the freezing water. The beaver dam at the edge of the pond was covered with frost. The area, with its grown-over bulldozer marks and downed trees, had been abandoned. But Paul had claimed this pond for his own little Walden, visiting it almost every week and making notes about what he saw.

The sun began to turn the haze at the horizon to vibrant salmon and orange colors, the sky's reflection showing in the frosty surface of the water. Paul stilled his thoughts, letting the place speak to him. He tried to train his eyes and body to see everything, hear and smell it. These were the things he wrote down in a notebook, what touching things felt like, how the air tasted, the music of the world.

Paul admitted to himself he felt a little hollow inside. He had finally been alone long enough to notice that it wasn't as much fun as it used to be. It was more enticing to steal time for yourself when you lived in a family and knew you would go home to a big rambunctious meal together. This was no longer true, but there was nothing to do about it.

Paul went home, made himself hot food and sat by the fire writing up his notes from the morning. He opened the small paperback book Arvi had pulled off his shelf one day recently, saying "Here, Paul. You must know this guy Bonhoeffer. He was a German Lutheran, executed for his part in a plot to kill Hitler."

"Executed?" asked Paul.

"Strange for a Lutheran pastor to be part of a plot against another human being," said Arvi. "At least it is hard for us Quakers to imagine. Though Hitler surely deserved it."

"They didn't succeed," said Paul, struggling to remember what had happened to Hitler. It was no surprise that Arvi would know about a German Christian caught up in the events of the Second World War.

"No," said Arvi. "There were a lot of them involved. All executed just before the Allies turned up, I think."

No one at Trinity College had told Paul about Bonhoeffer or his *Letters and Papers from Prison*. The book was startling. It was like the Christ-centered theology Dad preached, but with muscular new ideas. It was amazing to Paul. In the extreme situation of being in a Nazi prison, Bonhoeffer was considering exactly the questions Paul did himself.

Paul was a slow reader, chewing over sentences slowly, thinking about them. Bonhoeffer wrote to his friend Bethge that he had been reading a book about physics. He wrote: "It has again brought home to me quite clearly how wrong it is to use God as a stop-gap for the incompleteness of our knowledge. If in fact the frontiers of knowledge are being pushed further and further back (and that is bound to be the case), then God is being pushed back with them, and is therefore continually in retreat. We are to find God in what we know, not in what we don't know; God wants us to realize his presence, not in unsolved problems but in those that are solved. That is true of the relationship between God and scientific knowledge, but it is also true of the wider human problems of death, suffering, and guilt."

Paul had spent a couple of weeks in Minnesota that summer. Not in the small town where Dad was a pastor, but at the northern Minnesota lake the family went to in the summers. At the lake, Mother and Dad and the younger girls lived the time-honored summer lives they always had, watching loons, herons and eagles on the lake (Mother); boating and swimming, reading and cooking (Kristen and Hanna); and improving the cabin (Dad).

Paul did all those things, settling quickly into the self he was in the family. It made him realize how alone he was in Alaska, but also why he was there. At home, he felt constrained by the self he had been, unable to consider his thoughts freely. It was not in his makeup to open up the questions Paul had in mind. He was afraid his thoughts were moving so far from Christianity that he did not want to bother Dad and Mother with them. Instead, he listened and watched for clues to what they thought in their daily life.

Paul also worked at his friends' resort on the Alaskan lake they called Ermine, where there was still incessant summer effort at building cabins, docks, sheds and amenities. The road had come through, and getting supplies and machinery in to the site was much easier. The resort had opened to touring students, hunters and adventurers, with the women providing meals.

The Ermine Lake resort atmosphere was vastly different from that of the Mikkelson family at Lake Michigami. Paul's Alaskan friends were young, idealistic and driven. They had been students together in Colorado. Making a life in the bush had led them into all kinds of areas, but their focus was more on mountain climbing, ecology and hunting than on art or literature. They did have a phonograph, powered by a generator, and sometimes, if they weren't too tired, everyone danced wildly to the music loudly playing in the bush!

But these friends had no Christian overlay. In fact, that was what Paul was in Alaska for. He wanted to see nature and science without any filters, to get below his Christianity to how he himself felt about things. Either everything was sacred, or nothing was sacred. In Alaska, everything felt sacred.

Bonhoeffer wanted to bring God into the center of life, to stop focusing on redemption. "This world must not be prematurely written off; in this the Old and New Testaments are at one. Redemption myths arise from human boundary-experiences, but Christ takes hold of a man at the centre of his life," he wrote. Paul was living as largely as he could, taking his life by the horns. He was determined that his life be his own and that his thinking be at one with his life. Bonhoeffer was a wonderful addition to Paul's list of inner mentors.

The questions the book raised for Paul were essentially about what he was meant to do in the world. It couldn't have been easy for Bonhoeffer as a young man in Germany during the war. Paul was trying to get his idealism to fit what was possible. He had no illusions that he could do innovative botanical or zoological research or push the boundaries of ecological thought. He simply hadn't the resources. And he was sure he couldn't lead a congregation as a pastor. Perhaps he was simply meant to be a teacher and that was enough. He just wasn't sure. It was like a pressure, gnawing at him.

Paul was reluctant to go to the Lutheran church, where he must tilt against the rigid and familiar language he suspected he would find. Well-meaning friendships and groups would soon take over his life, as they did at home in Minnesota. He did miss choral singing, but he had tried to make up for it by playing the guitar and singing folk songs with his friends. Going to Quaker meeting with Arvi's family attracted him. Arvi was still the best person to talk to about philosophy.

At his new place, Paul would have a roommate, a guy who was studying biology at the university. Paul wanted to take classes himself. He was trying to leave everything open, to let his future come to him. But of course, he must be ready for it.

Paul laid down Bonhoeffer's book, letting the fire die down. When it felt safe to leave, he made sure the cabin was shut up properly and went and stood out on the road with his thumb out. The first person who drove past stopped for him. It was Carol, Arvi's wife, with her daughter, going in for some groceries.

"Where are you off to?" Carol asked, smiling.

"I'm going to stop by Brian and Linda's house and see what Brian's doing. Maybe some music or a chess game," said Paul. "Probably won't be back tonight." He did not tell Carol that both he and Brian had been in on a game of five-card stud on Saturday nights recently, with a bunch of great guys. Paul was, after all, a teacher.

"That sounds like fun," said Carol. "Arvi told me you're moving," she said. "It's been nice having you in that cabin," she said.

"It's not that I want to leave," said Paul. "Your family has been wonderful to be around. But I'm hoping to take some classes this winter at the university, and it's kind of hard to get around without a car." He had already bedded the old green station wagon he used in the summer under a tarp for the winter.

"Oh I understand," said Carol. "I'm surprised you stayed as long as you did! The kids are all champing at the bit now that they're getting older." She smiled at her daughter. Carol, a horsewoman, had been the instigator of the Kukkonen horses. "Rich as our life is," she said, "we are well aware there is a big world out there."

"Linda's had a baby," said Paul. "Six months now, did I tell you?"

"That's great!" said Carol. She pulled into the big market parking lot. "This good for you, Paul?" she asked. "Give my love to Linda!"

"Perfect," said Paul getting out of the car. He went in and bought a six-pak of beer so he wouldn't arrive at Brian's house empty-handed. When he knocked on his friend's door, Brian answered.

"Hey, Paul," said Brian. "I was wondering when you'd turn up. I'm making my famous lasagna."

Behind him Paul could hear Linda. "He can't make a small amount, Paul," she said. "If you didn't come to help us eat it, we'd be eating it for a month!" She looked more disheveled and attractive than Paul had ever seen her, cradling the new baby in her arms. She had no one to watch the baby during the day, so she was taking the year off from teaching.

Paul pulled back the blanket, "Son's getting big!" he said. Onion and meat smells came from the kitchen. "Can I help?" he asked Brian.

"Open one of those beers for me," said Brian. "And maybe put on my new album. Is that okay, Linda?" He called toward the living room where Linda was watching the news.

"Sure," said Linda good-naturedly. "The news is the same every day!"

It was true, Paul thought. The Vietnam war dragged on, though Nixon said he was ending it. A judge had lifted the injunction against the Alaska oil pipeline project, but on appeals by environmentalists another court stated the EIR didn't follow the Minerals Leasing Act and wouldn't allow the large right-of-way needed for the pipeline. Nothing ever got resolved.

Linda fumbled through a batch of record albums and handed Paul the new one, with a large photo of the singer on the cover. *Sail Away* recorded by Randy Newman. Paul didn't know a thing about Newman, had never heard of him.

"Side Two!" yelled Brian from the kitchen. "You won't believe it!"

Paul didn't. The mix of beautiful piano and satire was explosive. "No one likes us. Don't know why. We may not be perfect, but heaven knows we try. But all around, even our old friends put us down. Let's drop the big one and see what happens!" Listening, Paul wanted to laugh, but it was a terrible thought.

"See what I mean," said Brian. "You don't know whether to laugh or cry!"

"He's so funny!" said Linda. "And so sweet, and so dark! All at the same time."

They played the whole album during dinner. But Paul couldn't get all the lyrics. Not when they were all together, talking. Another day he would take time to listen.

"Doug's poker game?" asked Brian, after dinner. "Linda's just as happy when I take off," he said. "Aren't you, babe? Have the house to yourself?"

"It's fine," said Linda. "I'm still not getting enough sleep," she said to Paul. "It's weird wandering around sort of half-baked like this." The baby was lying in its crib. "But it'll get better," she said hopefully.

"Boom goes London, boom Paree. More room for you and more room for me!" Brian sang as he and Paul struck off down the street toward the house a friend was crafting.

"How does he do it?" Paul asked. The song was already playing in his head.

"Howdy strangers," Doug greeted them. Tall, dark and bearded, with a rakish red bandana handkerchief tied around his forehead, he led them through the unfinished house he was building toward the living space. Crafting was the word for what he was doing. Taking it slowly, Doug built the log house's barely-enclosed structure around a base. Out of a tall spruce tree raised in the middle of the central room, he was carving circular steps to go up to the upper levels. The smell of new wood and shavings was strong, cutting through the cold air.

The walls of the living space at the back were lined with pine, tight and cozy, warmed by a wood stove. Around the wooden table were three other bearded men. Eyes sunk in ruddy, hairy faces looked merry and lively by the light of kerosene lamps. One on the table threw long shadows around the room. Another lit up the bar on one side.

"Well now, if it isn't the Daddy and the Big Spender!" Joe, the dealer greeted them, taking a thin cigar from his mouth.

"What'll you have, boys?" Doug asked. On shelves behind the bar was a sparse collection: a bottle of whiskey, one of gin, small glasses and several beers.

Paul felt, as he usually did on these nights, as if he was walking into a movie. Poker was a time-honored ritual game which had been enacted in Fairbanks, and all over the American West for that matter, since adventurers had come out with horses, packs, gold-digging equipment. Paul had grown up folding church bulletins on Saturday nights, being quiet so Dad could work on his sermon. Card-playing and drinking on a Saturday night were the antithesis of his childhood. Paul perversely loved it.

Paul settled in with a beer and pulled out his change. There wasn't much. He stacked it in front of him, looking up sheepishly. He was the Big Spender, never risking much. The game had nothing to do with winning for him. It had to do with the guys, finding out who they were and what they were like. He loved the cryptic talk, the silences, the looks that fell between them.

Joe dealt them each a card. Paul admired all of the men. Alaska, known for its freedom and space, was full of men in their twenties like Paul. There were many fewer women.

Each of these guys had a reason for being in Alaska, which had been teased out over the nights they played together. Keith's grandfather had been a stampeder, come out for the Gold Rush with his brother in 1899, floating down the Yukon from Canada's Klondike and finally settling in Alaska. Keith told them, "When I was ten I offered to scare up the gold pans and shovels if he would finance the joint mining venture."

"'Don't forget food for a year, horses, oats, a steam boiler, dynamite, the other tools, tent, and ...'" his grandfather told him. "Our partnership died a-borning," Keith said. He was on Brian's surveying team.

Joe, a Vietnam vet, had seen worse than any of the rest of them had. He worked in lumber camps, trying to forget and drinking more than anyone should. He covered his inner trauma with a veneer of disdain. His partner Bob, a wonderful craftsman like Doug, was quiet and tried to look after Joe. He'd been in the army too, but, since he managed to learn the Vietnamese language, he'd spent most of his time at a desk in Saigon.

Paul saw Brian looking over at him. "Ah, the holy game of poker," Brian quoted Leonard Cohen. "I told you when I came I was a stranger."

"All right you strangers," said Joe, dealing out the face cards. "All in?"

Paul was in. He pushed in all his dimes, nickels and pennies. His hole card was a King and so was his face card. He looked around at the poker faces each of them put up. He was sure he was giving away his secret elation at being in this company. These guys were whole people. Bonhoeffer would probably have approved.

11

With a scoop, Line dug deep into a barrel of the oats she was buying to make granola. Christopher stood at her elbow, "helping" by holding the bag into which she scooped the oats.

"Why does it smell like this," asked Christopher.

"Smell like what," said Line.

"Like new bread," said Christopher. "Or mushrooms. It's beery."

The Santa Cruz health food store did smell like yeast, Line realized. Or malt. An earthy smell. "Maybe it's the vitamins," she said. "Or the soaps and herbs."

"I like it," said Christopher. "It smells better than the other store."

The Cohen family hardly ever went to the "other store," Safeway. Today, Stephen and tiny Heather were out in the car, waiting for Line and Christopher to finish shopping. "Come on, Christy," Line said. "We need vegetables."

Shopping was very important to Line. It was one of the few areas in which she had any choice. She had a family of four and a very small budget. She was also very much against the food industry which tried to process everything people ate. She would not buy packaged cereals or Minute rice or little boxes of raisins, when she could prepare all of these things herself. Bulk foods cut out the middlemen and the manufacturers. Line also hoped that they were closer to the source, the farmer.

Line bought "organic" fruits and vegetables displayed in the health food store for the same reasons she didn't buy packaged foods. They were often brown and bruised, but they were grown without the benefit of fertilizers. Here they were in California, near some of the richest farms in the world. Surely some of what she bought came from nearby.

It was chilly in the produce section which was half-open to the outdoors. A man smelling of patchouli and wearing a tie-dyed tee-shirt smiled indulgently at them as he stocked a huge pile of prickly artichokes.

"Christy," said Line. "Pick us some apples from that pile." She pointed to the organic apples. She could make applesauce, apple betty and apple pie. It didn't matter what Christopher chose. She could cut out the brown spots.

Line grabbed potatoes, cabbage, carrots, onions, winter vegetables. She considered the artichokes. She and Stephen would eat them. She chose a few.

"Straight from Watsonville," said the man as he arranged boxes of them.

Line smiled at him. Watsonville was just down the road. "I'm not sure Christy here will eat them. Or my baby!" she said. "But my husband and I love them."

"I can eat artichokes," said Christopher manfully. He had to stretch to reach the apples and put them in their cart.

"Good!" said Line.

When they had moved away toward the checkout, Christopher pulled on Line's skirt. She bent down to hear him. "Why does he smell like that?" he asked. "It smells like that in the dorm."

"That's patchouli oil," whispered Line. Students wore it to cover up their pot smoking, which Line was sure Christopher also got good whiffs of in the dorm.

A skinny young girl with beautiful brown skin helped them check out, weighing their sacks of grain, flour and beans. In a tank top and dreadlocks, she looked as though it was dead summer instead of January. But the sun always felt warm when it came through in the middle of the day, even in the winter in Santa Cruz.

Line let Christopher push the cart with their week's groceries out to the car. He was lanky for his age, but still only three and a half feet tall. It was a funny sight to watch him, hardly able to see over the cart.

Stephen had the doors open to their ancient Chrysler and the radio turned on. "Nixon says they're suspending offensive action in Vietnam," he said. He gave Line an eloquently sardonic look.

Line looked at little Heather asleep in her basket. "Wouldn't it be wonderful," she said, "if our kids knew nothing of war?!"

Stephen sighed. "It certainly won't be for lack of trying!" he said.

"I got us some hamburger," said Line.

"Good!" said Stephen. He stood up and shaded his eyes in the sun, helping load grocery sacks into the trunk. "Barbecue, huh Christy?! Looks sunny enough."

They drove back up to campus, Christopher sitting solemnly beside Heather's basket in the back seat. Line had impressed upon him his role in watching his sister and he took it quite seriously.

Line unloaded groceries into the cupboards, while Stephen set up the grill on their small deck. Line watched, frowning. The danger with barbecue was that some of the students would invite themselves over. Line did not usually have enough food to spare for extra people. They only had meat once a week, and she wanted to make sure Stephen and Christopher got it. For that matter, she herself needed meat, as she was nursing Heather. She steeled herself to tell anyone who showed up that they were welcome to bring something with them to put on the coals.

Christopher seemed to take an interest as Stephen fired the coals with lighter fluid. Indoors, Line mixed oats and chopped almonds and stirred in oil, honey and a little vanilla. She spread the whole mess on a cookie sheet and put it in the oven at very low heat. With a few raisins and some coconut, it would make granola for the week.

Sure enough, the doorbell rang. Line melted as she opened it. There stood Rita, a student Line had recently taken to the Birth Center as she was pregnant. Rita was crying. Line took her in her arms.

"What's the matter?" she asked. "You poor thing," she said as she pulled Rita into the room and walked her over to the couch.

Rita's long dark hair was tangled around a blotchy red face. She looked as though she had just gotten out of bed. "I think I lost it," she said. "There was lots of blood and I had cramps. I think it's gone," she whispered.

"Did you see it?" asked Line. The baby would have been very small, in any case.

"No," said Rita. "I just went to the bathroom and there was lots of blood."

"I'm sorry," said Line. She was sure Rita was relieved, but the tension she had been living with, and the trauma of the morning would obscure any lightening of her burden. "Just sit here. I'll get you some hot tea. Do you need anything?"

The comforting smell of sweet grains toasting rose in the air. "No," said Rita. She slumped in her jeans and a musty sweatshirt on the couch, wiping her face with her sleeve. "I'm fine now, I think."

Line heated hot water and poured it over that morning's tea leaves. She looked apprehensively out at Stephen and Christopher. Stephen lifted the coals with a tongs, spreading them out and setting the grill on top of them.

Fresh convulsions of tears poured down Rita's cheeks as Line handed her a mug of hot tea. Line said softly, "It's going to be okay, Rita."

"Oh God, I feel so bad," said Rita. "I think this is what blue means. Or black and blue."

"Just stay here and rest," said Line. "We're making hamburgers for lunch. Do you want one?" She was glad it wasn't one of the male students. They would undoubtedly want more meat than Rita.

Stephen and Christopher came in the sliding glass door. "Fire's ready!" announced Stephen. "Hello, Rita," he said. Then "Are you okay?"

"Yes," said Rita struggling. "I'm fine."

Line looked at Stephen significantly. He probably knew what the problem was.

"Okay!" said Stephen. "Got those burgers ready Line?"

"No, no," said Line. "But it will only take a minute." She quickly cleared the table they ate on and put out bowls of salsa and guacamole. "Christy, can you pour out the tortilla chips?" She handed him the bag. They were an old standby for filling up students.

Stephen sat down by Rita on the couch as she sipped her tea. She was taking a class in European history from him. Line stood near the kitchen counter at the edge of the room, slapping hamburgers. From the bedroom came a whimper.

"Christy, please go and talk to Heather," said Line. She did not know how seeing Heather would make Rita feel, but the reality of their family life must be comforting.

Stephen stood up and returned in a moment with Heather, Christopher right behind him. He jiggled the little five-month-old, who usually woke up happily from naps. Stephen brought her to the couch. "Want to hold her?" he asked Rita.

Rita put down her mug of tea and lay back against the cushions, holding up her arms. Her eyes were big, her face blotchy, but she took Heather, wrapped in a little blanket. Christopher stood beside them protectively, staring at Rita.

Line looked on as she washed the hamburger grease off her hands. "Here you go," she said to Stephen, handing him the tray.

"Salt and pepper?" asked Stephen.

"Yes, I did," said Line. She knew that Stephen wanted his burger just so, as long as he was taking his precious time to make them. She gave him a tray of split buns to put them on. He liked to toast his bun on the coals as well.

Line watched the little tableau on the couch closely, but it seemed to be going all right.

"She's my sister," said Christopher to Rita.

"Yes, I see," said Rita. Her face was clearing, growing less red, more peaceful.

Line laid plates on the table. She imagined Rita's hormones responding to the baby. It was probably the most healing thing in the world to hold a tiny one. She went over and sat for a moment beside Rita.

"Her eyes are so big," said Rita.

"Momma said she can see me," said Christopher. He twitched around in front of Heather, watching to see if her eyes followed him. He picked up the dried gourd baby rattle and shook it a little too hard on one side of Heather and then on the other. "See!" he said. "She knows where I am!"

Line stroked Heather's skin. "Smell her skin, Rita," she said. "Nothing like it." She wrinkled her nose from a faint ammonia smell and laughed. "I do think she needs changing!" She went and got a little rubber sheet and a clean diaper. Taking Heather from Rita, she laid her down on the floor and changed her quickly. "Want her back?" she asked. "Christy, go ask Dad if the hamburgers are about done." She was counting on the smell of barbecued beef to turn his little head.

Rita took the cleaned up baby back into her arms and settled against the sofa cushions, rocking her a little. "Thank you Line," she said. "I'm feeling better."

"A little less blue?" asked Line.

Rita made a face. "Less Prussian blue, maybe more cerulean."

Line smiled. "You'll be depressed for a while," she said. "We'll go to the Birth Center tomorrow. It's a good idea to talk to people about your feelings right now. But you are doing okay physically? How many weeks did we figure it was?"

"Only six or eight weeks," said Rita. "I think I can manage okay."

"It'll get better," said Line. "Just relax. Did you ever tell Dan?" Rita shook her head. "Good," said Line quietly.

When Stephen and Christy came in with the burgers, Rita didn't want to come to the table. "You guys eat," she said. "I'll hold Heather until you're done."

"Okay, but your burger is ready," Line said. It was a beautiful day, she thought. A ripple of pleasure went down her spine as she lifted Christy into the little step-up chair which allowed him to sit at the table. She was pleased with her ability to dispense largesse of different kinds to meet the needs of people coming into her domestic orbit. She sneaked a kiss on the top of Stephen's head as she passed him. He was the ultimate source of this hard-won happiness.

That night Line stood ironing while listening to Stephen talking to his father in New York. Christopher was asleep in his own little bed in a closet and Heather lay on a blanket on the floor, looking up at her parents.

Line always learned things listening Stephen talk to Poppa. They had heart-to-heart conversations about what each of them thought and what they were doing.

"Even trying to look at things from the point of view of the times," Stephen said, "I can't understand Muste's position!" He had learned that A.J. Muste, the man he was writing his dissertation on, had withdrawn his support from Bayard Rustin after Rustin was arrested and served 60 days in jail for homosexual activity in a car in Los Angeles. "I thought he was bigger than that!"

Line didn't hear Jacob Cohen's reply, but he seemed to be justifying Muste. Line's father-in-law was a lively man of 63 who had worked all his life as an immigration lawyer out of his Brooklyn home. After his wife died, he continued to work every day, representing Russian, Italian, Greek and Portuguese immigrants, but also, as he told them, increasingly people from India, Korea, Pakistan. He was lonely without his wife and had taken to going out to the movies at night.

"The Fellowship of Reconciliation paid for a therapist for him, but they expected a certain result!" said Stephen. "And they did drive him out in the end. It's outrageous! Rustin grew up Quaker!"

Line knew that Stephen identified with Bayard Rustin, who had done a lot of the organizing for Martin Luther King, even, Stephen said, writing some of King's speeches. Rustin had been mentored by A.J. Muste, the venerable man Stephen was writing his dissertation on. But, having discovered this rift between Muste and Rustin, Stephen seemed to be siding with Rustin.

"Muste was a prude! A puritan," said Stephen. "It just doesn't sit well with me."

In the silences, Line looked over at Stephen's long body stretched out on the couch listening, the black phone cord tangled around his arm. Stephen, despite all his political work, had a hard time empathizing with people's irrational sides. Religion seemed to play a part in Muste's makeup and Stephen didn't want to come to terms with it. Stephen, who had spent many years as an administrator in SDS, also respected Bayard Rustin's great success in making coalitions and organizing protests.

"I will talk to Bernie," said Stephen into the phone. Bernie Freeman was Stephen's mentor and had suggested Stephen work on Muste in the first place. Muste had died in 1967 and Bernie felt they all owed him something, that his leadership should be researched and acknowledged.

"So what are you doing, Poppa?" asked Stephen. A long silence followed. Line was glad they could talk together so freely. They were the only ones left in their family.

Line had long ago lost the ability to discuss what she thought honestly with her own Mother and Dad. If she had things to say, it was best to talk to Marty and Paul. Mother and Dad had not had the experiences that drove Line, Marty and Paul. The generation gap, it was called. Also Mother and Dad still had young children at home. Kristen would be 16 this year and Hanna 13. In the Mikkelson family, everyone protected the younger kids from things that would spoil their innocence. This too kept Line from arguing with her parents.

Mother and Dad had, Line suspected, commended them to the Lord in his mercy. Line knew they loved her, but Dad was a pastor steeped in the language and culture of the Bible and the Norwegian Lutheran Church. Mother totally supported him. It was a closed system. Wittenberg College was trying to open it up when Line was there, but not enough for her. Marrying someone from a different culture had blown the doors off for Line. She could never go back.

Line lifted the last shirt out of the ironing basket, and smoothed it on the ironing board, beginning with the collar, the sleeves and then the flat parts of the shirt. Where did I learn to iron, she wondered. Home ec? She could not remember Mother ironing, except as an aspect of sewing. Seams must be ironed flat. That must be where she had learned. She had no clothes that needed ironing. Only Stephen's cotton shirts and sometimes little shirts for Christopher. She imagined the little dresses Heather would wear. Marty still did a lot of sewing. Perhaps she would make a dress for Heather.

Line's ears pricked up when she heard Stephen say, "Page Smith is quitting. He doesn't want to work at a university where Paul Lee can't teach, he says. Lee took on Huey Newton, if you remember. But Lee didn't publish, so he's going to perish. I think it all goes back to Line's gardener friend Allan Chadwick. Lee was so attached to him, and Page too. Chadwick left last year." Page Smith was the provost at Cowell, Stephen's college, the first of the residential colleges at UC Santa Cruz.

A silence ensued, and then Stephen said, "Page doesn't seem surprised. He says the university is hardening, becoming an institution. They had five years of openness and experiment at the beginning. But it wants to be a research institution." He went on, reassuring his father, "Don't worry, Poppa, I'll hang in there. There's nowhere else for me to go. But I will miss Page Smith."

At last it sounded as though Stephen was saying goodbye. Line looked over at Stephen, hoping for a summary of what Poppa was doing. "How is he?" she asked. She and Stephen could talk about almost anything.

Stephen sat up. "He's doing fine. Every day interesting people with stories walk into his office. He loves his work. I'm very glad for him. He'll never have to retire. But he is alone. He was telling me about *McCabe and Mrs. Miller*. Made me want to see it!"

Stephen and Line watched a little television, but Line thought their lively house was more interesting than most movies. "Why?" asked Line.

"He said it was an anti-Western. The hero is a putz. But it's got Julie Christie in it." Stephen came over and put his arms around Line, making her set the steaming, hot iron to the side. "Thank you sweetheart, for ironing my shirts."

Line relaxed into him. "Just let me finish this one, and then I'll come to bed," she said. "I didn't know Page was quitting."

Stephen's body tightened. "It's a black day at the university," he said. "But what are you going to do? I can't quit. I'll be the one to write the history, though," he said darkly. "No one is going to stop me."

"That sounds like my husband," said Line. "What are you going to do about Muste?"

"Talk to Bernie," said Stephen. "He's more objective than I am. You may think I'm not, Line, but I want to be. I want my work to be rooted in reality. You've shown me that, my lovely wife," he said. "And of course Poppa. Events properly sifted down to reality as best we can; that's the only history that lasts."

In the morning it rained heavily. Line lay in bed listening as it drummed on the roof and sluiced down the drainpipes to land hard on the concrete. Stephen was already gone. Line saw little of him during the week. Rain was good but she wondered what she would do with Christy. He wasn't good at staying home all day. And, indeed, later in the morning, when Christy saw the maintenance truck pull up, he told Line, "I'm going out to help George."

Line was breast-feeding Heather on the sofa, enjoying the feeling of the tiny mouth connected to her. She let Christy go. George didn't seem to mind a bit of Christy at his heels. Line felt nostalgic. In the fall, Christy would go to school and that would be the end of their intense partnership. Christy kept moving outward, his curiosity driving him. Line was happy he was so bright and everyone liked him.

114

Christopher was relaxing a little in the family also, Line thought. Heather had been the answer. Stephen didn't pressure Christy, patiently gave him enough leash to do as he wanted to. Christy had finally seen that he was not Line's partner, that he and Heather were free to be the little kids. Line felt sad it was that way, that she had weighed him down with her life. But on the other hand, the alternatives might have been worse. She did not regret anything she had done.

When Christy came back in an hour, he had Rita in tow. Dark clouds filled the sky which was so visible through the second floor glass patio doors. It made the apartment feel dark, damp and dreary. It was still pouring outside, as if the sky had opened up and wanted to make up for the dry months they had been having. Line was vegetating, glad she didn't have to go running after Christy. She was not surprised to see Rita.

"How are you doing, Rita?" Line asked.

Rita made a face and then looked sheepish. "Terrible," she said. "I can't seem to get up and go to class."

Line raised her eyebrows. "Did you find George?" she asked Christy.

Christy was evasive. "He's washing the floors," he said not looking at Line.

Line decided not to ask what he'd been doing. "Well, I think we all better have some lunch." She stood at the refrigerator pulling out things for sandwiches.

"Oh," said Rita. "I'd love some of your good brown bread."

Line considered what to say to Rita. It was the beginning of a term. Perhaps a few missed days wouldn't be so bad. But on the other hand, if she didn't dive in Rita would get behind. She piled cheese, bean sprouts, lettuce, tomatoes and peanut butter on the table. "Come on Christy," she said. "I'll make you a sandwich."

"Where's the baby?" asked Rita.

"Sleeping," said Line. "Thank goodness. So what are you taking this semester?" she asked. Rita was not one of the students Stephen talked about.

Rita sighed. She slathered a thick slice of brown bread with butter. "I want to be a marine biologist, so I declared biology as my major. It's tough," she sighed again. "Gaaaah," she put a hand to her head dramatically. "I'm going to be so behind!"

"Sounds heavy duty," said Line. She had no idea what a marine biologist did. "Math and biology and chemistry, I bet? Are you a surfer?"

"Yeah," said Rita. "Lots of math and science." She looked up at Line. "Line, don't laugh at me," she said shyly. "I'm from Salinas and I want to study whales and dolphins and marine life. I do love surfing. That's what got me in this mess!"

"It's not a mess yet," Line said quietly. "It depends on what you do with it." She looked at Christy, who had a ring of peanut butter around his mouth. "Apple?" she asked him. She began cutting an apple into pieces.

"If I were at home, I'd turn on the television and just space out," said Rita.

"Television? In the middle of the day?" asked Line. "No way, my dear. Not at my house. Naps are fine. Let's have some tea and a nap. Such a good day for it," she indicated the floor to ceiling patio doors where the clouds had still not parted. Sheets of rain came down. It made Line feel droopy. She would like nothing so much as a nap and when she looked at Christy, it seemed he felt the same way.

Christy took a blanket into his corner and fell asleep while Line made tea. She heard Heather waking up in the next room. She looked at Rita, who nodded. Line picked up the tiny baby and handed her to Rita to hold. "Put her on your shoulder," she said. "Babies like it up there."

Rita softened as she took the baby.

"Did you love the guy?" asked Line as she put a mug of tea beside Rita on the table. "Are you sorry you aren't having his baby?"

"No," said Rita. "I don't think so. It was more of a drunken accident." She took a long drink. "I know the miscarriage was a good thing. I told my Mother and she didn't know what to do about the baby either. We were trying to decide."

"The baby decided," said Line, wrapping a shawl around her shoulders. "It gave you back your life. But now you know what you have to do, don't you?"

Rita looked at her.

"You have to make its brief little life worth it," said Line. "You have to do what you are meant to in life. If that's marine biology, go for it." Line leaned back. The hot tea was a nice contrast to the cold rain outdoors.

"It feels so nice to hold Heather," said Rita, humbly. "It's like she's saving me."

"She's saving us too, in some ways," said Line. She looked over toward Christopher, sleeping with his blanket pulled up around him. "That little guy sleeping over there was something of a surprise. And it did almost make a pretzel of us." Line cupped her hands around the warm tea. "You're in the thick of your life, Rita. It is all going to work out in the end."

12

"I've been thinking," said Erik. "Why don't we get married?" Marty and Erik were having a quick dinner at an old trattoria on Green Street.

"Married?" Marty was so surprised that her fork slipped and a lump of basil pesto landed on her white blouse. She looked down, chagrined. They were going to a lecture on architecture that night. She dipped her napkin in her water glass and dabbed at the spot.

"Surprised you, didn't I!" Erik said, laughing. But he looked up furtively. "You do want to, don't you?"

Marty had never said so. She kept her fervent desire to be married to herself. She was 27 and had more or less been with Erik since she first met him five years ago. "I do want to," Marty said solemnly. Emotion rose up in her. "I do very much. Thank you for asking me, Erik," she said, reaching her hand across the table to touch his. She would have liked a bit more ceremony to the moment, but it would have to do.

"Good," said Erik, kissing her fingers. He dug into his pasta. To his right, across an aisle of austere tables, taking up most of the wall was a lurid painting of Marilyn Monroe, stretched out, her golden skin bright against a red velvet robe.

"So, what are you thinking about it?" asked Marty. She drank the bitter, earthy red Italian wine from a small peasant glass.

"I'll bet you want to go out and have your Dad marry us," said Erik. "Like Line did. So I thought we could drive out, get married and take the southern route back."

"Would your folks come?" asked Marty. "Or your brother?" Erik, a lapsed Catholic, had little to do with church and probably didn't care what sort of wedding service they had.

Erik frowned. "I'm not going to ask them. But I guess I could ask Brad." Brad, his brother, was an attorney in Los Angeles. Marty had met him once. He was younger than Erik, but less golden. Erik had gotten the charm in the family, while Brad was bull-headed and arrogant. Marty suspected he was effective however.

"I'd love to have Dad do it," said Marty. "It's exactly what I want. But it doesn't have to be a big deal," she said. "I'd just like to meet your parents."

Erik sighed. "We can stop in Palm Desert and see them on the way back," he said. "I suppose they'd want to meet you too," he conceded.

Marty tried to imagine them. Erik's father wrote for television and lived in Los Angeles during the week. The major antipathy was between Erik and his mother. Marty suspected that Erik's mother thought he robbed her of her youth. But how could she not love Erik. As a tiny baby, she had given Erik to her mother to raise, and then taken him back. Marty felt this was the source of his lack of ease in life.

"When do you want to do this?" asked Marty. It was April and investigations into the Watergate leaks were revealing cracks in Nixon's administration. No one Marty knew was sorry.

"How about next month?" asked Erik. "Aren't you due for a vacation?"

Marty nodded. She hadn't been at Lipman, Mancuso and Pierson that long, but she had probably accumulated five days or so of vacation. "That sounds great, Erik," she said with feeling. She was glad he didn't want to wait. Who knew what would happen if they waited! "I'll call my folks," she said. Did she have to make any other plans? Not really. She would buy a dress. She was ready.

"We'll get the license here," said Erik. "And then your Dad can marry us." He stood up to pay the bill. "We better get going. The lecture's going to start!"

Marty put on her jacket, fluffing her long hair down her back. She looked at Erik fondly as he held the door open for her, his wry face so funny and full of thoughts in the dim light. She wondered what had sparked his desire to be married. They were growing closer, made more plans together. Marty had begun to hope that Erik wasn't dealing any more, but she had also been disconcerted by seeing him drunk. One evening he had come home from a nearby bar so drunk he could hardly get up the steps to their flat.

Marty took Erik's arm as they walked down the street. The lecture was held in a large empty room with dark purple walls, once a restaurant. The room was full of people in folding chairs, packed closely around the speaker, who stood near an abandoned bar and spoke without a microphone. Bill Stout, a local architect who ran a bookstore out of his house had set up the series. Why not? Everyone flocked to them, excited to hear their colleagues describe the theories behind their work.

That evening Lawrence Halprin, a landscape architect, presented his method of working with people to plan a project. He called it making a "score," as in a musical score. Marty was a bit dazed by Erik's proposal, her mind wandering. But seeing architecture as music was intriguing. "The musical analogy comes from working with my wife, Anna," said Halprin, a relaxed man in his fifties. There was a little silver in his beard. Marty knew of Anna Halprin, a dancer who organized Movement Rituals to explore the kinesthetic possibilities of awareness and empathy.

"We like to start with an awareness walk, which gets people on common ground," said Halprin, rolling up his shirtsleeves. "We just walk the space, talking about it. We say 'what are your feelings about the place?' or 'what are your feelings about how it should be used?'

"And then we score them," he said, turning to a blackboard and beginning to write. "We don't have a point of view, and we don't make judgments. Each person or group puts some ideas on the wall and describes it, then tells us how they feel about it. People may ask questions, but we never get people standing up and saying, 'that's terrible.'"

"Even in contentious situations?" asked Bill Stout.

"We have contentious situations all the time," said Halprin. "But they disappear during the workshop. People with different points of view suddenly have a common language."

"I would have said Justin Hermann Plaza had some contentious aspects," quipped an architect in the second row.

Halprin laughed and so did everyone else. "Yeah, it'll be a while until I live down the Vaillancourt Fountain. But you just go over there at lunch, anytime, and watch the little kids prancing under the waterfalls. Big smiles on their faces!"

Marty did love the fountain. It was a massive construction of stone slabs, ugly and brutal against the double-tiered concrete freeway behind it. But yes, Marty had walked through it, photographing it, herself. It was not something she would have chosen, but when you were there it demanded a reaction. Overall it was exciting.

Marty was aware of Erik, sitting close to her at the edge of the crowd. She wasn't sure if he was awake. His somnolence could be intense awareness or not! She wasn't really sure where he stood on this. He had studied programming at Berkeley's architecture school.

Erik was complicated. He liked working out details, understanding structures and was meticulous about drawing, but he was content to collaborate, letting someone else do the major design. He often seemed uncertain about whether he was good enough to be an architect, while at the same time putting on the hauteur when necessary! He had the persona down: the hot-shot young architect you wanted on your project. Marty thought being cool was the most important thing to him, that architecture offered him a way to live in beauty, as well as use his gift for drawing.

Marty still found Erik unreliable, secretive and protective of his time and space. Nevertheless, she had entirely accepted him. He was outgoing and had awakened her sexually. All around them these days, in the air, even in Halprin's presentation, was the idea that the body reflected the mind, that the body was the unconscious, that only through the body could you find your real self. Finding self-knowledge through the body justified their sexual and drug exploration. Even rock and roll! It was the opposite of the idea college had given Marty, that you should find a partner with your head, who had values like your own.

Erik didn't always act like a partner, but their profound physical relationship had convinced Marty that they could get there. My body doesn't lie, she thought. Marriage would help. She was sure that her unconditional love would eventually allow Erik to become comfortable and peaceful in himself. Marty didn't expect him to be ambitious any more than she expected a career for herself. She wanted the stability of a relationship to allow her to pursue ideas. She did not know where they would lead.

When Halprin had finished answering questions, Bill Stout thanked him and everyone stood up. Erik and Marty put on their jackets and walked up the steep Kearny Street steps home in the cool, spring night, Erik directing with a practiced hand. While he didn't always seem sure of himself in his work, he certainly felt sure of Marty.

Erik was nonchalant about the meeting. "Gestalt group think," he scoffed. "Halprin's only got a limited number of ideas. I don't think he has a sense of classical pattern. It's like he's just out there in the wild west, laying out stones and fountains and trees to see what happens! The Vaillancourt fountain is a monstrosity!"

"He didn't design it," said Marty.

"No, but he picked it out of hundreds of possibilities!" said Erik.

Marty fit her steps to Erik's. It was easy to do. Houses came right down to the edge of the sidewalk they were walking on.

"On this trip," Erik went on, "I want to come back through New Mexico and see some of the pueblos. Some of the adobe buildings. I've been to Europe. But I've never traveled that much in our own country!"

Marty sighed. "Yeah," she said. "I want to see the cathedral in Santa Fe, the one Willa Cather writes about." Under a street light Marty stopped and turned to Erik. "I'm so happy," she said. "It will be lovely to be married. We're going to have so much fun!" Marty was thinking about children, a child with Erik's charm and good looks, plus her own straightforward intelligence. But there was plenty of time ahead for that.

Erik's hands reached under Marty's clothes, fumbling for her skin. "We're already having it," he said. "No 'going to' about it."

Mother and Dad were both on the phone when Marty asked them about coming out to get married. She found herself crying. She knew considerably more about Erik than they did and was going into it with her eyes wide open.

"If you wait until the end of May," Dad said proudly, "Paul will be here. We're hiring him for the summer to work on cabin construction."

"Oh, that would be great!" said Marty. "He can be the best man if Erik's brother doesn't come."

When it came down to it, Brad didn't come. He was deep in a case that meant a lot to his career and he didn't want to take the time. The trip to Iowa was as quick as Erik and Marty could make it. They stayed in cheap hotels in Utah and Nebraska and arrived shortly after Paul did.

Mother greeted them when they arrived in the evening with her usual graciousness. "My goodness, Marty," she said. "It's so good to see you! Have you had any dinner?"

"Yes," said Marty. It was already eight o'clock at night but the sun was still in the sky. "We stopped for a bite since we knew we'd be late."

Everyone stood in the big tiled foyer. Erik looked like a fish out of water with his longish hair and a soft handsewn leather jacket he had gotten from North Beach Leather. Kristen and Hanna gawked at him. In contrast, Paul looked like he had stepped off a logging truck in a red plaid shirt and suspenders holding up his jeans! He was clean-shaven, but his shaggy hair looked less like a rock and roll star and more like someone who lived in the woods. I'm half way between them, Marty thought.

Mother pointed everyone into the living room. Even Aunt Rose was there, just retired, but still vigorous. The last rays of golden light slipped in through the drapes. Two guitars were propped against the sofa.

Kristen looked like every other 4-H member Marty had ever known, clear-faced, peaceful and a little shy. Hanna, almost a teenager, taller, slim and boyish, could not have been more different. A light shone from her defying definition. She seemed delighted that they were all home. Who is this stunning young girl? Marty wondered.

Hanna picked up one of the guitars. "Paul and I are practicing some songs to sing at the wedding," said Hanna. "Do you have any favorites?"

Marty was nonplussed. She looked at Erik. She had no idea at all what should happen at her wedding. "Give me a minute, Hanna," she said. "Do you have any that you usually do?"

Paul sat strumming at the edge of the couch, quiet. He was finger-picking the classical Spanish rhythm underneath a Leonard Cohen song. Marty heard the words under her breath, "It's true that all the men you knew were dealers who said they were through with dealing every time you gave them shelter." Marty looked at him warningly. He was too close to the truth! He was probably trying to imagine how to interact with this sophisticated new brother-in-law. Marty put her hands on the strings. Paul stopped playing, a silly grin coming over his face. Marty flashed a look at Erik, who seemed annoyed.

"I can play 'Amazing Grace,'" said Hanna. "But I sing better than I can play." She began picking out the notes. She had a strikingly individual, mordant way of plucking the strings. Marty could have watched her forever.

"I don't think it's for weddings," said Hanna, looking up.

Marty looked at Erik, who shrugged his shoulders. But Paul began picking out what Marty had recognized as Pachelbel's 'Canon in D.'

"That's the only classical one I know," said Paul.

"It's perfect," said Marty. "And 'Amazing Grace' too!"

"I'll sing," said Hanna, "and Paul can play."

Marty didn't feel Mother and Dad had changed at all since she last saw them. Mother was glad to be out of school where she taught in order to help her kids get through college. She had taken up weaving and showed Marty a small loom she bought. On it was a beautiful piece of red and black wool she said she would make into a handbag. Dad was full of construction plans for the summer. The family seemed to be thriving.

"I'm working on a big resort down in Arizona," Erik told Dad when he was asked what he was working on. "I didn't think about bringing any drawings with me." He seemed relaxed and had toned down his most obvious attempts to be charming. Sensitive, he tried to match the Mikkelsons' authenticity with his own. "They're so warm," he later told Marty. Marty could see that he respected Dad.

"Well I've got some to show you," Dad said, pulling Erik and Marty into the study. "I think if I hadn't felt the call to be a pastor," said Dad, "I would have liked to be an architect." He pulled out drawings he had done for a building at the lake. They would be supported by his experience of many years working with his own father who was a contractor.

Erik looked closely at the drawings, which were hardly more than schematics. "Can't quite imagine it," he said. "I'd need to see the site."

Marty wondered what life would have been like if Dad had not been a pastor in very small towns. Only cities could support architects. She wondered how many there were in the Twin Cities.

Mother left Marty and Erik the basement level of the commodious house. There were two rooms, one with a double bed and one a big family room with a couch. As they brushed their teeth in the tiny bathroom, Erik asked Marty, "What was your brother up to?"

Marty brushed it off. "I don't think anyone recognized it," she said. "I'm sure Paul didn't know what he was doing." She could not explain how close she felt to Paul. "I notice that Aunt Rose took quite a shine to you," she teased. Aunt Rose always liked young men.

The wedding was simple, a Lutheran service which Erik later told Marty was not very different from the Catholic weddings he had gone to. Paul, in a suit and tie, stood next to Erik, and Kristen and Hanna in their Sunday dresses next to Marty, with Dad, in his robes and a green silk stole around his neck, looking benevolent behind them. Mother played the organ and Paul and Hanna sang. Aunt Rose was the only one in the pews. She helped Dad take formal photographs after the service.

Marty had agonized over clothes for herself and Erik. She didn't want to wear a white dress, as it was obvious she was no virgin. "Don't buy a dress," said Erik. "Just wear that little black sheath that looks so nice on you. There'll be flowers and they'll stand out against it."

"Married in black, you'll wish yourself back," said Marty. "I can't do that." She wore a long, gingham dress she had found at an outlet store. Erik had beautiful suits and looked great in a tie, but Marty thought it might be too formal for the down-to-earth Mikkelsons. She chose a crisp new Oxford shirt for Erik and a modest suitcoat which looked good beside her cotton dress.

The flowers and a tiered cake made by a local bakery were exactly what were expected for a large wedding. "It's just like Line's," whispered Hanna to Marty as they set the table at home for a wedding supper.

Marty suddenly realized Mother was used to such weddings by now. It was the third time one of her girls had come home, bringing unknown men who would become their husbands. Ellie's husband had been better known than either Line's or Marty's. Ellie and Bruce still lived in Italy, where Bruce worked for 3M Corporation and their two girls were growing up. Marty had not seen them for years, though they usually spent part of every summer in Minneapolis.

Marty was overwhelmed with grateful feelings for her parents. Here they were, upholding all the cardinal virtues while she was off experimenting in the golden west. But she was too excited to be able to express herself. She would try to write them when she got home. After supper and the lovely cake with fruit punch, Erik and Marty drove off to the noise of tin cans tied to the bumper of their car. A sign in the window made by Hanna said "Just Married."

"What a trip!" said Erik. "It was a real wedding! Your family is wonderful!"

"Yes," Marty said. "You can count my family. Thank you Erik," she said, putting her arms around him as he drove, though the bucket seats of the car prevented her from getting very close to him. She felt chagrin as well as relief and happiness. Her family was her community. It could not be helped that their friends and Erik's family were not present, that almost two thousand miles separated their daily lives.

When she woke up the next morning in a motel in Nebraska, Marty realized that she was married. She was wearing the filmy embroidered cotton and lace nightgown she had bought for the occasion. Erik's blonde head stuck out of the white pillow next to her. Marty curled toward him in the comfy bed.

Marty's name was now Margaret Ruth Mikkelson Wilson. She could use any of these names as she pleased, but legally she was now Margaret Wilson. An obscure relief settled around her. If their apartment was busted or something terrible happened, the newspapers would not scream out the Mikkelson name. Her family was now safe from any trouble Marty might cause. The common name of Wilson was a good one.

Erik seemed to find the whole thing funny. "Yes," he said. "I can now call you wife! As in, get me my pipe and slippers, wife!"

Marty giggled. What she and Erik most shared was an ironic, often sardonic look at American culture. Marty thought she must have gotten her iconoclasm from Dad, who loved his work in obscure places and never wanted to become important in the Lutheran church. He had the connections, but preferred to stay where he was.

Marty had no love of pomp and circumstance herself. She had seen little of it and had no need for it. It sounded like Erik's family was full of pretensions, cocktail parties for bigwigs in Los Angeles, expensive homes, cars, clothes. His family played the game to the hilt, but it made Erik uncomfortable. The counterculture had come just in time to rescue him.

"Well, in the absence of pipe and slippers, what would you like me to do for you, my dear husband," Marty asked lightly. They both thought marriage wouldn't make any difference to them. But it did, a tiny bit. Marriage was one of the conventions they wanted to remake.

"Nothing you don't already do, my darling," said Erik, stretching lazily. "Let's get up and get going!"

Marty tried to untangle the sheets. It would be nice to sleep in that morning, but they had few days left and lots of miles to travel.

It took them a couple of days to get to Santa Fe, long hard driving through Nebraska, Kansas, Colorado. Marty had the road atlas on her lap. She loved navigating. Finally they were in the dry deserts of northern New Mexico. Marty could see snow on the peaks of what must be the Sangre de Cristo Mountains. The blood of Christ, she thought. They did look reddish in the setting sun. But after a blissful day in Santa Fe, they were back on the road to Palm Desert.

As they drew near, Erik seemed to get more agitated. "We need to get there about the middle of the day," he told Marty. "A lot depends on timing in that house." He had also timed it so they would arrive on Sunday, when his father would be there.

Marty caught Erik's nervousness. But she outwardly grew more calm. I can rise to this occasion, she told herself.

"It's really just a big country club," said Erik the next morning as they drove past manicured golf courses. "Second homes, resorts. It was all master-planned." Towering palm trees edged the roads. The houses were all one color, a sort of warm tan. In front of each house were grass plots, neatly mowed, flanking big driveways.

"Where do they get the water for all that grass?" Marty asked. It was the desert after all.

"The Colorado River," said Erik darkly. "Stolen, flat and simple. But I think they also have some deep wells."

They pulled into a driveway in front of one of the clay-colored houses which looked very modern with palms and flowering cacti in front of it. "Come on," said Erik, straightening his back. "Do or die."

Marty smiled at him and pulled a brush from her handbag, giving her hair a quick run-through. She was often impressed with the dramatic streak Erik must have gotten from his father. "They are expecting us, aren't they?" she asked.

"Yeah," said Erik nonchalantly. "I spoke to Dad. You look great, my lovely wife. Don't worry. No matter what she says."

Erik's father opened the front door, giving Erik a big hug. He looked relaxed, in a loose silk shirt and slacks, his hair waved back into place with grease. "How is everything?" he asked.

"Good to see you Dad," said Erik. "My wife Margaret."

Marty felt very self-conscious as she offered her hand to Mr. Wilson, who took her in with a quick glance. She wore only the lightest of makeup, and her hair was damp on her neck. Mr. Wilson led them into a cool, air-conditioned foyer which opened onto a spectacular sunken living room looking out toward the empty desert.

On a sinuous couch in front of a brick fireplace, Mrs. Wilson nursed a glass with beads of water on it. She was thin, with bleached blonde hair. Her expensive shirt draped down onto a pair of slacks. She did not get up. "Oh, Erik," she said coolly. "And Margaret, is it?" Mrs. Wilson was not quick about looking Marty up and down. "So you're the little minx that stole our Erik," she said, in a husky, slightly rough voice.

Marty was astonished. She had thought that Mrs. Wilson cared little for Erik. She couldn't think of an answer, so she just said nothing. The men ignored the elder Mrs. Wilson.

"Martini before lunch?" asked Mr. Wilson. He busied himself in front of a sleek bar, and handed Marty and Erik each a triangular glass with two pimento-stuffed olives in the silver liquid. "To the two of you!" he raised his glass in salute.

"And to us!" said the hoarse voice on the couch. "To the continuation of the Wilson line!"

Marty took a sip. It might not relax her, she thought, but it might smooth out the rough edges. She stood awkwardly, her shoulder bag weighing down one shoulder.

Erik paced about, looking out the window at the view. Marty went over to him. "It's beautiful," she said. The sky came down to the low hills beyond what looked like more palm trees. Perhaps a golf course. "How long have you lived here?" she asked Mr. Wilson politely, who had come to stand beside them.

"Oh, I guess we've had this place about ten years," Mr. Wilson said. "Makes a nice rest from that sink hole over there," he indicated the west with his glass.

"Oh, you love it," said Mrs. Wilson acidly. "Doesn't want to retire. Can't wait to get back on Sunday nights. Doesn't think there's life off the studio lot!" She sniffed audibly behind them.

"Well, is there?" asked Mr. Wilson rhetorically. "You can't play golf every day!" Marty wished she knew more about Mr. Wilson's work. But this did not seem the place or time to display ignorance. In the background, Marty saw a plump olive-skinned woman laying the table in the dining room. She wore a white apron and her black hair pulled back tightly into a bun. She smiled at Marty.

The lunch went off with some formality. Mr. Wilson joshed the housekeeper, Estella, who teased him back. He asked Erik about his work and complained about Los Angeles.

"Did you get to any of those Laker games?" asked Erik. The NBA title for the year had just gone to the rival team, The New York Knicks.

Mr. Wilson sighed. "Nope. Can't win 'em all, I guess," he said. "Exact reversal of the way the games went last year!" he said. "Now who could predict that?"

"Brad saw a game," said Mrs. Wilson meaningfully. Was she taunting Erik with his successful younger brother? "We watched for him on television, but we didn't see him."

"Sounds like Wilt the Stilt is moving on," said Erik, ignoring this. "Coaching next year?"

"Yup," said Mr. Wilson. "Amazing career. Amazing. But he's gonna go with the money. I'm not too surprised. Anybody would."

Mrs. Wilson, picking at her Caesar salad, agreed. "Quite a guy," she said. "Fun to watch."

Marty was amazed by the conversation. So that was what sports were good for, to keep people from letting themselves show. She wondered what was so scary, what everyone was protecting themselves from. The family was successful, obviously. Marty realized that everything about the Wilsons was indeed on view, in their artificial bodies and expensive tastes. Truly the unconscious was revealed in the body.

After the salad, Estella triumphantly brought in a baked ham, studded with cloves and slices of pineapple. The mashed potatoes didn't taste very good to Marty, and the green beans must have been frozen. Marty imagined the two women, caring for the big, empty house during the week. Lunching together, conferring, planning their days. This must be Mrs. Wilson's real life, Marty thought. Her name was Rosalind, but Marty could not imagine calling her that. Art, Erik's dad's name, was easier. Someday, Marty thought. Someday we'll bring home a baby, and all this artifice will melt.

13

Paul inched along the roof of the 'barn' he and Dad were building at Lake Michigami, nailing shingles one after the other as he worked his way up. Below him, Dad nailed siding into place on the building.

Paul tried not to waste any motions, slide the shingle into place, pick up a nail, hammer it in. He had been working since early in the day, but at midmorning the sun was hot and moist. Breezes through the birches and poplars provided some relief, dappling the roof with leaf shadows. Paul was protected by a cap and considered taking off his shirt. He loved being up in the trees. He loved the piney smell of the new wood. And he loved working with Dad.

The building was set across the driveway from the cabin. It had several levels, the lower one to become a garage, and the upper ones to become studios and craft spaces. A craft barn, Dad called it. On the second level, windows looking off into the woods would be a bird blind where Mother could ensconce herself. The third level was to be a combination artist's studio and library.

They had some help from neighbors with the heavy roofbeams, but mostly, with Dad's contractor's knowledge, and Paul's experience, they built it themselves. Dad had been impressed at Paul's agility. Dad was only 54, strong and able, but Paul, at 25, made use of his powerful arms to hoist himself around. Paul had done construction work in the Alaskan bush for the past two summers and he had many ways of compensating for the leg which had been weakened by polio more than twenty years before. If a task didn't involve running, Paul could master it.

Paul and Dad were rushing to finish enclosing the surface of the barn by the end of the next day when Paul needed to be on a red-eye flight to Seattle and Dad would head down to Iowa to go back to his work as a pastor. It made Paul's stomach tighten just to think about it. He hoped that nothing would delay their trip to the Minneapolis airport. He didn't want to toy with expensive airplane flights.

It had been a great summer, but the tough part was that Dad wasn't at the lake much. Because most of his parishioners were busy farming during the summer, Dad could stretch his two vacation Sundays into many days, but it wasn't enough. Paul had done the best he could, and his sisters Kristen and Hanna had helped, but they had only been able to build the structure and external shell of the barn this year.

With his bird's-eye view, Paul could see all around the woods. There were Kristen and Hanna, setting off from the little beach house with their guests, Ellie's daughters, Brenda and Rhonda. All four girls headed to the lake in bathing suits, carrying towels. Frodo, the family's black Labrador, followed, tail wagging. Brenda and Rhonda were only slightly younger than their aunts, but the younger girls admired Kristen and Hanna. They had wedged their sleeping bags into the beach house for a week-long slumber party.

And here was Ellie herself, coming toward the barn with a plate of bars and a thermos of coffee. It was strange being on another level than people. Paul heard, as if in the distance, Ellie say to Dad, "It's too bad you are so rushed all the time!"

Ellie looked more American than any of them, Paul thought, though she had been living in Italy for the past several years. Her blonde hair was pulled up in a curly ponytail and she wore a sundress that fit her rounded curves perfectly. She probably had more leisure than Mother did, and certainly more money. Living in Europe had increased his oldest sister's self-confidence.

Dad laughed. "We'll be in for lunch. Don't you worry." Paul heard the rope and pulley system they had rigged creaking. "Hey Paul," he yelled, "coming up!"

Paul lifted the sweet bars wrapped in a paper towel out of the basket they used to get the shingles up on the roof. "Want some coffee?" shouted Ellie up to him.

"Just put a little in the cup and send it up," Paul said, leaning over. Even though they couldn't stop for coffee, it was a miracle they had it! In the bush last summer, the people Paul knew worked like savages and fell asleep on the floor when the sun finally slipped below the horizon for a couple of hours. Paul had learned to pace himself, working carefully and steadily to the measure others set.

Summer in Minnesota had been comparatively leisured. People came and went and visits and talk happened all the time. Ellie and her girls had been at the lake for a week and Aunt Rose's friend had come the day before to pick her up and take her home. It was August. Almost time for school to begin.

The early part of the summer it was just Mother, Paul and his sisters. Mother brought her small loom with her and worked on intricate white cotton panels. Kristen embroidered a wall hanging. Sometimes Hanna read to them all in the evening from T.H. White *The Sword in the Stone*. And sometimes Paul played the guitar and Hanna sang along.

Paul swung himself around and took a swig of coffee. The sweet bars were made of oatmeal, coconut and sugar with a layer of chocolate in the middle. They were heavenly and the coffee wasn't bad either. From Paul's vantage on the roof he watched Ellie go inside the building and look around.

"How does it look up there?" asked Dad from below. He wanted to know how much time Paul thought it would take to complete the roof. Paul wondered himself. In the middle of the job, he couldn't think about anything else. Just one shingle at a time. He stood up and looked at the expanse.

The roof was simple, but huge, covering the big building in one piece with flashing around a chimney. The angle wasn't too sharp, just enough to let the snow slide off. "Well, maybe I've covered a third of it," Paul said.

"Great!" said Dad. "If we get it mostly today, that'll leave tomorrow for cleanup. I need you to help me with some of these big pieces of plywood here."

At lunchtime everyone sat around the table which had once been a door back in North Dakota. There were potato salad and cold cuts for sandwiches. Paul's body cooled, after being hot and sweaty. The young girls in their shorts and wet hair had just gotten out of the lake. Brenda and Rhonda whispered to each other, which seemed to be their primary method of communication. Ellie ignored them.

130

"Can Kristen drive us to town for a Dairy Queen this afternoon?" asked Hanna. She was the spokesman for the group, the one they all felt confident could sway the grownups.

Mother looked at Dad, who looked at Ellie. "What time do you want to leave?" Mother asked Ellie.

Ellie sighed, which seemed to be **her** favorite means of communication. "I don't think we have to go until 5 p.m.," she said. "It would be nice to be home before dark." It took three hours to get to the Twin Cities where the Morlands lived in a company apartment while they were stateside. Bruce was in meetings at the office, but they too would soon go back to Milan where Bruce managed a lab and the girls were in school.

"You can go if you don't stay long," said Mother. "We don't need groceries, since everyone's leaving." Paul was surprised that Kristen, 16, was now allowed to drive. She had done some of the grocery shopping in town that summer in Mother's car.

"Yay!" said Hanna, looking toward Brenda and Rhonda who giggled.

"I bet you girls can't wait to get back to school," teased Dad. "Now, where did you say it was?"

"It's right downtown," said Brenda, as if Dad should know.

"It's in an old building in the center of the city," said Ellie. "It's nice, but we've been trying to find money and a place to build a real school. The playground isn't big enough and the parents want space for athletic fields. To have a real school!" American parents were the originators of the school, which, it seemed to Paul, could have been in Minnesota. Just as his school in remote Fairbanks could have.

"It's amazing to have an American school right in the middle of Milan!" said Mother. "There can't be that much space in such an old city."

A cloud came over Ellie's face. She broke down, as if here at least, in the bosom of her family, she could complain. "I'm afraid we won't be there long enough for the new school to get started. The company is making noises about transferring Bruce." She looked tired, as if this were an insult, as if her resources had been strained to breaking already.

"Where would they send you?" asked Mother gently. She looked over at the little girls. Wasn't this adult conversation? Should they be hearing that their mother was tired and fearful?

"I don't know," said Ellie. "But we keep hearing about South America. Mines down there. Copper, I think. The company needs copper." Her voice trailed off.

At the mention of copper, Dad perked up. "Of course they need copper," he said. "Copper is the best electrical conductor on the planet! And what's that stuff on the magnetic tapes?" Dad was off and running.

"I don't think it's copper," Paul said. "It's an oxide, but I'm not sure what metal they use." Certainly it was no use to ask Ellie! 3M Corporation made the reel-to-reel magnetic tapes on which Dad recorded music and their Christmas celebrations.

Mother brought the conversation back down to family level, asking Brenda, "How was the lake this morning?"

"Warmer," said Brenda. By August the lake usually absorbed enough sun so it wasn't too cold for swimming. "But Frodo wouldn't leave us alone."

Everyone laughed. Frodo was tireless. Paul himself had once thrown sticks in the water for two hours, trying to tire him out. Frodo did get tired, but he wouldn't stop jumping into the water after the sticks, splashing back up onto the dock and laying them at Paul's feet, ready for another go.

Dad stood up. "Well, Paul, I guess there's no rest for the wicked!"

Paul stood up too. He badly wanted to finish shingling the roof by evening.

On the roof that afternoon, up among breezes soughing through the birches and poplars, Paul sang to himself: "Oh Shenandoah, I hear you calling. Ah-ah-way, you rolling river. Oh Shenandoah, I long to hear you. Ah-way, I'm bound away, 'cross the wide Missouri." It was a song from a Harry Belafonte album Mother sometimes played. All summer there had been no radio and no television. Only the music from albums they played on an old stereo. Paul had picked the melodies out on his guitar.

It was a beautiful song. Paul had no idea what the relationship of the Shenandoah River was to the Missouri, but he loved the mournful lyrics, which could mean many things.

The sun seemed to stay high for a long time. Shirtless, Paul watched Kristen and the younger girls get into Mother's car and drive up the two-lane grass track out to the gravel road that led to Walker. He had no desire whatever to go into town. He wasn't even interested in Dairy Queen, which tasted like chemicals the last time he'd tried it.

It was fun to imagine places like Milan while you were here, way back in the woods, but Paul didn't want to go anywhere. He was happy where he was, deep in the Paul Bunyan state forest. Forests stretched from here into the boundary waters between Minnesota and Canada and then further north.

Paul had taken an ecology class at the University of Alaska that year and found out more about the interdependency of species, especially on tundra. Hundreds of biologists converged on Alaska. Paul did not think, however, that anything he learned (other than the names of many species and ways of defining an ecosystem) was really new to him. Mother and Dad's nature ethics were no different. Paul attributed this to the ecological consciousness of the Scandinavian culture.

Paul did love studying an area as a whole, as if everything that happened there affected everything else. The worst things about the Midwest were the long distances everyone drove and the chemicals farmers used to get high yields on their mono-cropped fields. Aldo Leopold had pointed this out years ago.

When Dad arrived at the lake this time, he told Paul that amendments favoring the Alaska pipeline project had just passed both the House and the Senate. No one was surprised. America could not get along without oil and gas. Trains were better, but there were not enough trains and people had gotten used to getting into their cars and going where they wanted to at the drop of a hat.

Paul was now getting around Fairbanks as much as possible by bicycle. He wasn't there enough in the summer to warrant buying a canoe, he had decided. He was saving a bit of money from his small teacher's salary, but he hadn't decided exactly what he was saving for. He was still not interested in hunting and didn't own a gun, though most of his friends did. Wildlife photography was becoming a big topic among Paul's friends.

More study was probably the thing for him, Paul thought. He was drinking up books. That summer, he'd brought Jung's *Memories, Dreams and Reflections* with him and Darwin's *The Voyage of the Beagle*. He got much more bogged down in Jung than in Darwin. Exterior adventures were more interesting than interior!

Mother directed Paul's attention to Sigurd Olson, a Minnesota naturalist who wrote books and lived in Ely. Olson extolled the value of wilderness and was a member of the Wilderness Society which tried to get public land protected. Paul's mentor Aldo Leopold had been a founder of the Wilderness Society, but Olson was also an effective writer.

By late afternoon, the end of the shingling was in sight. Paul's body ached from holding it in one cramped position after another as he climbed down the ladder to say goodbye to Ellie, Brenda and Rhonda. He wanted to go jump in the lake, but not quite yet. Hold your horses, he told himself.

Everyone stood in the clearing between the barn and the cabin. Surrounded by tall birches, poplars and the occasional pine, the cars were parked in a row. Dense undergrowth under the trees butted right up to the space that had been carved out. A few piles of dry brush and dirt were left pushed up against the woods by the bulldozer which had leveled space for the barn.

Paul stretched, leaning one way and then another as family members hugged each other goodbye. Paul could hardly remember when he had last seen Ellie, and had no idea when he would see her again. Brenda danced around and snapped her little camera at him as Paul grimaced.

"It won't go," she said, handing the camera to Paul to fix.

"I think that you've taken all the pictures," Paul said as he peered at it. "You'll have to take it to a shop to get them developed and buy another film."

"Okay," said Brenda. She hugged Paul and everyone else, one by one. She got in the back seat of Ellie's company Chevrolet beside Rhonda who was already settling into the nest of pillows and books which were there to amuse the girls on the drive. Paul remembered the long car journeys of his childhood, on which, stuffed into the family station wagon, they had only each other to amuse themselves.

Ellie put her keys in the ignition and rolled down the window, waving as she slowly pulled out. The shady birch trees waved their shimmering leaves and shrubby branches slapped against the car in the lush woods. "See you next year!" the little girls called out the open windows as the car pulled away down the rutted two-lane track.

The remaining Mikkelsons, Dad, Mother, Kristen, Hanna and Paul stood in the clearing, watching the small hands which poked out of the open windows until they couldn't see the car any more, waving. Frodo moped at Kristen's feet. Emptiness was left in their places. Mother looked bereft, but she roused herself and headed toward the new building.

The barn looked raw, but its plywood walls smelled clean and piney. The roof was the most finished thing about it. A few windows had been inset under the eaves and on the back wall. Paul followed Mother and Dad into the building.

"There won't be a door this year," Dad said. "Just an opening in the side. I'll close it off tomorrow." The bottom floor was uneven gravel and dirt, but a few steps climbed up to the room at the back. The windows looked directly into the woods, letting in the afternoon light. "We can put your loom here," Dad said gesturing. "Darkroom here. But that means I'll have to get water to it." The years marched away in front of Dad's excited eyes. Everything would flow from his powerful hands.

"We can bring all our old *National Geographics* up here and I'll finally have time to read them!" Mother said, taking the plywood steps up to the third level, the library. "Shelves here, right? Plenty of space for storage." The roof sloped right down to the upper level floor making deep eaves. No walls had been set into the open building, just the studs and the floors.

"It's beautiful just like it is," said Paul.

"I don't think Old George will be enough to warm this big space up," said Mother. Old George was the pot-bellied iron stove which had lived for so many years in the basement of the cabin, helping to dry it out. Paul and Line built fires in it to warm themselves on cool June mornings.

"Oh, don't worry Lois," said Dad. "We'll insulate it, finish it off. It's going to be great."

Mother smiled at him with girlish enthusiasm. "Well," she said, "I'm impressed. So much work! I can't wait until we can use it! How's the roof, Paul?"

"Another couple of hours would do it, I think," said Paul. He looked at Dad who nodded.

"Yeah," said Dad. "We'll make sure everything is tight before we leave tomorrow." The winter would have its way with the building when they left.

Paul left them plotting and planning. He headed toward the cabin to see whether there were any bars left. The empty cabin echoed with silence, but there were chocolate oatmeal bars in a pan on top of the fridge. Paul popped a couple in his mouth as he watched a hummingbird dip its long beak at the sugarwater feeder Mother had set up outside the window, its iridescent green body visible, though its fast-beating wings were not. Paul drank a tall glass of the water which tasted of northern minerals, grabbed another sweet bar and went out, ready to finish the roof or die! A marathon day, but he would finish.

After nailing the last shingle, supper and a welcome swim, Paul fell into bed. In the morning, he helped Mother load boxes and luggage into the trunk of her car.

"It's been a great summer," said Mother. "Thank you Paul for coming and helping so much!"

"Loved it," said Paul. "Couldn't have been better. And thank you guys for paying my way!" It was harder to say goodbye to Mother than to Ellie, whom Paul hardly knew. Kristen and Hanna were somewhat nonchalant. They hugged Paul, but they had their lives ahead of them and weren't worried about when they would next see Paul. Hanna, in the front seat beside Mother, would help navigate. Kristen was in the back in order to placate Frodo. He would not have this much fun again until next year at the lake.

Finally, as Mother's car drove off down the two lane track through the trees, it was just Paul and Dad standing in the clearing on a bright August morning, the trees shimmering around them in the sunlight.

Dad was all energy. "Come on, Paul," he said. "Some of these panels are so heavy I need your help." That morning they made sure the building was fully enclosed, though some of the panels were temporary. Dad also started draining the plumbing so that the pipes wouldn't freeze and burst over the winter.

Paul made a dump run with tin cans and bottles. Mother had left them sandwiches for lunch. Paul then took the last of the milk next door to let their neighbors know that they would be leaving. While Dad packed, Paul cleaned up the lakefront, stowing things in the beach house for the winter. "Time for one more canoe ride," said Dad when everything seemed packed and ready.

Paul stood on the dock. In the afternoon, the wind came up across the long fetch of the lake, deepening the troughs between waves so it was less fun to canoe. The dock would have to be taken in so as not to be broken up when the ice went out in April or May, but Dad paid someone to do that. A dragonfly skimmed the water. Paul braced himself for the conversation he knew he could not avoid.

"Did you get enough canoeing in this summer?" Dad asked as he pulled the light fiberglass craft around with a rope. It was unusual for the two men to go out together these days. Usually they each went out with Mother or one of the girls. Dad got in the stern and Paul sat in the bow, looking out over the water.

"Yeah," said Paul, turning around. "I got out early most mornings when you weren't here. That heron, or its son or grandson is still flapping across the lake every morning and evening." The wind was stiff enough that he had to speak loudly.

"Good!" said Dad, paddling expertly, feathering his stroke at the end so they stayed at an angle to the troughs.

Looking down into the thick yellow-green water, Paul saw algae, and a black spotted leech undulating just below the surface.

They paddled east toward the pine forest where an old trolley-car had once been parked at the top of the hill. The owner was famous for not wanting to sell his property to pastors. Line, Marty and Paul had braved the angry owner only to find the trolley-car empty, derelict. When he died several pastors bought lots on the property. New buildings more like houses than cabins now graced the top of the hill. The floor beneath the trees was covered with thick pine needles and duff, crowding out any underbrush.

They passed the mouth of the creek where the mud was so full of iron that as kids they painted their faces with it. "Ferrous oxide?" asked Paul as they passed it. It was the same red-brown color as the tapes Dad used for recording. Paul deferred to Dad as the local expert.

"I think they call it red ochre," said Dad. "Iron or hematite in the presence of oxygen and water." They were at the edge of the Iron Range, a huge area along the Great Lakes where iron ore was mined from taconite and hematite deposits. It was also what made the distinctive taste of the water they drank.

"Guess we better turn back," Dad said finally. "Probably not time enough to get over to Preacher's Point."

Paul concurred. He was still nervous about delays occurring in the process of getting to the airport. Dad was always getting deflected by one thing and another.

Dad held his paddle in the water, turning them around, and paddled quickly back. When they got to the dock they took everything out of the canoe and lifted it together, turning if over. "We'll come back for those," said Dad, regarding the paddles and the light anchor they sometimes heaved over the edge of the boat to stabilize it. Together they headed up the path carrying the canoe on their shoulders, zigzagging up the hill to the car.

"So Paul," asked Dad as they strapped the canoe to the top of the car. "Have you thought any more about the seminary?"

Paul fastened his strap with a metal buckle. "I have," he said as resolutely as possible. "But I don't think it's for me. I love teaching," he said. His stomach constricted. Here it was.

"Well," said Dad, mildly. "It isn't always so easy for me either, lately. I really don't understand what these kids are thinking," he said. "My confirmation classes, for instance. Maybe they're just not thinking!" He dusted off his hands on his work pants.

Paul laughed. "So many influences out there," said Paul. "For my kids too. Alaska is changing so fast. I hate to think what this pipeline is going to mean."

"The eternal truths, though," insisted Dad. "They don't change. Maybe they're getting pushed aside by all these other things."

"What other things, though, are you seeing?" Paul asked.

"Oh, this whole interest in pop culture," said Dad. "As if it were important."

"Yeah," said Paul. "But some of it is. Like the anti-war protests. And civil rights." He was pleased with himself. And with Dad. Here they were, having a substantive discussion.

"Oh I know," said Dad. "Lots of room for improvement there, I agree. It just seems as though it's taken over. Kids don't seem very interested in their inner lives."

"Yeah," said Paul. "Maybe you've put your finger on it." They were leaning against the car. Paul looked toward the lake, nervously. "I better go down and get the paddles and stuff."

"Yup," said Dad. "We better get going. Keep an open mind, though, Paul. Don't cut off your nose to spite your face." They started walking toward the cabin. "I'll make sure everything's locked up," he said.

Cut off my nose, thought Paul as he headed down the path to the lake. It didn't feel like that. He wondered whether he understood Bonhoeffer's letters well enough to discuss them with Dad. Bonhoeffer focused on this life instead of heaven, though he believed God spoke to men, especially through his Son. Dad's thinking wasn't that different. Well, thought Paul, hitching up his courage, no better time than the present.

14

When Line became pregnant that winter, it was clear that Cowell College's residential staff apartment was just too small. Stephen appealed to his father, who provided a down payment and the Cohens began to look for a house. Or rather, Line began to look for a house.

In January, every day when she picked up Christopher from pre-school, Line cinched him into the car with Heather and trolled the streets of Santa Cruz looking for houses for sale. The main part of town, near the beach, was built in the 1920's for vacationers. The houses were solid, wooden, cute, but tiny, on small lots. North of the freeway which bisected the town, newer houses had been built which were bigger, but you couldn't walk to shops. A big elementary school was nearby however.

"We don't need tiny and cute," said Stephen. "We need a big house. I'd like Poppa to come out sometimes and stay with us, if he ever retires."

Line agreed. "I want to be close to the school," she said. "If we can walk to school, I don't mind having to take the car to get groceries."

"I can bike to the university from almost anywhere," said Stephen helpfully.

"And all your books and papers?" asked Line. Stephen was still skinny as a rail and he looked like a scarecrow with a heavy pack full of books hanging down his back.

"I'll leave them there," said Stephen. "I promise. As soon as I finish this dissertation, I promise I'll spend more time with the kids." Stephen was almost there. Bernie Freeman had helped Stephen focus on writing about A.J. Muste's life and work in the labor and peace movements. "For your sins," Bernie told Stephen, when Stephen went down to Santa Barbara to visit him. "Concentrate on Muste. Learn how he used non-violent direct action. Learn how to write history." Bernie Freeman, perhaps Stephen's best friend, was referring to Stephen's lean toward violence during the latter part of his SDS leadership in Chicago.

If he was willing to look for a house in Santa Cruz, Line thought that Stephen must be confident he could teach at the university for a long time. Even though his mentor Page Smith had left, Stephen was realistic about his academic goals and his growing family. Line was grateful to Bernie and Kay Freeman for their influence. She was thankful that the family could settle.

Line looked among the bigger houses in the northern part of town. Driving around in the rain with Christopher keeping his eyes peeled and Heather napping in the back seat, Line despaired. Almost no houses were available. She stopped in to see Mr. James, the real estate agent she was working with.

"Don't you worry," said Mr. James. "Come spring something will open up."

Line looked down, "But," was all she had to say. She put her hands on her growing belly. As if to emphasize the point, she felt the baby kicking inside her. This one was particularly active, Line thought.

"When are you due?" asked Mr. James.

"End of May," said Line.

"I promise you, come March, we'll find something. I've got my ear to the ground," he said. Line liked the man. She had never in her life dealt with a broker for anything, but she felt sure this man would help them.

Line tried to relax. Everyone at the Birth Center knew that she and Stephen needed a house. At the health food store Line peered through the ads on the bulletin board, but these were mostly for rentals. You couldn't expect sellers to advertise there.

When Patty Hearst was kidnapped by a gang who called themselves the Symbionese Liberation Army, it captured everyone's attention. Stephen fumed, "They're a bunch of idiots! Who would kill Marcus Foster? They're a bunch of egotistical, media-hungry creeps! They're not going to accomplish anything! They will just give blacks and the left a bad name!" The media was having a field day.

In March, Line got a call from Raven Lang. "Come down to the police station if you can, Line!" said Raven's insistent, harsh voice. "Midwives are being arrested!" It turned out Linda Bennett and Jeanine Walker had been called to see a pregnant woman who was actually a police officer. Entrapped by the police who forced money on them and confused them, they were handcuffed and arrested for practicing medicine without a license.

Kate Bowland, Linda and Jeanine were taken down to the police station and stayed there several hours while their friends gathered in the street. Raven had called everyone she could think of to tell them about the situation, including a radio station. She watched while police searched Kate's house, looking for heaven only knew what evidence. At the police station Line stood in solidarity with Raven and others, with Christopher at her side and Heather in a stroller.

"They have no idea what they are doing," said Raven. "They are going to be sorry." Women and children milled about. Raven's daughter, who was Christopher's age, came and stood by him in a little red sweater, offering him a licorice whip.

"Why are we here?" Christopher asked Line, pulling at her skirt and chewing on the licorice.

Line leaned down, "Because we want these men to know that they have done something wrong. They took our friends to jail."

"Why," asked Christy.

"Because Linda and Jeanine and Kate were trying to help a baby get born, and the police only want doctors to do that," explained Line. She felt sad. Police oppression was the last thing Line wanted her kids to know about.

A lawyer and Linda's husband emerged from the station. "They're going to be let out on misdemeanor charges soon," said the attorney. Raven dragged Line and her brood toward the front of the group. "Power to the people!" she said loudly.

Christopher imitated her. "Power to the people!" he said, raising his little hand in the Black Power salute he had seen others do. Raven's daughter raised her fist too. "Power to the people!"

When Kate, Linda and Jeanine emerged, Raven hugged them, turning to raise their arms in a victory salute. "These men don't know what women want," said Raven, shouting above the crowd. "We do! Join us!" she called to people passing in the sleepy street.

Raven lifted Heather who was now a year and a half out of her stroller and held her high. "This healthy little girl was caught at birth by a midwife just like these women," she said to the crowd.

Line felt sick to have Heather embroiled in this fight, but it was true. Linda Bennett took the chubby Heather and bussed her on the cheek, then handed her back to Line. Line could see fear in Linda's gentle eyes. "Sorry Linda," Line said low. "This is terrible."

Linda summoned courage and hugged Line, touching her bulging tummy. "Don't worry Line," she whispered. "We'll be there for you." Line remembered her own midwife Nina's hands, tender and helping.

Raven seemed to revel in the commotion. "Well I hope you are all ready for this," she said grimly. "We'll all be at your court dates!" She took her daughter's hand and everyone began to head out.

"Good girls!" said Stephen when he heard about the scene that evening. "Now that's some action I can get behind!" He quickly corrected himself. "I mean, good women!" he said, laughing. "Or 'brave women' or something."

Line didn't care. She still thought of herself and her friends as girls. "When did we become women?" she mused. "I've forgotten." They were at the supper table, eating spaghetti. Heather's fingers and face were covered with red sauce. Heather didn't talk much yet, but she was good at eating!

"In Chicago," said Stephen the historian, ruefully. "At the SDS convention in 1967. I remember it well."

"According to you," Line said, giggling. "and your friends." She sighed. "Raven and the other midwives are brave, though," she said. "The medical establishment, the AMA, is at least as entrenched as the military industrial complex. They scared the one doctor who would do home births away from it."

"The AMA is a worthy opponent," said Stephen. "We've got to shake them all up!"

Christy stabbed at his spaghetti with a fork, winding it as best he could. Line looked at him and sighed again. "I do hope Mr. James is right and some house will open up for us soon," she said changing the subject. All else paled in relation to her family's well-being.

Within the week, Mr. James called to say that he was trying to keep a house from going on the market until Line had looked at it. "I think it is just what you need," he said. "When can you come and see it?"

The down side of the house was the fact that it was on Morrissey, facing the concrete wall which edged the freeway. Other than that it was perfect. It was around the block from a big elementary school where Christopher could go next year, had three bedrooms and a large, fenced-in garden. It was 35 years old and affordable. When it was built, no one had known what the highway in front of it would become.

"I think we have to take it," Stephen said when he saw it. He and Line stood in the back garden, which was bare, except for a tree Mr. James said was an apricot. White blossoms showered off every branch. The house had been remodeled to add a two-car garage, which left an L-shaped building sheltering the large back garden. Tall evergreens on the lot at the east side of the house shaded the space in the morning.

Line went over to the apricot tree and put her nose in the light pink blossoms. They were probably a little past the height of their bloom. It was a good omen. "Someone must have liked apricots," said Line. "I wish I could pick the house up and put it somewhere else," she said tentatively. The house was okay, but she wished it didn't face the freeway. It was all fine for Stephen. He wouldn't even be there.

"We really need the house," said Stephen. "We'll take it."

It took a month to settle the fees and the paperwork, by which time Line was getting nervous. Where would the baby be born, she wondered? It was due in about a month. Line called Marty, who had promised to help if she could. Stephen was swamped with end-of-term papers and finals.

"It isn't that we have so much to move," said Line on the phone. "We don't have anything, really. But I need to make the house livable, and I need to have this baby!"

"Is there a carpet?" asked Marty. "Fine, I'll bring a sleeping bag. I'll take a week off."

Line tried to relax. Marty would be a great help. In fact there was no furniture, nor money to buy any. The staff apartment had been partly furnished, but they couldn't take the furniture with them. There were only dishes, books, clothing, a few toys, a rocking chair, the television. Christopher's small bed. Heather slept on a thin mattress. Line bought a thick futon for herself and Stephen.

Marty came down on a Greyhound bus as she still didn't have a driver's license. She stood in the cramped Cowell College kitchen wrapping newspaper around Line's motley collection of glasses. She looked small, dark and competent, her long dark hair in a horsetail down her back. Just watching her allowed Line to rest.

"The new house will feel gigantic to the kids," said Marty, "after this cozy space where you all live on top of each other."

"Yes," said Line. She was tired. "I don't know myself how I'll manage when I can't see what the kids are doing. Christopher is really too little to look after Heather, though he tries." Heather sat on the floor looking up at them, placid as a little cat, but Christopher was in pre-school.

"Is he getting better about Stephen?" asked Marty.

"Sort of," said Line. "If it's a family thing, if it's generalized, Christy will listen to him. He's still stubborn in a one-to-one situation. The thing about Christy is that he's too outgoing. The college has been a protective bubble for him. The students all know where he lives, and he can go down the hall and find people to talk to. I worry about how he will be when we live in a stand-alone house. He's always exploring, always looking around the corner!"

"Protected?" asked Marty. "Are you sure he's not smoking second-hand pot?"

"No," said Line. "I'm not sure. But at least he isn't out in the street."

Line hired a guy to move them. When he showed up, they threw all the boxes and bits of furniture in the back of his truck. A few loose things were stuffed in the trunk of the car and Line drove the three miles to the new house, picking up Christopher on the way.

"Will Stephen know where to go?" worried Marty.

"He'll figure it out," said Line. "He took his bicycle this morning." She couldn't worry about Stephen. He certainly didn't seem to worry about her!

The new house was quiet, cool and spacious. Thick, creamy carpet covered the living room which had a fireplace at one end. At the other, was the kitchen, also painted white. "A monochromatic house!" said Line. "I'm not complaining, mind you. I'm just so glad we are here!"

Heather had not had a nap on this exciting day. She fell asleep almost immediately. Marty found her little sleeping pallet and put a blanket over her.

Christopher helped unload boxes and then headed for the back yard. "Don't wander off!" yelled Line. "We'll come exploring with you after we get settled!" She sat down heavily in the wooden rocker they had bought to rock children to sleep. It was positioned between the kitchen and the living room. Boxes littered the kitchen and lined the walls.

Marty pawed through kitchen boxes, looking for the teapot. She put the kettle on. "This is one of my favorite things," she said. "Having a new space and finding out where the light is going to lie and how you feel there." Mugs and a colorful little cardboard box of Good Earth teabags emerged from her efforts.

"I will miss the view," said Line. The old apartment, on a second floor, had looked out toward sky. On a good day, even the ocean was visible. "But having a garden will make up for it. Could you pull those drapes, Marty?" she asked. "They make me feel claustrophobic."

Marty pulled the wall of pale custom drapes open, revealing a sun-soaked bare front lawn with a yellow-leaved willow smack in the middle. A slanted rectangle of light fell on the carpet. "I think you need to plant some trees out here," she said. "It's weird when a house is set back so far from the road. Like a Midwestern house. The front yard of a house is almost unusable!"

"I agree," said Line. "It's probably because the highway is in front."

"I would have made a good architect," said Marty. "Or designer." The teakettle was shrilling in the kitchen.

"It is so good to have you here!" said Line. She had no idea what Marty's life was like any more. Living with Erik, going to an office every day and becoming absorbed in architecture. Line cradled her big tummy. She could feel the baby kicking and turning in its amniotic soup. "I'm just so exhausted by all this!"

"How do you feel?" asked Marty bringing Line a steaming mug and sitting down on the carpet.

"I'm fine," said Line, swilling the drooping teabag through the water by its tag. "Now that we're here. The tension was getting to me. Not good for the baby. This one's got some kick to it!"

"Tension is never good," said Marty. "So have you seen the midwives since the bust?"

"Yes," said Line. "At the Birth Center." She looked around. "I think this house will be fine. I should get Nina out here to have a look. All we need is a comfy place on the floor. And someone to take Christopher and Heather."

"There was an article about the bust in the *San Francisco Weekly*," said Marty.

"It's not very encouraging," said Line. "When the kids get older I want to go back to nursing, and maybe even being a midwife. I was always trying to get into obstetric wards. Birth is so magical! For everyone!"

Marty looked shocked. "That's down the road a bit!" she said.

"I know," said Line. "At least five years. But kids do grow up." Marty seemed more worried about Line having to handle three kids and work, than that she would get into trouble as an illegal midwife.

"Hard to imagine," Marty said. "I can't think any further than next week!"

"I do try to remember to love how things are right now," Line said wistfully. Her tendency was to be a little ahead of things. "I love how the kids are," she said. "I like being with Heather before she can talk. I've always liked communicating without words. And Christy is so interesting too." She looked out the window. "Could you go check on him?"

Line shut her eyes gratefully as Marty stood up and stepped out into the back yard. They had done it, gotten moved during the last weeks of school and the last weeks of her pregnancy. She didn't have to do another thing until the baby came. She looked over at the sleeping Heather, who seemed far away, off in a corner of the living room. It looked like acres of space.

Marty came in with Christopher. "The apricot tree is amazing!" said Marty. "There're already small fruits on it!"

"Apricots are early," said Line. "What did you find, Christy?"

"Nothing," said Christopher. "The doors are all locked."

"You mean the doors to the garage," said Line. "Well, we'll figure all of that out later when your Dad gets home."

"I'll start unwrapping the dishes, so we can have some dinner," said Marty. "Come on Christy. You can help me."

"I think it might be a pizza night," said Line weakly.

"Pizza!" said Christy, jumping up and down. He probably associated it with students. There were always late night pizza parties at the dorm.

The rest of the week that Marty was there, Line did as little as possible, except for driving. When no suitable tables were available at the secondhand shops, Stephen said they should go to the unfinished wood shop. They bought a trestle table with two chairs and benches for the sides so it could accommodate more people. "Students," said Line. "I'm sure we will have students over."

When it was delivered, the table was beautiful and blonde and smelled great. With no time or energy to finish it, they covered it with a length of red handkerchief-patterned oilcloth. It was the brightest thing in that white-painted house!

"Now we are set," said Line. "We can live here." The living room was still one big expanse of pale carpet with a fireplace at one end and the fitted drapes, but there were places to sleep and eat.

"I wonder whether one of those kids from the university garden would come and help me double-dig a garden," Line mused. Though Alan Chadwick was long gone, students maintained the gardens he had started, especially two of his apprentices. Line knew them. "It's not too late to start a garden and seeds are cheap."

Marty laughed at her. "You've got your priorities straight, Line! You don't care if there is any furniture or if the kids have clothes on their backs. You just want to make sure there's a garden!"

"Darn right!" said Line laughing. It was true. She didn't worry about the kids as much as about the environment they lived in. The compost, water and light, in effect. She was like Alan Chadwick, double-digging a place for her family!

"Thank you so much, Marty! For coming," Line said. They were easy together, now that each of them was happy in their own lives. Marty was leaving in the morning.

At the beginning of May one night, Stephen came home to tell Line that the Symbionese Liberation Army was under siege in Los Angeles. He would not allow Christopher to turn on the television that night, but after supper he went out to a bar. He returned late at night to tell Line that every member of the SLA in the house had been killed after a horrendous shootout and fire. Patty Hearst was not among them. Stephen looked sick. "A meaningless travesty," he said. Line was glad she hadn't seen any of it.

After school was out, little Fern Marie arrived in the middle of the night. There was no time to send Christopher and Heather away. Stephen carried Heather and her little pallet in to sleep beside Christopher and closed the door. Line hoped they slept through the commotion when the midwives, Nina and Annie, arrived. And Line didn't need to yell so much anyway. Birthing was quite familiar to her and Fern was quick. Nina hardly had time to scrub up before catching her.

Line slept with Fern beside her when Christopher stumbled into her bedroom in the morning. "Is that our new baby?" he asked.

Line stroked the baby's dark head, guiding Christopher's hand. "This is Fern, your new sister," she said. She could smell coffee and hear Nina, Annie and Stephen talking. "Isn't she a sweetheart?"

Christopher ran out of the room saying excitedly, "I'm going to tell Heather." In a few moments he dragged his toddling sister with him toward the bed. "See, I told you!"

Line wondered whether Heather talked to Christy more than she did to Line. She doubted it. Christopher probably imagined what Heather said and thought, just as she did. They were very close.

"Could you ask Dad to bring me some coffee and toast?" Line said. The sleepy Heather, her thumb in her mouth, curled up on the futon at Line's back.

Stephen arrived with breakfast. Nina and Annie took Fern to measure her and record everything about the birth. "She looks like a scrappy little one," said Annie.

Stephen sat with Line, stroking her sweaty hair. "My wonderful wife," he said. Luckily, no one had to go anywhere.

Annie put the wrapped baby into Stephen's arms. "Where'd that dark hair come from?" she asked. Everyone else in the family was either grey blonde like Stephen or red blonde, like Line.

"God knows," said Stephen. "Russians, Lapps, old Norskies, who knows." He looked very contented. "Another little Amazon," he said, putting his nose to Fern's soft red face.

Line sighed. She felt tired and grateful. Though they had agreed it didn't matter if the baby were a girl or a boy, she thought Stephen would have liked a son he could cleave to, to make up for some of the pain that he and Christy caused each other. Stephen was a great dad. He gave almost all of his attention to his work, but other than that, nothing was as important as his family. "Thank you Stephen," Line said. "For everything."

"And you," said Stephen. "Another beautiful kid. It's absolutely wonderful."

"You can give her to me whenever you want," said Line. She was actually yearning to hold the new baby.

"I will," said Stephen, cradling little Fern. "I will in a minute."

Line put her arm around Heather, drawing her toward her. What a beautiful crop of children, she thought to herself. What a thrill to watch them grow and change.

When Nina and Annie got ready to leave, Nina bent down and hugged Line. Sun was streaming through the trees on the eastern side of the house and laying leaf shadows on the walls of the bedroom. "I'm so happy," Line said. "Thank you for risking your freedom to come, Nina," she said.

"Nothing will stop me helping mothers," Nina said. "My husband is proud of me. He's totally behind me in all this." Nina's husband worked for the park service. They had no children of their own.

"Rest, Line," said Annie. "You'll be up and around for the court date next week. Everyone will be there."

Line heard them saying goodbye at the front door. "Power to the people!" said Christy's small, shrill voice. Line pictured his little fist, raised in salute.

15

One clear twilight evening skiing with Denise, whom Paul had met in his geophysics course, Paul pointed out the stars. When they got back to his apartment and rustled up some beer and popcorn, Denise said, "You know, Paul, you're perfect for crew on the Adventuress. Angel would love you. You are an astronomer, you sing and you're a teacher! You should apply!"

Paul was thrilled when Denise, small, white-blonde and tan, asked him to do things with her. He had begun to wonder if he didn't want a little more female company. Denise was from Seattle and all of her interests ran to water and oceanography. Like Paul, she was taking the geophysics course to learn about snow, ice and permafrost. It seemed that Denise just wanted a friend, but you never knew. She was among the many fascinating, forthright, adventurous people Paul met in Alaska.

Most of the year Denise served as crew on the tall-masted schooner Adventuress, which sailed out of Port Ludlow, Washington, providing overnight trips for "kids of all ages" who wanted to learn what it was like to be sailors.

"I don't know anything about sailing," said Paul. "I wish I did!"

"Angel can teach anyone," said Denise. "I didn't know much myself when I started. She takes out these groups of at-risk kids, and before the end of the week, they're sailing the damn boat! Which is no joke, I might tell you. We stay on the Sound, of course, don't get out into the Pacific. But 110 feet of mast and several thousand square feet of sail, plus the lines are dangerous. All that weight! And Angel does it anyway, over and over. Some weeks she just takes women."

That spring, Denise could not stop talking about the Adventuress. Angel turned out to be Angeline Donleavy, who ran "Sailing Adventures." Paul received a positive response to his application and an invitation to come down and talk.

Denise made him study his knots and taught him to read nautical charts, but she counseled him not to say he could do things he couldn't. "Angel isn't big on phonies," said Denise. "You, Paul, are among the least phony people I know! Your problem," Denise told him flatly, "is that you hide your light under a bushel! I've seen that light," she insisted. "And I think Angel will too."

Paul flew down to Seattle and hitchhiked out to Port Ludlow. The Adventuress, sitting in harbor rigged for her first outing of the year, sent a thrill down Paul's spine. From somewhere deep in his past he remembered a funny tune, "A little boat can be anything you please, but a full-rigged ship's a lady!" This two-masted, wooden ship with her rectangular sails rigged to long spars, gaffs above and booms below, was a lady indeed. Denise had told him that the crew just called her a 'boat,' though the feminine pronoun did apply!

Angeline was a generous, brusque woman in her mid-fifties. She sat down with Paul for a few minutes in the harbor office. He could feel her sharp eyes watching him as she said, "The interesting thing about a boat is that it's a closed system. Absolutely everything on the Adventuress affects everything else. When you've got ten crew and twenty passengers, you have to convey that right away. A ship is run in a hierarchical way, but ability is very visible. Sailing always has an element of meritocracy to it."

Angeline did need crew, and when she heard Paul was familiar with engines as well as his other qualifications, Paul was hired. The crew used a motor to get around at various times. "When we first take people on, they're deck hands," said Angeline. "You'll shadow Charlie, our engineer, to start with. Then we'll see what happens. You'll be a bit behind since you can't come until the end of May," she said. "But we'll put up with it. We've got several teachers on the crew."

Everything in his life felt different to Paul after talking to Angel. She told Paul to go out and introduce himself around, but he sat for a while at the edge of the harbor looking at the beautiful ship at anchor. A grey and weathered totem pole stood sentry, with cedars, hemlock, Douglas fir in the background. A crow picked through the briny-smelling seaweed-covered rocks along the edge of the Sound.

The magnitude of what Paul didn't know sat squarely on his stomach. He did not like it. He would have to cram, read everything he could get his hands on about sailing. He had always loved the idea, but, growing up in the middle of the country, hadn't put much effort into it.

When Paul got back to Fairbanks there were guys sleeping on his living room floor. His roommate had given them the space in exchange for cooking meals. Fairbanks was becoming a wild place. Work on the Trans-Alaska Pipeline between Prudhoe Bay and Valdez began in March and people flocked in from all over the country. Rents were sky-high as everyone tried to make a buck off the boom. The high school was planning to run two shifts in the fall, one in the morning and one in the afternoon, as students were taking the jobs in town that everyone else was too busy to fill.

Paul was glad he had a job in the Lower 48 for the summer and a mission. Denise gave him books on sailing, he found others in the library and the lengthening light helped. Paul ticked off the days on the calendar, reading until late every night. He also made sure his song notebook had a few sea shanties in it.

Denise left soon, reminding Paul, "Be sure to call things by their right names. It shows you're a sailor. Lots of pride in that!"

School was a blur, but everyone, including Paul, got through it. The day after school was out, Paul again flew to Seattle, breathing a sigh of relief at leaving the burgeoning town of Fairbanks. He would be back in the fall ready for the onslaught, but for now he would learn to crew on a schooner.

Once again, there was the Adventuress, with her towering masts, moored in a light drizzle in the Port Ludlow harbor. Paul felt jittery and self-conscious wearing a new yellow rain jacket, and carrying a duffle bag and his battered guitar case. He was sure he would be thrown to the lions immediately.

Luckily Denise's blonde towhead under her damp visor shown like a beacon. "Hey Paul!" she said. "I got you a present," she said. She handed him a worn leather sheath with a rigging knife and a marlinspike embedded in leather slots. "I got a new one, so I'm giving you my old one." Paul knew every sailor carried a knife at his belt. The lines were so heavy they could take off an arm or a finger. You had to be ready. "Micah, the first mate, is good at knots. He's been teaching us," Denise said as she deftly palmed the marlinspike, which was used for ropework.

"Can't wait," said Paul, opening his belt and slipping the leather sheath on it. "That's a very handsome present! Thank you so much."

"Just in time. Crew meeting about to start!" barked Angeline when she saw the two of them.

Ten weathered and tousled people of all ages sat wedged around the table in the main cabin drinking from steaming mugs. One of the girls poured Paul a mug of hot water and handed him a teabag. Angeline introduced him: "Paul Mikkelson," she said, "landlubber out of Minnesota and Fairbanks. But also engineer, biology and chemistry teacher, guitar player and amateur astronomer. Make him welcome!" She looked up the companionway. "This is supposed to clear up by tonight or so, which is a good thing because we've got a group of artists coming on board!"

She went on to explain the course the boat would take that week. "This group will be doing sketching and watercolor painting, so you'll take them to all of our most picturesque anchorages. Their leader, Mr. Kennedy, says they'll be interested in the Adventuress also. As always, be your most gregarious selves and tell people everything you know," she said. "Everyone who has ever been on the Adventuress is part of the community. We need all the help we can get!"

Paul knew she meant what she said. Denise had explained the amount of work and money that went into repairing and restoring the Adventuress to her original lines. She had been built in Maine in 1913 and sailed around the Horn. But as a workboat in San Francisco bay for many decades, her masts were cut down to deal with heavy winds and treacherous waters. She sat as junk in Sausalito harbor for ten years before someone bought her and brought her to Seattle. These men restored her masts, her gaff rigging and bowsprit, with the intention of offering sail training to Sea Scouts.

Angeline Donleavy got involved when she sought training for her daughter. Extending the community reach of the schooner through fundraising and volunteer help, by this time she was running the place. Denise said she had bought the vessel. Angel was adamant that women could sail just as well as men. Paul could tell right away that gender equality was important on the Adventuress.

Captain Wayne was skipper that week with Angel working dockside. Charlie, the engineer and second mate, took Paul under his wing, showing Paul around. "We're responsible for the boat's operations, comforts and infrastructure. Usually it's all fine, but there are tough things about it." In the toilet room he explained how the toilets pulled up seawater to flush. "When the pumps on the heads don't work, we have to fix 'em," he said, laconically. "We're not so much about deckhand work, but because we're such a small crew, we do get orders from the first mate or the bo'sun sometimes. There's a crew meeting every morning."

By the time the passengers came aboard and assembled, it was evening and the sky had cleared. The crew stood out on deck. Captain Wayne, tall and bearded wearing a grey woolen hat from a European university, talked about the Adventuress and explained that they should watch out for slippery decks, pay attention to the booms and be gentle with the marine toilets.

"Okay," said Wayne. "Micah's going to divide you up into watch groups. The watch groups are the eyes of the schooner at night. You'll do bilge checks, check the fathometer and the deck light, and make sure the pilot light on the stove is still on. You'll look for anything unusual, ships around us, wind coming up or whistling. The thing is, there's only one boat, and we're all in it together. Got it?"

Charlie and Paul stood beside the glassed-in charts and Charlie pointed. "We're motoring up into Oak Bay tonight. Tomorrow we'll be under sail," said Charlie quietly. "You can just hang with the passengers and learn, since this is your shake down. But right now, come on down to the engine room." The engine room was a cheerful accumulation of archaic and modern dials and equipment in the wooden bowels of the boat. Paul listened with his whole body as Charlie explained what was what.

Later that night, when the Adventuress sat at anchor, dinner was served on deck in the chilly air. The sun was still out and the shore was sandy with pebbled beaches and Douglas fir, the water still and shining. You could see the Cascades to the east where the trees weren't in the way. It was late May and there were no mosquitoes. Salt water, thought Paul. Paul slipped into his bunk, which had hardly any headroom. It was claustrophobic, but Paul told his mind to shut up and get used to it.

Paul didn't sleep much. It felt too new. The heavy wooden timbers creaked and waves washed against the side of the boat. Swells rocked them and a heavy can fell in the galley. Charlie got up to check. Paul could hardly stay below deck. He wanted to know what was going on!

At midnight Paul followed the passenger watch group around, observing. They recorded the bearings in the logbook, sighting along a compass needle toward the bearing points chosen by the captain. Walking forward, they listened to the anchor to see if it was dragging. They checked the bilge and the pilot light on the stove. Between midnight and one a.m. the sky changed from very clear and starry to misty.

Paul went back to bed, slept a little, but then was up before the sun. A sliver of waning moon hung high in the sky. Fog thickened along the shoreline, then receded. The deck, the wooden benches, everything was covered with dew. The sun began to come up, lightening the sky. Every sound was magnified on the water so people who were up only whispered to each other, allowing each other to enjoy the hush of the morning. It was very still, like a morning at Lake Michigami in Minnesota.

Denise wore a faded Norwegian sweater, her bare footprints leaving tracks in the dew on the deck. Whispering to Paul, she pointed out an otter which had come close to check out the boat. The sleek little otter went under, came up to play and then swam away. There was lots of birdsong. The mountains were blue in the distance.

One of the artists pointed out to Paul the sun shining on the foresail boom in watery reflections, playing on it like flame. The sounds of

Megan and Fritz singing as they chopped fruit for breakfast echoed up the companionway. "My father was the keeper of the Eddystone light. He married a mermaid one fine night!" They didn't care how much noise they made. "Yo, ho ho and the wind blows free. Oh for a life on the rolling sea!" The smell of coffee sent a pang down through Paul's stomach.

When the first mate called "All hands on deck!" after breakfast Paul went. Captain Wayne explained the names of the sails, mainsail, foresail, jib and stay sail. "It'll take all of us to set the sails and get the ship underway," he said. Everyone lined up on the port and starboard sides so they could haul on the lines together.

"Ready on the peak, haul on the peak," Paul heard. The peak halyard was laid out on the starboard side, the throat on the port side. The throat side of the boom partly encircled the mast and slid a little as it went up, the sails attached by wooden mast-hoops.

Once the mainsail and foresail were up, "Haul on the jib," came the word and one group hauled, making some lines fast and easing up on others with Micah's help. Underway, the sails took the breeze and the Adventuress danced on the water before her.

"A perfect day," said Wayne, standing at the wheel which was set at an angle toward the stern. "Doesn't get much better than this."

Paul stood near him and Wayne let him take the wheel and feel the boat under his hands. He could hardly feel that he was controlling her.

"Nope," said Wayne. "Can't exactly stop this baby on a dime."

Farther out in the Sound it was windier and the boat heeled. A passenger came up to Wayne and asked whether they should all move to the other side of the ship. "Don't even think about it," said Wayne. "She's so heavy she doesn't even notice us."

Mary Beth, known as M.B., her dark curls tied up in a red bandana, taught Paul to coil the lines. A big Flemish coil, clockwise, was made of the main halyard. "When you get to the middle, layer it," she said. Halyards raised and lowered the boom. The sheets were used for tacking and trimming.

"Get ready to come about," shouted Wayne. The boom and all that heavy sail swung around and filled with wind. Nothing was more romantic than a large canvas sail belling on a wooden boom.

Under sail, either Wayne or the first mate, Micah, had to be on deck at all times. The artists gathered in their own group. Paul was impressed at how the crew never quit: the deckhands polished the brass and the kerosene lanterns, washed the anchor chain, scrubbed down the soles (the below-deck floors). Megan, the cook, and her mess cook Fritz chopped vegetables, made soup, baked pies and cookies.

That afternoon they anchored off Marrow-stone Island so the artists could take the dingy to shore. M.B. climbed out on the boom to furl the sail. "I'm always a little scared walking the leech," she told Paul. "Or climbing the mast. I can do it though. I never want to leave her." Paul could understand. The Adventuress was growing on him too.

By late summer, Paul was walking the leech barefoot himself, carefully pleating the heavy sail between the lazy jacks which corralled the sail as it was lowered. He realized that a boat was a good place for a slightly lame person. His arms took up the slack for his legs, and there wasn't a lot of space to traverse.

Nothing happened aboard the Adventuress that summer that Paul didn't love: quiet early mornings with people drinking coffee, doing exercises or meditating and enjoying their surroundings; working with kids and grownups to get the ship under sail; navigating around the Sound; the evenings of songs and skits.

Paul did feel lonely, though, and restless. On off days, most people had somewhere to go. The communal apartment shared by the crew was crowded, though it was good to get a hot shower now and then. Paul found himself looking for places to be by himself, to perch for a moment, read, write in his notebook and gather his thoughts.

In early August, Paul borrowed a tent from Wayne and hitchhiked up the road to the industrial Port Hadlock, where there was a lumber mill and a lot of boat-building and cabinetry going on. Just west of town was a lake where the campground was not very crowded even in August. As he pounded in the tent pegs with pieces of wood he had collected, Paul fumed softly to himself. He was 'in a mood.' It was all very well to have Thoreau as a mentor, but Paul wasn't sure he was meant to spend all his time studying and observing. He made himself a fire and sat in front of it a long time.

Denise was falling hard for Micah and Paul had to watch. He was often dense about these things, but he couldn't help but notice this. Micah had come from the Clearwater, a boat Pete Seeger had built to sail up and down the Hudson, calling attention to pollution. Micah was going back to the East Coast soon and Denise would go with him. What about me? wondered Paul. How many times had he watched others become attracted, decide they were meant for each other and go off into the sunset. Or, in this case, the sunrise.

Paul felt uncertain about his life. Like a fishing line thrown far out into a trout pool, he wanted to reel himself in. He wanted to settle in Alaska, but he had yet to spend a summer in Fairbanks. Fairbanks was deeply interesting, moving from left to right politically and geographically! From Arvi and his liberal neighbors on Chena Ridge, to the university, and then further east out to the U.S. Army's Fort Wainwright. Paul was getting an understanding of the two kinds of responses to the Alaskan wilderness, the indigenous one and the European. The future would be a mesh of the best of these two.

Paul wondered whether Dad, if he had taken the pastoral call to Washington State, would have felt the pull back toward his folks and to Minnesota. Neither Dad nor Mother ever expressed regrets. They always seemed contented with their work and the lives they had invested in kids, home, church and their larger families. It seemed to Paul that Line and Marty were also settling, Line with three kids and Marty now married.

As the fire sank down to coals, Paul began to look up. The Perseids were just beginning. The waning moon would not come up until morning and Paul laid his bag outside the tent, trying to stay awake. There was hardly any extraneous light. A few of the meteors fell like fireworks around him.

I hope it stays this clear, thought Paul. The coming week on the Adventuress, it would be new moon and he would be able to show off the Perseids. Even with all the comings and goings of the crew, the volunteers and the passengers, the Adventuress was a community. Paul loved it.

In the morning Paul rambled around the lake, eating the hot, tangy blackberries off the bushes in the sun. He wished he could find huckleberries, but they were at higher elevations up in some of the old logging clearcuts. Paul had no car. He felt like a bear, going from one bush to the next in the sun, having breakfast.

That week's batch of passengers was a group of women. Angeline came aboard as skipper, but Micah, Charlie, Paul and a few other males were on board. So far, Angel had not found a female engineer.

The crew was primed for working together. When they stopped to refuel, to take on drinking water and food and get rid of garbage, Angeline said, "I want this to be a pit stop. I want it to go like precision clockwork. As if we were at a NASCAR race." Paul pulled the big fuel lines out of the underground tanks, attached them to the boat and turned on the pumps. Everyone hustled boxes, bags and tanks on and off board. They were out of there in no time.

When the passengers came on board, Angeline gave them a pep talk. "These beautiful old schooners are sailed by an ancient method," she told them. "It is rigorous, unforgiving, meticulous. But if you learn it, if you are willing to become part of this ancient lore and culture, you too can be a sailor." The boat had a good safety record. The worst accident Paul had seen that summer was someone getting hit with the boom. The kid had been knocked out, but had come around. No one held it against the crew.

The night of the new moon Megan made a pot of coffee after dinner. As they waited for it to get dark, Paul brought out his guitar, but Kathleen, the program director introduced the songs. She turned out to have been in Australia and loved the Seekers. She taught Paul one of her favorite songs, which used an old Russian folk melody. The guitar part was simple. G, C, G7, C7, F. Paul found it hypnotic. "Like a drum my heart was beating, and your kiss was sweet as wine. But the joys of love are fleeting, for Pierrot and Columbine. Now the harbor light is calling. This will be our last goodbye. Though the carnival is over, I will love you 'til I die." Who were Pierrot and Columbine, wondered Paul.

"Again," said Kathleen, standing in the afterglow in the sky which reflected in the water and illuminated all the faces. "High above, the dawn is waking, and my tears are falling rain. But the carnival is over. We may never meet again."

"It sounds Russian," Angel's big voice called out over the water. "Haven't you got a happier one?!"

Kathleen laughed. "It's the melody I love," she said. "But Paul's got one he wants to teach us. It's an old Quaker hymn, he says, but Pete Seeger's revived it. These old hymns and songs are in our blood. Let Paul sing it first and then we'll sing it with him."

Paul belted it in his favorite range, remembering Arvi in the sauna as he sang:

"My life flows on in endless song;
Above earth's lamentation,
I hear the sweet, tho' far-off hymn
That hails a new creation;
Thro' all the tumult and the strife
I hear the music ringing;
It finds an echo in my soul —
How can I keep from singing?

Some of the stronger singers picked it up right away, had perhaps already known it. "Stand up," yelled Kathleen. "You can't sing this sitting down!"

When the glow had finally gone down, the stars began to come out. Paul pointed out the evening stars. He had Charlie's telescope on board, but it really wasn't necessary. He was so fearful that a mist would come up in the middle of the night that he begged people not to go to bed. Late at night, around 11 p.m. most were still on deck. The Milky Way flowed kitty-corner across the sky, a river of brightness flowing through the summer triangle.

With Paul's eager direction, most of the passengers could see the Great Bear with its pointer stars toward the pole star. Cassiopeia was also easy, making a 'w' in the sky. Paul also managed to make most people see the triangle made up by the bright stars Altair, Deneb, and Vega.

All the while, little 'oooohs' and 'aaaahs' came from people pointing out shooting stars. "The Perseids are named for Perseus," said Paul. "You can kind of see him running away from Andromeda there, whom he is supposed to marry, under the watchful eye of Cassiopeia. See? He's got two legs. The big star in his hip, Algol, is a double star," said Paul. "Two stars circle around each other and if you watch closely, sometimes over a period of nights, Algol will appear either brighter or darker depending on which one is in front."

The Perseids were in the vicinity of Perseus in the northeast, but not entirely. "Actually the Milky Way covers all of this clandestine activity," said Paul.

"Good one, Paul," said Angeline's big, unmistakable voice.

It was a night of wonders. Megan, who had early cook's hours and was half asleep drooping over the gunwale, noticed it first. "Look!" she said loudly, pointing. All eyes came down off the heavens. White edges of light lapped up the beach as the small surf came in.

"It's not stars," said Paul. "It's phosphorescence!"

Angel confirmed it. "If we're lucky, we see it when the water's really warm," she said. "Something about the temperature in August brings out the phosphorescent phytoplankton. But it has to be really dark to see it."

Everyone was now hanging over the gunwales. "Look," said one. "There's an otter!" The otter made the disturbed plankton light up. Paul could see the outline of two of the small mammals swimming. They looked like ghosts outlined in a bluish glow.

"I saw it in the toilet," said a passenger, coming up the companionway. "Swirls of light in the head!"

The night couldn't last, however. Finally people began slipping away to their bunks and so did Paul. For him, it was the last voyage of the summer. The carnival was over.

"See you next year, Paul," said Captain Angel when they debarked the next day. It wasn't a question.

Paul smiled. "I hope so!" He hugged Denise, thanking her profusely for the summer. "I never would have known about this if it weren't for you," he said.

Denise lifted her visor and squinted at Paul in the sun. "Catch you later," she said, her voice a little thick.

And my tears, like falling rain, Paul said to himself dramatically. The song, the music, the summer, would stay with him.

16

At the airport Line looked around at her family waiting in line to check in and hand over their luggage. Counter-culture they certainly were, with that educated, gypsy look that Line loved. Stephen, with sandy beard and wire-rimmed glasses slipping down his nose, was wearing Fern, who was only six months old, in a green corduroy Snugli, an ingenious little pack with straps over the shoulders. Even though he was now a professor, Stephen still wore second-hand shirts and sweaters Line found for him.

Christopher held firmly to Heather's hand, bending down to tell her, "I've been on an airplane before. When we went to Alaska to see Uncle Paul. It's just like sitting in a car." They both looked like roly-poly little animals in the thick sweaters they wore under their jackets. Line was sure they would not be warm enough in the bitter cold of Iowa, but she hoped Mother could help her find warm clothes if the kids needed them.

Line herself wore a thick Mexican sweater belted over two other sweaters worn over a long skirt. She carried an old Scandinavian Airlines bag stuffed with diapers, plastic bags full of wet rags and snacks for the kids. Line had not been home for a couple of years and, because Mother and Dad didn't travel, they had not seen either Heather, now two, or Fern.

At last the ticketing agent put their bags on a belt that disappeared to the right and handed them boarding cards. "Gate #A8," she said smiling at the eager faces of the little kids.

"I can find it!" said Christopher, looking in all directions at the signs overhead.

"So proud of our kids," said Line quietly, holding on to Stephen's elbow as they followed Christy and Heather down the grey halls thronged with people. "Thank you Stephen," she said. "I've dreamed of this." Flying was terribly expensive, but, Line thought, if you insisted on living so far from your folks, you just had to do it.

"We're a motley crew of Cohens, to be sure," said Stephen, smiling. Most of the families they saw traveling together were dressed in their best, neat Sunday clothes; but so were the Cohens.

At the gate, Line piled their coats and sweaters in a seat and they all stood by the window and watched the huge silver jets roll on their tiny wheels toward the gates. The noise of the jets wheeling and tumbling around them was tremendous. In the distance, Christopher pointed out the ones speeding down the runway and lifting off. The air was grey and foggy, with rain threatening, but it didn't seem to stop the airplanes.

On the plane, the air was fuggy and a high-pitched whirring drove anxiety up. Stephen stood, jiggling Fern, who didn't like the noise. Line buckled the little kids into their seats and sat down between them. "The captain will tell you to keep your seatbelts on," she said. "In the air, we have to do what the captain says." Heather looked at Line solemnly, but Christy's face was glued to the small rounded window, watching the luggage being loaded into the bottom of the plane.

Line looked over toward Stephen, who was settling in across the aisle. "I'll take Fern when she gets hungry," said Line.

The flight seemed short, an anti-climax to the fevered pitch of excitement which led up to it. Line looked out the window over Christy's shoulder. Mostly they were above the billowing white fluff of clouds and you couldn't see through it. But at one point, Christy yelled, "Mom, Mom!" and there below were jagged, snow-covered mountains and a huge-looking lake. "The Sierras," said Line. "Someday we'll go see them."

After a while, Line traded seats with Stephen, so she could nurse Fern. The older lady next to her, in an actual hat Line noted, didn't seem to like this, but Line covered herself and Fern as well as she could with a cotton blanket.

The stewardesses came down the rows in very short mini skirts carrying trays of hot food. Stephen must be watching the nylon-clad thighs going up and down the aisle at eye level, Line thought, but at least he was tucked up between his two young children. The sounds of tinfoil and plastic crackled and Line could smell chicken. Line let her meal sit under its tinfoil on the little tray table until Stephen had eaten.

Stephen wrapped up the kids uneaten food and handed their trays to a stewardess, standing up to switch places with Line. Line tucked herself into the small seat between the kids and took a few forkfuls of chicken and rice. Heather's head was falling. Line wrapped her in a grey blanket, and she fell asleep, her head on the little airline pillow.

When the captain's voice came over the loudspeaker saying that they would land soon, Line looked over Christy's shoulder down on cold snowfields, punctuated by forests, far below. Twilight was coming down as the plane descended slowly among the frozen lakes, houses and snowy parks of the Twin Cities.

"That's the landing gear," Line said when they heard mechanical sounding thumps. "It stays in the bottom of the plane while we are flying, and now it's coming out."

"What if it didn't?" asked Christy. "What if it got stuck?"

"I guess the plane would have to land on its belly!" said Line.

"Wow," said Christy.

The plane hit the slippery runway with a roar, its tiny wheels bumping the plane up and down. The flaps on the wings tipped up to stop it. Christy looked up at Line. "That was a good landing," she said. "We should thank the captain!" She looked across the aisle, where Stephen sat with a book propped up on the baby's back. At least it was a paperback, thought Line.

Gathering up all of their bits and pieces and walking out into the garish airport light, Line was quick to see Dad. And Hanna! Hanna jumped out at them, hugging Line.

"I promised to do the dishes all week if I could come to the airport," she whispered to Line. Her pale face was lit by her excitement.

Line hugged Dad, who looked a little older, his crew-cut gray at the temples, but his face was ruddy with active health. Dad greeted Stephen and each of Line's little ones gravely.

Hanna took Christopher and Heather's hands on either side and headed for the baggage claim. The airport was warm enough, but Dad told them to bundle up when they went out to the car. He was driving Mother's big Plymouth. "My new Rabbit is too small to carry everyone!" Dad said. "But you'll see it in the garage. Mother drives this to school every day." There was plenty of room, but not enough seatbelts for all of them.

The car warmed up as they drove and before long, Heather and Christy were asleep in the back seat with Hanna and Line on either side. Line tried to remind herself where Hanna was in school. "What year are you?" she asked, as the car rolled through the dark. Snowy fields glimmered under the cloudy sky. In the front of the car, Dad asked Stephen about his work.

"I'm a sophomore," said Hanna. "I'm going to be an only child next year. Won't that be weird?!" she asked.

"So Kristen graduates this year?" asked Line.

"Yes. She's going to nursing school. I'll be the only one home next year," said Hanna.

"Wow," said Line, shaking her head. "I can't imagine."

Heather was small enough to carry, but not Christy. Line woke him up when they got to Haroldson. He had to walk into the house on his own two legs.

The house was warm, steamy even since they were still all wrapped in sweaters. And there was Mother, gracious and welcoming, beaming at the whole family. Kristen too. Kristen was beautiful, Line thought. Seventeen and blooming, with long golden-brown hair and pink cheeks. A black Labrador followed her around, its toenails clicking on the tile floor.

Line stood in the big foyer, Heather asleep on her shoulder. I'm like Mother now, she thought. There were more Cohens than Mikkelsons.

"It's hot in here!" said Christy, sleepily pealing off his coat and sweater.

Line put Heather down on the sofa in the living room. "He's used to our freezing house," said Line. "It's huge and the heating bill is enormous. So we don't use the heat much."

"Do you want some cocoa?" Mother asked. "Or a snack? It must have been a long day!"

"That sounds good!" said Stephen. Little Fern, sleeping on his chest in her Snugli, seemed not to even notice where she was. He followed Mother into the kitchen.

We were married out of this house, thought Line. She remembered arriving with Stephen and his parents, six years ago now. She had never lived in the house. She looked around. The Christmas tree was fragrant on one side of the living room. Piles of presents, wrapped and ribboned, stood under it. Mother's maple dining set and hutch looked almost new. A Sears and Roebuck house. Except for the guitar, propped against the wall behind the sofa.

On top of the blonde piano was a manger scene, smooth plaster figures of Joseph, Mary and the baby Jesus in the stable, flanked by shepherds, angels and wise men. There was not much sign of the scruffiness in which Line had grown up, or, for that matter, in which she was raising her own children.

Kristen handed Line a cup of hot cocoa. "Do you want a marshmallow?" she asked. The black Lab was right behind her. Conversations were going on all over the house. Christy examined the presents under the tree while Dad watched affably. Stephen was talking to Hanna and Mother in the kitchen.

"No thank you, Kristen," said Line. "It's so warm and comfortable here. I just heard that you are going to nursing school!"

Kristen smiled, her pink skin glowing. "Next year," she said, dipping her head modestly. "I have to graduate first."

Across the room Dad asked Christopher, "Can you find your name on all those packages?"

Christy, who had been to preschool, did manage to find his name.

"You know why we give each other presents at Christmas, don't you?" asked Dad. "We want to share in God's love because of his gifts to us."

Christopher nodded gravely in return, Line was happy to note.

Line took Fern from Stephen when she wakened and lifted her sweater to nurse the dark-haired baby. "Isn't she beautiful?" she asked Kristen, who had stayed to watch. "What kind of nursing do you want to do?"

"Oh, I don't know," said Kristen. "I'll have to wait and see what's available."

For Line the week at home was relaxed and wonderful. The ratio of grownups to kids was higher, and she could count on them. She didn't worry about Christy and Heather, who were entertained by their young aunts.

She was also surprised and pleased that she didn't slip back into her old role in the family, as now her own family's needs were so intense. She saw the Mikkelsons now and their Christmas traditions through Stephen's eyes. They looked totally different from when she had once been so immersed in them. Christmas seemed to go on forever.

Because Stephen wasn't observant of his Jewish religion, and left so much of their holiday-making to Line, Christmas in California was pretty simple. Instead of opening presents on Christmas Eve, the kids hung stockings by the fireplace and even put out milk and cookies. It wasn't that the kids believed Santa would come down and fill their stockings. It was just a game. Stephen and Line, when filling the stockings, took bites out of the cookies.

On Christmas morning the kids found their stockings full of oranges, chocolate and nuts. Line made pancakes and then they opened their few presents. That was Christmas for the Cohens. A morning of unlimited candy and a few toys as per cultural dictates. But that was all she wrote. Stephen did not approve of the commercialism of Christmas and Line agreed.

In Lutheran homes, as Line well remembered, anticipation of Christmas began in early December with the advent Sundays on which a candle was lighted in honor of the coming Christ Child, along with Bible readings. All during December the family decorated the house, sent out Christmas cards, purchased or made presents and sang Christmas carols for presentations and parties.

By the time the Cohens arrived, Christmas was well underway. Though her children knew the story of the Christ Child, Line had never emphasized that he was the Son of God, come to save them from their original sin. They knew some of the carols as well. But this special Scandinavian Lutheran Christmas atmosphere must be new to them. Line waited to see if Christopher said anything about it.

Mother served a special dinner on Little Christmas Eve, December 23, at which each person opened one gift. "We used to have secret friends," Line said. "We were supposed to do nice things for them all through December. Do you still do that? We found out who they were on Little Christmas Eve when they gave us a present."

"That was when there were eight of us at home!" laughed Mother. "I think we were trying to get you kids to be nice to each other! There're not enough of us any more!"

"I remember the time we painted walnuts gold and hung them on the tree with the names of the secret friend in it," said Kristen wistfully.

The next day, Christmas Eve, after another splendid dinner, Dad recorded the family Christmas presentation on a tape recorder. He read from the Christmas story in the Gospel of Luke. Hanna played her guitar. She had taught Christy and Heather one verse each of "The Friendly Beasts" to put on tape. Christy was clear and definite as the donkey, but Heather's voice was so soft you could hardly hear her verse about the dove in the rafters high, who cooed "Jesus our brother, kind and good" to sleep. Dad held the microphone close to her mouth.

Mother played the piano and they all sang carols, "Silent Night," and "Hark the Herald Angels Sing." Line watched Stephen, who seemed to know these more familiar songs!

After this, the presents were handed out, one by one. A wash of paper, ribbons, and piles of presents accumulated around the room. Line noted that Mother seemed to have plenty of money to spend. Of course, no one was in college right now.

When they woke up on Christmas morning, the Mikkelsons and the Cohens went to church, where Dad preached in his warm, joyful voice a sermon about the great gift God had given in his Son. The choir was ambitious enough to lead the congregation in the "Hallelujah" chorus from Handel's *Messiah*. Line was impressed.

At home, Mother pulled out the turkey stuffed with her own mother's famous sage and cracker stuffing. Christy and Heather helped make the place cards which indicated where each person should sit around the table, along with candles, a centerpiece and tiny paper nut-cups filled with mints and nuts. There were vegetables and a pumpkin pie. Finally, Christmas appeared to be over!

"You have to remember that this started in Scandinavia," Line told Stephen as they went to bed that evening. "It was very dark for many months, and Christmas was a way of lighting up the world. Here too it's darker than it is in California."

"It's hard to believe it until I've experienced it," said Stephen. "All the sugar and food too. Poppa would dig it!" Poppa, Stephen's father, was the only remnant of his immediate family left.

After the holiday, things were more relaxed. Kristen and Hanna played games with the little kids and helped Christy make the model airplane he had gotten for Christmas. Heather used her crayons to color any sheet of paper the older kids produced.

When the weather turned clear and bright, they wrapped the kids in jackets and mittens and sweaters and went out to a nearby park. Kristen, Hanna and Frodo the dog showed them how to use the old green fiberglass saucer which even Line remembered. The small town was on very flat ground, but Kristen and Hanna found a small rise to slide down. Line went out to watch when Fern was sleeping. "Show them how to make snow angels," she begged Hanna. And Hanna, lay down in the snow and moved her arms and legs, getting up carefully so as not to disturb the angel she had made, glistening blue in the sunshine.

"Do you remember 'fox and geese'?" she asked Kristen.

"We play 'red rover' even in high school," said Kristen. "But I don't remember 'fox and geese.'"

Line made a big circle by walking around a piece of new, unbroken snowy lawn. Then she walked across it, cutting it into pie pieces. "Now, one person is the fox and tries to catch the geese," she said. "But everyone has to stay on the paths I've made. Try it Christy," she yelled.

Heather didn't want to stay on the paths. She lay down in the middle of the circle and waved her arms and legs, getting up to see what shape she had made. Christy, Line, Kristen and Hanna ran around the circle, their faces pink and their breath making little clouds in front of their faces. But the game didn't last long.

Another day Dad and Stephen put the beautiful old wooden toboggan on top of the car and took the kids to the nearest place where there were actual rolling hills. They also brought three pairs of cross-country skis with them. "I'm sure you can wear my ski shoes," Dad said to Stephen. "Bring some warm socks."

"I'd love to," said Stephen. "I've never been on skis!"

Line didn't feel she could leave the tiny Fern for an uncertain amount of time. She sat with Mother, helping her tie knots for the warp on her loom using dark wool. "There's a herringbone effect I want to try," said Mother. "I think it would make a nice handbag."

Line watched Mother's fingers, a tiny diamond on her left ring finger. They were growing old and the veins showed, but they had a gentleness Line recognized. "Your hands look like Marty's," Line said. "Not like mine." Line had Mother's hourglass figure, with big hips, and had luckily gotten Mother's healthy eyes. Marty had the Mikkelson figure of Dad's mother and sisters, but her poor eyes were as lovely as Mother's, and so were her hands.

"Do you see much of Marty?" asked Mother.

"Not so much," said Line. "She comes down once or twice a year. She doesn't have a driver's license or a car. And of course she's working a lot. She helped us move, just before Fern came. I really appreciated it! It was quite a process!"

As if Fern had heard her name, she made swimming motions on the little pallet of blankets Line had put on the floor. Line picked her up and held Fern against her shoulder, letting her wake up slowly. "And how are you," she smiled at Fern. "What do you think?" she asked. Fern looked a little dopey, a little sleepy, but she smiled.

"And what do you think of this fellow Erik?" asked Mother, looking up. "He was nice enough when he was here for the wedding."

Line couldn't help but grimace. "I don't mind telling you, Mother," Line said. "He doesn't seem like a very reliable person. I think Marty's carrying the emotional burden of that relationship. She certainly does love him."

"Your family is just lovely," Mother told Line. "After all the anxiety, doesn't it feel great once in a while to just look at them and see them for who they are?"

"You are so right," said Line. "I feel lucky that we can get by without my working right now. And we love Santa Cruz. Stephen has made a place for himself at the university."

"There's so much talk about women lately," Mother said. "We were always taught that women made the harmony in the family, between a wife and her husband, and also for the rest of the family."

"Harmony," said Line, thinking about it. "Nobody thinks about that now. It's all about getting everyone's needs met. Your husband's, your own, your kids."

"Providing a harmonious place to live does help," said Mother.

"Oh, I agree," said Line.

"My mothering style, when there are lots of kids around is, I think, one of benign neglect," said Mother a little ruefully. "But it works. I like following you kids."

"But you managed us," said Line. "Organized us. You did most of it by example. You didn't say much." Line looked down on Mother's dignified face, bent over the loom. "You were wonderful," she said. Line's own mothering style was more invasive. She had no problem wading into a scrum of kids if she felt someone was getting the worst of it.

"Thank you, Line," said Mother. "You kids are all so far away. It isn't what I wanted. I don't think Kristen will stray far, though who knows about Hanna!"

"Yeah," said Line. "The friendly beast she should have chosen is the tiger! Hanna's got a tiger in her tank for sure! I'm starting to think Fern's a little like her. Much less placid than Heather. Heather's my Kristen!" Line laughed.

"And what do you hear from Paul?" asked Mother.

"I don't hear," said Line. "But because I was up there, I have a pretty good idea of how things are. Really nice people." Line talked to her family on the phone on special occasions. It was her only way of keeping in touch during their long absences.

"We get letters," said Mother. "The pipeline is making Fairbanks boom, it sounds like. And he loved the sailing ship he was on this summer. I do hope Paul finds a nice girl. I mean woman." Mother laughed.

"Oh, I think he will," said Line. "Fairbanks is going crazy, I've heard. But there are many more men in Alaska than women. That was obvious when I was there even for a few weeks. The women come to Alaska as part of a couple!"

"Well, we just hope the best for all of you," said Mother.

"It means a lot to us," said Line. "I'm more aggressive as a mother than you were, I think. But I'm kind of on my own. I get what I need from Stephen, but I hate to ask for much more. It's a big job to support us, after all."

"Dad worries about your spiritual lives," said Mother. "But in the end we've had to commend you all into His hands."

"Thank you for that, Mother," said Line. She suspected Mother helped convince Dad to do this. Dad had been miserable to see his kids straying from the Lutheran fold.

"It really doesn't seem so long ago that I was 30 and had four little kids." Mother shook her head in wonder, her face reflecting some of her anxiety. "I was overwhelmed. I'd never even changed a diaper when I got married." Mother stood up, stretching her back. "And then Paul got polio," she said. "How's that little one," she said, reaching for Fern. "Are you awake yet?"

Thirty! Line thought, handing Fern to Mother. I'm thirty, and I have three little kids. She tried to imagine being Mother, working in an orphanage in the dark winters and trying to take care of her first baby, Ellie.

"Is Ellie's family still in Italy?" Line asked. She had helped Ellie with her kids when she was in high school.

"They are," said Mother. "But this is the last year. When they come home this summer they will be going out to Chile, where Bruce is going to start a 3M operation."

"Wow," said Line. "It's been so long since I've seen them."

"They're fine," said Mother, kissing Fern's dark hair. "The girls are growing up fast. Like your kids. It's so great to see Christy and Heather and this little one. Christy is doing well too! For all your worry."

"He's a wild one," said Line. "But I have to trust him. He likes school." Line loved this deep talk with Mother all to herself. It was so rare.

A car pulled into the garage, and pretty soon the little wild one was at the door, stamping his snowy feet on the tile. People came in through the kitchen. "How was the toboggan?" Line asked Christopher.

"Fast!" said Christy. "The more weight you have, the faster it goes! So we had to have Kristen and Hanna and Grandpa on it!"

Line laughed and looked at Stephen. "Thought you'd seen the last of snow when you left Chicago, didn't you," she smiled at him.

"Quite a bit more benign here!" said Stephen, putting his arms around Line. "I don't mind it a bit!"

Kristen helped Heather with her little coat. "Such a sweetie," she said. "I think I'm going to keep you!"

"Oh no, you're not," said Christy solemnly. "Heather's in our family."

Everyone laughed. "I didn't mean it," said Kristen. "Don't worry Christy."

At this a light went on in Line's head. What fun it would be to have Kristen stay with them and help with the kids this summer! She resolved to ask.

"How about making everyone some hot cider, Kristen," said Mother. "And weren't you girls going to make lefse? We can't let Stephen get away without tasting some Norwegian lefse."

"Oh yes!" said Line. "We can help! Christy likes baking. Don't you Christy."

Christopher looked at her. "I can answer for myself," he said. "You don't need to talk about me."

169

Line leaned down and rubbed his nose with hers in an Alaskan kiss. "Okay," she said. "I won't talk about you."

<h1 style="text-align:center">17</h1>

Marty sat beside Erik on a rock wall at the edge of the Mediterranean, watching him sketching in the town of Ladispoli. It was not the quaint old town climbing the hills that Marty saw in Italian postcards, but neither was it totally modern. Erik had declared he would be happy anywhere in Italy and so here they were.

The light was fast settling over the sea. It was April and the sun still angled to the north. The surf coming in was noisy, rushing over large rocks and leaving sea wrack behind. Familiar seabirds settled on the beach, gulls and terns. It felt like California, Marty thought. Indeed Italy and California were on almost the same latitude. Facing west as they did, it felt similar, though the Mediterranean was not the Pacific.

Erik found old things to sketch. Stone houses with closed, painted shutters. Ancient churches. He sat with his back to the sun, shading his work with his body. He had affected wire-rimmed glasses, though not with the strong prescription Marty's had. With his unkempt blonde hair and a tightly-fitting Italian suitcoat over an open-necked shirt, it was hard to know he was American. Marty was dressed simply too, in a sleeveless dress, dark cardigan and sandals. Europeans, Marty hoped. They were too old to be students, but architects, photographers, yes.

Against the buildings on the street, tables were laid for the evening outdoors. At some, patrons were having an aperitivo or a late afternoon gelato. The temperature was perfect. It was the magical time of day when Italians came out of their houses and walked around before their late dinners. The passeggiata, the evening promenade. Mothers and fathers pushing prams stopped to talk to older people they knew. Young, thin girls with their arms linked. Toddlers holding hands walking in front of their parents. Everyone walking slowly, dressed up to have a look at each other, taking their time.

In this larger town it wasn't as ritualized as when Marty had first seen it in Greece eight years ago. Then Marty and Kate had been waiting for a ferry, fascinated to see the townspeople circle the main square as if in procession. Older people in black, young people and children. Marty had been dying to know what was happening and Kate asked someone who looked like he spoke English. "Oh," said a young man who was probably not Greek, "it's the *korzo*. Everyone out for a turn around the square. They do it every night."

The passeggiata looked as satisfying as Marty imagined it, even through her now slightly more sophisticated eyes. Were people compelled to come out every evening? Did they do it to satisfy their families? Did they look forward to it? She understood that young women especially needed the outlet, protected by their families. It was like a daily parade, a way of telling their friends and neighbors how they were. No need to use words. Presence is worth ten thousand words.

Erik and Marty had flown to Rome and had a car for a few days until they ended up in Brundisi where they would take the ferry to Patras. Erik had convinced Marty to take extra time off work as they traveled, looking for ancient architectural details and, later, in Greece and Turkey, for interesting houses, architecture without architects, as Rudofsky had termed it: the spontaneous building of peoples of a region with common resources and a common heritage. "So much more beautiful than our chaotic cities," noted Rudofsky.

Marty struggled with traveling more than Erik did. She was up early, hungry, waiting while Erik slept, used to her normal work day. But after a few days in Italy, she found she couldn't fight it. "It's the Mediterranean way," said Erik. "When in Rome, after all …"

Erik nosed around, asked questions in bars, trying out bad Italian, discovering the older, sketch-worthy places they should go. There was no rush to see things, simply a meandering. Everything was interesting. Everything had its reason. They took their time in the late mornings over a leisurely breakfast, wandered around, laid low if it were hot and stayed out at night.

Marty enjoyed seeing Erik in action. The cool, young architect, slinking into shadowy places, using men's lingo. She felt much less cosmopolitan. She wasn't as slim and beautiful as the woman she imagined Erik should be with. But he did trust her and she was as ready for adventure as he was. He took Marty into bookshops, buying thick books Marty had no idea he wanted to read. "Buy some thick novels," he told her. "We're going to need them."

While watching Erik sketching, Marty fell back on her books and notebooks. She had a camera, but she took few photographs. It felt rude to take them of people. Yet few unpeopled scenes were worth a photograph. Photos of people in their homes in the Italian magazine *Abitare*, which Marty loved, were black and white, realistic. Kid's rooms were messy, there were dogs and older things sprinkled in among new furniture. Much more artful than the American magazines in which every color photograph was pristine, every item new and shiny.

The light on the combers as they rolled in began to reflect the opalescent sky, the pale pinks, purples, almost greens and blues, frothing white at their edges. On the shore, lights became visible in the bars and restaurants. Without many automobiles, with people walking about, the evening felt civilized.

Erik, meticulous and intent once he had found something he wanted to sketch, took his time. Marty put her chin on his shoulder, looking into his work, disturbing it. "I'm hungry," she said. It had been a long time since brunch.

Erik sighed. "Okay, okay," he said, taking a last look at the scene. A sketch was always finished, he had told Marty. Or never. He put his pencils and sketchbook away. "Come on," he said. "Time for an aperitivo."

They settled themselves at an outdoor table only a few feet away from the wall on which they had been sitting and ate for what seemed like hours. The food was as remarkable as Marty remembered, except that this time she wasn't coming from a banal Midwestern cuisine. Italians had settled San Francisco and Marty had come to expect the amazing tastes: pizzas with intense tomato sauces, layered with herbs, onions and olive oil; fluffy foccacia bread; vegetables stuffed and baked; seafood stews. On her earlier visit she had hated olive oil and longed for butter. Now she loved good olive oil!

Marty was having a wonderful time. But what am I doing here? a secret voice asked. Learning, studying, she told herself. This is what people do with their free time. She thought of the Magnussons. All of their travel was directed to specific aspects of history and culture they wanted to study. Irene was just as involved as Dr. Magnusson.

And how about me? wondered Marty. What am I doing here with Erik? It was clear what he was doing. He was studying architecture, perfecting his skills. And Marty was being a wife, a companion. But was it enough? It was a pressure, a question. She had to admit that Erik wasn't as generous with his thoughts as Dr. Magnusson. Or perhaps they had not been married long enough to share everything.

A few days later they took the ferry to Patras, passing islands and miles and miles of Greek coastline. Marty told Erik about the odd Easter weekend on Corfu she had spent with Kate. Erik had been to Spain and Italy, but never to Greece. A bus took them along high ridges above the sea to Athens. The city was blossoming after its first democratic election in a decade. Flags with a simple cross and stripes in a very dark shade of blue and white flew everywhere.

Marty and Erik went to American Express, where Erik picked up letters and dealt with money. They dropped their things at an inexpensive hotel near the old part of town, the Plaka. "Amazing how cheap everything is," Erik said.

In the evening, they went down and sat at a table set out in the big open Monastiraki square near the train station. Erik ordered ouzo and snacks. "I think the Greeks finally understand what they have to give," said Erik. "Abundant sunshine, gorgeous landscapes, history. Tourists bring in money!"

"The last time I was here," said Marty, "there must have been a dictatorship, and I didn't even know."

Erik sniffed. "Two girls by themselves aren't going to find out much."

"We were so relieved," said Marty. "In Athens people spoke English! Everything was painted blue and white. The window frames and doors on every café. Out here too, in the Plaka. Everything was blue and white. I bought a blue shift dress, plain cotton edged with dark Greek-patterned braid." Marty thought she still had it, folded up in a square at the bottom of a drawer.

"The Greek key pattern?" asked Erik. "I think I remember it."

"Yes," replied Marty. The key pattern edged everything, the tops of buildings, vases, floors, textiles. Sometimes two sets interlocked, forming swastikas. She looked around her. "It felt more open then," she said. "Not so modern and ugly. Even eight years ago." The colors were still dominantly blue and white, but red Coco-cola signs were visible and many other advertising signs as well.

"Modernity is ugly," said Erik. "But you can't blame people. Plumbing, electricity, cars. It's all our fault," he said. "I just draw them out of the picture," he laughed. "Or sometimes put them in."

Marty sat heavily in her chair in the hot sun, pushing up her hair with her hands. The cold ouzo was pungent with the licorice taste of anise.

"You're tired of traveling, aren't you," said Erik. "Do you like the hotel?" he asked.

"It's beautiful," said Marty. "So fresh." The hotel was modest, but comforting. White curtains, thin white coverlets on the twin beds, bath and shower down the hall. An open window with shutters and a little balcony looked out on the street below. "I could stay there forever."

"That's kind of what I was thinking," said Erik. "Would you stay and wait for me here while I go on to Istanbul?"

Marty was shocked. What was he talking about?

"Just a few days," said Erik. "I want to send some packages here, the books we've been collecting. It would be a good idea if you were here to pick them up."

"When?" gasped Marty. "Shouldn't I come with you?"

But Erik acted as if it had already been decided. He leaned forward, conspiratorial. "We'll walk around the Acropolis tomorrow morning. I'll do some sketching, and then I'll fly out to Alexandroupolis, take the train to Istanbul."

It was like a switch in him had flipped over from indolent sketcher to someone brimming with purpose. Marty was a little frightened. "You're not doing anything dangerous, are you?" she asked.

"I don't think so," said Erik, smooth as butter. He smiled. "Athens isn't dangerous," he said. "Istanbul might be. I think it would be a good idea if you stayed here."

"But Erik!" said Marty. "Did you know about this?"

"Plans have been forming," said Erik enigmatically. "I'm not asking you to do anything, but I really need you to be here."

Marty was both shattered and fascinated. Since their marriage, she had thought Erik more interested in architecture and less in the clandestine dealings of which she was never apprised. She had been excited about this trip which, though rather sudden, she thought would cement their ability to study together, to take on adventure together.

But here she was, confronted with something outside of them which she didn't understand. Marty's idea of love was that it was unconditional. She had hoped that, like a white blood cell surrounding and disarming illness, her love could get around Erik's problems and neutralize them. It was still her hope. But this evening she had the feeling that Erik might be something bigger and darker than she could deal with.

They had dinner together and a leisurely morning, but there was little talk. Marty was relieved when Erik left in a taxi for the airport and she was alone. "I'll be back in less than a week," he said. Marty said nothing.

She did not know what to say that wouldn't splinter between them like glass shards.

Marty sat out in the square that evening alone. She didn't drink ouzo though. A glass of water and a plate of dolmades dipped into a fragrant minty yogurt sauce was enough. Back at the hotel, she sat watching the sky darken. People walked lazily in the street below. A breeze came up and the evening star came out beside a tiny waxing crescent moon. Just like it did in California.

In the morning Marty felt better. Walking through the Plaka, she stopped and bought round bread topped with sesame seed from a woman who sold them off a cart. Koulouri they were called. With a cup of coffee, Marty felt more herself. She hiked up the hill to the Acropolis where the Parthenon stood out starkly against the blue sky.

Marty sat on the broken stones near the Erechtheion, beside an olive tree, the lone tree on the hill. The sun on her body felt warm and sensuous. With a big hat to cover her thin scalp, Marty had found she could enjoy as much sun as she wanted. Grass grew between the stones which littered the space. A little clutch of what looked like British kids followed their teacher around. Otherwise the place was empty this early in the morning.

Marty walked down into the more wooded Agora. The long red roof of the Stoa of Attalos no longer looked as garishly new as when Marty had seen it eight years ago. Trees surrounded the building, an open portico which housed a museum. The reconstruction had been funded in the 1950's by the Rockefellers and the American School of Classical Studies. Marty walked toward it, up the steps and into the cool marble colonnade of the building.

Using a guidebook, Marty tried to place it in history. It had been built before the birth of Christ, but long after Socrates and Plato had taught in the Agora. It housed shops, an Athenian marketplace. Citizens strolled there, shaded from the sun and protected from the wind and rain.

Marty sat on the shaded marble steps, writing in her notebook. What effort had gone into re-imagining classical Greece, based on the writings of men and the remains of its buildings. Western civilization, Dr. Magnusson had said, was a result of the confluence of a Greco-Roman heritage and the wandering Jewish tribes which resulted in Christianity. Dr. Haatvedt, Marty's ancient classics professor, must have been in Athens many times.

Marty's own problems were small and simple. But they're not simple to me, she thought. For her, marriage was foundational, at the root of life. Finding cracks in this foundation so early was devastating. Though she had known, she had to admit. She had known Erik, as attractive as he was, was not a safe person.

Marty was certain Erik's trip to Turkey had something to do with drugs. The books, the packing materials he had been collecting. Yet drugs of all kinds had been used even here, Marty thought. The oracles consulted by the Greeks may have used drugs. She herself felt that hallucinogenic drugs had helped her overcome barriers to her inner self.

What was really wrong, Marty decided, was that Erik wouldn't confide in her. Trafficking in drugs was dangerous and illegal. He was probably trying to protect her. And he also didn't want to know what she thought about it. Marty would certainly have protested his continuing to endanger his life by dealing.

But Marty wasn't going to ask Erik for information he didn't want to divulge. He was allowed a life of his own, even though they were married. She must keep communication lines open. Over time, she hoped, they would become partners.

A girl with an American accent stopped to ask Marty whether she knew the way back to the Plaka. She carried a cloth Greek tourist bag over her shoulder, but to Marty's eyes, the map she pulled out was upside down, the north arrow pointing south. Marty helped the girl right the map and pointed down the mountain. "Oh, thank you! Thank you!" said the girl. "I was afraid I had lost my friends!"

Marty pulled herself together. A vivid mind and healthy body helped her. No use in succumbing to fears. She thought of Mother and how the quick arrival of four kids, and Paul's polio, plus making do on a pastor's salary, had challenged Mother's early marriage. Mother had persevered. Line's marriage had looked tenuous for a long time, but Line was now settled with her husband and had two little girls in addition to her son! Marty must be patient. Things did change. She must stop worrying!

Marty walked down the hill, lingering in the streets and walking until she could see the sea. In the square Marty noticed the girl with the Greek bag and the map at a table with her friends. Marty stopped to talk to them. It turned out they were from Middlebury College in Vermont. During a semester in Italy, they had come for a week's visit to Athens.

"And what about you?" asked the girl, whose name was Olive.

"Well my husband was here," Marty looked rueful. "But he took off. He'll be back soon."

"Do you want to come with us tomorrow? We're going to take a bus to Delphi," asked one of the girls.

But Marty had not looked carefully around Athens yet. There was much she could study. "I better not," she said. "But I'd love to have dinner with you."

"Sure! We heard about this place that has good moussaka we want to try," said Olive.

Marty was delighted by the evening. English-speaking people she didn't know from the East Coast. The girls were a little younger and wanted to know about California. California had a reputation for blonde surfers, engaging counter-culture people and fabulous music. Marty did not think she was a good representative of California, but she did not dissuade them from this romantic veneer on reality. All of it was true, she said.

Marty drank wine, talked and smiled. When everyone dispersed toward their hotels Marty thanked them. "Have a great trip to Delphi!" she said. "I'll see you tomorrow evening, if you are in town."

In the twilight Marty found her hotel. Take that Erik, she thought to herself. I can have fun without you!

Marty found a rhythm to the days. She studied at the museums in the morning and walked or sat dreaming in the afternoons. Brown paper packages in the shape of books arrived from Istanbul. Marty piled them in the corner, not touching them, as if they were combustible.

Marty found a laundromat and washed all her clothes. She hunted for newsstands and read the New York papers. What was she doing here, miles from home? She thought of Hemingway's first wife, Hadley, who was a soft, Midwestern woman living in Paris. I'm a woman, Marty thought. I'm just being, she thought to herself. I'm just being a woman.

But Marty remembered that the objectives of her first European trip had been set by Kate. Yes, she was indeed a woman who let other people plan the agenda. "You're like a reed in the wind," Dad had lamented. "Blowing whatever direction the wind blows!" Mother and Dad would have liked her to fulfill her promise as a teacher or librarian. They were pleased she had found the job in architecture that she wanted, but she knew they expected more of her.

One night a man followed Marty, asking whether she wouldn't join him for a meal. His English was leavened by a dose of what Marty thought may have been Russian. Marty flashed her gold wedding ring at him, but it didn't have much effect. She went back to her hotel and spent the evening looking out the windows.

Eventually Marty got nervous. Erik had been gone a week. He had sent a flock of packages and one postcard, a photograph of an intricately carved and beautifully painted tile, postmarked a few days ago. "Having a great time," it said. "Hope you are too! Love, Erik." It was something, Marty thought. She put it up against the mirror in the hotel room.

Athens, she thought. It could have been worse. But it also could have been better. Who was Erik? Who was the real Erik, she wondered. Was he the playful and loving husband she had seen in Italy, the faux intellectual he had been showing the world? Or was he the intent, risk-taking dealer who had picked up his directives from the American Express office? But I'm no better, thought Marty. Am I the person who lets other people set the agenda, a polite, sedate married woman? Or do I have something inside myself I'm not acknowledging.

Solitude made Marty philosophical. She wasn't panicked yet, but she was beginning to wonder about getting home. She pulled out her airline ticket. She and Erik were booked to leave the Paris airport in seven days.

Two days went by. Marty was having trouble sleeping and she was running out of travelers' checks. But that night, at 3 in the morning, there was a knock on the door. It wasn't Erik, but the man at the night desk at the hotel. "There is a phone call for Mrs. Wilson," he said. "It is a customs official in Alexandroupolis. He wants to ask you some questions."

Marty pulled on a robe and ran downstairs. Yes, Erik was her husband. Yes, he was an architect studying housing in Turkey. He had lost his papers? His passport? No, he had a passport. They just wanted another identification. They just wanted to make sure. Marty breathed deeply. "May I speak to him?" she asked.

"No," said the man. "Mr. Wilson isn't here. I believe he'll be on a plane to Athens today. You can talk to him then." The phone call was abruptly cut off.

Marty put the phone down and looked at the man behind the desk. "Thank you," she said. "Do you know what time the plane arrives from Alexandroupolis today?"

"I think 4 p.m.," said the man.

"Thank you," said Marty. She clutched her light blue robe around her and ran back up to her room. No sleep came that morning, however. Marty sat in the window, watching the sky become light, writing recriminations in her notebook. She did not know what she would say when Erik showed up. Or even if she should be there waiting for him. She was angry.

In the morning she fell into a late, heavy sleep. Waking in the tangled white sheets, Marty thought: "But this is Athens, the birthplace of philosophy. What if I have been abandoned for more than a week. Have I learned nothing? Am I not a woman with resources?"

Marty purchased coffee and koulouri on the square, heading for the newsstand she had found on Adriano Street. At the back of the stand was a small selection of books, some in English. Marty pulled out the one she had been reading about the Greek philosophers. The Stoics, she read, took their name from the Stoa Poikile, or Painted Stoa where Zeno taught about 300 years before Christ. It was very near the reconstructed Stoa of Attalos, the museum Marty had used for study all week. According to the Stoics, destructive emotions resulted from errors in judgment. A sage would not suffer such emotions.

I'm not a sage, Marty thought. But I want to be impeccable. I don't need to be so sour. Looked at a different way, who wouldn't want to be abandoned in the sun of Greece?! She could make of this experience what she wanted. She remembered Zorba the Greek, his elemental joy, his dancing. Erik is my Zorba, thought Marty, leading me into my depths. Erik was drawn to darkness as well as light. Heaven preserve him.

Around 5 p.m., when she thought Erik might arrive, Marty sat in a cafe under an umbrella near the hotel entrance, drinking a glass of wine. In a dark sundress and a big hat, she felt cool and collected.

Erik, when he got out of the taxi, was anything but. Marty had hardly ever seen him so dirty and disheveled. He didn't see her, but she stood up. "Oh, Mr. Wilson," she called as he headed up the steps, carrying his suitcase. "Can I buy you a glass of wine?"

"Marty!" said Erik, turning, surprised. He looked as though he was thrilled to see her. "Oh, my God. Do you look great!"

Marty smiled. The shoe was on the other foot, for once. But Erik, in all of his aliveness, looked good to her too. He came toward her and leaned in to kiss her under her hat. A pungent, sweet, undefinable smell came from him. "So the baraka is still with you?" she asked sweetly. The baraka, as Marty understood it, was the blessing of life.

"Yep," said Erik. "Got out with my filthy skin. And you did help. I don't even want to touch you until I've taken a shower!"

"Oh, never mind," said Marty. "It's just dirt."

"Turkish dirt," said Erik. "I've never felt so unwashed in all my life!"

"No water in Turkey?" asked Marty.

"No water and no soap," said Erik. "At least not that I could find."

"Or that you cared about," said Marty. She handed him her cool glass of wine, which he finished in one long swig.

"And what have you been doing?" Erik asked, "in all this long time?"

Marty's smile came up from her inner self. "Studying philosophy," she said.

18

Angeline was right about Paul. He was back on the Adventuress the very next summer. He did not like boomtown Fairbanks. The school year had been tough, with Paul spending long hours, teaching both morning and evening classes. He was dedicated to the students and wanted to help. But when people who worked on the pipeline came into Fairbanks on their off time to spend their money, they were often rowdy. The shifting population doubled and housing, policemen and tempers were stretched. Paul was glad he could leave for the summer.

At the end of May, Paul went to Port Ludlow, humping a duffle bag and a guitar down the gangplank onto the Adventuress. She was as beautiful as ever, at anchor with the sun shining on the polished wood and her shrouds slung along the towering masts. At least he wasn't quite such a greenhorn this year.

He almost collided with a dark, thin girl pushing a cart toward a pile of groceries on the dock, bags of onions, potatoes, cartons of milk, paper bags full of bread, and big jugs of drinking water. "Hi," she said. "I'm Marie. Are you Paul? M.B. told me you'd be coming aboard soon."

"I am Paul," said Paul. "I'm so glad to be back!"

"Great!" said Marie. "I love to sing! I'm in the galley this summer, prepping for Megan. We'll have lots of time to sing, I hope!"

Marie wore two old-fashioned black braids bound across the top of her head. Paul all of a sudden wondered what her hair looked like down around her face. But he caught himself, becoming instantly wary. "Sounds good," Paul said as he stomped off to his bunk. A feeling of loss reminded him how friendly Denise had been last year and how she had run off with Micah, the first mate.

Paul had time to walk the 133-foot Adventuress from its long, graceful bowsprit to its sculpted stern. Every boom, sail and piece of rigging felt familiar. He remembered how on a few days toward the end of last summer, he had felt so connected to every part of the schooner and her crew that he could almost sense what each creak of the timbers, each metal rattle of the anchor chain meant. He had never seen her hauled out as she was sometimes in the winter. The Adventuress was not his life, as it was Angeline's and the many other people who worked with her. But Paul had missed her.

Except for last year's first mate Micah and Denise, most of the crew was back. Charlie the engineer, Megan the cook and M.B. with her bandana and dark curls were all well-known to Paul.

Angeline called everyone out on deck for introductions when the first batch of sailors arrived. She liked to captain the weeks the inner city kids from Seattle came aboard. She knew many of them from having worked with them before. Some of them were tough and scrawny, but others were big and soft, Paul noticed. Living on French fries maybe.

"Okay," Angel said. "This is a non-smoking sail," she reminded them. "You kids are young. I know you don't have to smoke. If we find someone smoking, we'll put them off the ship then and there. Wherever we are. With a life jacket of course!"

Paul looked around. He could tell the kids were imagining themselves stuck in the cold Sound with nothing but a lifejacket. Wry smiles went from one crew member to the other. All of them knew just what Angel was like under her bark. She made leadership look easy.

"Now what do we want to do?" asked Angeline. "We want to get this gorgeous boat out into the Sound and watch those sails in the wind, right? And what's it going to take to do that? All hands! And I do mean yours. Because we're all in this together, I need your absolute cooperation. If someone asks you to do something, just do it. Don't ask why. We'll tell you, but maybe not while it's happening.

"You will each have your turn at the helm while you're on board. Such a great feeling, holding the wheel, with everyone's well-being in your hands. But we're not going far tonight," she said. "We're going to motor up into Oak Harbor and have some supper. Bill, our first mate, and M.B., our bo'sun, will split you up into watch groups and explain your duties. Tomorrow we'll get underway."

Paul helped unmoor the ship and then went down into the engineering room to see if Charlie needed anything. He could hear Megan and Marie singing as they chopped vegetables for salad and baked lasagna.

"Down the way where the nights are gay and the sun shines daily on the mountaintop. I took a trip on a sailing ship and when I reached Jamaica I made a stop." Marie's voice was interesting, full of color. Paul could hear lots of things going on in it, even over the chugging of the engine and the churning wake of water they left behind. He knew the song from an old Harry Belafonte record.

"I love it when I can just let go," Paul heard Marie say to Megan. "When there's enough noise that no one minds."

I love it when you let go too, said Paul to himself. She sounded delicious. He wondered what playing the guitar with her would be like.

After supper the dishes were done on the deck, supervised by Marie. Later, the "Jamaica Farewell" sounded melancholy as Megan and Marie scrubbed down the pots in the galley. "Sad to say, I'm on my way. Won't be back for many a day. My heart is down, my head is turning around. I had to leave a little girl in Kingston town."

Paul met with the YMCA program director, Matt, and M.B. a few minutes before everyone gathered on the still sunny deck for skits and singing. M.B. had a ukulele this year. Paul felt like he had parted from her just yesterday.

"We should keep it simple tonight," Matt said. "What do you guys usually do?" he asked.

"Well, charades, singing, sometimes skits," said M.B. "But I agree that it might take a day or two before we all coalesce. Paul just got here. Marie's been great at singing. She sings in restaurants in Seattle," she said.

"What does she sing?" asked Matt.

"That's the thing," said M.B. "Some of the pop stuff might be a little raunchy, and I know Angeline wants us to include everyone. So what do you suggest?" M.B. strummed the ukulele with a little pick as she talked.

"Well we don't need 'Onward Christian Soldiers' or anything like that, but maybe 'Amazing Grace,'" said Matt. "And no 'Puff the Magic Dragon'!"

"I can play 'Amazing Grace'," said Paul.

"It's a good sundowner," said Matt. "We do some singing after our meetings in town. You could do one entertainment thing, just you guys singing alone."

"Do you remember 'Michael Row the Boat Ashore?'" Paul asked M.B. "We used to make up verses for that one, put in a verse for each of the crew."

"Yeah," said M.B. "I like it! We'll get everyone in on that one. I wish Marie were here. She did a great 'Me and Bobby McGee' the other night. No guitar or anything. Can you play that, Paul? I tried to do it, but I'm not so good."

"Yeah," said Paul. "That one's easy and I really like it. Starts G, C, D7, I think." He began strumming. Kristofferson was a great lyric writer but not very inventive on the guitar chords, which made his ballads easy. "These kids probably all know it," said Paul. It was a hippie anthem. "Freedom's just another word for nothing left to lose."

The sun was still high when everyone assembled on deck. Paul jammed the Greek fisherman's hat he had found over his blonde hair and tilted it to a rakish angle to shade his eyes. He loved being second fiddle, or even third fiddle. Just so he didn't have to get up and talk too much.

Matt introduced them and got everyone to sing. He knew the kids' names, who he could count on, dragged some of them up front. There was no microphone, just the still air over the water.

Paul felt the rush of energy Marie brought. And yes, a mass of dark unruly curls floated around her face. She was like Paul, a little self-conscious, but she had a loud, amazing voice which came from her whole body and she gave herself completely to a song. Paul stood beside her, deadpan, not betraying the emotion he felt. He played the guitar and came in on the chorus. "Feeling good was easy, Lord, when Bobby sang the blues," Marie crooned. "Feeling good was good enough for me." Paul could hear the ache in her voice and looking out over the kids he could see that they did too. "Somewhere near Salinas, Lord, I let him slip away."

On "Amazing Grace" Paul took the harmony, letting Marie's strong voice carry the melody. Matt then bid everyone to their bunks. "Up bright and early tomorrow!" he said. "Listen for the bo'sun's whistle! That means breakfast."

Adrenalin coursed through Paul's veins. How could he go to bed? Marie too seemed excited. "I wish there was a place to talk," she said to Paul. "Just for a minute?"

Paul put his guitar away. "I've got to stow this. The air gets so wet overnight," he said. "I'll meet you by the anchor chain." If there was anywhere to be alone, it might be there.

Paul emerged from the crew cabin and went out toward the bow. The sky was very light. No chance for stars for quite a while. Clouds were somewhat illuminated and Paul could see the horizon clearly. Paul leaned over the gunwale. When Marie came and stood by him he whispered, "Do you know about nautical twilight?"

When she said no, he explained that when ships used to navigate by the stars, it was the time when you could no longer distinguish the horizon and only vague outlines of things were visible without illumination of some kind. "The sky's not there yet," he said.

"You're from Fairbanks?" asked Marie. "What's that like?"

"It was great," said Paul. "Long dark winters, of course. But it was beautiful. And I did lots of skiing! Lots of music there too. Now, since they're working on the oil pipeline, it's not so much fun. It's crowded and crazy." He turned toward her. "You have an amazing voice."

Marie looked down, dipping her head and spoke very quietly. "It's gotten me in trouble," she said. "I thought I wanted to be a professional. Like Joni Mitchell or one of them. I'm French-Canadian. But it was too tough and I got involved with the wrong people." She tossed her head, dark recalcitrant curls flying up. The afterglow lit up her tawny skin. "It's just for fun now," she said.

Marie was two years older than Paul, and called herself the black sheep of a large, strict Catholic family. She had left home early, gone to Toronto and then Los Angeles. Now she worked in restaurants in Seattle. Angeline had pulled her out to work on the Adventuress for the summer. "I'm kind of a hard luck case," Marie said. "Everything you can imagine has happened to me."

"I guess that's what I hear in your voice," said Paul. "Not a bad thing if your tough times are in the past."

"I've got to get to bed," said Marie, yawning. "Wakeup time for me is right around the corner!" Her hand brushed his shoulder which warmed to her touch. "Night, Paul."

"Good night," said Paul. He felt uplifted, awed by meeting this vibrant woman. When he stumbled into bed, he could not sleep. He tried to tame his feelings. She might like him, but it was hard to tell how much.

At breakfast, M.B. looked at Paul significantly. It was impossible to hide anything from any of the crew. Paul nodded and smiled. Yes, he didn't have to say it. Marie was something.

That week Paul's awareness shifted from the Adventuress to Marie. Whether he was doing the inventory of parts for Charlie, lubing the engine, or up on deck helping the kids coil lines, pleat sails, and climb the rat lines, he was always aware of what Marie was doing. She was busy. Prepping, cooking food and cleaning up after 30 people took a lot of time. But she had off time too. She might go ashore in the dingy or Paul would come across her curled up like a cat on deck, shading a book with her body. It wasn't that he wanted to know where she was! He didn't like this feeling. It felt scary. Unfamiliar.

And then in the evenings, she unleashed that powerful voice. Whew! But Paul also felt a knowing in his thoughts about Marie. As he became comfortable around her, she felt a little like a sister, kind of a cross between Line and Marty. He felt that way about M.B. too, but between them there wasn't the shimmering electricity Paul felt between himself and Marie.

When the inner city sailors left the boat, Paul fled. He went straight to the showers in Port Ludlow, borrowed a tent and stuck out his thumb on the highway toward Port Hadlock. The summer before he had gotten to know people there and found a lake he could camp beside.

Paul stopped in at the boat works to say hello to Robert, the boat builder. Paul loved the smell of wood shavings and the lovely shells being built in the covered boat works. Robert was having a Scotch and marveling at a piece of purple heart wood he had gotten from Brazil. It would be used for the decking on a yacht he was building. "Would you look at that, Paul," he said. "Extremely dense and water resistant. Have to use carbon steel blades on that. I never saw anything like it." The wood was a lovely chocolate color. Paul hung around, looking at everything, glad to be free of emotion in the workmanlike atmosphere.

The air was damp that evening and moisture dripped off the trees. Paul stayed in his tent reading a while, but his book didn't hold him. He came out and coaxed a fire together. What was happening to him, he wondered. Was this the much-vaunted love affair he had been waiting for, which seemed to make everyone so happy? It was painful! Loneliness was easier, he thought. Not so much responsibility. Eventually, using bigger and bigger pieces of deadwood, Paul had a crackling, snapping fire for company.

It did feel delicious to think about Marie. Paul turned over every day, one after the other. What she had looked like, what she had said. She was really tiny, though she ate a lot. High metabolism, she said. When she wasn't singing she was pretty quiet. Paul loved overhearing her and Megan, cooking together.

One day she had started singing, "I've been warped by the rain, driven by the snow, I'm drunk and dirty don't ya know, and I'm still, willin'. But if you give me weed, whites and wine, and you show me a sign, I'll be willin' to be movin'." Paul was listening hard to get the words, which weren't very clear.

"Angel would kill us if she heard you singing that," said Megan's shocked voice, low.

"Yeah," said Marie. "It's Linda Ronstadt. It's a truck driver's song. But she just belts it. It's sort of my song."

"What are 'whites,'" asked Megan.

"Bennies," said Marie. "Uppers. Truck drivers use them to stay awake."

"Oh, yeah," said Megan. "Maybe you can sing it on another trip."

It was a mesmerizing song. "I'm still, willin', to be movin'." The stops, the words. Paul had never heard it. And the place names. He loved place names in songs, "I've been from Tucson to Tucumcari, Tehachapi to Tonapah." Southern desert names, Paul thought.

Paul sat in front of his fire a long time, watching the logs burn down to cinders and the sparks fly up. He needed to 'get his grits together,' as he had heard it said. Face the music.

A day later he went back to the apartment the crew used on time off. People had been wondering where he was. "I'm looking for that chess game, Paul," said Captain Wayne, who lived with his wife and kids in Port Hadlock. He would captain the next sail. "Remember? You beat me last year and that is not going to be the last of it!"

Marie's eyes followed Paul. She was lifting hot cookies off a cookie sheet with a spatula. They smelled heavenly. Someone handed Paul a beer, which he didn't open. There was a game of hearts going on in the corner.

Paul went up to Marie and said, "Would you like to go for a walk? It's a little damp out, but it's nice." He did not want to have another week like the last one, another week of not knowing if Marie felt what he was feeling.

Marie looked over at M.B. "Could you finish the cookies?" she asked.

"Sure," said M.B.

Paul put the beer back in the refrigerator and stood waiting by the door while Marie got a sweater. "Catch you later," said Paul to the group. And then, in front of everyone, they walked out into the wet, damp twilight.

"I was camping up near Port Hadlock," said Paul as they walked toward the marina and then along the water. "I like it up there. There's a lot of woodworking and boat building going on. It's less of a resort and residential place, like this. There's a great café in an old building up there too."

"I've heard of it," said Marie. "The Ajax, right?" She was wearing a thick, creamy sweater with a blue heart pattern knit into it.

"Good music on the weekends," said Paul. A bench along the waterfront loomed and Paul headed for it. "Sit for a minute?" he asked. The air was wet and dark with the smells of pine and salty sea wrack washed up on the beach. Lowering clouds lay over the grey water.

Marie sat down, drawing up her legs and putting her arms around them. She smiled at Paul. Against the grey sky and water she looked very alive.

"I just want to tell you that I like you," said Paul. "I'm not very good at this, but I need to know more about you. We've never really been alone." He looked out toward the water. "Do you want to write songs?" he ventured lamely.

Marie laughed to break the tension. "No," she said. "I'm more of an interpreter. But it's just a hobby now. A way to meet people and to have fun. I'm really getting interested in food. Did you see how malnourished those kids were last week? Broke my heart," she said. "I just want to feed everyone."

"I did see," said Paul gravely.

"And what do you want in life, Paul?" asked Marie.

Paul thought about it, answering slowly. "My folks wanted me to be a pastor. But I can't. Not in a traditional Lutheran church. I really like teaching. But if I could do anything I wanted, I'd do something like we're doing on the Adventuress. Maybe with canoes. Kids are fun to work with. And they need so much!"

"In Alaska?" asked Marie.

"Maybe," said Paul, darkly. Would Alaska be the same after the pipeline?

Metal halyards clinked in the distance and birds dived toward the rolling water, screeching. Marie looked out to sea. This isn't easy, thought Paul. I want you, he thought. He wanted to say it, but he didn't know how. "Do you miss Montreal?" he asked.

Marie laughed again. "I miss French," she said. "Speaking French. Singing in French. But that's it. I'm not sure I could live there any more."

"French?" asked Paul.

Marie put her legs down, her hands in her lap, and turned toward Paul. "Tu me plais. Je pense que vous êtes doux," Marie said softly. "It means that I like you. I think you're sweet."

Paul melted. It was Marie that was sweet, sitting there in her thick sweater, her dark skin so beautiful. "May I take your hand?" he asked, touching them. Her hands were warm. They were thin, working hands, but right now they lay still, pliant. She's like a flower, thought Paul. I'm the bee. He moved closer.

"Tell me one thing I should know about you," said Marie.

"I had polio," said Paul. "One of my legs is really skinny and one is strong. It works, but it makes me lopsided. And I can't run." It felt good to let it out, the thing he was always trying to hide.

"M.B. told me," said Marie. "No one notices. You work really hard, and you're so strong."

Paul slid closer to her, their bodies touching all along one side as they looked out to sea. Paul put an arm around Marie's shoulder.

"I have something I need to tell you," said Marie. "I'm divorced. I was married in Los Angeles to a musician. We didn't have kids. It was sort of silly." Marie looked into Paul's eyes to see if he was scandalized. But Paul just held her closer. "I'm Roman Catholic. Or I was. So it seems really terrible to me."

"I'm sorry," said Paul. "It's not terrible. There are worse things." He smiled down at her. He certainly hadn't thought she was innocent.

"I made a vow to myself not to have anything to do with men again until I meet the right one," Marie said. "The divorce was terrible and I don't want anything like that to happen again." Memory rose into her face and Paul felt her thin body shudder.

"That's why we are getting to know each other," said Paul. "To see if we are the right ones."

"Might be," said Marie. "It feels really nice to be with you."

"Yes," said Paul. "I've never had a real girlfriend. I always thought I was immune, like a monk. Or Thoreau." He smiled. Marie felt very warm and her hair smelled like pine. They were whispering into each other's faces over the sounds of the wind and the waves.

"Did you want one?" asked Marie.

"I think so," said Paul. "I don't know." He leaned over and kissed Marie's soft neck. They were wrapped around each other, kissing.

"I hate everyone on the crew looking at us and wondering," said Paul. "But if we know, if we've talked, then I don't mind."

"I think we know," said Marie.

"Maybe you'll come camping with me the next time there's a break?" asked Paul.

"Yes," said Marie. "We don't know each other yet, but we will," she smiled. "And we have talked. Ce sera notre secret. It'll be our secret."

"Cold nose, warm heart," said Paul as he pressed his nose into Marie's cheek. "It's okay," he said. "We can go back." They were inside the force field now. It could not be broken. All of their atoms strained toward each other.

Paul knew it wasn't a secret when they went back to the apartment, faces red and shining with cold. But he could rest. He didn't care what anyone said, or didn't say.

That week he hardly talked to Marie, but their eyes met often. The ship was like a Bunsen burner making a new compound out of their two elements, Paul thought. And everyone supported them. There were two short sails that week, one with a group of Sea Scouts and one with a group from Boeing Corporation. The guys from Boeing kept comparing the Adventuress to the 747's they were building. Paul was in the thick of it.

Scared as Paul was at opening himself up, the feelings between himself and Marie did not go away over the summer. During the sail trips, they both had duties, Paul working with Charlie, the engineer. And Marie being mess cook for Megan. They hustled with the rest of the crew to take care of the hordes of passengers, sang together at night, and Paul gave astronomy talks. On the weekends, they sneaked off together in Marie's little truck, often up to Port Hadlock. Marie brought cookies to Robert at the boat works and they made friends of the cooks at the ancient Ajax Café.

One dry night, over a campfire, Marie taught Paul the song "Willin'." She had told him she didn't want to play the guitar. She felt it hampered her full-on singing. But she did have a tambourine for the rhythms and she knew music. Even just tapping one piece of wood against another, her body was the most alive thing Paul had known! Her hair tumbled over her face in time to the beat.

It would have been easier if Paul had heard a band play the music, but there was no way to get the record. They worked out the chords, starting with G, some version of a D chord and a C chord. Paul understood it, now, though.

"It's got some great slide guitar in it. A guy named Lowell George from Little Feat wrote it," said Marie.

"Was he a truck driver?" asked Paul.

"No, but I think he worked in a gas station," Marie said. Her eyes darkened as she seemed to be looking back over her past.

His Marie, thought Paul. Battered, traveling, but still "Willin'." So am I, said Paul to himself. "And if you show me a sign ..." Well, there it was. It was an American song.

"How did you get to be so American?" asked Paul.

"I don't know," said Marie. "It just happened. Somewhere along the way."

"My folks took us up to Winnipeg when we were little. It seemed really exotic. I always loved the Mounted Police in their red coats!"

"I think it was the desert," said Marie. Her face looked wistful. "I loved driving in the desert at night. The sky. 'Tucson to Tucumcari, Tehachapi to Tonapah'. They're all desert towns. I haven't been to most of them, but we did drive to Tucson."

"It's a mouthful," said Paul. "What great writing!" He didn't care how American or Canadian Marie was. He was glad he was no longer alone.

19

At eight in the morning Marty locked the door of the flat and ran down the stairs into the street, leaving Erik still asleep. It was chilly and Marty could almost see her breath in the watery light. She walked past the restaurants and bakeries on Green Street, the sun rising in the misty atmosphere along the Bay. North Beach hadn't waked up yet. Passing Malvina's the smell of thick, bitter roasted espresso wafted out into the street. Marty's office was down the hill and north toward the water.

Many people Marty knew didn't like doing the same thing every day at the same time, but habit stabilized Marty. She loved watching how things changed around her daily pattern, like the light which, in February, was slowly increasing each morning. She loved having the same walk through town each morning, noticing other people's repetitive morning tasks, plants growing and blooming, cats slinking along.

On the green lawn of Washington Square park, homeless people wrapped in old sleeping bags sat on benches, their hair matted and their eyes closed. On the corner, she passed Mama's, the delightfully kitschy painted restaurant where you could get breakfast at any time of day. A few people on their way to mass went up the steps of the lovely white church of Saints Peter and Paul, with its arched doorways, towers and rose window.

Turning north on Powell Street, Marty passed the shop of the flamboyant designers, husband and wife, who used the brand Jeanne-Marc. Their clothing hung in the old-fashioned bay windows. Most shops on the street were now empty, except for the sign of a photographer's studio or a small architectural firm. Marty angled toward Fisherman's Wharf, making sure to go down Water Street, where people would not give up their tiny, wooden dwellings and embellished the rickety balconies with gardens and hanging potted flowers. North Beach, at least parts of it, was known for its human scale.

Marty was at the office on Beach Street by 8:30 a.m. A huge room on the second floor built into an old warehouse with acres of drafting stations where people, mostly men, labored to draw plans for hospitals and hotels. Around the edge of the room were various planning, interior and specification departments with more conventional workstations. Marty's was just outside the library. Fluorescent light poured down on the desks, but at the end of the room, a few windows admitted the low-slanted winter light.

Across from her, Shantanu, the Indian mathematician and programmer, nodded sleepily over his cup of coffee. "Friday," he said, making a peace sign with his fingers. "TGIF!"

Jill, who took two buses and Bay Area Rapid Transit all the way from east Oakland, was not there yet. Marty pawed through the pile of work in her inbox and began to type up the meeting notes she had been given. They must be copied, distributed and filed immediately.

When Jill arrived, Marty was all attention. Jill, a small pretty blonde, was the daughter of one of the early leaders of IBM. From her father she had absorbed an understanding of data processing, and had taken degrees at UC Berkeley in architecture and mathematics. To Marty, Jill's pretty, placid face hid weighty thoughts and authority. She had introduced Marty to the seductiveness of databases, an entirely new way of looking at things.

This morning they worked on an inventory for the new King Khalid Military City hospital to be built in the Saudi Arabian desert. It was a fabulous project and would keep the big architectural firm in funds for a year or more.

Marty sat in the narrow computer room at a terminal, typing. Beside the door was a photo of Mikhail Baryshnikov, her current favorite dancer. Connected by a telephone line to an IBM mainframe, she typed data into the fields Jill had prepared for each record. In this case, a record represented a piece of equipment which would be specified for a hospital. The fields were descriptors for the item, color, manufacturer, dimensions, cost, power requirements and all its other attributes.

Jill wrote Fortran and APL programs, or sometimes Shantanu did, parsing the data into lists and reports. The equipment was sorted, quantified, specified in categories such as manufacturer, cost or electrical requirements. It was no longer kept in laborious paper notebooks, copied and faxed. The new computerized inventory could be added to, changed, sorted and saved throughout the life of the complex hospital project.

Through the door Marty overheard Jill having a fight with the project manager, Leonard Bailey. One of the most spirited architects in the place, he was middle-aged and vigorous. But he expected that when he stated his needs, they would be met, pronto.

"We'll try," Jill said, when Leonard said he must have the revised inventory to go out to Riyadh with a package of drawings next Friday. "But I can't promise."

"What do you mean?! Can't you assure me your team can meet a deadline?!" shouted Leonard, his face growing red.

"If the mainframe isn't down and the program runs, you'll have your data. But I can't promise," Jill stated quietly.

"That's incredible!" said Leonard. "Why can't you make a deadline?"

"There are too many variables," said Jill, reasonably. "I can't absolutely control them."

Marty could see that she was driving Leonard crazy. He stomped off toward the front of the room where the offices of the principals were ranged along the wall.

Jill came over to Marty to let off steam. "At Berkeley, I'd see the computer spit out the cards and they'd be all over the floor!" she said. "I can't give him an absolute promise of anything! If there's a comma in the wrong place in the Fortran it could throw the program into a tizzy."

"And we're depending on a processor miles away to which I am connected by a tenuous telephone line," Marty agreed. But she could see that it wasn't a matter of language. It was a culture clash, in which what one generation had gotten used to could not be done in the same way by the new generation. There was nothing Leonard could do about it. They were giving him something he had never had before.

At lunch time, Marty headed out toward the Art Institute just up the hill. A venerable old Spanish-style building built around a beautiful courtyard, the Institute had a bold new addition on the back with a concrete deck overlooking the water. A small cafeteria, run by a hippie crew, made whole grain bread sandwiches loaded with tomatoes, avocados, lettuce, sprouts and bacon! Marty's favorite.

Because it was Friday and Marty felt daring, she decided she would have a cup of coffee. Marty could no longer drink coffee, as it made her stomach ache. This light French roast didn't seem to bother it so much. She stirred brown sugar and cream into it and took a sip. Sweet and aromatic, it was delicious. Marty took her lunch out onto the concrete deck. The sun was strong in the middle of the day and warm enough, even in February. No one seemed bothered that Marty might not be a student. The students were not self-conscious and none of the architects came up from her company.

Except, there was Ming-Yue! Ming-Yue was a winsome architect, one of two Chinese women recently hired to do design and drafting. Marty had only talked to her a little, but she was impressed at how direct and simple Ming-Yue's conversation was. She had grown up in Hong Kong and gone to a Catholic high school in California. She had gone to a prestigious architectural school and worked in New York.

Ming-Yue was alone, sitting on a series of steps which was the roof of the auditorium below. Marty asked if she could join her. Ming-Yue was drinking coffee, but she had a piece of paper in front of her, upon which she wrote in beautiful Chinese characters.

"What are you writing?" asked Marty.

"I'm trying to help my brother," said Ming-Yue. "He's working on a movie and needs ideas for music. I'm making a list of music that might work."

"Wow," said Marty. "That sounds like fun." In the interview of Ming-Yue LMP had published in its newsletter, Ming-Yue said she liked to sketch. "You like sketching, don't you?"

"Of course," said Ming-Yue. "I like process. Sketching processes, like flowers blooming and then decaying. You learn something from it." She stretched her thin, black-stockinged legs under her. "Do you come here because of the food?"

"Yes," said Marty. "I love these sandwiches. And the coffee." She held up the cup and took a sip of the sweet liquid. Even in the take-out atmosphere of the café, it was a real ceramic cup which she must return.

"I like Chinese food," said Ming-Yue. "But this place makes nice salad. I love salad." She raised her coffee cup to her lips with delicate hands.

Marty wished she liked salad more. If she did she would be thinner! What Marty really liked was bread and butter.

"Why are you working at LMP?" asked Ming-Yue. "What did you get your degree in?"

"English and Latin," said Marty. "I'm really interested in architecture. I love the photographs in the Italian magazines. And lately they've had these great articles about surrealism in *AD*. How the streets and buildings of Paris affected the surrealists. They were magical to them." She considered. "I'm glad to be working in architecture. And I like learning about databases." Databases imposed pattern; Marty was good at patterns.

"This is not the kind of work I want to do," said Ming-Yue. "I was much happier in New York. Here I just get to design and specify a console, or a piece of furniture. I was given much more work to do in New York." She turned up her nose expressively. "But I try to learn from everything. I never stop learning."

The sun shone down, warming them. But lunch hour was short. They must go back. Walking down the hill, the coastline of the Bay spread in front of them with its tourist haunts, parks and marinas. "Sometimes I buy a packet of lemon drops and eat them all afternoon," confessed Ming-Yue. "That's how unhappy I am at work."

Marty looked at her sympathetically. She must be younger, Marty thought.

"There's a lot more intellectual activity in New York too," said Ming-Yue as they stepped down the hill. "Lectures and exhibits and discussions. It isn't as exciting here."

"There are the AIA lectures," said Marty. "And Bill Stout's." Bill Stout's magical bookstore was stocked with architectural books. He rented an empty restaurant on Broadway, with purple walls, a casual space for lectures. Everyone flocked to them.

"Yes," said Ming-Yue. "It's something."

"Did you think of the music for your brother?" asked Marty. "I'm sorry I interrupted you."

"It's a process," said Ming-Yue. "I'm working on it. Movies take a long time to finish, but William edits to music. It sets the tone of the piece."

They climbed the steps to the office. "Do you have your lemon drops?" asked Marty quietly.

Ming-Yue nodded, smiling, sharing a moment of complicity.

At 6 p.m. Marty shut down the computer terminal and left the office. In an architectural office, unlike an attorney's, lunchtime wasn't paid, but LMP was on an innovative plan to give people an extra Friday off every other weekend. This was achieved by having people work an extra half hour every day. Everyone agreed it was worth it.

But it was not a Friday off, and Marty had to hurry. She was due at the ballet in a couple of hours. She rushed out to a bus stop in the deepening twilight and hopped on an electric bus which lurched up Van Ness. The Opera House was half an hour away.

Stopping along the route, Marty went into a restaurant and ordered soup. It was hot and smelled of vegetables, a fragrant bowl with a spoonful of unctuous pesto on top. Marty took her tray to a high metal stool in front of the glass window walls looking out on the street. Traffic poured forth in both directions during rush hour.

Buttering a piece of sourdough bread, Marty thought about the day. Ming-Yue had strong ideas about where she wanted her career to go, but Marty had none. She saw herself as a complex, rounded, whole person, willing to give all of her talents to the company. She was concerned about money, though she knew LMP could not afford to pay her what she was really worth. LMP would only pay her as a project secretary. They did not want more, and she could not expect to do more.

Erik too was more like Marty, than Ming-Yue, Marty thought. He liked architecture, especially drawing. He liked the idea of being an architect, the life it afforded him. But he wasn't idealistic or ambitious. He didn't care deeply what he worked on. He would not be at the ballet, as he preferred sports. He and Marty each did as they pleased, meeting at home. It was part of the freedom they allowed each other, even as married people.

Car lights illuminated the dark shapes of people crossing at the corner as the traffic lights changed. This is my city, thought Marty. She could not imagine wanting to be in New York as Ming-Yue did. If Marty wanted to be anywhere else, it would be somewhere in the wild, with trees and big skies.

Lately, Marty was homesick for Minnesota. She realized that, now that she was married, there was no going back. Erik was not a Minnesotan and never would be. She missed the birch trees and lakes of northern Minnesota, the puffy cumulus scudding across the summer skies, the sun leaving a golden path across the lake as it set. She missed lying out under trees, which lost their leaves in the winter and became new and leafy in spring. Her chief complaint about San Francisco was that there were few trees, certainly none you could lie under, unless you went out to the park, which was no longer anywhere near Marty and Erik's flat.

Many weekend mornings, Marty felt desperate waking up in the apartment half way up Telegraph Hill. There was nothing wild near by, no natural places that she could walk to. When Erik woke up, he might take the day and go out to the country with her, but she could not count on it.

Nevertheless Marty was glad she had been enticed out to California by the Chertoks. The Bay Area fed her mind and independence and gave her more than she had been able to imagine. Of all possible cities, she felt most at home in this one. Marty's life was layered in it. Wherever she went, especially in the northern part of the city, she could see in her mind's eye the friends who had accompanied her, the things they had done, the photographs she had taken. She could see Line and Paul there. And of course Erik. The edge of the Pacific, with its fresh winds and its beauty, was the place to be.

Marty finished her soup and walked down to the Opera House. Light flooded from the upper recessed windows and lower levels of the white columned building. People arrived in limousines and taxis, some dressed in shimmering gowns and even furs. Marty had bought season tickets for the San Francisco Ballet with Lana, who waited for her inside near the curving marble stairway.

"I came straight from work," Marty said as she slipped off her coat, by way of explanation for her plain clothes, a white shirt with black wool slacks and a black sweater. Her thick dark hair waved down her back.

"Oh," Lana waved her hand. "You look fine. I came from the yarn store myself." Lana's colorful dress almost reached the floor, and she was wrapped in a luxurious shawl she had woven of thick, fleecy red and gold yarns which matched the sheen of her curly hair.

Marty touched the shawl. "So lovely," she said.

The ushers helped them find their seats and handed them programs.

"There's a Twyla Tharp ballet tonight," Lana said. Lana was the expert. She had had tickets the year before and knew all the gossip about the company dancers.

"And who's Twyla Tharp?" asked Marty, flipping the pages of the program. She was hemmed in by a perfumed and powdered lady to her right, digging pills out of her handbag.

"She's a modern dancer and choreographer from New York," said Lana. "She's becoming really famous."

Lana pointed out the photographs of two of the dancers in the program. "They're husband and wife," she said. "But they say her breasts are really too big for classical dance. She'll probably have to quit."

Marty was all ears. She felt her own breasts were too big to wear clothing well. Most fashionable clothing looked like it had been made for boys, draping simply from the shoulders and hip bones that you could almost see. Marty resolved to watch Pat Simmons carefully, to see about her breasts. Dance was very difficult. Few dancers made it out of the corps of dancers. Anything could stop you. Marty had not heard from her college friend April in many years, but she did not think April was still a ballet dancer.

Marty turned over the pages of the ballet program, turning her attention to Lana, who she had roomed with long ago. Lana had done white-collar organizing at Cardigan Shores, inviting a printers' union in to organize clerical workers. At one point she rebelliously gave up her copyediting job and became a library page, walking around to the attorney writers' offices delivering books and mail. She enjoyed it and could still live on the small wage she got!

Lana went from that experience to working in a yarn store. "I'm downwardly mobile," she said. But she could pay for her room in a communal apartment and she was becoming a weaver, using the yarn store as a base. She was often at the store alone, managing the whole place. Marty liked being able to go there and find her. Marty herself was doing needlepoint these days, buying yarns from the store.

Lana enjoyed living. She was independent, but she wasn't particularly interested in working. She loved stories and gossip and was wonderful company. What drives people like Lana and me? Marty wondered, as opposed to her friends Jill and Ming-Yue, who were bent on having careers and making a mark in the world.

The orchestra took up the music for one of the favorite ballets of the company, Balanchine's choreography to *Symphony in C* by Bizet. Lana, who had seen it before, indicated her excitement to Marty. The velvet curtains parted and the dance began. It was exactly what one expected of the ballet, women in white tutus and tiaras, partnered by men in black.

Marty sat quietly, unsure of exactly what she was supposed to feel. She looked at first one dancer and then the other, trying to pick out Pat Simmons. Sometimes the whole smiling company seemed to be on stage. At others, two dancers arched around each other in a pas de deux. At another time, three male dancers made a spectacular leap together behind a woman kneeling, arms upraised, setting them off.

Marty was close enough to hear the thudding of feet on the wooden floor. She knew that toe shoes had stiff boxes in them to encase the toes, that dancers' feet were usually battered. But April had also told her that it was much more fun to be on stage dancing than to watch from the audience.

At intermission, Lana and Marty stood up and climbed the steep steps out to the balcony level where people milled and talked. It was good not to be so cramped, to stand for a few moments looking at all the amazing city people. "I'd really like a chocolate truffle," said Lana. "I know they have them at the dress circle bar."

"I'll go get two of them," said Marty. "If you think we have time." She raced down the steps and managed to purchase two thick lumps of chocolate, carrying them in paper cups, before the lights began to blink indicating people should return to their seats. The truffles were the best kind of chocolate, thick with cream.

After two shorter ballet pieces, Marty was surprised by recorded music filling the hall. It was the Beach Boys! Slowly dancers came out on stage, some jolting and jazzy, full of attitude, in loose, creamy colored costumes which flowed around them. One dancer stood in the middle, doing the classical ballet positions one after another. The others danced and acted around her, as if they had met her on a street corner.

The music mesmerized Marty. She had never had a Beach Boys' album, but their music leaked into the atmosphere. It was so rich, surrounding Marty and filling her body with allusions to modern dancing as well as classical ballet. The dancers used it, animating it, moving through it, shimmying and using every part of their bodies. The combination lifted Marty almost out of her seat! She wanted to be dancing. She wanted it never to stop! So this was Twyla Tharp's work.

But of course the dancing did stop. The curtain came down, applause calling the dancers from the wings over and over. The conductor, the director of the ballet, the stars all took bows, bouquets of roses greeting them. Marty stood, clapping, all inner and outer smiles. At last she and Lana moved up the aisles and out into the thickly populated hallways. Marty noticed several young children, dressed up and sleepy. How would it feel to be a city child, Marty wondered, brought up in this opulent atmosphere, this rich night life.

Limousines were pulled up to the curb outside the Opera House. It was exhilarating to see so many festive people out on the street late at night. Lana bid Marty goodnight. "I had a lovely time," said Marty. "Thank you for getting me to buy tickets this year." Lana headed to the lot where her car was parked. She would drive home and search for a parking spot on her street.

For Marty, there was no easy way to get home through the rough Tenderloin on public buses late at night. Part of the cost of the ballet was an expensive taxi home. Marty waited her turn, watching men in livery hold doors open for elderly ladies in their best clothes who awkwardly settled their creaky limbs and canes into the cars. The air was thick and wet with moisture, but not cold. Light glistened and gleamed where it fell on wet pavement, the shiny paint on the vehicles, the flash of patent leather.

In the taxi, Marty was tense. She was never sure whether she would have the right cash to pay for one, and also didn't know how much to tip. It was so rare for her, she couldn't enjoy it. But the distance was short. Soon she was climbing the steps to her own flat on Sonoma Alley and letting herself in. There, in the dim light of the television, lay Erik, asleep on the beautiful Turkish carpet, a pillow tucked under his head. The sweet green smell of marijuana hovered in the room.

Erik seemed to wake. Marty slipped off her shoes and knelt down to kiss him, her long hair falling on the carpet. The stars of remembered music and dance played around her eyes. She reached for the knob on the television and turned it off, then slipped down on the floor, and stretched out beside Erik. "How are you?" she asked. His body felt loose and easy.

"Good," said Erik. "How was the ballet? That's where you were, right?" he asked.

"Yes," said Marty. "Such a wonderful dance by Twyla Tharp! To the music of the Beach Boys. I couldn't believe it!"

Erik yawned. "The Beach Boys?"

"Yeah," said Marty. They were too poppy for her, a little before her time, and probably for Erik, who had grown up in Los Angeles. "Did you like them?"

"Oh sure," said Erik. "For a while. As a teeny bopper. I was something of a beach bum, a surfer. And now they're making ballet out of it?"

"She's from New York," said Marty. "It's a new kind of dance. I think she could make dance out of anything. She uses jazz sometimes."

Erik got to his feet lazily and reached a hand down to Marty. "What is it you always say?" he asked. "Tomorrow is another day?"

"Yes," said Marty. "It's what my mother said when we wanted to stay up too late." Erik's hands were on her tummy, feeling for the skin under her pants.

"I think, Mrs. Wilson," said Erik. "That you should come to bed with me."

"Yes," breathed Marty. "Yes."

20

Paul breathed in the fresh, soft air as he and Marie skied down the street in a light snow to their friends' house a mile away. He had been looking forward to spring, mostly for Marie's sake. It was her first winter this far north and in this much darkness. But now it was broad daylight at suppertime in Fairbanks, almost the March equinox. The light was rapidly encroaching on the days though it was still freezing.

Linda opened the door and greeted them as they stood their skis and poles on end in the snow outside the house. "Hey, you two," she said. "Brian's not home yet, but I've got a bunch of muffins in the other room who would love to see you!" Marie was a favorite with kids, who brought out her performing instincts.

Nicholas, almost four, came running from the living room, his hands embedded in sock puppets. "Marie! Marie! We need you," he said. "Sing us the song again. Little Rabbit Foo Foo!" He grabbed Marie and dragged her into the other room where there were two slightly older children. Linda had opened the doors of the ranch house she and Brian bought to a daycare while Nicholas was little.

Paul shook the snow off his shoes and went into the steamy kitchen, redolent of the smell of meat cooking. Caribou stew filled a black cast iron stew pot. "Can I help you with anything?" he asked. Linda wiped her hands on a big apron and stirred the stew with a wooden spoon. From the kitchen Paul could overhear Marie establishing the characters and going over the song with them.

"Those kids' mother is working on the pipeline," said Linda, shaking her head. "They've been here for a week already. Brian drops them off at school in the morning, and I pick them up at night. We just lay out a row of pallets on the floor. It's tough on the kids, but no one is happier than Nicholas!" she said.

"Father?" asked Paul.

"I'm not sure," said Linda. "I've only talked to the mother. Everyone's behaving like maniacs."

Paul shook his head. "Boom town. People think they're saving up. I'll be glad when the pipeline's done and things get back to normal." It was scheduled to be done in about a year.

"Normal?" laughed Linda. "I doubt that things will ever be normal again! There's too much money floating around!"

"Money's not a bad thing," said Paul. "I'm hoping they start building schools in the villages. That ought to be the top of the agenda. Keep the kids in their homes."

"Would you go teach in a village, Paul?" Linda asked.

"No, I doubt it," said Paul. "I've been committed to the new West Valley high school for quite a while. It's supposed to open in the fall."

With a slam of the door, Brian entered and shook feathery snow off his jacket. "Hello, all!" he said, bussing his wife on the cheek.

"Paul, Linda," came Marie's voice. "Please come. We need an audience."

"Come on Brian," said Linda. "The kids have made a puppet show."

In the living room, Marie, little Nicholas and the other two kids tried to hide themselves behind a brown paper box, their sock-covered hands sticking up as characters. Brian, Paul and Linda sank down on the floor in front of the box.

"Little Rabbit Foo Foo," began Nicholas, "running through the forest, scooping up the field mice and bopping them over the head," he giggled, his stockinged hand pounding at two other little stockinged heads which stuck up.

Marie, the narrator, said "Down came the Good Fairy," and a Barbie doll in a long dress, held by little Peggy, whose brown face showed she was about six, wafted out of the sky. "I'll give you three chances. And if you don't behave, I'm going to turn you into a goon." The story was long, it was repetitive, it delighted the kids!

Brian hooted from the audience, "You're using up your chances, little Rabbit Foo Foo. Aren't you going to straighten up and fly right?"

"No!" shouted Nicholas. "Little Rabbit Foo Foo, running through the forest …" He bopped two little sock field mice over.

Paul was laughing. They all knew the story. But it never seemed to get old. Paul watched little Peggy and her brother Mike, giggling.

"And the moral of the story is!" said Marie slowly, nudging her little counterparts. "All together now."

The three kids' hands stood up, as well as the Barbie doll and shouted out the moral: "Hare today, goon tomorrow!" Nicholas tumbled over backward, and then jumped up to greet his father, who rolled over and over on the floor with him.

Paul thought again, as he had all year how much fun it was to have a woman to live with. Marie had brought him so much. Most especially a kind of clarity that he hadn't expected, the chance to quit worrying about things and think, really think, about his life. It was scary, though. He wasn't sure he could trust this happiness.

Everyone gathered around the table in the kitchen for stew and beers. Marie mused about food, as she often seemed to do. "Up here, people seem to balance the year, not the meal, or even the day," she said. "Like I hear now is a time to go looking for greens. One of the people I work with calls this season 'ducks', because it's the time they go out to the marshes to shoot migrating ducks. And then there's fish camp, and berry camp in the fall. I guess the human body adapts!"

"You're not kidding," said Linda. "In the winter your body wants fat and sugar!"

"And beer!" said Brian. "Washes down all that fat."

"Well, I'm ready for some greens," said Marie. They hadn't seen green stuff that wasn't frozen or canned for some time.

"I guess you're pretty busy, Brian," said Paul. "What are you working on?" Brian was now on a geological survey team attached to the University.

"Over near Mount McKinley," said Brian. "They've just designated the park an international biosphere reserve, through UNESCO. It doesn't change anything. It just means they're studying the area. They want to exchange research and experience across international lines. It's pretty interesting. I'm working on mapping, as usual. Keeps me closer to home, for the present," he said, looking toward Linda, who nodded appreciatively.

"I'd love to come out and hear you guys sing some time," said Linda. "But how could we ever get out so late at night?"

"Oh yes," said Marie. "You have to come some night to the restaurant. It's so much fun!" She worked in a restaurant run by a big warm Greek who loved his staff and managed to make an ethereal moussaka, even in Fairbanks. "There's not so much alcohol involved, you know, so we don't have the fights they have in the bars. But people stay late to sing and dance. Even Paul, on the weekends." She reached over and tugged at Paul's rough blonde beard. "He does a mean horos!"

"Wow!" said Brian. "I'd like to see that!"

"Kind of lop-sided," said Paul ruefully. He loved the Greek dance, but if it required prolonged weight on his skinny leg, it was tough. He was notoriously an early-to-bed type but the restaurant had become like a family. He could not refuse to bring his guitar and sing with Marie. He was often sleepy, up early and then late, but he was young. He wasn't worried about it. Everyone else was doing the same.

Linda looked at Brian. "We have to go," she said. "Now that it's going to get warmer. We'll just ship the kids to Anna's house?" she said questioningly.

"Maybe Marcia's," said Marie. Marcia had married Leon from Minto. They had an apartment in Fairbanks where Marcia, who was pregnant, thought it might be safer for her to have a baby. Marie's French Metis ancestors gave her an emotional investment in this dark little baby which would come to Marcia from Minnesota and her Athabascan husband. "Marcia and Leon's place isn't far from the restaurant."

"Well, we'll figure it out," said Brian. "With things getting warmer, everything gets easier. Pretty soon we'll all be running around in mudboots!"

It did get lighter and warmer, but the snow stayed on the ground. It was a great time for cross-country skiing. Paul and Marie went out to Arvi and Carol's house on Chena Ridge. Paul showed Marie the little log cabin where he had spent his first two winters, and the sauna where people still came to sweat the dirt off and to talk. "I had a little red fox that first year for a friend," said Paul. "He kept stopping by and I'd put my frying pan out for him to taste the leavings." They looked in the cabin windows. Someone obviously lived there, but they weren't home at the moment.

Paul heard Arvi's voice. Arvi had seen them skiing through the woods. "Paul!" he yelled. "Stop by for a cup of tea. Carol's just put the kettle on." No one was more sociable and welcoming than the Kukkonens.

A pungent smell filled the warm kitchen. "Juniper tea," said Carol. "The Athabascans use the branches, but I like the berries." She filled mugs for each of them and they sat down at the long table in the big room surrounded by wooden shelves of jars, cans, boxes of food. Books lined the shelves on one side, sliding off the sides. "We never throw anything away," Carol had told Paul.

Marie had met the big, affable Arvi and his petite wife Carol before. "Juniper berries?" she asked. "Don't they use them to flavor gin?"

"Sure do," said Arvi. "But they make a nice tea too."

"I'm ready for anything living, green or otherwise!" said Marie.

"Come on, Marie," said Carol. "I've got a few things growing in a cold frame on the south side. A few shoots make all the difference, sometimes." Marie followed Carol out to the back of the house.

"I've been reading that Minnesotan of yours, Paul," Arvi said. "Sigurd Olson. He's doing great work, as I hear."

Paul could never get enough of Arvi. He was always bringing up things Paul wanted to think about. Arvi knew all aspects of science, but also anthropology, and history, theater and politics. He had reputedly read all the books in the house. "I connect everything," Arvi told Paul. "It's like a spiderweb up there. Everything fits somewhere in my brain, connected to something else." Arvi had worked as an electrician, was an educator, and was involved in countless service and community projects across Alaska. Arvi was what Paul wanted to be, though Paul knew he would never be as sociable.

"Yeah," said Paul. "My mother has Olson's books."

"Olson's helping get Alaskan wilderness land set aside, and also the boundary waters area between Minnesota and Canada," said Arvi. "Did you ever spend time up there, Paul? Is that boreal forest? Or not?" Growing ecological interest was resulting in intense study and definition of geographical ecosystems, now called biomes.

"Part of it may be boreal, in Canada. You don't find much boreal forest south of the fiftieth parallel. Our lake is in central Minnesota, not that far north," said Paul. "I've canoed around our lake, but I never get Dad to take much time for exploring. He's always building."

"I know the feeling," said Arvi. "But I do agree with Olson that wilderness has a power over us, a power to connect us to ourselves. I've heard Olson is none too popular with people in his hometown. And of course he doesn't know as much about Alaska as we do. But it is helpful to have people like that working at the national level. The Wilderness Society and all."

"It's mining country up around Lake Superior," said Paul. He wished he knew more about it. Arvi respected anyone who stood firm. Arvi himself was usually at the head of some grass-roots liberal campaign or other. A little lightbulb began to go off in Paul's brain, but he didn't have time to think about it now.

"So Arvi," asked Paul, changing the subject. "Do you think they're going to start building village schools as a result of all this money pouring into the state?"

"Yes," said Arvi. "Won't take long now. They've got to settle that Molly Hootch class action. I think the time is right. We'll see it soon." A group of students' families had sued the State for discrimination, saying that it did not provide local high school facilities for predominantly native communities when it did for the same-sized, predominantly non-native, communities.

Marie returned with Carol, displaying a few precious greens in a plastic bag. "See!" she said.

"Nothing like a homestead," said Carol. "You can try anything!" The Kukkonens had lived on Chena Ridge since the 1950's. By now their holdings were very developed.

"Like horses!" said Arvi. "No one thought you could have horses this far north. But Carol does."

"I love to hear them snuffling in their stable against the house. Keeps us tied down, though," said Carol. "We've traveled a lot, but not right now. The kids need to finish school."

Paul rose. "Well," he said, Minnesota-style, "We shouldn't keep you. Thank you so much for inviting us in." He and Marie wrapped themselves up again, against the cold.

On Wednesday that week, Paul found himself forming a question in his mind as he stood in front of the room where he taught, chemistry book open on his desk. When had men begun to work against nature instead of with it, as indigenous cultures did? Somewhere in Europe, for sure. Was it the Scandinavians? But students began ranging into the desks in front of him. It was these types of questions that got him in trouble, Paul knew. Why couldn't he just stick to the book?! The bell rang and he called the class to order.

Paul did stick to the book. It was safest, and students needed to know the basics: how scientists looked at atoms and molecules, the properties of elements, how gases and solutions worked, what were the various states of matter. Essential for scientific purposes. Paul applied them to life as much as possible, but who was he kidding. What education really did was help a few students go on to college. The rest of them would forget it as soon as they got back to their own lives.

Lathrop high school was a mix of all kinds of students, the kids whose parents were officers at the US Army's Fort Wainwright, professors at the University, homesteaders, pipeliners and miners, as well as Eskimo and Indian students boarding in from the villages.

Here was Jerry Field, whose father made him "drop and give me 20" pushups for the least infraction. Here was Jean Jones, female track star from homesteading parents on Chena Ridge. And here was Chrissy Jansen, an ambitious, bossy socialite who had her heart set on a preppy college on the East Coast. Randy Alexander, Leon's brother and one of Paul's star Athabascan students, was now attending the University of Alaska. Everyone had pulled strings to get him scholarships to go to school. He worked part time, of course, but so did everyone.

Trying to reach the students where they lived was tough, but Paul was good at it. He was a moderate, understanding discipline but lenient where necessary. He was beginning to feel he was a good teacher, but he liked sticking to basic science. It was impossible to keep up with everything that was going on. He did try on his own, taking at least one class at the University every year. But he was more interested in philosophical issues than in the details of how acids and bases were being used in creating new substances, or the esoteric uses of thermochemistry. He did worry that as time went on, his homemade, holistic teaching style would be overwhelmed by those wanting high-level reductive science.

Paul was sure that, with good textbooks, most Eskimo and Indian kids would be better off in their own villages in high school. Fourteen was too young to get thrown into a different family as a boarder, with completely different cultural ideas. Having your community, your family around you was more important than having the highest academics, with some exceptions for bright, ambitious kids. It was difficult to do serious academic teaching, even in the city.

At lunch Paul brought his tray into the tiny teachers' lounge and put it down beside Alf the shop teacher. Students talked about teachers out in the lunchroom, and here teachers talked about students freely! An English teacher was complaining loudly that no one cared about grammar any more. Paul stole a look at Alf. They both thought grammar was the least of their worries! Paul did get his students to write as often as possible. It helped comprehension. But he wasn't too worried about perfect English.

"How are they going to get into college?" railed the English teacher.

"Colleges don't care either," said another. "Spoken English, written down, is the future. If you get these native kids to speak at all, you're lucky."

Inuit and Yupik kids had a language of facial gestures Paul had tried to learn. He found it fascinating. What he loved most about all of the Eskimo and Indian kids was the quality of attention they could command, if they happened to be interested in something.

"High school is about standards!" said the English teacher, looking around for support.

Paul had trouble keeping from smirking as Alf kicked him under the table. Détente and courtesy ruled in the teachers' lounge. Teaching was difficult enough without the teachers battling over molehills. After finishing their food Paul and Alf went and stood out in the back while Alf had a cigarette.

"She's kind of right, of course. But also not," said Alf, dragging on his smoke with the corner of his mouth.

"I agree," said Paul. "Marcia, who's been here a lot longer than I have, has shown me how the Athabascans teach their kids to be ready and alert to change, especially in the environment. Things are always changing. English changes too. Keeps it interesting!"

"Standards are a base, but they have their limits," said Alf.

The diverse population of students made all of these questions have more dimensions than could possibly be nailed down once and for all. Paul felt lucky to have had Arvi, with whom he could talk about anything at all, as a mentor in the early years. Arvi always took the time for it.

By evening the wind had shifted. It was clear from horizon to horizon with prospects of an aurora later that night. Paul wondered whether he would be able to stay up late enough to see it.

The apartment Paul and Marie shared with their roommate Jake was empty, as was often the case. Marie was at the restaurant. Jake, who had an administrative job for Alyeska, the company building the pipeline between Prudhoe Bay and Valdez, was in Anchorage. He moved around a lot.

Paul turned on the oil stove. He was glad for time alone to unwind and think about all the things he had been too busy to turn over in his mind. In the refrigerator was a leftover pot of chili. Paul took it out and put it on the stove burner.

Slowly Paul's brains opened into the space, his own space. He was thinking about Sigurd Olson. He thought Olson's writing about wilderness was mushy compared to Athabascan and Eskimo stories, which were very direct. The Alaskan natives were practical, moving about to find food during different seasons. They believed all creatures, and some inanimate things, had spirits. Their quests involved intimate knowledge of the interlacing of their environment. No one had to explain ecosystems to them!

Olson's romanticism about wilderness had to do with civilization, with the divorce between men and their environment. When did it start? Paul wondered. It was happening in Alaska now, as people forsook the old subsistence ways and relied more on technology. Paul wondered what work Marcia's husband Leon would find when pipeline construction was finished.

And what about me, Paul wondered. Where do I fall in all this? The main thing, he realized, was that living in Alaska helped him unlearn the intense Christianity which, growing up, had been his only reality. The world was much larger than he had supposed as a child. It could not be divided up into who was saved by belief in Christ and who was not. Paul had sloughed off this dividing line, central to his early thought, along with the language surrounding it.

Athabascan customs, those he knew most about from his visits to Minto, were still confusing to Paul. He could not really get a feel for how they understood money and property. Ownership was a deeply ingrained habit of Christian culture Paul knew he had absorbed! At the same time, Paul had been raised not to put much stock in possessions. "Lay not up for yourself treasures on earth where moth and rust corrupt," Christ had said. In the Mikkelson family, a fine inner life, kindness, altruism were more valued than property and wealth.

Paul wondered if he needed to make more money if he wanted to have a family with Marie. He had always made enough to make himself happy and do the things he wanted to do: buy books, study, some left for travel. But teacher's salaries were small. It might not be enough for a family. Did he dare talk about this with Marie? No, he wasn't ready for that!

Paul sighed, spooning up chili in the growing twilight. The oil heater glowed in the corner. He hated to turn on the lights, much preferring natural light. Not much moon tonight, but the snow would be glowing. He wondered what his own path should be. Arvi's mention of the boundary waters between Canada and Minnesota had set up a pang of homesickness. He guessed there were probably twenty degrees of latitude between Fairbanks and Ely. Paul set about looking through books and maps, trying to figure this out.

Fairbanks was 65 degrees north of the equator, as near as he could tell, while Ely, Minnesota, headquarters of the boundary waters area and home to Sigurd Olson, was about 48 degrees north. Thirteen degrees. The difference between boreal forest and coniferous forest, he noted.

Paul remembered how keenly he had wanted to go canoeing on the boundary waters as a kid. He had never done so. But he also remembered how ubiquitous church membership and culture were in Minnesota. What he wanted, to the extent it was possible, was to see the world unfiltered by any religion or pre-existing cultural assumptions. Would that be possible in the thick religious atmosphere of the Midwest?

In Alaska, cultures bumped up against each other. Eskimos, Indians, remnants of the Christian missionary and Russian cultures, as well as Greeks and Quakers, gold-diggers and boomers. You could not make assumptions about anyone you met, and no one made assumptions about you. Paul had found himself sensitive to the conflicts, even when not expressed.

Bonhoeffer's *Letters and Papers from Prison*, which included much questioning of Christian institutions, had helped Paul think about his own beliefs. Bonhoeffer never gave up on revelation, and used dedicated Bible study, especially the legacy of Christ's words, to find his way. Jung too had veered away from his fundamentalist Christian father, wanting direct experience rather than faith.

Marie had left her Roman Catholicism behind in an attempt to meet the modern world face to face. It was something they shared. Paul felt grateful to know her. How simply she had agreed to come to Fairbanks with him, driving her little truck up from Seattle. She was a rolling stone for certain.

The next thing Paul knew, Marie was shaking him. He raised his head from where it was pillowed on his desk on the papers, maps and books. He had fallen asleep!

"Paul," Marie's voice was urgent. "It's so beautiful out. You must come. The aurora is waving like a green banner across the sky!" Her hands were cold. She stood there in a parka and boots, her face ruddy and glowing.

Paul stood up and stretched. "What time is it?" he asked, scratching his beard.

"Maybe two o'clock," said Marie. "But you have to come out. It's hardly ever this clear! And the stars are amazing."

Paul pulled on boots and parka. He and Marie went out and stood in the middle of the wide street. Heaps of snow along the road wavered and flickered with a green glow. A strong green band spanned the sky to the west, undulating like a curtain, alive and changing. Ragged spruce roughened the edges of the narrow road, but there were big spaces between them. There was no moon and the Milky Way looked as dense as the aurora. Looking east between the trees, the stars looked like they might fall on them.

Marie's eyes, stuffed back in her hooded parka, were bright, but it was cold enough that it was hard to understand her. Paul thought she was trying to thank him for the experience. He caught her hand with his bare ones and brought her gloved fingers to his lips. Marie put her hand on his shoulder, and he reached up to hers.

"Ta daaaaa," Marie began in rhythm like a Greek mandolin. Paul could hear the music in his mind. "Ta daaaaa, ta daaaaa ...." Lifting their other arms expressively, they stepped slowly together in their thick boots. She was a master, had been doing the syrtaki every night all winter.

Who knew, Paul thought, that I would be doing Greek dances under the aurora borealis in Alaska with a beautiful girl, in my life. Who would have thought it possible?

21

Line stayed home from the Santa Cruz parade, watching instead on television as Marian Anderson read the Declaration of Independence in Philadelphia on the two hundredth anniversary of its signing. The newest little Cohen, one-week old Ivy, who had been something of a surprise, lay in her arms.

Line was delighted to be alone for a moment with Ivy, who ferociously sucked at her full breast as she sat on the sofa. It was a warm day and light shimmered behind the creamy drapes on the south-facing windows. After Anderson's rich voice read, President Ford described what had happened to those who signed the Declaration while an armada of British ships lay in New York harbor: prison, sons lost, homes destroyed, death. Line thought how blessed she was, holding her tiny daughter in her arms while the rest of her family watched a peaceful parade on the main street of their town.

Yes, America isn't perfect, Line thought. Yes, corporate interests prevail. Yes, we have a long way to go in alleviating poverty, racism and poor education. But really, couldn't we all, for just one day, be grateful?! She was. America was a two hundred year old experiment.

Line stroked the little head. Ivy wasn't as dark as Fern, who had gotten her black hair from some unknown ancestor, but she was an intense little thing. All of the kids are, thought Line. Ivy would be the last. After her birth Line had let a surgeon put little rings on her Fallopian tubes, clamping them off so she could not have more children.

Luckily she had been able to import her sister Kristen from Iowa for the summer, to marshal the other kids, cook and generally help out. Letters flew back and forth between Kristen and a boyfriend who had only grown more important the longer Kristen was away. Line knew she was miserable so far from home, but she would probably survive. Kristen would go back to finish nursing school in the fall. She had been thrilled to be present at Ivy's home birth a week ago.

Line stretched out on the sofa, Ivy resting on top of her. She was tired, but she too would survive. When she opened her eyes, the room was full of kids, Christy dancing in front of the television on which several tall ships were parading down the Hudson, Heather sweetly climbing up on a chair to reach the bowl of cherries and Fern, holding tight to Stephen's hand.

"How was the parade?" Line asked.

"Hot and sticky," said Stephen. He sat down on the carpet and made a circle of his long legs for Fern to sit in. "But it will be nice tonight for the fireworks, unless the fog comes in."

"Kristen?" she asked, looking around.

"I think she went into her room," Stephen said.

Line nodded. Kristen always dove into her room when she returned, looking for any message Line would have left on the little desk. She was getting a lot of messages, but none today.

"Hey," said Christy. "Look at this one! So many sails!" He stood aside so the rest of them could see the ship on the screen in front of them. "There're sailors up in the sails!"

"Up on the masts, " said Stephen. "So many ropes! Every sail must have four or five ropes. Imagine keeping all that straight!"

"Is that the Hudson?" asked Line, peering at the screen.

"Well," said Stephen. "New York Harbor. I think that's the Verrazano Bridge in the background. They were building it when I was in high school."

"It's in New York?" Christy asked, excited. "Do you think Poppa is there?" Poppa, Stephen's father, had visited California that summer, raising in Christy a lively picture of New York City.

"I am sure he is," said Stephen. "He goes to everything."

Line thought of her father-in-law, all that remained of Stephen's family. The son of Russian immigrants, involved in immigration law, no one would appreciate the Bicentennial more than Poppa. Line felt blissfully happy, thinking of everyone she knew and all her own family safe around her. Mother and Dad might be going to a hometown parade today. Marty? Maybe not. Paul was in Fairbanks doing construction work for the summer. There would surely be a parade there.

Kristen slunk out of the dark hall and into the living room. She sat down on the sofa beside Line and reached for tiny, precious Ivy. Line handed her over, smiling. "And what do you think your Scott is doing today?" she asked.

Kristen mumbled, smiling shyly over the baby which she had lifted carefully to her shoulder. "I think he went fishing with his brother," she said. She wore shorts like everyone else, and a sleeveless button-up shirt, her blonde hair cut short. "I think their Dad let them off for the day." Scott's dad ran a big farming operation in northern Iowa, with livestock and fields planted to feed. Of the brothers, Scott was really the farmer. His brother wanted to study electronics when he got older. Line thought of all the information she had gotten out of Kristen about this family she had never met. Kristen would be a farmer's wife, thought Line. Did she know what that meant?

Ivy slept. She seemed happy as long as she was in someone's arms. Not too choosy about it. But that had been true of the others too, thought Line. Babies just want to be held. Line stood up shakily. The birth had been fairly easy, but she had two small incisions in her tummy which were healing from the tubal ligation.

Line went into the kitchen. She had hardly done anything for the last week, leaving the childcare and cooking to Kristen and Stephen. The ever-fastidious Heather carefully deposited cherry pits in the trash. Line looked about the kitchen Kristen had neatly battened down. Nothing had to be done today either. She could relax.

All of a sudden Stephen stood up, quieting the kids and paying attention to the television. Harry Reasoner introduced cameras on the People's Bicentennial celebration in Washington, D.C. Yellow flags printed with a black rattlesnake waved in the breeze and people in the crowd wore the black tri-corner hats of the time of the first revolution. The commentator described a peaceful protest on the capitol mall, with speakers warning against the growing power of multi-national corporations.

Stephen smacked his fist into his hand. "Yes," he said. But the coverage was brief, no more than two minutes. As if he had been waiting for this bit of news coverage, Stephen swung into action. "I'm going to set up the barbecue," he said.

Line followed Stephen outdoors to the backyard to catch a moment alone with him. It was rare these days. She reached around his skinny chest, hugging him. "I'm feeling very grateful today," she said. "Thank you, Stephen. For everything." He must know that she meant for the baby, for their life. Like her, he was surprised to find himself, 34 years old with four kids!

But Stephen never complained. The deal they had tacitly established over the years was that they could each have their work. It meant that Stephen spent long hours at the university, while Line ran the household. They were both happy and thriving.

"I'm going to get small again," Line said, leaning into Stephen as they walked out to the garage. She couldn't wait. It seemed she had been pregnant forever.

"As small as me?" teased Stephen.

"No way," said Line. Stephen was a stick, his second-hand clothes hanging on him. He did not seem to care about food, tucking an apple in his backpack and taking off on his bicycle in the mornings, coming home late in the evenings. "But smaller," she said. "I don't want to be Jack Spratt's wife!"

"You are my beautiful wife," said Stephen, putting his arms around Line and kissing her. "You're not that big. I'm proud of you and of our kids. I too am grateful today, to those men who created our country. If they only knew."

"But we know," said Line. "As you've said." Teaching history had given Stephen perspective, as he told Line. It had shown him that generations could only build on what they had been given. He did not regret his revolutionary past as part of SDS in the last decade, but felt it had gone as far as it could go. He was now sifting that past, writing about SDS and its contributions. The Vietnam war was finally behind them.

"When I was watching television this morning, I was grateful that it wasn't Tricky Dick trying to tell us about our history!" Line said. "Can you imagine?" The enemy was no longer silence and moribund tradition. Since Watergate, it had shifted to political corruption and the surging power of multi-national corporate interests in the great military-industrial complex the United States had become.

Stephen shook his head. "Today I'm going to think about John Adams and Thomas Jefferson," he said. "I think we're allowed." He headed for the garage where he hauled out the Weber grill onto a little patio. The house was too old and the windows at the back too small to have a nice relationship between the house and the backyard. But against the garage was a patio with a picnic table where they often ate, shaded by an old wisteria vine.

Line turned toward the garden. Evidence of drought was everywhere. The grassy area was dry and yellow, covered with toys. The leaves of the trees were yellowed and brown, showing their burnt edges. A pine tree was losing its needles, which made the garage roof look almost red with the dried refuse. Under the apricot tree, bees buzzed over the last squashed fruits which were turning to dried, sweet leather. Line and Kristen had harvested hundreds, making pies, cakes and many jars of jam. Some were on drying racks in the garage.

Line knelt down by the garden. Not only did she need to get smaller, she thought. She also needed to get back the strength in her legs. But she would. Kids were good exercise. She clucked over her squashes, her melons, the poles of green beans and the dry-looking carrot tops. In the potato patch, the strong stems looked wilted, and so did the tomatoes. Heat was good for them, of course, but only if there was enough water for them to make fruit. Line saved the water from while the shower was getting hot and any other water she thought safe for her garden, watering sparingly.

Heather came over the hot grass toward Line. "Kristen's making lemonade," she said. She had a need to keep Line posted at all times!

"Is the baby sleeping?" asked Line. She had hardly spent any time away from Ivy in the last week.

"Yes," said Heather. Kristen had pulled Heather's blonde hair up in a pony tail to keep it from being sweaty. But her skin was damp when Line reached around to hug her.

"And what's Fern doing?" asked Line, releasing her. Heather was somewhat placid and chunky. Line did not think she would be a stick like her father. Fern and Christy had skinny little bodies more like his.

"Nothing," said Heather. "She's just watching TV."

Line propped up a plant here and there, removed a leaf so as to give another light while she listened to Heather. There were a few borage plants for tea, mint, chives along the borders, parsley, oregano. Line had learned how much sun each of these herbs wanted in the two years since they had bought the house.

"Okay," said Line absently. She did not need to ask about Christy. He displayed a lively interest in the outside world and could not be torn from the television if it were on. Some boys his age would have leapt to help light coals in the barbecue, but not Christy. He still didn't willingly hang out with his father, though Poppa, when he came out from New York, had set up a model airplane workshop in the garage and succeeded in interesting Christy.

Taking Heather's hand, Line walked around to the front of the house. The wide stretch of lawn which went out to the sidewalk was hardly used. At the border with their neighbor were some hardy old roses, a few rosemary bushes and sage. On the east side was an alley, shaded by tall pine trees. Smack in the center of the yard was a low weeping willow tree. It suffered from the heat, but must be getting water from deep below. Heather went to it immediately and was lost under its long fronds.

It was an odd house. The original garage had been converted into the large living room and a new two-car garage added off the alley. It worked well, but Line wished she could use the front yard better, maybe making a series of raised beds. No one would care, Line thought. A cement wall across the street blocked the noise and traffic on the thru-way, but the neighbors did use the front of their houses for show. One was lavish with roses and another served up a crepe myrtle which was beginning to bloom in brilliant cerise. But this was not the year for enlarging plantings. Line sighed. She would have to wait. She felt that she did nothing but wait!

Now that Ivy was born, Line felt she could look ahead to the time when the kids were more grown up and she was more free. She wanted to go back to work as a nurse, or as a nurse-midwife. The court case for her midwife friends still dragged on. Kate Bowland had had two babies by this time. "I've had more court dates than neonatal appointments!" she said. Line had been in court with her, pregnant herself.

The front yard was hot. Line crept in under the willow tree with Heather. Her legs hurt and her stomach hurt. But she had to start living sometime! "What are you playing?" she asked Heather, who sat plump on her knees, holding nothing in her hands but some willow leaves, swaying back and forth.

"Laura and Mary," said Heather. "I'm Laura and you can be Mary."

Line lay down on the ground under the tree, looking up into its drooping branches. How lovely they were. Probably all little girls wanted to be Laura, she thought. Laura was the active one, the one who took care of her sisters and wrote the *Little House* books. Line would have liked to lie under the willow tree forever, but she was feeling twinges of fear, worrying about whether Kristen was all right, whether the baby had fallen. "I'm going back," Line said. "Are you coming with me?"

Heather seemed reluctant, but she crawled out from under the willow fronds after Line on the dry yellow grass. "We should go back," she echoed. "Pa might be looking for us."

"Or Ma," Line said. She giggled to herself. She was the Ma of the family, after all. Every strand of relationship in the house connected directly to her. She could not escape, nor did she want to. She was the spider constructing her web, partly by accident, partly by choice. "Remember the picture of the bed covered with wrapped up babies in the Big Woods where Laura went to the dance at Grandma's," she asked Heather. None of them, Line reflected, had been born in a hospital!

"We have a wrapped up baby too," said Heather solemnly.

Line felt buoyed up by her tiny escape. She hugged Heather. "Help me up!" she said, reaching a teasing hand up to her four-year-old daughter. Heather tugged, but she wasn't much help. Line struggled to her feet.

Back in the house, no one seemed to have missed them. Kristen was patting ground meat into hamburger shapes, while Fern sat in her high chair eating crackers. The television droned on and Ivy lay on a blanket on the living room carpet. Line attached all her various strands again. "Christy, please turn off the television, and go out and see whether Dad has the fire ready. Heather can you help Kristen get picnic plates and cups?" She leaned down and picked up little Ivy.

That night when it grew dark, firecrackers and sparklers could be heard popping and dancing around the neighborhood. Christy was beside himself, but Stephen did not want to drive down to the beach and get involved in the press of people and cars. "We'll go up behind the house, up on the golf course," he said, "And see what we can see."

"Fern should go to bed," said Line tentatively. Fern's little dark eyes were droopy. She was only two.

"I'll carry her," said Stephen. "After all, when is this going to happen again?"

"Put some sweaters on," Line chided. Line watched the little party set off, Kristen with Heather on one side and sturdy little Christy on the other, Stephen carrying Fern. "Have fun!" she said.

Line followed them mentally up into the hills. Their residential neighborhood was blocked off from the center of town by the Cabrillo Highway, and it was impossible to get to a grocery store without a car. But north of them was a big elementary school and beyond that an old vineyard trail, the golf course and parks. Hopefully Stephen could find a high place from which to watch. The air was clear and it might be possible to see fireworks for miles.

Line had had enough television. She put a Buffy St. Marie album on the record player and danced a little with Ivy in her arms in the middle of the spacious living room. There was still no furniture except for a couch. Line liked it that way. "So appreciate a dedicated baby, but boy you are a lucky man," she sang with Buffy, stomping her bare feet. "It's just 'cause I got a little crush on you."

Joni Mitchell lyrics were interspersed with Buffy's own songs. But "The Circle Game" was ubiquitous, everywhere, insipid by this time. Buffy's songs were wonderful. Line would never tire of them. "I'm not a queen, I'm a woman, take my hand," she sang. "We'll make a space in the lives that we've planned. And here we'll stay until it's time for you to go." Buffy's long vibrato stretched out the words. Yes, Line thought. Life is good.

But she was asleep again when the door burst open and Heather said loudly, "Christy's gone!"

Line opened her eyes. Ivy lay on the floor below. "So what else is new," she said in what she hoped was recognized as Poppa's clipped New York accent. She knew it sounded a little callous, but she couldn't help it. "Did you see the fireworks?" she asked.

"A little," said Kristen. "They were kind of far away."

Stephen carried Fern into her bed. "Put her on the potty first," called Line. "You should go to bed also," she said to the girls.

"Come on Heather," said Kristen, catching Heather's hand, two blonde girls. "I'll help you."

When Stephen emerged he went into the kitchen and reached up high on the shelf. "I think I need a gin and tonic," he said. "Do you want one?"

Line considered. She knew that everything she ate and drank passed into the tiny body of her new baby. But probably a little gin wouldn't hurt either of them. "Sure," she said. "Just a little one." She could hear the ice cubes as Stephen prepared the glasses.

"Does Kristen want one?" Stephen asked.

"Wait until she comes back," said Line. "I'm not sure she's coming back." Stephen handed her a glass.

"To freedom," Stephen said, reaching out to touch her glass with his. "To diversity, equality, fraternity."

"My comrade in arms," said Line. "To you." She drank the cold, fizzy liquid. "Oh my god this is good," she said.

"So what about Christy?" asked Stephen. "We looked all over, and called. But he had just disappeared." He sat down on the carpet beside Ivy.

"I'm really not worried about him," said Line. "I can easily imagine him lured off by his friends and some smoke bombs or something. He knows this neighborhood like the back of his hand. Eight years old. On a farm he'd already be driving the tractor."

"I do think you are letting him get away from you," said Stephen.

"That kid, like me, needs a long leash," said Line, taking another swallow from her glass. "Is Kristen coming?"

Stephen looked down the hall. "I think she's in the bathroom."

"I was thinking about how different I was from Kristen," said Line. "I had a farmer boyfriend. I used to ride my bike out five miles to see him. Remember? I think I told you." The beautiful undulating fields, plowed to the contours of the hills to prevent erosion and striped in colors of gold, green and black, unrolled in front of Line's mind's eye. "But I knew I couldn't stay there. I was nothing like Kristen."

"But you're both nurses," said Stephen. "That's interesting."

"Exact same parents," said Line. "But there are seven years between us."

"Do you think the times were enough to catapult you down South? And then to Chicago and California?" Stephen asked.

"What else could it be?" asked Line. "Kristen can't wait to get home."

Kristen emerged from the dark hall, looking anxious.

"Want a glass of something?" asked Stephen.

"No, thank you," Kristen said. "I'm sorry about Christy. I just turned around and he wasn't there!"

"The little sneak," said Stephen.

"Kristen, go look in his bed," said Line. "Maybe he came in when I was asleep." She and Stephen exchanged looks. "I promise I'll talk to him in the morning," Line said. "I bet he looked around for you too and couldn't find you."

Stephen looked exasperated. "Quite a day," he said. He looked toward the kitchen. "Another?" he asked Line.

"No thanks," Line smiled at him. "You can't wait to get back to work tomorrow," she said.

"Well at least I know what I'm doing," said Stephen. "Kids, man," he said. "You're just like the momma cat here, surrounded by kittens."

Line giggled. "You've had a tough week," she said. "But I think we are all going to make it." Stephen had stuck with her, helping with everything. "I love you so much, my darling."

When Kristen returned she looked much more relaxed. "He's there," she said. "Sleeping in his clothes."

Stephen's face tightened scornfully. "I'm telling you Line," he said. "That kid is on your hands."

Line turned solemn. "I know," she said. "I'm sorry Stephen." She looked up at Kristen. "So how was your day? Are you celebrating your freedom?"

Kristen sank down on the sofa beside her, but she hung her head a little. She didn't seem to like attention being turned to her. "Okay," she said. She leaned down and picked up Ivy.

Line let Kristen off. "I'm sure Scott is thinking about you while he's fishing," she said.

Kristen heaved a big sigh. "He could call," she said.

Line had trouble not laughing. "You talked to him a couple of days ago, didn't you?" No accounting for taste, she thought. How many girls would kill to spend the summer in Santa Cruz! She looked sideways at Stephen who stood up and went back into the kitchen for more ice, gin and tonic.

Kristen nodded her head. "The time just seems long," she said.

"Time is tough when you're in love," said Line. She patted Kristen's arm. "But look what it leads to!" She opened her arms. "Houses, kids, husbands, happiness!"

Stephen laughed at her. "Only one husband, please, my dear."

Going back to their earlier conversation, Line continued: "I see the kids as a garden," she said. "Each of them needs something different. Water, shade, sunlight." She leaned over toward Kristen and into Ivy's short field of vision to see if she would react. "And what are you going to need?" she asked. "You little girl?" Line shook her red-gold curls at the tiny baby. "Her skin's not so red any more, is it?" she asked.

22

Line heard Fern screaming from the bedroom. That was not so unusual, but Stephen yelling, "Line! Line!" That was. Line put Ivy in her little bed and went out into the kitchen. "Fern's been scalded," said Stephen. "She pulled a cup of hot tea on herself! I'm calling an ambulance."

"Scissors," said Line. She ran to her sewing kit and back to the screaming Fern. Ceramic shards littered the floor. She cut off the little turtleneck t-shirt Fern was wearing. Red and white water blisters were rising on her chest and neck. Christy and Heather stood watching, transfixed. Line wrapped Fern in a cotton blanket, poured milk into one of Ivy's bottles and gave it to Fern to suck. She was shaking. "There, there," she said, laying her on the sofa. "It's going to be okay." Not right away, she thought. But someday. She could not tell exactly how badly Fern had been burnt.

Stephen cleaned up the shards of ceramic, barking at the kids to go get dressed and put some shoes on. Line rushed into the bedroom, put on layers of sweaters and tucked Ivy into the Snugli. It was February and cold. When she came out the emergency technicians were at the door.

"They want to take her straight to Stanford," said Stephen low to Line. "There's a burn unit there. It's only 45 minutes away."

Two-and-a-half-year-old Fern was so little she only took a third of the stretcher. Line kissed the small, contorted face. She climbed in after the stretcher to sit on the bench beside it.

"You can't take that baby into the burn center," said the EMT. He bound down Fern's little hand and attached an IV to it. She started screaming all over again.

"But I can't leave her," said Line. She wasn't thinking too straight, she knew. She hoped there was a painkiller in the IV.

"You can't take her," said the EMT.

"But I'm a nurse," said Line.

"You can't take any children under 12 into a burn unit," said the EMT flatly. "Too much danger of infection. Come on, ma'am," he said. "We have to go!"

Line stepped out of the ambulance, giving Stephen, who stood at the door, an anguished look.

"I'll go," said Stephen who stood at the door. "Call the university," he said. "Tell them I'm not coming in."

"I'll bring the kids in the car," said Line. "Stanford, right? The Medical Center?"

"Take it easy," said the EMT as he shut the door on Line and her kids standing in the driveway. "Don't rush. Your daughter is going to be all right."

Line knew he was right. She tried to remember what she knew about burns, hoping she had done the best she could for little Fern. The ambulance took off with its lights flashing.

Christy was crying too and Line saw that Heather was still barefoot. "It was my fault," Christopher said. "We were horsing around and the cup flew off the table."

"Get some clothes on, and some shoes!" Line said, shepherding them back into the house. "None of us will go to school today," she decided. "Let me see your feet, Heather," she said. She wanted to make sure they weren't cut. She made phone calls, leaving messages for teachers and Cowell, Stephen's college.

Now that it was quiet, Line tried to move slowly so as not to make more mistakes. She put Ivy in her infant carrier and buckled it into the passenger seat of the car. She made sure Heather had her seatbelt on and told Christy to buckle his. Then she headed in the general direction of Palo Alto. "Keep an eye out for signs to Stanford Medical Center," she said to Christy. "Or I'll just ask someone, if we can't find it."

The Medical Center was a warren of buildings. "Pediatrics. The burn center," said Line clearly, and an attendant directed her to a parking lot. Line had no idea how she had gotten there.

Inside, the familiar smell of Lysol and plastic met Line's nose. There was a big waiting room full of little kids and grownups, but no Stephen. Line sighed. The burn center was on an upper floor. "You can't go up there with those kids," said nurse attendant.

"My husband's up there," Line said. "Could you page him and ask him to come down?" She settled the kids in a corner and Heather picked up a coloring book. Christy had gone into protective mode. He scanned the room, looking for trouble to point out to Line, trying to be the little father of the family.

After half an hour, Stephen got off an elevator. All of the Cohens stood up to receive him. "Second and some third degree burns," said Stephen. "Mostly on her neck. But she's going to be fine. They are filling her full of fluids and nourishment. They'll need to keep her about a week, they told me."

"That damned little turtleneck," said Line, shaking her head. "I couldn't get it off quick enough." She handed Ivy to Stephen, who put on the Snugli and stood in the corner with the kids while Line took the elevator upstairs.

The nurses made Line put on a mask, gown and cloth booties on her feet. Fern looked tiny in a big white hospital bed. Her chest was swathed in bandages, her eyes were shut and her little dark face looked wan. She was attached to two IV's, one for fluid and one for nutrients, Line

222

guessed. What a lot of pain for a little girl, thought Line as she kissed and stroked the little face. The skin was such an important organ, maybe the most important.

A nurse came in. Speaking through her face mask, she said, "We measure all the fluids in and out." She showed Line the little catheter collecting Fern's urine. "We don't want her to have kidney problems later in life," she said. "So much of the body's fluid goes to healing the burn we really have to pump liquids through."

When Fern didn't wake up, Line realized that Stephen couldn't come, so she would have to go down. When she got there, she took Ivy, who looked restive and hungry. Line sat down and gave her a breast.

"I called Poppa," said Stephen. "He's going to come out for the week. He'll watch the kids and we can come up here in the evenings. I think we both have to come because of Ivy. We can take turns."

"Oh, that's wonderful," said Line. "I was trying to think how we were going to manage." Stephen's level head did come through when she needed him.

That night Stephen picked up Poppa at the airport. Line found him as chipper as ever, his grey hair curling back from his high forehead, a little bow tie at his neck. Christy had refused to go to bed until he arrived. But after the kids finally went to bed, Line made Poppa a cup of tea. The grownups sat talking at the kitchen table.

"Christy thinks it's his fault," said Line. "Though I've tried to tell him it was an accident." Ceiling lights shone down on them and the electric heat hissed in the units along the wall.

"I should have been watching," said Stephen, shaking his head. "Shouldn't have put my cup there."

"I'll settle that little guy's hash," said Poppa. "Fault doesn't help anyone. Not you either, my son."

"Do you think we can go in to the hospital tomorrow morning?" Line asked Stephen. "I'd like to watch them doing the dressing." It was still Friday, and tomorrow would be Saturday. She wanted to assess for herself the skin underneath Fern's dressing.

"Sure," said Stephen. Saturday was usually his day for catching up at his university office. But the term was just beginning.

"It was so horrible," said Line, struggling to relax. The scene at the ambulance that morning passed in front of her eyes. "Having to choose between my children." She looked down at the sleeping Ivy who lay in a little padded basket.

"That little girl is in God's hands," said Poppa. "Sounds like she couldn't be in a better hospital."

"Thank you Poppa," said Line. "Of course you're right." She sighed. "I should try to get some sleep," she said, rising. "Your bed is all ready for you," she said, putting her arms around Stephen and giving Poppa a kiss on the top of his head. Poppa slept in one of the two beds in Christy's room. She picked up the basket carrier and left the two men in the kitchen.

The week passed very quickly. In the mornings, Line sent Christy to school and Heather to pre-school. Poppa was on the phone all morning, talking to Ashik, his assistant in a busy immigration law practice. Stephen got back as quickly as he could from the university and he and Line drove to Stanford hospital, taking little Ivy, while Poppa walked over to school and picked up the other kids.

On Thursday, Line sat with Ivy in her lap, waiting for Stephen to arrive. She was emotionally exhausted. Beyond the window, the apricot tree was beginning to flower, its lovely soft blossoms almost white in the sun. The apricots might do well this year, but Line still felt apprehensive. It had been another very dry winter and the snow pack in the mountains, upon which the reservoirs down below depended, was very light. The drought would be even deeper that summer.

Another cause for low spirits that winter had been the California Supreme Court's decision that midwives attending births were practicing medicine without a license. Many midwives had been arrested and prosecuted based on the decision. It had also put a wrench into the study group Raven Lang had put together. Nurse midwives were legal, however, and schools were starting to train Certified Nurse Midwives. Line's friends who could afford the time and money were going that route.

Midwifery was about time. It was about women banding together to care for each other during pregnancy in ways doctors wouldn't take time for, to support a mother's emotional needs as well as her physical ones. Supreme Court justices in black clothes had no idea. Apparently they had the right to regulate lay midwives, however.

Line did not want to be arrested. She loved spending time with pregnant women and attending home births, but she had too many other responsibilities to do it any more. Perhaps when Ivy and Fern were in school, she too would be able to go back and add midwifery to her vocational nurse training. It was a little early to think about it. It all made her very angry.

And now this, thought Line. Poor little Fern, only two and a half and knowing intense pain.

When Stephen arrived, they got into the car and drove north in companionable silence. When one of them went up to Fern's room, the other held Ivy. Fern had been sedated for the first couple of days, but then, as the blistering on the skin began to go down, the hospital staff wanted her to get up and move around a little.

Line sat by the bed coaxing Fern to eat and drink, feeding her with a spoon as if she were a baby. The more she ate and drank the better. The little girl looked as though she were only half awake, and she refused to talk. Perhaps it hurt to move. Burns took a long time to heal.

"We can do a skin graft in a couple of weeks on her neck," said a smiling Dr. Kenneth, a young woman who looked both motherly and competent. "We'll take a little skin from her buttocks and put it on her neck so she'll have less of a scar."

Line inwardly recoiled. "Surgery?" she asked. "She's already had a lot of trauma."

"Well, we'll see," said Dr. Kenneth, making notes in her chart. "See how it progresses."

Line and Stephen came home with pizza for dinner, finding Christy and Heather's natural effervescence had been ignited by Poppa. All three of them were down on the big, empty living room carpet pretending to be eland.

"It's a kind of antelope," said Christy. "Me and Heather are a herd of eland, and we're hiding out from Poppa, who is a predator."

"What predator?" asked Stephen, standing in the door with the cardboard box of hot pizza.

"Maybe a cheetah," said Christy. "Or a lion."

"I want some water," said Heather solemnly. "I'm looking for a watering hole."

"Come on in the kitchen," said Line. "I'll get you some!"

"What do eland eat?" asked Stephen.

"Grass and leaves," said Christy. "They're herbivores."

"Hmmmm," said Stephen. "There is sausage on this pizza. I guess you don't want any."

"Oh yes I do!" said Christy. He was always hungry these days.

Poppa stood up. "No pizza on the savannah," he said. "I guess we're back." He laughed sheepishly. "It's a combination of *Where the Wild Things Are* and *National Geographic* specials around here!"

"I want to be an elephant," said Heather. "I like elephants."

"You can be an elephant another day," said Poppa. He had brought a big picture book full of animals for the kids. "We'll do elephants later."

Line was glad Poppa was not afraid to discuss predators. Predators were a fact of life. But it reminded her that she had not allowed the kids to watch *Roots*, a week-long television miniseries about Alex Haley's forebears, going all the way back to Africa. Christy was not even nine yet. Line did not want him exposed to the violence of slavery this early, though everyone was watching it. Line had agonized about it and Stephen watched it with one of his fellow teachers.

The next day, Friday, Line and Stephen went to the hospital prepared to take Fern home.

"Monday," said Dr. Kenneth, when Line went up first. "Give it another couple of days. I know you have all those kids at home," she said. "Lots of chance of infection. And playing rough. She'll be fine though. She's doing very well."

Line was sad. "We hoped to bring her home today." Line was sure Fern would perk up at home. The hospital was cold and white. "I'm a nurse, and the other kids will be careful of her. I'm sure we can take care of her."

"Monday," Dr. Kenneth said again. "I'm sorry." But she also wanted to discuss the skin graft.

"I have to check with my husband," said Line. She was inclined not to do it. She had called a friend who had burned himself badly with a kerosene lamp on a camping trip and he said his skin came back well enough without grafts. "I don't think we want to subject Fern to surgery if we think she can get along without it."

"Okay," said the doctor. "We'll make that decision later."

Driving home without Fern, Line felt empty. It was strange. Each of the kids had become part of the whole. She could not do without any one of them. She remembered what it had been like when Paul had been put in the hospital with polio and none of them could go see him. It had always been hard. She now knew the anguish Mother and Dad must have felt at the time.

At home, the animal for the day was the ostrich. "It can't fly," Christy told them. "But it can kick!"

"Where's Fern?" asked Heather. "I wanted her to be an ostrich with me."

"I don't think Fern is going to play ostriches with you," said Stephen. "Or anything else right away. We hope she'll come home Monday. But she's been pretty sick!"

Line moved disconsolately about the kitchen, cooking hotdogs and making salad for a simple supper. "Come on Christy," she said. "Help me set the table."

"I think I know what we need," said Poppa. "I noticed that they were playing *Butch Cassidy and the Sundance Kid* tomorrow night at that little rep theatre downtown. I loved that movie!" he said.

"Who's Butch Cassidy?" asked Christy.

"A gun slinger," said Poppa. "And a bank robber. But he's this very funny guy!"

Christy looked at Poppa hopefully. Line put out wineglasses for the grownups.

"Let's all go!" said Poppa. Since his wife died, he had made a hobby of movies. Especially foreign ones; but also the best American ones.

Line had never seen the movie he mentioned but she knew it was a western, reputed to be good. She hardly saw any movies. "So it's sort of comical?" she asked. "Not too violent?"

"It's violent," said Poppa. "But no more than was the case. These guys just had a great attitude in the face of fate. Puts a smile on my face just to think about it! Christy's not too young for it. And Heather will just fall asleep."

"I haven't seen it either," said Stephen. "I agree. I think we should all just go. We'll go see Fern and then we'll just bloody well go to the movie." He looked at Line, who knew she had been overruled. The strain was telling on all of them. Stephen had thought Christy should be allowed to watch *Roots*, but then he had grown up in Bedford Stuyvesant!

With something to look forward to, the family had a merry meal. Line quizzed Heather about the ostrich. "Do ostriches have predators?" she asked.

"Lots," said Heather. "All the big animals."

"But they can outrun most of them," said Christy. "And they fight if someone comes after their chicks."

"Did you show Poppa that book you found in the school library?" Line asked Christy. "About the kids in the museum?" she asked. Christy had been excited about a book set in New York, *From the Mixed Up Files of Mrs. Basil E. Frankweiler.*

"No, I forgot," said Christy.

"These kids run away to live in the metropolitan museum!" said Line. "They take baths in the fountain and stand on the toilets in the bathroom when the guards are checking at night!"

"Wow," said Poppa. "I doubt they could get away with that for very long."

"Have you been to that museum?" asked Christy wistfully.

Line smiled at him, remembering how kids always wanted what they didn't have. If he had lived in New York, he would have wanted to come here, to California.

"Sure," said Poppa. "Hundreds of times. So has your dad." He looked at Stephen.

"Yup," said Stephen. "Practically grew up there. But the museum I really liked was the Natural History Museum. Near Central Park."

"Someday," said Poppa. "Someday, Christy, I'll take you there."

"Salad, Christy," said Line. "Have some salad." Line was always trying to push vegetables, on the kids especially.

"You know," said Poppa, his eyes alight with ideas. "Do you kids know anything about Purim?" He turned to Stephen, who put up his hands as if fending off the question.

"It's a Jewish holiday," said Line. That was all she knew. Stephen did not care whether the kids were Jewish or not. He had told Line he didn't even think they were, as the Jewish racial line ran through the mother.

"Ah ha!" Poppa said. "It's almost Purim. Purim is the happiest holiday, the closest thing to a carnival we Jews ever get!"

Line looked at him. Poppa never ceased to amaze her. "A carnival?" she asked.

"It's a celebration," said Poppa. "Feasting and making noise, drinking. It's about reversal! It celebrates the plot against the Jews foiled by the beautiful Esther. Sometimes people dress up and have plays. Everything's topsy turvy. Fern's coming home on Monday, right?"

"Hopefully," said Stephen.

"Let's have a Purim carnival to welcome her home!"

Line tried to imagine poor little Fern coming from the silent, gauzy world of the hospital to a bunch of lunatics! The poor girl. It couldn't be helped though. Life was for the living, and Fern would soon be back in the thick of it. "Poppa!" she said. "You should have had lots of kids! You're so good at it!"

"Line, my girl," said Poppa. "I'm good at grandkids! I only wish Sima could have been here," he said. "She made me think of Purim. She loved the story of Esther."

"Tell us about Esther!" said Line. "I don't think I remember the story. If I ever knew it."

"She was chosen by a Persian king to be his queen. When her family heard that Haman was plotting against all the Jews in the country, she took her life in her hands and went to the king and told him she was Jewish. She asked that he spare her life and those of her countrymen. He did, having Haman hung instead of her uncle Mordecai, who had once saved the king. He also allowed the Jews to arm themselves and kill their enemies. Purim celebrates their deliverance."

"When was this?" asked Stephen, a little suspiciously.

"About four or five hundred years before Christ," said Poppa. "There probably is more legend than history to this story. It doesn't occur anywhere except in the Hebrew book of Esther. But Purim is fun. We should celebrate!"

"I do remember Purim," said Stephen. "Especially Mum. ..."

"Your mother liked the part about giving to the poor," said Poppa. "But she was always one to celebrate." He looked at Christy and Heather. "She was your grandmother," he said softly.

"Plenty of opportunity for giving to the poor in Santa Cruz!" said Stephen dryly. It had begun to seem that the streets downtown were overrun with dirty people camping out, begging for food. They weren't just hippies. These people had been living on the streets for a long time. Of course the weather on the west coast made it easier. It almost never froze and the warm winter sun lit up the middle of almost every day.

On Monday, Stephen carried little Fern from the hospital out to the car in a cold rain, while Line tried to manage a big umbrella over all four of them. Line had brought clean clothes and Fern's favorite quilt. Wrapping her up in the quilt, Stephen belted her into the back seat and Line sat beside her with Ivy. They had rejected the idea of more surgery. The scar on Fern's neck would just have to be there.

Fern was wan and quiet, but she had only one light dressing at her neck. "Do you like that red shirt?" asked Line. Somehow, dark little Fern needed strong colors, red, orange and greens, while Heather needed softer ones, blues, pinks and greys.

Fern looked down and patted her shirt. She nodded but didn't say anything. In the front seat, Stephen had put on a jazz station rather low. Dave Brubeck's light piano in the rain seemed to be just the thing to welcome the little girl back into life.

"Christy and Heather have been missing you," Line said. "And Poppa is here. He's been staying with us this week."

Fern's big eyes moved around, listening to Line. Line wondered when she would talk and what she would say. Line was thrilled by the rain. They had had so little of it that winter. Hopefully it would be a long, wet spring.

At the house, Stephen carried little Fern in and sat her on the couch. An odd group surrounded her, with Line holding them off.

"Well," said Poppa, in a high pitched old crone's voice. "If it isn't little Fern. How wonderful to have you back home." He wore a blonde wig, a long skirt and a shawl. "Now if I were a fairy godmother, I would touch you with my wand and make you all better, but since I'm not, I'm just going to give you a little kiss." He kissed Fern lightly on the top of her head.

"Just let Fern be," said Line to Christy and Heather, who stood gawking. "If you have made a play, she can watch." Christy wore a pirate costume, an eye patch rigged over one eye, ragged pants, a wooden sword at his waist. Heather had little cat ears and whiskers painted on her face. A long feather boa was pinned to the back of her pajamas as a tail.

"There's no play," said Poppa. "But it's Purim. I'm going to read the story of Esther, and whenever you hear the name Haman, the villain, everyone makes noise!" Somehow he had found a kazoo for Christy and a noise-making ratchet for Heather. He handed Fern a drumstick and put a little drum beside her on the couch.

Line and Stephen sat on either side of Fern, watching closely to see that she was okay. Such a bizarre scene, thought Line, after the sterile, white hospital!

Poppa opened a large book and began to read while Christy and Heather stood, noisemakers at the ready. Whenever he came to the name Haman, he paused first, raising his finger so that everyone knew he was about to read it. Crash, buzzth, boom. Christy wouldn't stop blowing his long, loud note on the kazoo. Even Stephen came up with a Bronx cheer, blowing through his fingers!

"Hey, stop!" said Poppa. "Let me read." He kept going, holding up his finger again when he came to Haman. And there was little Fern, hitting the drum with her stick while everyone else banged or buzzed or cheered. Fern's eyes were shining. Line laughed to see her.

When Poppa finished the story, he fell on the floor as though exhausted. "Again!" they heard Fern's little voice croak. "Again!" It was weak but harsh, as if she hardly knew how to use it.

Poppa's eyes peeked out from under his wig, smiling. "Again?" he said. "I don't think I can do it again. But we can give you a treat. To celebrate the deliverance of Esther's people. Our people." He stood up and bowed, gesturing, offering the world to his grandchildren. "Follow me to the kitchen. We're going to eat Haman's pockets full of money!"

At Poppa's insistence, Line had found hamantaschen filled with prune and poppy seeds at a bakery. She could have made better ones herself, she thought, but not this year.

Line leaned back against the couch, Ivy nestled in the Snugli on her chest and Fern resting in her blankets. Again, Line thought to herself. May all the gods keep my children safe from harm. Again.

23

Marty walked from window to window in her flat on the flanks of Telegraph Hill, carrying a cup of tea. It was an "off Friday" and she was home alone. Heavy April clouds hung over the world, but they would probably not result in rain. Way too little rain had fallen that winter and there had been so little snow Erik had not been skiing. A shaft of morning light came through, illuminating the dense streets and trees below.

Marty was happy to be alone. Erik was in Reno, doing a punch list for a hotel project with his employer, Andrew Murray, whom everyone called Bud. Bud ran a big architectural firm, Murray Costa. He saw Erik as a son and enjoyed showing him off. Erik was classy and cool; just the right mix of California bohemian and prep school graduate to help Bud sell his services. Erik could whip out a pencil and do a sketch in the middle of a meeting, if necessary.

Marty went back to the kitchen. She washed the dishes lovingly and swept the floor. Perhaps the counters were getting dingy in the corners. Five years was a long time with no new paint or changes. She could hardly "see" the flat any more. It was still lovely, had changed little. It was a shell, empty, in which people slept, ate, contemplated the world. Erik wanted it to be a retreat, a hideaway, so they rarely entertained.

Moving into the bathroom, Marty reminded herself as she scrubbed the toilet, the sink and the tub, that in Erik's world, women didn't clean their own houses. It was why she liked to do it when he wasn't around. She was glad to see Erik working with Bud Murray, finding his professional feet. Erik even made a plan to study for his architectural licensing exams. Marty had begun to wonder if he ever would. But Marty also saw huge gaps between herself and Erik, which worried and saddened her.

For one thing, Erik seemed interested in easy money. Condos, hotels, office buildings where there was little art involved. He liked the wheeling and dealing Bud Murray did. Power and playing the game interested Erik more than the work. Marty hardly knew how to behave around this. What had happened to his love of Christopher Alexander's architectural dictums?

By contrast, Marty's friend Ming-Yue saw architecture as art. Work was hardly worth it to Ming-Yue unless she was putting spirit into it. Marty understood life as Ming-Yue did. She still did not know what her own work would be, but daily life was a zen koan, like a tea ceremony. Everything mattered. Art and spirit were everywhere.

Marty's general idea was to pay for a sensual and spiritual life with the steady money she made doing administrative work. Discrimination was interesting. She was trying to find her way to her own individuality. This search was easier to share with Ming-Yue than with Erik. Marty never knew when she would touch a hot button with Erik.

Cleaning made Marty love the flat more. She polished the mirror with glass cleaner and then moved out into the living room. At least she and Erik agreed about keeping the place simple and empty. He had a fine stereo now, but there was little else in the room beyond the Swedish fireplace, a few bookshelves, the two Barcelona chairs, a low table and the beautiful Turkish carpet. Marty got out the vacuum cleaner. This room only needed dusting.

When it was just the two of them it was easy for Marty to find the place where she and Erik had first met, the sexual intensity, the interest in exploring. My body doesn't lie, Marty often told herself. It had wanted Erik all these years. Marty trusted it. But by this time they had few friends in common and few things they liked to do together.

Marty sighed as the noisy vacuum sucked into the corners of the room. Initially, Marty's lack of judgment of him, and Erik's trust in her, had tied them together. But now, there was less and less she could talk to him about. He heard judgment in many of the comments she made, whether intended or not. There was also the pressure of children. Erik didn't want any, he flatly said. Certainly not now.

They would go to Hawaii in a couple of weeks. Bud was sending Erik and another architect on a reconnaissance mission. They would meet a developer on the big island to scope out a resort. Marty had never been to Hawaii. She and Erik would have a weekend to themselves. It would be warm, tropical. Marty looked forward to it. She was already preparing the books she would read while she waited for Erik to be done with his meetings. Architectural magazines had led her to surrealism. She was saving two paperbacks, Henry Miller's study of Rimbaud and a book called *Age of Surrealism*, by Wallace Fowlie, for this trip.

Marty put the vacuum away in the closet and got ready to go out, putting on leather boots, a skirt and sweater. Ming-Yue had badgered Marty to throw out her polyester blouses. Only cotton, wool, silk, linen were allowed. Marty needed little urging. Could she afford silk? Perhaps. Raw silk, she thought. She was keeping her eyes open for it.

Marty brushed and combed her hair. It was the death of her. She had cut it and now rolled it on hot rollers for a few minutes in the morning, trying to get some bounce to it. When it was long, it hung heavily around her round face. As Ming-Yue said, hair is meant to frame the face. Marty's fine dark hair was straight and after a shampoo each day, had no volume whatsoever. Especially on a rainy day, it was limp as a dishrag. Marty sighed and tucked it behind her ears. She put on her glasses. There was no getting around thick glasses either.

Locking the door with a slam, Marty went down the steps and into the street. The air that greeted her was cold, but alive, edged with damp.

She walked down the Kearny Street steps toward the canyons made by the tall buildings in the Financial District and swung off onto Sutter Street.

As she headed down the street, past book shops, art supply shops, restaurants and retailers, Marty reminded herself that walking around San Francisco was a privilege. In her own mind, it was as fine as Paris, where the Surrealists had made their experiments and the flâneur, the stroller, was recognized. San Francisco lay on the Pacific, the result of a mixture of cultures. The fact that it was stacked into a small peninsula made every block of interest. Ming-Yue hated its architectural conservatism, its pandering to developers and tourists, but to Marty, who had grown up on the Midwestern plains, it was a great city.

Marty ducked into Caravanserai, a purveyor of exotic foods. The downstairs shop smelled tempting, with shelves of packaged teas, teapots, coffees and spices. Imported candy, wine, and gifts delighted Marty's eyes, but she didn't stop. Imported things were often stale compared to the wonderfully fresh things she could buy in North Beach near her apartment. The expense wasn't usually worth it.

Upstairs, Marty looked around the small room toward the wall of windows looking out on Sutter Street. Ming-Yue wasn't there yet. Marty ordered from the sullen young woman at the espresso machine. "French roast," she said. "And a brioche, please. With butter." She took her coffee to a table at the window which allowed her to look down into the street, as if from a balcony.

Across the street were art galleries and shoe stores, designer clothing stores and a jeweler's shop. Cars drove up and down the street under an overcast sky. And people. Marty loved watching them walking, stopping when something caught their eye. There was the flamboyant Marc, from Jeanne-Marc, dressed like an oriental pasha in a colorful Russian shirt, pants and boots. And there was a well-dressed woman with a shopping bag marked Gump's, the hundred-year-old shop which sold fine gifts and housewares, many from China and Japan.

Marty buttered the soft eggy brioche. And here was Ming-Yue, very stylish with a raincoat belted around her thin figure, her black hair brushed into an airy bouffant around her face. Ming-Yue dropped a package of books and newspapers at Marty's table. "You've been to Bill Stout's!" said Marty.

"Yes," said Ming-Yue. She lived and breathed architecture.

Marty looked over the front page of the *New York Times* while Ming-Yue ordered. The remaining members of the Baader-Meinhof gang were being sentenced in Stuttgart to life imprisonment. This group had insisted that they were a political force, the Red Army Faction. Ulrike Meinhof had committed suicide in prison a few years earlier.

When Ming-Yue returned Marty pointed, "I never understood what they were trying to accomplish," she said.

"Me either," said Ming-Yue brushing it off. She picked up her cup. "Such good coffee!" she said. "I have news! I have decided to leave LMP. I'm going to work with Anders' parents on their projects, for the time being." Anders was the partner Ming-Yue lived with. They had gone to school together and Anders worked at SOM.

"I'm glad for you," said Marty. She was not glad for herself. She would miss knowing Ming-Yue was behind her at a drafting station where Marty could stop to talk any time.

"I'm thinking of taking my Western name now, as a professional name. I want to get off on the right foot for my career."

"Meredith Shen?" asked Marty.

"Yes. It has a good sound, doesn't it? I like Meredith because it can be either the name of a man or a woman, an androgynous name."

"It'll be hard for me to get used to," said Marty. "I like Ming-Yue, and I like knowing what it means. Bright moon."

Ming-Yue laughed. "My parents were trying to tone down the effect of my being born in a dragon year. But I'm getting used to Meredith. It looks nice on business cards. Ming-Yue is a child name. Time to give it up."

Marty felt sad. She loved how unsentimental Ming-Yue was, but it was also sudden. "I'm sure you are not sad you won't be coming to LMP any more," she said. "But I'll be sorry."

"Your name is androgynous," said Ming-Yue. "There are many men called Marty, for Martin or something."

"Yeah," said Marty. "It just kind of happened. My sister called me that. I don't even think of myself as Margaret any more. I can't imagine using that name."

"Marty Wilson," said Ming-Yue. "It's a good name."

"Used to be Mikkelson," said Marty wistfully. "Marty Mikkelson."

"Better!" said Ming-Yue. "You can use whatever you want professionally."

"Where will you be working?" asked Marty.

"Just out of my house," said Ming-Yue, "trying to get some projects together. Working on a brochure. I'm certainly ready. Look at this book I found." Ming-Yue pulled a book of paintings by Giorgio Morandi from a brown paper package and thumbed through it, showing Marty reproductions of very simple still lifes of bottles, vases, bowls, flowers.

"Beautiful," said Marty. She too was drawn to the textures of the lines, the purity and simplicity of the forms. The beautiful book made Marty want to stop, just stop and sink into the pictures. Her head bent over the book next to Ming-Yue's. Neither of them spoke.

"It helps me to look at things like this when I am designing," said Ming-Yue, finally, and there was wistfulness in her voice now. "To open my eyes. The volumes," she said.

"He doesn't use much color, does he," said Marty, staring.

"Just enough," said Ming-Yue. "There are drawings too. I love his drawings. He lived in Bologna his whole life with his sisters."

Marty bent her head over the book, now associating it with Ming-Yue. She imagined a life lived in one place, focused entirely on one's art, drawing the spirit out of life. The monastic purity of it was attractive. So different from my own frantic uncertainty, Marty thought. What should I be doing? "The drawings are wonderful."

Ming-Yue closed the monograph and put it carefully back in the package. "So where are you going today?" she asked.

"I'm going to go look at photographs to start with," said Marty. "At the gallery across the street. Caponigro. He does landscapes and nature photography. I always think of his sunflowers."

"Hmmmm," said Ming-Yue. "I guess I could have a look." Marty knew that Ming-Yue was most interested in urban landscapes.

Marty cleaned off the table with her napkin and carried her used dishes to a tub near the espresso bar. Ming-Yue belted her raincoat and the two of them went down the steps. Marty was so happy to be with her, to be sharing their experiences of art. It was exciting, like being with Erik in the early days when he had showed her so much.

Two weeks later, Erik and Marty got off a plane in Hilo with John, a slightly older architect Marty liked. The air was just as damp as in San Francisco, but much warmer. None of them had been to Hawaii, and they were all delighted to be greeted with fragrant-smelling leis at the rental car company.

"Look at us, the flower children," said John derisively. His perfectly-trimmed hair was graying at the temples, but he was thin and dashing. Handsome, Marty thought.

"It's amazing to have enough orchids and plumeria that you can waste them this way," Marty said. Flowers made her smile.

The three of them drove seventy miles north to Waimea, which was slightly inland and a couple thousand feet up Mauna Kea. It was an old fashioned town with a country lodge. Bud thought it way too expensive to stay at the nearby Mauna Kea Beach Hotel, but the next day they went there for breakfast.

Breakfast was a smorgasbord served at long tables by middle-aged Hawaiian ladies who stood behind them, ready to help. You could take as much as you liked, many kinds of eggs, potatoes, sausages, smoked fish, bacon, and Danish, breads and salad vegetables. The dining tables were open to the breezes, which washed in from the sea, cooling off any heat from the sun.

"You can stay here and we'll meet you around cocktail hour," said Erik. He looked tousled, blonde and sleepy. Sexy as hell. "Just wander around as if you belonged," he said. "It'll be fine."

John was sympathetic. "I wish I was you," he said. "Able to stay here and be in the sun all day."

"Oh, you love it," Marty joshed him back. "You'll love your Japanese developers and your ritual meetings. You can't wait to get started."

"Of course you're right," said John, looking around at the relaxed people in light tennis clothes, already drinking piña coladas with their breakfast. "It's the perfect atmosphere. But I'd probably get island fever if I had to live here."

Marty wore a sleeveless black tee-shirt and a short skirt. She had no swimming suit with her, but she did have her books and journals in a basket she used as a handbag in the summer, and a big floppy hat. She was happy to move from one lovely spot to another, walking along the edge of the beach, basking in the warmth and letting her mind go where it wanted.

When the sun got hot just after noon, Marty sat in a shaded lounge on a deep sofa, her bare feet up on a hassock, her nose pressed into Wallace Fowlie's small blue paperback, underlining certain paragraphs with a pen so she could go back to them quickly.

What interested Marty about Surrealism was that it seemed to be trying to get at the same thing Marty was working on, the idea that the body IS the unconscious, that subject and object are not split, that the body and soul were one. The experiments of the surrealists were strange to her, Breton walking about Paris with a friend trying to predict when they would next see a Bois Charbons sign, the significance of a lady's sky-blue glove, or their unplanned meetings. It all seemed silly, lost in time. But the impetus, the attempt to see the spirit in matter, drove Marty as well.

It was not that the body had been degraded in Marty's early understanding. Mother and Dad honored it. They had not been shy about showing their affection for each other and Marty remembered seeing the look of bliss on Mother's face as she took a nap with Dad one Sunday afternoon. But they did not condone selfishness, or excessive self-interest.

And the prevailing Midwestern Scandinavian culture carried a sense of shame about the body. It was talked about as little as possible, the medical book with the colored plastic pages of human organs hidden off in a closet. As young women, she and her sisters had watched their friends dress up and done the best they could themselves. But to the Mikkelsons, it was always clear that the body was just a carrier for the more important soul, which was immortal and would go to heaven. The more circumspect one was about the body, the less it interfered with the journey of the soul. It was not what Marty now felt.

On the contrary she was led by her body and trusted desire to show her the way to herself. She had learned to listen to her body, indeed could sometimes not ignore it, it clamored so loudly! The early acid trips she had done with Erik helped, quashing judgments which rose up in her, allowing her to see more than she could with her everyday eyes. The body was indeed the unconscious, one with the soul. "Surrealism, in stressing the relationship between and even the identity of spirit and matter, differs from supernaturalism," said Fowlie.

Marty was half asleep, dreaming, letting her book fall from her hands when Erik came over in his crisp linen shirt and put a drink down in front of her. "Gin 'n tonic, my dear?" he asked. No pink drinks with paper umbrellas for him, thought Marty. Her Erik was rich, austere, sometimes powerful. She smiled up at him.

John joined them, carrying his briefcase and a similar drink. He too wore blue jeans with a dark knit polo shirt. "I'm in love, I'm in love," he gushed. "I'm just bowled over by the history of this place!"

"The place you are designing the resort for?" asked Marty, sitting up and taking a sip of the bright, acerbic drink.

"Yes!" said John. "It was owned by a famous Hawaiian politician and athlete, Francis Hyde 'Ii Brown. He sold the property to the Japanese developer we're working for, but he had had it forever. His grandfather had been a companion of King Kamehameha II. Brown bought the property from one of the Parkers. He knew the ancient Hawaiians kept it for royalty and he wanted a place of retreat for himself."

Marty listened, wishing she could see the place for herself. "Is it similar to the way it is here?" she asked. "White sand beaches, winds washing in from the west? I can't imagine anything more refreshing."

"White sand interspersed with lava beds," said John. "It's incredible. Brown just died and the place has been derelict for some time. But there are these fish ponds! Some of the existing buildings are built with local lava rock."

Erik agreed. "A fabulous place. Wish I'd seen it in the 1930's when he was living here and working on it. Separate buildings for sleeping, cooking, eating."

"It's a project to sink my teeth into," said John. "It's a huge place! It could last the rest of my natural life! But we've got to find a way to save those ancient fish ponds," he said. "A remnant of old Hawaii. The area was kind of dry and desert like, with the lava flow and all. So the fishponds helped the Hawaiians survive, supplemented their ocean fishing."

"They just walled off pools from the ocean and made sluice gates for seawater to circulate in," said Erik. "A long time ago. This local guy explained."

Marty tried to imagine the ponds. "Walled up with lava rock?" she asked. It was a long way from Paris!

"Built up with lava rock edges, a few palm trees. It's a huge area with paths around them and between," said John. "But it's not in good shape now. We've just got to make sure they don't dry them up and build on top of them!"

"Sounds great!" Marty said.

Erik and John had another day of meetings. This time Marty brought her bathing suit and was able to get in the water. It was so warm she could bob all she wanted in the salt water, only worrying about her fair, Norwegian skin, which would turn lobster given a chance. She wore round wire-rimmed prescription sunglasses so she could see. Letting herself lie on the beach a little, Marty turned herself like a hot dog. But then she retreated to a shady lounge chair and her books. What a day, Marty thought to herself.

John left that night for Waikiki, but Erik had arranged for Marty and he to stay over the weekend. "I've got a special treat for us," he told Marty. On Saturday morning they went down to a big public park on the west side of the island, Spencer Beach: a long strand of white sand with forested parkland above it. A lava rock reef cut off one side, but the beach seemed to go on forever on the other.

"It's a beautiful day," said Marty as they picnicked up under the trees above the beach at noon. She had shown Erik how she could bob in the salty water.

"You look like John Lennon in those glasses," Erik said. "If your face were a little thinner."

Marty laughed. "Well you don't look like Yoko Ono! Maybe more like Rod Stewart." She looked out toward the hot sunny beach, the ocean green beyond it. "Is this weather legal?"

"Must be," said Erik. "I'm not sure this is though." He pulled out of his hip pocket a small clear plastic envelope. "Pure windowpane," he said. "I saved it for us. For today."

Marty eyed it and looked up into his face. "You trust it completely?"

"Absolutely," Erik said. "You take one. I'll take two 'cause I'm used to 'em."

"Wow," said Marty softly. She hadn't taken acid for ages. They were outdoors, but it seemed pretty safe. And they had just eaten. "Do you think we're ready for this?"

"Sure," said Erik. He looked around. "Couldn't be better."

Marty took one of the thin gelatin squares in the tiny container and popped it in her mouth. She smiled at Erik. There was no going back.

Marty need not have worried. It was a lovely afternoon. She lay back, resting on the blanket under the thick leaves of the tree and looking out on the stretch of golden beach below them, the warm green water beyond it. As she lay there, her body softened. She curled up toward Erik who lay with his arms behind his head. There was no chance of the wild sex they used to have on acid, but it was luscious being together.

The thick, dark green leaves in the tree above were each distinct, like a tree in the Garden of Eden. Marty thought she could see every single one, pinnate along their branches. A pea variety, she thought. The tree burned into her consciousness. A bright blue jeep drove along the road above them, like a toy.

A long time went by. The sun began to sink lower on the horizon. "This is what we came for," whispered Erik, looking out toward the shore. "Come on." He took Marty's hand and they made their way down to the beach. Marty didn't trust herself to move very fast. Her heart was pounding in her breast.

"The tide's going out, isn't it?" Marty asked, her words echoing through her mind. She never felt sure about the ocean since she hadn't grown up around it.

"Yep," said Erik. He headed up the beach, his bare feet squinching in the warm sand.

Marty stood at the edge, watching the water. The surf washed up in round poufs, as regular as mathematics. Each wave poufed in, separating as it came into smaller, distinct scallops, in a crocheted lace pattern. Marty watched, mesmerized, sitting down at the water's edge. How have I never seen this before? Marty wondered.

Erik walked up the beach, which was becoming less populated, a black figure in the sun. "Don't look at it," Erik said as he came up to Marty.

Marty nodded, but she couldn't help it. "I'm looking around it," she said. "And the glasses protect me. I want to see the green flash." Marty felt delicious, her body fluid and loose. A golden sun path went from her to the round orange ball on the horizon.

The sun set slowly, like a time lapse, irrevocable. A little spray of green light went up as it settled into the ocean. The few puffy clouds had pink and flame gold under their edges. The colors reflected in the darkening water. The white-capped grey poufs kept coming in, but they were harder to distinguish.

Holding hands, Marty and Erik went back to the blanket under the tree. They lay down together and Marty wrapped the edge around herself. Looking toward the ocean, a few dark tree shapes framed the scene, palms and more of the thick-leaved trees. The sky remained bright, the line of horizon clear as the breezes washed up fresh and free. Time had disappeared. Marty had melted into it.

Slowly shape returned to Marty's body. It was actually her favorite part of a trip, the slow waking up, when you knew you had been somewhere. She and Erik had gone together. Marty breathed deeply. "I'm getting hungry," she said quietly to Erik.

"That's a good sign," said Erik. "Shall we go back?"

"Yes," breathed Marty. Her mind was washed clean. Free, empty as a teacup.

24

On a Thursday night in May, Paul came home to find Marie fervently packing. "Help me, Paul!" she cried. "I have to catch the evening flight. I have to go home."

"Go home?" asked Paul.

"To Montreal. My mother's sick. My daughter," Marie was barely coherent.

"Your daughter?" asked Paul. He knew much about Marie, about her large austere family who were spread out across Quebec, and her black-sheep years in Los Angeles, but she had never told him about a daughter.

"I'm sorry, Paul," Marie said as she struggled to zip up a suitcase. "I meant to tell you. As soon as I could."

Paul took over and squashing the bag, zipped it up. Marie already had her coat on. They went out to the pickup and made a mad dash for the airport.

"I had her when I was 18. She lives with my mother, but my mother is very sick," said an anguished Marie as Paul drove. "I'm afraid one of my sisters will take her, but one of them would be better than the others. I have to go." She wrapped her arms around Paul's neck. "I'll write. I'm sorry Paul. I have to go." She was half way out of the car. "Please tell Nikolas that I'm okay. I'll be back." She stopped a moment. "I hope I will be."

Paul was left on the airfield, watching the plane for Seattle as it lifted off in the setting sun. He could not have been more shocked. A daughter. What is her name, he wondered. He did not even know if he had an address for Marie's family. He leaned on the ancient pickup. A flock of mallards flew overhead, their honking a reminder of friendship to Paul's sudden feeling of loneliness.

The light was now long in the evenings but the fields were a sea of muck. Paul drove back to downtown Fairbanks in the twilight, to the restaurant where Marie had been working.

"I was wondering where that girl was," said Nik, her boss. He shouted at Angela to call one of her friends in to help. "Thursday's not a busy night, but I have a hard time without Marie," he told Paul. "Sit down, sit down. Have a drink." He made Paul sit in a booth at the back. Nik's drink was there, but he hardly sat down, his watchful eyes on the house full of diners and the waiters rushing back and forth with plates of food.

"So explain again?" said Nik, sweating as he put a beer and a plate of hot meatballs and rice in front of Paul. The place was warm, but he wore a suitcoat, which minimized his respectable paunch.

Paul told the story again.

"That girl," said Nik. "Always taking care of everyone. She's a wild one. She's told me a lot of stories. But she loves you," said Nik. "I think you can settle her."

"If she comes back," said Paul. The cold, hard reality was beginning to dawn on him. He could hardly swallow any food.

"Awww, she'll come back," said Nik. "Where else is she gonna go?" He jumped up and went over to help carry steaming plates to a customer.

A daughter. The fact felt completely unreal to Paul. Marie had never talked about a daughter. She could not have more children, Paul knew, because her Dalkon shield, an IUD used for birth control, had given her such an infection they had taken out her uterus a few years ago. Part of the nightmare of her years in Los Angeles. She was only 31, two years older than Paul. But she had a whole life behind her. As do I, thought Paul.

"So what are we going to do when all these pipeliners go home?" asked Nik, when he returned. Oil was scheduled to start flowing through the pipeline that summer. "What does your roommate think?"

Paul shook his head. He couldn't think about anything. His roommate, who worked for Alyeska, had told Paul there would be plenty of money in Alaska when the pipeline was finished. "Taxes," said Paul. "The oil companies will be paying taxes. Alaska will be rolling in dough," he mumbled. "I'm supposed to work on a village high school building project this summer."

"Now there's a good use for it," said Nik. "I was wondering about the people. What will happen to my customers? Will they all disappear?"

"Nah," said Paul. "All that money will buy enough comfort for people to stay in Fairbanks. I don't think they're going anywhere."

"Yeah," said Nik. "Maybe you're right. Could be a great place."

But Paul was weary. "Thanks, Nik," he said. "I've got to go. You wouldn't happen to have an address for Marie, do you?"

"I'll go look," said Nik. He threaded his way back through the kitchen. "Just the Fairbanks address," he said when he returned. "Don't worry. She's a honey. She'll come back."

Paul felt bereft. What had he been thinking? What did he know? Nothing! He went home to the cold, empty apartment and stretched out on the bed under the sleeping bags he and Marie used as a comforter. He felt like he had been kicked in the stomach. He had had no idea how vulnerable he was.

Only last weekend, he remembered, Marie had been singing a Beatles song as they stomped home from the university library in the rain. "Two of us chasing paper, getting nowhere, on our way back home." She was laughing. "Exactly like us," she said. "Two of us wearing raincoats, standing solo, in the sun." There hadn't been any sun, but it was warmish, humid and there were drops in Marie's lively dark curls. It's how I'll remember her, Paul thought.

On Saturday, Paul went out to the little lake in the Cripple Creek marsh area that he had used, years ago, to call his own. He was heavy-hearted and hoped to lose himself in the wild as he had done in the past. Cripple Creek no longer flowed, as it had been dredged and dammed by gold mining operations. What was left was a maze of stagnant pools and beaver ponds, where at this time of year, migrating swans, owls and sandhill cranes mated. Paul parked by the side of the road and hiked in through the wet, muddy undergrowth.

The heavy skies had cleared somewhat and patches of blue allowed bright sunlight down onto the reedy edges of the ponds. Nothing was dry but it was greening. Paul saw crocus and pasque flower. In the shade were patches of dirty snow. Shrubs and trees burgeoned with new leaves. Reeds were no longer brown and clacking, but green and dense. In time to help with nesting. Nature's timing was always perfect.

Paul, climbing over deadfall and hummocks with his binoculars, didn't want to get too close. He made out a mated pair of sandhills nesting on the ground. Researchers thought they mated for life, though they migrated long distances, down into Nebraska and Texas. How did they know their mate, Paul wondered. How did he know? What internal compass had helped him find Marie?

As Paul watched, the male and female, who looked much the same, grey, worn plumage with long necks, a bit of red on the forehead and on their long bills, stood together and made a long, trumpeting call. Eerie, Paul thought. If only he could show Marie.

No other people were visible. Creamer's Field north of Fairbanks, where barley and corn fields had been planted to attract sandhills away from the airfields, was becoming a tourist attraction. In the fall, thousands of migrating cranes gathering out at the field were celebrated. Ugly birds, flying with their necks straight out, they were majestic together as they moved on the thermal air currents.

Paul liked backwaters like this damaged marsh area where no one went, where he could watch nesting birds alone. He had used to come often, keep observation notebooks of what he saw and heard, what the temperatures and water levels were like. Everything was important, everything counted.

It didn't help, though, to think about mated birds. Paul's heart ached. He had never wanted much, had been afraid that if he wanted anything badly, he would jinx it and would most assuredly not be able to get it. He knew now he wanted one thing, Marie. You could not prove by Marie's background that humans were like birds. She had been with several men. But perhaps humans were more complicated.

Paul wanted it to be true that there was "a cover for every pot," as the Germans said. He thought he had found his, though he had never said so. He and Marie had been playing together, living together, exploring. Her going made things serious. And did she trust him? Did she feel he was just another passing stranger? What did she want? The abrupt cut off in communication was agonizing.

The clear morning out by himself didn't help. Paul could not still himself. He could not sit quietly without his skin crawling with anxiety. He went back to town and knocked on Marcia's door. She lived in both Minto and Fairbanks with her Athabascan husband Leon and their year-old baby. Marcia had given Paul the idea to come to Alaska in the first place. Would she be there?

"Hey, Paul," said Marcia as she opened the door. She held her toddler with his bright black eyes and a shock of black hair on her waist. "How are you?"

"Not so good, truth to tell," said Paul. "Marie left. Did she tell you?"

Marcia drew Paul into the kitchen. "Come on in, have a cup of coffee," she said. "No, I haven't heard anything." She looked happy and confident, maybe a little plump.

Paul sighed. He pulled off his muddy boots and left them at the door, walking in in his woolen socks. "It was kind of sudden. She went back to Montreal, said her mother was sick and she was worried about her daughter." He looked at Marcia significantly as he sat down at the formica table.

"Ah," said Marcia. "I'm glad she finally told you. She was scared to. You've accepted so much, and have been having such a grand time." She put her little son in his highchair and turned the stove burner on under a teakettle. "Leon's out on shift," she said. "But he'll be home tomorrow night for a few days. They're really driving hard to finish this summer," she said.

Paul nodded. He had suspected Leon would be working. "Do you know her daughter's name?" he asked.

"Grace," said Marcia. "Grace Angelique Bernadette, or something like that," Marcia laughed. "You know how many names Catholic kids have. I think she calls her Grace. You know, by the grace of God. She must be about 13." She put pieces of toast in front of Tadzi, who clumped them in his fist and tried to stuff them in his mouth. He was named for Neal Charlie, a chief in Minto, but Leon and Marcia called him Tadzi, little loon.

"How could she spend so much time away from a daughter?" asked Paul. He could not understand.

"Her family convinced her she was bad for Grace," said Marcia, stirring Folger's instant coffee with a spoon. She hunted in the cupboard and came up with a package of cookies. "I think she believes it. And she had that desperate need to sing. And she kept moving."

"Her family sounds hard-working," said Paul. "And austere." He had tried to imagine the farm Marie described. The family sold poultry and eggs and also butchered pigs and cured bacon, sausages and hams. Some of the family also had a maple syrup operation. It sounded wonderful to Paul, though he knew there was little to spare and that rivalries had split the brothers. Marie's mother was devoutly Catholic. She had taken her youngest daughter, Marie, to mass with her almost every day, until Marie grew old enough to refuse.

"Don't worry," said Marcia. "I know she wanted to tell you about Grace. It will come out all right, I'm sure."

"I don't even have an address for her!" said Paul. "I don't know what to do!"

"You, my friend," said Marcia, smiling. "Are going to have to wait. I know you men don't like to wait. But I don't think there's anything else you can do."

"Arrrrgh!" said Paul, putting his head dramatically in his hands. He rarely gave away his feelings, but he had known Marcia a long time. He tried to push it all away, tried to relax. He shook himself. "You at least look great," he said. "You're probably happy as a clam."

Marcia beamed at him. "I am happy. We're hoping that Leon gets to stay on with Ayleska when the pipeline's done. He likes the work! And I'm hoping I can go back to teaching soon. There are all those aunties in Minto to help take care of my kids." She tickled Tadzi's plump cheek with a maternal hand.

"So you don't mind how tacky Alaska has gotten?" asked Paul. "I mean, there's money, but I'm not sure it is being used well." You could buy almost anything now and the grocery stores looked like those in the Lower 48. Paul's students were running the stores, however. The grownups had taken higher-paying jobs. Fairbanks had a sort of sleazy opulence.

"Knowing about Minto protects me from all this," said Marcia. "I love Minto. But it's been nice to have a place in Fairbanks. People are always coming through. These big families. I get to see some of Randy, who's over at the university, and their uncles are setting up cultural history programs. It's really an exciting time!"

"You are wonderful, Marcia," said Paul. "Everyone loves you and you've made the right choices."

"So, what are you doing this summer?" asked Marcia. School was almost out.

"I had two possible school districts to do construction for," said Paul. "I wanted to go out to Gambell on St. Lawrence Island, but I didn't want to be so far from Marie." Paul hung his head, a little shamed.

Marcia nodded, smiling.

"I've never been out on the islands, or that far north. But instead I chose the Gateway School District because I could get back and forth more. I'm supposed to work in Tetlin, in that beautiful marshy area on highway 2, almost to Canada." Paul sighed. "Now I don't even want to do that! It's a four-hour drive from Fairbanks. I won't save money if I drive back and forth all the time. I just want to stay here!"

"You better go," said Marcia. "Work will make time go faster."

Paul looked at her. He knew she was right. "But what if she comes back and I'm not here?" he asked. "Or she sends a letter and I'm not here to get it?"

Marcia sighed. "I know it's painful," she said.

"I'm already writing her letters in my head," said Paul. "But I don't have anywhere to send them!"

"Good God," said Marica. "And I thought I fell hard. Here you are, melting down in my kitchen all these years later!"

Paul stood up. "Sorry," he said, regaining his dignity. "You know her so well. And you know me. I don't have anyone else to talk to about it."

Marcia put a hand on his arm. "Paul! Sit down!"

Paul sat. Tadzi was throwing food on the floor. Marcia picked him up, emptied his grubby little hands and handed him to Paul while she cleaned up. Paul got a silly grin on his face. "So how are you?" he asked Tadzi. "Little loon. Little half Norwegian, half Athabascan." Tadzi smiled, fascinated by this new blonde bearded face so close to his own.

"You're going to have to go out to Tetlin and work," said Marcia. "And I'll certainly hear from Marie if she comes back. I'll contact you. I'll even go and check on your mail now and then. Do they get mail in Tetlin?" she asked.

"There's a mail plane, I think," said Paul.

"Okay," said Marcia. "I'll forward your mail, or send you a letter. Or try the bush telegraph. Send me a message when you find out what's the best way."

Paul sighed, smiling at the sweet boy in his arms.

"I'll tell you a secret," said Marcia, beaming at him. "To show you that things do turn out all right. I'm pregnant!"

Paul looked at her. She did look radiant. "Congratulations," he said quietly. "I'm glad for you. You look wonderful."

Paul pulled himself together and left, letting Marcia know he would contact her as soon as he got to Tetlin. She would be his lookout.

It was a tough summer for Paul. The Athabascan village was isolated, but it couldn't wait to get its school. And its basketball court! "It's going to be a basketball court with a few school rooms attached for looks," said Gary, the construction foreman. They worked long hours, six days a week.

Paul didn't even try to get away. He grew numb, living in a dream. Nailing floorboards, Paul thought about his future. He had managed to save some money, as he had few needs and worked both summer and winter. Not much, because he had done what he wanted, the Adventuress had not paid well, and he hadn't taken advantage of the big money jobs available. But he did have some money. Am I a pipeliner, Paul wondered. Pipeliners took the money they made in Alaska and spent it elsewhere. He hadn't intended to be.

Days were very long, and Paul was at a disadvantage because he didn't play basketball. Often the construction crew played the locals on an outdoor court late at night as the sun struggled to set. But Paul couldn't run. He holed up in his bunk in the crew trailer and wrote in a journal to keep a rein on his feelings. Addressing Marie, he told her about what had happened during the day, what he was thinking. About his dreams. About the part she played in them.

Mostly Paul admitted to himself that he did not want to stay in Alaska. He was being teased instead by what he heard about the boundary waters between Canada and Minnesota. Ely, Minnesota, was the jumping off place for canoe trips into the area. Paul also thought Northern Minnesota might be a little quieter culturally, the conflicts between people not quite so raw. The strain of the many different people tussling over resources and ideas was wearing on Paul, as well as the pace of boom-town Fairbanks. The Alaskan wilderness was wide, but you could not get away from people.

Paul wanted to go back to Minnesota, and he wanted to take Marie. He thought he could find work there, either as a teacher or a helper to an outfitter. He did not care whether Marie could have children or not. He wanted her for his mate.

That was the dream. "Now put foundations under it," ran Thoreau's refrain through Paul's head. He could do nothing about Marie. But he could begin thinking and planning for the rest of it. It might take another couple of years, he thought. Another year or so at West Valley High School, a few more courses at the university. Alaska had been all that Paul had asked of it. It was making a person out of him. He would take that person, his whole self, back to Minnesota.

During the day, Paul kept an eye out for the mail plane. If Gary was nearby, he teased him. "Eagle has landed, Paul," he would call. In the evening, Paul went to the store/post office to see if there were any letters.

Paul wrote to his sisters, because who else would listen to your troubles. "My Alaska has disappeared," he wrote. "The cabin I first lived in on Chena Ridge, the nights skiing home, that empty purity. It isn't coming back, either. People are moving in, making themselves comfortable. You can get anything you want. Lots of people are thriving, but somehow I'm missing northern Minnesota.

"Every inch of the state is being measured, mapped and surveyed. Some good is coming of all this attention. The Alaskan native corporations are becoming politically active. They are demanding high schools in their own communities, and native cultural education for their kids. This is great. I love the way they express their beliefs, their languages. But I'm finding less and less place for irredeemable generalists like me," he wrote. "Or maybe I'm just making it all up to justify going back to Minnesota!"

Paul had hinted to his sisters about the girl he was living with before, but now he described Marie. "I'm in love with a beautiful girl," he wrote. "She's French Canadian, a great singer. But she's also got quite a past. She tried to have a singing career, was married and divorced in Los Angeles. I just found out she has a daughter named Grace, who lives with her parents. Marie's gone back to see her. I don't know what will happen, but if she comes back, I will ask her to marry me.

"Please write!" he begged. "We're working hard out here, but I don't have people to talk to much. Thanks! Hope you are all fine."

Marty, for whom it was easy, wrote back right away. "Thank you so much for your thoughts," she said. "I hardly ever get to hear them! I'm an 'irredeemable generalist' myself and I'm also unsure what I am supposed to do in the world. It isn't going to be photography. Professional photography is too technical, involving light and equipment and competition! I just like photographing people, friends and family. But I'm not going anywhere! San Francisco is the place for me. I'm glad to hear about Marie."

Paul wrote Marty back that wildlife photography was seeing a surge of interest in Alaska. Paul viewed it as a good alternative to hunting, which also continued unabated. "There is an amazing Japanese guy at the university," said Paul. "Michio Hoshino. Everyone talks about him and I've met him. Very nice, humble guy. He goes out in the wild alone, stays there until he gets what he wants, braves all kinds of conditions. Keep an eye out for him in magazines. His subjects are grizzlies, moose, other animals."

Line sent snapshots of her family, all six of them! The baby, Ivy, was a year old, just walking. They seemed to be playing in an enclosed garden. One picture was of an empty lawn chair. Line had written on the back, "a chair waiting for you." Paul's heart melted. He would have liked nothing more than to go to California and see Line's family. And Marty, at home in San Francisco with Erik.

At last, in the middle of August, a letter arrived from Marie, having wended its way, through Marcia, to Paul. He was chilled as he opened it. Terrified of the rip in the fabric of the dream he was weaving. But, ink on blue paper, the world falling away, Paul took in the words.

"I have thought about you so much," Marie wrote in a large, childish hand. "And I want to see you and talk to you so badly. My daughter, Grace, will go back to school soon. She's going into 9th grade. I wish you were her teacher! We've all decided she should stay here with my middle sister while she's in high school. She likes the idea of Alaska, but stability is better for her. She's a little timid. My mother is better, but she and my dad can't do as much heavy work any more. My brothers do most of the farming. It is good to see them, but I can't tell them about anything.

"I haven't told them about you. There's nothing to tell, really. Not that they would understand. They don't want to hear that I've met another guitar player! I'll be back at the end of August, when school starts. It has been wonderful to spend the summer with my Grace. And I got to town for a wonderful music festival! I can't wait to tell you about it! Give my love to Marcia and Nik and everyone. I will see you soon. Love, Marie."

That was it. It was plenty. It was enough for Paul. He now had an address, but she would be back in Fairbanks before he could send a letter. And so would he! He helped lay carpet and paint, but Paul had to get ready for his own school. Instead of staying until the last week, when the Tetlin school would open with a huge potlatch, Paul took the mail plane back to town.

Paul looked around Fairbanks with anticipation, with reverence. The trees were rapidly turning color, the nights growing short and cold and the sandhill cranes were on the move. Paul tried to be present, looking around him with new eyes. He liked Fairbanks people. They were genuine and warm. Nik's restaurant was thriving. Oil moved through the pipeline. Marcia was now visibly pregnant.

But Paul found himself still focused on one single point. What would Marie say, he wondered, if he asked her to marry him. What would she be like? Every moment opened up on vistas Paul had never imagined. Fear and trembling were real, he thought. It wasn't like facing a firing squad. That would be easy, he thought. This was like facing a life.

At school, Paul organized his science room at West Valley High School. He was still teaching two sections of biology and one of chemistry, as well as a basic math course. He ran a science club with Karl, who taught advanced math courses. Students at West Valley, while obsessed with sports, did have a more academic bent. The school's location at the edge of the University of Alaska didn't hurt.

Karl flashed a *Popular Electronics* magazine at Paul. "We've got to get some of these kits for science club," he said. He showed Paul an ad for a kit to build a personal computer. "My students will surely be interested."

"But what do you use it for?" asked Paul. He had heard about computers, but doubted that they would solve any of his existential problems.

"Oh, I don't know," said Karl airily. "They'll figure it out. I brought back some of these *ComputerWorlds* too. I got them in San Francisco. Have a look when you have a chance."

Paul sighed. He liked observational projects, but they were darn slow. Kits and engines did engage students more quickly. He would have a look. He carried the magazines home to his apartment, where Marie had just arrived!

There she stood in all of her actuality, brown eyes snapping, electric dark hair cut short and wafting around her face, brown hands in the warm woolen sweater with the blue hearts on it she had first worn on the Adventuress. Paul just stood there, the dream falling away in the face of her strangeness. Who was this live woman?

Marie came over to him, however, and they hugged. It was a long hug, neither saying a word. Marie broke away and looked up at him. "Two of us chasing rainbows," she sang, softly.

"We shall be one person," Paul said, reaching up a finger to trace her eyebrows and sealing in language their bond.

25

Line pulled clothes off the umbrella-shaped line in the back garden, enjoying the smell of sunshine on the clothes. Stephen's shirts were already on hangars, as there wasn't room for them amidst all the little t-shirts and pajamas. Ivy was still in diapers. Line washed a load of clothes several times a week, though the drought had lasted so long the kids wore their clothes longer than usual. Clean clothes were a luxury.

Heather stood below her, trying to separate the clothes into piles. "Don't worry about it, Heather," Line said. "We'll sort them out later." In the sandbox nearby, Fern drove little cars over roads she had made, and tried to stave off their destruction by Ivy, who was scooping up sand and didn't care where it landed.

Line sighed. The kids couldn't bathe every night either. There was sand on the floors, sand in the beds. The house was barely under control at any time, and since she was trying to save water everywhere, it was even worse now. Line watered the apricot and the willow tree with buckets of water she had saved from the shower. She had herbs which could stand some abuse, but she had not tried to grow vegetables this year. Even the toilets generally had a bit of yellow pee in them, since the kids were not encouraged to flush the toilets unless the water was "brown."

Carrying the clothes into the house, Line put the basket on a chair near the dining table. "Now," she said to Heather. "Please collect all of the girls' clothes and put them away." Heather made piles of her own things, Fern's and Ivy's, all of which went into drawers in their room. The three girls had the biggest room, what would have been the master bedroom. Christopher had his own room, with an extra bed in it for Poppa when he showed up. The third small bedroom was for Stephen and Line.

It was late on an October afternoon and still very warm, though the days were already much shorter and the heat dissipated as soon as the sun slipped off to the southwest. When the clothes were put away, Line took her book outdoors and sat at the table under the wisteria vine near the garage.

Heather followed with her own book. She was in kindergarten. Of all the kids, she was the most pliable and quiet. Turning over the pages of a picture book which had been read so many times she had it memorized, she whispered the words as she looked at the pictures. "I'm in the milk and the milk's in me," Line could hear her whispering to herself as a pudgy finger tracked the words in a cartoon cloud over Mickey, who fell into a giant milk bottle.

Like plants, Line loved finding out what her children were like. Each might need something a little different, some shade, extra water, a bit of fish emulsion to develop into the flower they were to become. Christy was a wanderer, always excited by new people and things. Heather a little homebody. Fern and Ivy were little hellions at this point, more like each other than Heather. But who knew what they would need in the future. Fern had a little scarring from the burn on her neck, but Line did not feel that it would be that noticeable as she grew.

"Why didn't Hanna or Kristen come this summer?" asked Heather, turning to Line, who was reading the entry on thyme in a herbal handbook. Line loved the writer, Juliette de Bairacli Levy, who wrote about her own

253

experiences with herbs, things she had learned from gypsies, not from books. Ivy had ceded the sandbox to her sister and came over to climb up on Line. She hardly talked at all yet. Line put down her book.

"Well Kristen got married," began Line, taking the dirty little Ivy on her knee. "You remember she kept getting those letters when she stayed with us? The letters were from a man who became her husband. She's going to nursing school now and has to take care of her husband."

"Oh yes," a look dawned on Heather's face as if she remembered. "She told me about him."

Kristen had gotten married in Dad's church, though the wedding was small. Hanna and two of her friends were her attendants. The photographs looked like that of a perfect, conventional white wedding.

Paul had gotten married in Alaska. He sent a photograph of himself with Marie, singing at their wedding reception. Paul, in a suit with a vest, the collar of his shirt open, played guitar. Marie sang into a microphone, wearing a dark print dress with autumn-colored flowers on it, a chrysanthemum in her hair. The photo looked like it was taken in a restaurant. Line had missed both of these weddings. There was simply no money to go. But also, Mikkelsons were not big on celebrations. Every day was a celebration.

"And I asked Hanna to come," said Line, brushing sand off Ivy and coming back to Heather. "But she got into some theatre camp in Minneapolis which was more important to her than sitting here in the garden with us!" Line had wanted the help and she felt it was great experience for her sisters. But Hanna was her own person. Line wished she knew what she was like now.

Stephen had spent a month in Santa Barbara over the summer, working with Bernie Freeman. They were trying to get Stephen's dissertation on A.J. Muste published. The Freemans were doing great work, starting up grass roots organizations and agitating for coastal environmental protection, solar energy and citizens' rights. Tom Hayden too, with Jane Fonda, had started the Campaign for Economic Democracy, which worked with governor Jerry Brown on these issues, as well as the election of forward-thinking local candidates.

With Jimmy Carter in the White House and Jerry Brown as California's leader, Stephen felt political strides were being made, though there was still a long way to go. He came back from Santa Barbara full of energy and excitement. Line had been delighted to see him that way, at least briefly, before the weight of his work and family set back in.

"Marty came for a week," said Heather. "That was fun."

"Yes," said Line. It was wonderful when Marty could come. Marty loved Line's kids. She told Line it was so different from the rest of her life that she willingly gave up half of her summer vacation to be there. "But a week is pretty short!" They were all deep in their grownup lives now. It could not be helped.

When shadows fell completely across the garden, Line heard Christy's bicycle on the loose gravel before she saw him riding nonchalantly up the alley beside the big pine trees. He was in fourth grade, about to be nine. Line didn't care how long he played after school, but insisted that he be back for supper. If he didn't arrive by six p.m. she started calling around to the mothers of his friends in the neighborhood.

"How was school?" Line asked as he dropped his bike on the brown grass.

"Fine," said Christopher. "I'm going to get some milk." He disappeared into the house.

Line did wish the kitchen and the back yard were more related, as they were in some California houses, with big decks and patios opening off them. This house was too old for that. But Line was happy for the house. It was an island where the values she shared with Stephen ruled.

Stephen didn't come home for dinner that night. He had a staff meeting at the Oakes College where he now taught. It was one of the newer colleges at the university, originally called College Seven. It had a focus on ethnic studies, as a compromise with the black students who wanted a college of their own. Stephen taught core courses in history there and one in civil rights issues. When he did get home, the kids were in bed.

Line made them both a cup of tea. "How's it going?" she asked. Oakes was full of stories which Line loved to hear.

"Well, the students want to rename one of the housing units Biko House," he said. "We're all for it, of course." Stephen Biko had been killed in custody in South Africa. He was an anti-apartheid leader, only 30 when he died a month ago.

The story about Biko had been sifting in slowly. The police said he had died as a result of a hunger strike, but Donald Woods, a white journalist had gotten into the morgue and photographed the massive head injuries he had sustained. 10,000 people had attended his funeral. Many more had tried.

"They say he came up with the phrase 'black is beautiful,'" said Stephen. "I also heard that Donald Woods had to leave the country. None of us had heard of Biko," Stephen said. "But this one white guy, his friend, is eloquent enough that twelve countries sent representatives to his funeral! Now that's the power of words right there!"

Line nodded sympathetically. "I'm glad the students want to remember him."

"I really think," said Stephen, "that we need a big mainframe in which we can plug in everyone's version of history, so that someday, we can get a really comprehensive view of truth." One of Stephen's mentors, Page Smith, was writing "people's history," as seen from below by common people, using original source material. It was the issue of Stephen's time: who gets to write history?

"I should have been a librarian," Stephen laughed.

"Someone has to sift that history," said Line. "That's what you do."

"True," said Stephen. "Though interpretation of the truth keeps changing. I do have more sympathy for the blacks than I do for the women just now, as you know," said Stephen. The women's liberation movement on campus was the bane of his existence. He felt it was devolving into hatred of, and competition with, men.

"Well the blacks do have grievances!" said Line. She didn't really understand why the women on campus were so strident. Women had had much success lately, in judicial cases and culturally. Women historians were finding and celebrating women who had not previously been recognized for their contributions. They wanted to write history too. Herstory, as they called it.

Line herself was angry about many things. She wanted to go back to work, wanted a foot of her own in the world. But she could not make enough money to pay for day care for four kids. She must stay home, at least until the kids all started school. Also, the courts would not recognize midwives and many had been arrested when births had sad outcomes. Lately she had been miserable about animal mistreatment, especially on big factory farms.

But Line saw these problems as coming from society's deep structure, not from men only. Caretakers and educators never made as much money as they ought. And science had become defined by what one could measure and see. It did not seem able to value anything else. Herbal healers, midwives and people who worked with nature, such as Alan

Chadwick, were shunned by the 'professional' establishment. Line felt in her bones that natural ways of doing things were better. But men and women must work together to solve these problems.

"How are the cherubs?" Stephen asked.

"Dirty!" said Line. "Can't someone do something about the rain?" she giggled and put her arms around Stephen. She loved their late night conversations.

Nature did do something about the rain. In November, storms began to roll in, washing the countryside and changing everyone's outlook. Line rejoiced. Rain hit the soil, which had become hard as a rock, and ran off down the streets flooding the gutters. Toilets were flushed, sand washed away and the children were cleaner. Slowly the soil began to soften enough to accept the water and the ever-responsive grass shot up little sprouts.

Line made carrot cake cupcakes for Christopher's birthday in November. "Do they have to be carrot cake?" Christy asked.

"Yes," said Line. "You just had all that Halloween candy. You have to eat something decent for a change." She topped each cupcake with cream cheese frosting. "You can put a corn candy on top of each one, if you want."

"If kids bring in carrot cake," said Christy, "everyone knows their family is a bunch of hippies." He leaned out over the table, his chin in his hands.

"Well? So what?" asked Line. "I'll bet there are lots of hippy families in your school."

"I wish we weren't one of them," scowled Christy.

"Oh?" asked Line. "What did you want us to be like?"

"I'd like to have Pop-tarts for breakfast," said Christy. "I want to know what they taste like!" Christopher was a scrawny kid with longish brown hair that curled exactly as Stephen's must have when he was little. He and his Dad weren't close, but Christopher looked like an exact miniature of him. It always made Line laugh.

"Wow," said Line. "They're terrible. But I will get some so you can find out for yourself!" Line never bought anything processed if she could help it. For breakfast there was always granola she had mixed and toasted herself. There was milk or yogurt, raisins and bananas. This week Line had made applesauce because apples were in season. "What else makes you think we're a hippy family?" She handed Christopher the empty frosting bowl and a spoon, licking the big spoon herself.

"Everything we do has to be 'politically correct'!" said Christy. "The 'natural' way, and all that. I'm sick of it," he said.

"Christopher Cohen," said Line looking stern. "Who have you been hanging out with? Where are you getting these ideas?" She knew, though. She could smell a whiff of one of the more well-off families in the area, the Summerwoods.

"I want a BB gun," said Christy flatly.

Line looked at him, shocked. He had named the one thing she could not imagine giving him.

"Andy has a BB gun and he won't let anyone else use it. The only people who can be in his club have a BB gun," said Christy.

Christopher tried to look innocent and righteous, but Line was not amused. Andy, Line knew, was one of the sons of John Summerwood, who drove over the mountain to San Jose every day to work. Line thought of Astrid Summerwood as her opposite in every way. They were definitely not hippies. Astrid had gone to law school, and now worked part time in a law firm. She had every appliance imaginable in her crowded house and a Hispanic woman who came in to clean and keep an eye on the boys in the afternoon. Astrid's best attempt at controlling her boys was: "Just you wait until your father gets home!" There were three of them, the youngest being Andy, and they were a force to be reckoned with in school.

"I think you better begin making your own club, Christopher Cohen," said Line decisively. "You are perfectly capable of doing that. You are not going to get a BB gun!"

"Awww," said Christy. "It's just for target practice!"

Line faced her son and looked at him hard. "If you think 'Make love not war,' is a hippy slogan," she said, "you may be right. But it is one of the ground rules of this family. Your father helped run an organization which demanded the US get out of Vietnam, as you know. Guns are not peaceful, and you can give up the idea right now." Line was calm and definite, keeping her voice down. She was surprised she had to make such an issue of this, but Christy was only nine, she reminded herself.

Christopher gave up quickly. He was interested in many things and the latest thing always took precedence over the previous one. Line could tell he hadn't really expected a BB gun. He was just testing, though Line had to laugh at his technique, calling their family into question first. Manipulative little kid, she thought. He wandered off.

In the morning, Line organized the kids. Stephen caught a ride with a friend as it wasn't safe to ride his bicycle in the thick rain. None of them had much rain gear, but getting wet wasn't a bad thing either. Line drove the few blocks to school, with the girls in the back and a cookie sheet full of cupcakes on Christy's lap. The windshield wipers slapped across the windows, but everyone drove slowly. The air was grey with mist.

When they parked, Line scooped up Ivy and held the big umbrella over the cupcakes as Christy carried them. "Come on Heather," she called. "Come on Fern!" The puddles collecting on the asphalt were attractive!

They stopped in Christopher's room first, where his teacher Miss Alcorn, admired the cupcakes. "Oh good," she said. "They probably don't have too much sugar. I'm telling you, 25 kids full of sugar is no joke!" Birthday treats were an obligatory tradition in California schools. Line didn't mind. She did want the kids to be part of things.

Christopher had absented himself from his mother and sisters immediately by joining a table full of boys in the opposite corner of the room. "Bye, Christy," said Line, waving.

In Heather's kindergarten room, Line and the girls were more at home. Christopher and Heather walked to school most mornings, but Line, Fern and Ivy came after school to pick Heather up. Line often talked to Heather's young teacher, Miss Hernandez. Rows of orange pumpkins, cut and colored by the kids, ran along the edge of the schoolroom. They would soon give way to turkeys.

Heather took off the rain slicker Line had managed to find for her and joined her friends near the bookshelves, Fern following her. Fern loved the idea of school.

"We are dropping off cupcakes for Christy's birthday," Line explained to Miss Hernandez. "But who can complain about the rain? Certainly not me!"

Miss Hernandez sighed. "It makes things harder for us, but I won't complain either. Everything has been so parched. We are really ready for it."

"Oh well," said Line. "What's a few muddy children?" The ground needed to open and let the rain in, reservoirs needed to fill, trees which had been straining for water needed to relax.

"Line," said Miss Hernandez, "I wanted to ask you. This time of year things start going so fast! At the staff meeting we decided to have a Christmas door-decorating contest in December. Could you possibly be the chairman for our room? Help the parents organize and prepare a great door?"

Line blanched, but of course she could. "Yes, I guess so," she said. Miss Hernandez was new to the school, but she had a lot of enthusiasm. Heather predictably loved her.

"I would really like to win!" Miss Hernandez said. "Don't worry about it right now, but I am sure you would have good ideas for the door." She looked over toward Fern. "And lots of help!"

"Fern!" said Line. "Come on, we must go home so school can start!" Line went over and took her hand, tearing her away from the crowd around a little train laid out at the edge of the room. Shifting Ivy, and managing the unwieldy umbrella, Line took her two youngest girls out to the car. A Christmas door? She was nonplussed. But she did have time to think about it.

The rain continued and people began to get used to it. One night the wind was strong and all the electricity went out. The electric stove quit in the middle of cooking pasta and there were no lights at all. Line looked for candles to light, telling the little girls to stay put. Christopher came up with a flashlight. Line would have been happier if Stephen had been home, but he would be late that night. She hoped he was all right.

The tomato pasta sauce was already cooked, but Line left the pasta in the hot water as long as she could, so that it would get a little softer. The kids didn't seem to mind eating by candlelight, and Line had to admit it was lovely. The only thing she was worried about was the mess. It was hard to see pasta sauce on the floor in the dark!

"It's like the olden days," Line said. "You know people didn't always have electric lights!"

"Did Poppa have them?" asked Christy, shoveling pasta into his mouth.

"Yes, I'm sure he did," said Line. "He lived in New York, and cities always had the new things first."

"What can we do without light after supper?" asked Christy.

Line laughed. "Well in the olden days, I think people went to bed early!" she teased. "But we could also have a fire in the fireplace, and that would give us some light." Also heat, she thought. The house had electric baseboard heaters, but it would stay warm for a while. "You've seen all those pictures of Abraham Lincoln studying by the fire, haven't you?"

"We could sing," said Heather.

"I want to sing," said Fern.

"Okay," said Line. "Everyone think of something to sing, or a story to tell. Or even a poem if you know one, and we'll sit in front of the fire before we go to bed. Christy, can you help me with the fire?"

Line had learned to build fires from Dad, and she taught Christy. Stephen, the city dweller, didn't have a clue. They had not had a fire yet this year. Fires were for special occasions. But there was wood in the garage, and even a little kindling left from last year.

Line made sure all the candles were too high up for Ivy or Fern to reach. "Heather," she said. "You're in charge of Ivy. I'll only be gone a minute."

Line and Christy rushed out to the garage under the umbrella in the wind and rain. Using Christy's flashlight, they piled the little red wagon full of wood and kindling. The light dwindled as they did so. "The battery's going," said Christy.

"I bet a tree fell on our power lines," said Line. It looked like all the houses around them were dark, and there were no streetlights.

"I hope they don't come back on," said Christy. "This is fun!"

With the fire going and candles on the mantelpiece, Line's little party sang songs and recited any poems they could think of. "I'm a little teapot," was a favorite, which Heather taught Fern. And Christy made them all giggle with a song which seemed to chiefly consist of the words "Shake, shake, shake, shake your booty!" Which he did, dancing in front of the fire.

"Come on, everybody!" said Christy. "I wish I had some music!" But Line had heard it, she could almost remember. "Shake, shake, shake, shake your booty!" he yelled. The little girls seemed to need no information at all about where their booty was. They stood shaking it! Even Ivy on her two, sturdy little legs jigged up and down.

"Oh I wish Daddy could see you," said Line, smiles and laughter streaming from her. She could not imagine herself at nine doing anything similar! "You know there is school tomorrow. It is definitely time for bed!"

Teeth brushing was difficult in the dark, but Line held candles and helped. She wondered just how long this problem would go on. "Good night, sweet girls," she said, as the girls fell into bed.

"Thank you Christy," Line said as she helped Christopher. His flashlight had gone out long ago. "You are a big help."

Line stayed up, trying to clean up the kitchen by candlelight. There seemed to be hot water, so at least the pilot light on the gas water heater hadn't gone out. She was thinking about Stephen. The great thing about Santa Cruz was that they had so many friends.

Both Stephen and Line loved the community raised around Alan Chadwick and the conflict over his garden. Alan was now in Covelo, California, working with his interns on other gardens, but friends, especially Paul Lee and Page Smith, Stephen's history mentor, kept in touch with Chadwick. These men were also starting restaurants and non-profit programs to benefit Santa Cruz. Line was still involved with the Birth Center, though it was changing. The more militant women continued to teach each other and work with pregnant women. Raven Lang was their leader. But others had gone back to school.

As Line rinsed dishes and put them into the drainer, Stephen walked in, dropped off at home by one of his faculty friends. "I was just thinking about how much I trust people in this community to help each other," said Line as Stephen came toward her in the dark and kissed her.

"I can see what you've been up to," he said, indicating the red coals of the fire in the living room.

"The kids loved it!" said Line. "But I am hoping the electricity comes back on before morning!"

"We'll see," said Stephen. "It was fine at the university, so it's probably just one power station. I'm sure crews are out at this very moment."

"Good!" said Line. "One night's an adventure, but morning might be a struggle."

"Page Smith told me that Paul Lee wants to hold a service under what he calls 'the sacred oak' over in a meadow in Pogonip on Thanksgiving day," Stephen announced. "I told him we'd come."

"Okay," said Line. "I was just thinking of those two. They're amazing!" Paul Lee was a Lutheran, a student of Paul Tillich at Harvard. "We can give thanks for the rain!"

"It'll be non-sectarian," said Stephen. Both Stephen and Line made sure their kids knew the stories from the Bible, but they could not drag the kids to church or synagogue services in which they themselves didn't believe. Stephen saw the old and new testaments as history and was interested in the light the Dead Sea scrolls were beginning to shed on the times.

"It's the very community I was thinking about," said Line. In her mind's eye, she saw her family in a green meadow surrounded by the people they knew, with the probable exception of the Summerwoods!

The actual day was not far from what Line imagined. The weather was mild again after weeks of rain, the sun warm and pleasant. Paul Lee had found 'the sacred oak' while riding his horse. He pointed out where a limb had been lopped off that looked like a head with a semblance of eyes and a mouth, the enormous limbs as outstretched arms, an image of Christ crucified.

For Line, all oaks were sacred. She did not need to personify them, but she was willing to go along with the idea if it got people together. A California live oak with spreading, craggy limbs, its little leaves had sharp points on them, almost like holly. It was made to stand a lot of drought. Not a deciduous tree, it retained its leaves all year, though they were brown and brittle now.

Paul Lee passed out bread and wine, and lyric sheets for songs he thought were appropriate. He spoke a little, and then everyone sang a Woodie Guthrie song to the music of a guitar. "This land is your land, this land is my land, from California to the New York Island." Line moved closer to Christopher. "Listen to the words," she whispered. "This is about you!"

For Line, the best part of the morning was singing "'Tis the gift to be simple, 'tis the gift to be free. 'Tis the gift to come down where we ought to be." She looked with smiling eyes across to Stephen, who held Ivy in his arms. "And when we find ourselves in the place just right, 'Twill be in the valley of love and delight." Yes, she thought. This is the place.

26

A large bouquet of branches with small pomegranates hanging from them interlaced with unfamiliar grasses and greens greeted Marty and Erik in the front hall of Chez Panisse. The restaurant was a two-story house in Berkeley with a monkey puzzle tree and a handcrafted metal gate in front of it. The host showed them to their favorite seat in front of a window looking out at the street. It was a weeknight, wet and raining, but for Marty the casual classicism of the café elevated the evening.

"Frank Lloyd Wright windows?" asked Marty. The windows were paned with thin wooden strips, the walls paneled in wood. Each table had a candle with a little square copper hood on it. Handmade copper lamps hanging from the ceiling gave the room a warm light.

"I think more Charles Rennie Mackintosh," said Erik. "He influenced Wright. This place is an extension of Berkeley's Arts and Crafts movement, what I know of it. Maybeck, Julia Morgan. If you look around, everything is crafted."

Stiff white tablecloths laid on the tables were covered with a square of white paper. The tableware lay heavily on thick white napkins. A smiling waiter with a towel wrapped around his waist placed a glass carafe of water in front of them as if it were gold. He brought a small dish of olives and a loaf of peasant bread with butter beside it. The menu for the evening was printed on a piece of creamy paper, but there were no choices except among the wines.

"It's like a monastery," said Marty quietly. "It's all rigorously correct, as if things couldn't be any other way." Marty had found the restaurant listed in the paperback *Little Restaurants of San Francisco*. It was now their favorite. Tonight they were celebrating the fact that Erik had passed his architectural exams and become a licensed architect. It was a big step for him and they were both very pleased. He had begun to look more like a professional too, his attractively chiseled face more mature, his hair shorter and not quite so blonde.

The set menu for the evening began with a plate of linguine with mussels. Marty broke off a piece of bread and dipped it in the rich, garlicky sauce. She did not know anything about mussels. Where did you find them? How did you cook them?

Erik was as interested in food as Marty was, as willing to take time and money for a meal in a good restaurant. He was not intimidated by the long wine list, and at the waiter's recommendation drank a glass of Sancerre with his mussels. Marty was too worried about the price to order one, but she took a sip out of his glass.

"I had a chance to look at Alexander's book today," said Marty. "Someone brought it in to work."

"You did!" said Erik. "I haven't even seen it." Erik had studied with Christopher Alexander, a professor at the University of California's architecture school. The book was published by Oxford University Press on thin Bible paper pages. It described a 'pattern language' which Alexander had discerned, with the help of his assistants, for making good buildings.

"It's full of little drawings and photographs," said Marty. "I like some of the patterns especially, like Light on Two Sides of a Room. Of course you can't see people properly if the light is from only one side. I never thought of it before." Marty detached a mussel from its shell with a fork.

"Yup," said Erik. "We've known about this for a long time."

"Do you 'wrinkle' the edges of your big hotels and condos to get light in?" asked Marty.

"Yes, often," said Erik. "The rooms on the corners are featured. They're the most expensive in a hotel. But you can't follow this rule in every room." A lovely little pile of dark mussel shells with opalescent linings accumulated on the plate in front of him.

"I suppose not," said Marty. "So many modern apartments are like caves, big window wall on one side, but not a shred of side light."

"True," said Erik. "Modernism at its worst. But glass and steel are here to stay. Alexander's getting to be more of an artist than an architect. He shoots concrete to get curves and rounded edges. It's not cost-effective."

The word 'cost-effective' jumped out at Marty. Erik was taking on the language of Murray Costa, the big architecture firm he worked for. They had helped him get the experience to take the exam. He could now put AIA, for American Institute of Architects, behind his name. He was a professional, if a lazy one.

Marty herself worked for a big architectural firm. Their jobs paid for their apartment, and the lovely food in front of them at Chez Panisse. But Marty hoped that their lives had bigger ideas to them. If they could only find one to share!

"You bought the rug under Alexander's influence, didn't you?" asked Marty. She was referring to the authentic Persian carpet which lay in their living room. It was thick, made of tufted wool in medieval patterns, in colors made with natural dyes. Marty loved it. She didn't think about it, but it filled the atmosphere of their flat.

"Yeah, I guess so," said Erik. "I thought it would be a good investment. Something whose value increases with time. Also," he smiled, "hard to steal."

"It has been a good investment," said Marty. "I feel that that carpet underscores our life. It's always there, somewhere in my field of vision, since we live with it every day. Like a popular song that gets stuck in your head."

"Yeah," said Erik. He looked noncommittal, as if he had moved on from the pre-occupations of his days in architectural school. "Looks like a ski weekend," he said, looking out at the rain. Storms had rolled through California for much of November and December and snowfall was heavy, relieving the long drought California had suffered for the past two years.

Marty nodded, unsurprised. She did not usually go up to the Sierras with Erik, as he was a downhill skier and liked to move fast. Lately he had been manic about it, leaving early on Saturday and getting in a whole day, sleeping in a cheap ski bum hotel and skiing Sunday before returning that night.

The second course was a duck breast with corn fritters, wild greens and mushrooms, beautifully dressed. The waiter explained that the hedgehog mushrooms had arrived that very afternoon, foraged up in the woods of Sonoma County. Marty shut her eyes as she tasted them, smelling the earthy oils and enjoying the crisp roasted edges.

"When my Dad and Mother picked morels on our hillside in Iowa, I wouldn't do more than taste them," she said. "Now I understand what a delicacy they are!"

"We might have had them creamed," said Erik. "My Dad liked prime rib, so every so often we went to Lawry's in Beverly Hills. They had creamed corn, creamed spinach, gravy, all that stuff. I bet my Dad still goes there. Nothing fresh. Stuff probably came out of cans. But the meat cart came right to the table. They sliced it in front of you."

"Such a different world," said Marty. She shivered, remembering the icy reception she had gotten in Palm Desert from Erik's mother.

"Believe me, it gives me the chills also!" said Erik. "I think I had to wear a bow tie. I'm not kidding! Mother made me."

"And your brother?" asked Marty. She tried to imagine the two boys tagging after their parents, like perfect little people out of a glossy magazine advertisement.

"He's quite at home there," said Erik. "He probably still goes to Lawry's." Erik looked incredulous. "I do like a little prime rib now and then though, I'll admit."

Dessert was a plate of pears and toasted walnuts, with a wedge of gorgonzola.

"Mmmmmm," said Marty. "I never even knew I liked gorgonzola!"

"It's like dinner in a fine home," said Erik.

"It is like the dinners the Magnussons served in Oxford," said Marty. "I swear! So many different tastes all melded perfectly together. I guess that's where I learned to eat."

"It's worth knowing," said Erik.

The spell of the transcendent had begun to wear off. Marty's stomach was uncomfortably full. "Coffee?" asked the waiter. Erik nodded but Marty demurred. The waiter scraped the breadcrumbs from the paper in front of them with a little knife before bringing the steaming cup.

By Friday the air had cleared and the sun shown down warmly as Marty stepped out for lunch. At the entrance to the reconstructed Cannery, in a niche which amplified the sound, stood a clarinet player. He had longish hair and confidently played New Orleans music which was all of a sudden everywhere in the city. It was as if people had just discovered Scott Joplin.

Marty smiled at the man as his fingers flew over the keys and the stops. He wove up and down, making music so good it made Marty want to dance. His clarinet case lay on the sidewalk open in front of him, full of green bills.

The Cannery was full of shops and restaurants. Marty nipped into the bookstore on the ground floor where she had been eyeing Edward Weston's *Daybooks*, in which he described his photographic life in Mexico and California. Marty splurged and bought both volumes. The second had a glowing pepper on the cover, as sinuous as the backside of a person. The books were beautiful, with prints of Weston's amazing photographs tucked in between the pages of his journals.

A quick bowl of soup and half a sandwich and Marty was back at work. Looking down the aisle of desks she noticed a Bartlett pear someone had put on top of the papers on their desk. It looked so alive, yellow tinged with brown in a suggestive shape, heavy at the bottom. All around it desks were piled high with paper and file folders, bookshelves above them spilling over with binders and books. The gorgeous pear stood out against black and white, straight lines and rectangles, begging to be eaten, touched, seen.

Trudy, Tib Thibodeau's assistant solicited Marty's attendance at a bar that evening. "Friday night," she said. "Tib wants to take us all out." Marty was one of eight people in the programming department, which did no drawing, but laid out the needs of a building project.

"Okay," said Marty. She tried to avoid the evening drinks routine, but once in a while she could not pass up an evening of gossip. Monday night that week she had stayed at the office until 3 a.m. typing Robin

Bradshaw's book on architectural programming the company was publishing. She richly deserved a drink!

Marty's piano-playing fingers were now good at typing. Robin Bradshaw, who was British, appreciated Marty's excellent spelling and grammar. The typed words were saved on cassette tapes. The program left a little room at the end of each line on the magnetic tape for additions, but if Robin wanted to add a whole sentence, which he often did, Marty had to redo several lines to tuck the sentence in. It was laborious, but better than retyping an entire page several times.

Jill pooh-poohed this method of word processing. "Random access storage will be much better," she told Marty.

After work, Marty slid into a big leatherette booth with her cohort. Jill and Shantanu, the programmer from India. Betty the librarian and Trudy, Robin Bradshaw and Tib Thibodeau. Fred Lee, a strait-laced Lutheran from the Midwest with a wife and baby, had not come Marty noticed. The rest circled around the table. Everyone ordered drinks, Marty a glass of sherry. Sherry reminded her of Oxford.

With a glass of iced gin and tonic in front of her, Trudy let out a breath and said, "Civilization!" She raised her glass. She was a single woman, a few years older than Marty, easily stressed by what went on in the office.

"I found some leis that I think we could afford," said Betty to Trudy. She was talking about the upcoming Christmas party, a Hawaiian luau to be held in the office. "The flowers are real. I really don't want plastic!"

"Can't wait to see you in your grass skirt!" said Robin.

Betty smiled at him. She was thin and pretty, though her dark hair was graying a little. Betty's father, Mr. Pierson, was one of the founding members of the company. She managed the library, with enough time to write a newsletter and also set up the social calendar for the company, often with an ethnic theme. Her family was Scottish, so the company celebrated Robert Burns birthday with oatmeal scones and tea. Betty read one of his poems!

"I do have a grass skirt," Betty said. "I hope you are dusting off your best Hawaiian shirt!"

"Don't worry," said Robin. "I'll find one!" Robin was at least as old as Tib, tall and rangey with a head of white-yellow hair. A transplant from England, he had a modern air and often wore bluejeans. Marty liked him, but he was quite reticent. He liked Marty too and treated her as if she were an equal. Robin didn't require ceremony, but professionalism prevented the group from talking about their personal lives.

"I want to thank you all for rising to the occasion of that deadline today," said Tib. "Couldn't have done it without any of you!" Marty had little imagination of Tib's life. He was a venerable architect who had found his niche developing this group to specify the number of rooms required, the furniture, electrical and structural requirements of big hospitals.

"Such redundancy," scoffed Robin. "It's like having two hospitals right next to each other." At King Khalid Military City Hospital, which the company was programming and designing for the Saudi Arabian government, all of the women's facilities had to be separate from the men's. Not just restrooms, but entire suites of offices, operating rooms and hospital rooms.

"It's deep in the desert, isn't it?" asked Shantanu in his sing-song, bitten off English. "Are we using the 'famous' interstitial space?" A thin slice of space under the floor, or sometimes in the ceiling, hid the electrical cabling, plumbing and other infrastructure. Temporary floor or ceiling panels allowed for the constant updating expected as departments moved around and technology changed.

"Of course," said Tib. "But the furniture and equipment inventory you're working on is really something new for us. Databases are surely the direction of the future." He raised his glass to Jill who designed them and, with Shantanu's help, programmed them.

Jill nodded, receiving his approval. Jill was a star. She had gone to Berkeley's School of Architecture also, though she was most interested in the data processing which could be done in the field. She was investigating the idea of drafting with computers. Though they spent a lot of time together, Marty could hardly conceive of Jill's world of math and science, so different from her own.

"Another drink?" asked Trudy. Marty could tell Trudy would be perfectly happy settling in to drink and eat snacks all evening. But both Jill and Betty lived across the Bay Bridge in the eastern part of Oakland.

"I need to go home," said Jill.

"I'd have another," said Betty, recklessly. "If I'm late enough, the kids will already be in bed when I get home!" Her husband was taking care of the kids. Betty and her husband had bought a palatial, old house in Oakland. Marty had once been there. The fireplace was as large as the ones Marty had seen in photographs of Hearst Castle. Betty's two kids danced around the fire but there was no furniture in the room. Like Line's house in

Santa Cruz. "One day we'll have enough money to furnish it," Betty had said.

"Go ahead," said Tib, standing up. He handed Trudy some cash. "Just give me back what you don't use in the morning."

"Thanks!" said Trudy. Everyone else prepared to leave. Marty was of two minds. Erik might not be home anyway. But she stood up too, leaving Trudy and Betty, who were old friends, to gossip.

Marty walked home through the clear, cold air. The office, her job, gave her a chance to scan the horizon to see what was happening in the world, what other people were thinking about. She was a little radar screen poking up from the deck of a ship, turning, turning, noting and recording blips in various directions. Her own inner life went on below this surface.

Marty was glad she wasn't teaching in a high school. Working as an administrative assistant, providing form to other people's content, gave her freedom. She did not know what she thought about anything yet. She was still peeling away the layers of the culture she had grown up in, and had not achieved any content of her own. This vulnerability was precious. She was glad she was on the West Coast and could make enough money to support herself. Paul, her brother, was probably a good teacher, but he must have to teach what was expected of him. Marty herself could be in free fall, as long as she got to work on Monday!

Marty longed to hear from Ming-Yue, who was now in New York. Marty had received one letter, but that was all. She felt closer to Ming-Yue than anyone else. Perhaps even closer than she was to Erik! My growing point, thought Marty. What she longed for showed her where she was growing. But what was it about?

It must be that she liked people who had traveled, who had grown up in exotic circumstances, as Ming-Yue had in Hong Kong. Ming-Yue was a world citizen. She told Marty that on Christmas Eve when she was growing up her family went to a Hong Kong night club to eat, drink and watch people perform. It shocked Marty. A greater contrast between Marty's isolated snowy Christian Christmases and Ming-Yue's could not be imagined!

It was also something about ambitions and ideas, Marty thought. Ming-Yue had been unhappy doing work which was beneath her talents and aspirations. In New York she took a job at Skidmore, Owings and Merrill, one of the oldest and largest architectural firms, which had pioneered the use of glass-walled skyscrapers, the 'international style.'

In her first letter to Marty, Ming-Yue pointed out what she had found lacking in San Francisco: "Everyone is very much interested and quite knowledgeable on the subject of design. All have a very serious, but almost humble attitude. Everyone is interested, confident and has the self-assurance of being in a good office, but that prevalent 'air,' as one immediately detects from SOM San Francisco is absent. ... Here I am surprised to see a slower, but very serious attitude. The importance lies in thinking, not speed. One is told to think thoroughly before one draws."

Marty was happy for her. She missed this kind of talk, this kind of aspiration. Erik certainly didn't have it, though she was proud of him for getting his license and settling in to a big, powerful company. He didn't seem to care as much about design as he did about the game, about wooing and working with big corporate clients. That was why Bud Murray liked him.

It wasn't that Marty thought of architecture as romantic. She saw it as an attempt to create space which transformed those entering it, making them excited and thoughtful and part of something larger. She thought she saw it in the 'pattern language' Christopher Alexander wrote about. Marty's own aspiration was more like that of Ming-Yue than that of Jill. Jill was interested in what science had to offer people, but Ming-Yue was interested in art.

Walking in North Beach at night always felt safe. The streets were full of people, bars and restaurants were open and warmth, talk and music came out of them. Marty could nip into any doorway if she were at all worried, and meld into the crowd. She generally didn't go to bars, but if she needed people, they were there. Between her own common sense and her general trust, Marty rarely felt frightened when she came home late.

Marty climbed the hill to the flat and went up the steps. The little lamp which lit the entrance was on. Erik did not seem to be home. Perhaps he had left for the Sierras already. Marty made herself an omelette, using fresh sage from the plant she kept on the roof and slices of Monterey jack cheese. She was thinking about how much Ming-Yue (now Meredith, she reminded herself) liked food. One night Ming-Yue had told Marty that she felt Japan got all the credit for beautiful Asian design, while in fact Japan simply took things from the ancient mother culture of China and refined them.

Marty wrapped a blanket around herself in lieu of a fire, and curled up under the lamp on one of the Barcelona chairs with Edward Weston's journals. His too was an inner life Marty understood. An American life.

The next night, Saturday, at 9:30 p.m., Marty slipped into a weathered forgotten building on Green Street which had been appropriated by the Old Spaghetti Factory. It was now a slim and dusty theater where flamenco guitar players and dancers gathered late on weekend nights. Two rows of wooden benches lined one side of the narrow room and on the other was a makeshift stage. The program couldn't start until late, as most of the dancers and musicians were waiters in the surrounding restaurants.

Marty sat on one of the benches, waiting as people packed themselves into the small space. At the end of the dimly-lit room, a man had begun playing the guitar. Just a man in a white shirt and black vest, playing a beautiful wood inlaid guitar. Stillness and sensitive sounds were followed by furious energetic strumming, and then back to the delicate melody. The man got everything he could out of the instrument which was a part of himself. Marty picked out the main melody which he played against a few small flourishes and ornaments, a low bass line at the bottom.

As they came in, people immediately became quiet and respectful because of the music. The dancers filed in and sat opposite the audience. No one spoke as the dancing began. The guitar was accompanied by the powerful voice of one of the men singing, as the others clapped.

First a younger girl in a wonderful red dress with tiered skirts and sleeves began slowly. Turning and twisting her arms artfully, she picked up the lower part of her dress with one hand and held it high. Her other hand turned at the wrist above her head, circling and gathering all eyes to her. A man beat on the wooden box in front of him like a drum. Finally, after furious clapping and stamping, the girl sat down, gathering her red tiers around her.

An older woman danced with the man who seemed to be the leader of the group. She was lovely, her black hair pulled back into a chignon, a flower at her ear. She raised her hands, clapping in time as her feet found the beat of the music, stamping in her heeled shoes. Turning her back to the audience, she moved her hips from side to side in the tight dress as the dance slowed. Her understated movements came from inside of her, in a language of joy and sorrow which everyone could understand.

Even better was the male dancer. He had little hair on his balding head and his clothes were very tight on his body: grey pants, a white shirt with blousy sleeves and a grey vest. When he danced by himself, his expressive body hardly moved, but you could see the hidden passion. Then he exploded into the stamping, clicking, and tapping of extraordinary footwork. Marty couldn't believe it. All of his life had gone into these formal movements which showed such delicacy and such power.

In the middle of the session, two men brought chairs out onto the stage and played guitar. One was visiting from Spain. Marty knew little of the music, the technicalities. She only knew her heart ached. She thought of the American pop music awards show she had recently seen on television, in which every act reeked with glitz, spangles and glamour. It had nothing of the art the flamenco guitar players and dancers created with only their bodies and a guitar made of wood.

Marty stayed until the last dance, listening, watching. She found it fascinating that the older people were so much better than the younger ones. In America, everyone looked to young people, their athleticism, their beauty and splash. But here one could see that beauty was not reserved for the young, and there were things, physical and emotional things, which could only be expressed after long practice, by inhabiting bodily movements which were repeated endlessly, but were always completely new.

It was late when Marty got home. She made a small fire in the Swedish fireplace and poured herself a glass of sherry.

The deep colors of the Persian rug glowed in the lamplight, protected by another rug on top of it where sparks might fly. The vermillion expanse was dense with patterns of what must represent fruit and flowers outlined in dark Prussian blue. An inner border and an outer border defined a thick black field at the edges of the rug. Marty knew little about it, except that it was Persian and made recently. Erik had bought it at Emmett Eiland, a well known rug company in Berkeley.

Flamenco dancing had come from gypsies, the turning and twirling, the rhythmic handclaps and furious stamping. Marty felt a bit bereft, as if they and the other Mediterranean countries had something she did not, she who spent most of her day surrounded by stacks of paper, plastic binders, and metal desks, under hideous fluorescent light. A place so ugly that a single Bartlett pear stood out in gleaming magic against it.

Marty had been inoculated against some of contemporary ugliness by Mother and Dad's preoccupation with nature. The Mikkelsons had never been well-off, but Marty's parents' innate taste had kept her focused on the natural. Even now, Mother was deeply involved in weaving wool and cotton fabrics and Dad made thick, rustic loaves of bread from grain he had ground himself.

Line's family lived on hand-me-downs from the thrift shops, but Line kept to natural materials also. The garden was everything to Line. Marty was happy the rains had come and Line could be assured of a garden next year. And Paul? Marty had no idea. The grandeur of Alaska, its snows, mountains, rivers and aurora borealis must make up his life. As well as music, it sounded like, since his marriage to a folk singer.

Marty had given herself to the simplicity and clarity of the Modern style which Erik espoused, but it did not preclude such things as this rich and marvelous carpet. Marty sipped her sherry, letting its warmth go down her throat. She pulled out the Weston book and turned the pages of the photographs slowly. She would not give up on the transcendent. It was really all there was.

27

Line looked at her family, sandwiched around the dining table in Poppa's crowded brownstone in Brooklyn. It was a little bit fuggy in the summer heat, Line thought, but exotic spices lifted a warm, pungent smell into the air. Big tureens of Basmati rice, and two kinds of curry, cooked by Sadia, the wife of Poppa's assistant Ashik Rahman, stood on the sideboard. There were also many other vegetable dishes, cucumbers, flavored yogurts and chutneys.

Line was proud of the kids. Christopher spooned chicken curry onto his rice with no help. He was excited by new tastes. The little girls ate mostly rice and yogurt, but Heather and Fern did taste the lentil curry. Line had put a tiny bit on each of their plates.

Heather turned up her nose. "It's hot!" she said.

Fern seemed to like it. "Do you want more?" Stephen asked her. She nodded, her eyes very large.

Tiny Ivy, two years old, sat on thick law books, spooning up rice, an apron tied around her neck.

Line smiled at Sadia, who hovered nearby in a blue cotton sari, woven with many other colors. "So good!" said Line. She had made curries herself, but none as good as these. "I would like to see your spice cupboard," Line said.

"She'll take you to the Indian market if you want," said Poppa. He had come down to the ground-floor dining room for lunch in his bow tie from his office upstairs. "She goes often."

Sadia smiled and spoke carefully in heavily accented English, "Yes, you will like it." Poppa had made room for Ashik and Sadia to live in the top level of the narrow building, helping them bring their kids to America

274

to get an education. They were refugees from the terrible poverty, famine and political turmoil going on in the newly formed country of Bangladesh. Their son was studying economics, their daughter wanted to be a doctor.

It was the middle of the day on a June Monday. The wet warm air was quite the opposite of what the California Cohens were used to. Poppa had grown impatient to see his grandchildren and paid for airline tickets to bring them to New York. The little girls were really too young, Line thought. They might not remember much. But it was eye-opening for Line to see Stephen's city.

Line tried putting Fern and Ivy down for a nap on the portable bed Poppa had put in the guest room. "Quiet time," Line insisted. "If you sleep a little we'll go out and look around later." The two little girls were becoming inseparable. Line lay down on her own bed with Heather beside her reading a book. Christy's bed was in Poppa's room. Line wasn't worried about him in this deeply interesting old house with Poppa and Stephen nearby.

If they stayed inside, Line felt fine, but the neighborhood was frightening. In the cab from the airport they noticed trash and beat-up cars lining the streets of Bedford-Stuyvesant. Every ground level window had black iron bars on it.

The house was nice, Line thought, trying to see the good in it. Big windows, high ceilings, spacious rooms. There was still an unused fireplace on every one of the four floors. The narrow garden in back was paved with cement tiles, though it did have an actual tree. Trash cans stood against the wooden fence, a few wilted potted plants, and two sad lawn chairs where people sat when it was hot, looking up into the back windows of the neighboring houses.

Line could understand why nothing was planted or visible on the street in front, but the place made her feel claustrophobic. Line wasn't anxious to go sight-seeing. She found it instructive to just be there, to feel the actual vibes of the place.

They did go out, though, when the kids woke up and the sun wasn't so high in the sky. Poppa was insistent that they see two things in New York. He didn't care about anything except the Statue of Liberty and the United Nations.

As he didn't keep one of his own, Poppa hired a car. "We want to go to Battery Park," Poppa told the driver. "But don't take the tunnel. Take the bridge, even if it's a little longer. My son and his family are from California. They've never been out here." The driver looked at them in the rearview mirror, but said nothing. Line guessed he didn't speak much English.

The streets looked like a war zone, graffiti and trash everywhere. There was a wide mix of kinds of people, but most were black. "You can see why I was right at home on the south side of Chicago," Stephen said as they drove through the neighborhood looking at the few pedestrians. "In the 1960's there were gang wars and race riots here, but mostly these are people with jobs."

"Robert Kennedy moved in to study the problems here in the 1960's, and lots of grassroots programs were developed," said Poppa. "Anti-poverty programs all over the country are based on them. The place is so interesting I've never wanted to move." Poppa's parents had bought the house in the 1930's and Poppa had run his immigration law practice from the first floor his whole adult life. When Sima, Stephen's mother, was alive, she did a lot of the work of Poppa's practice, but now Ashik did it.

"A couple of years ago, they were laying off everyone at the Seatrain Ship Builders, but Shirley Chisholm stepped in and helped the company restructure their loans. They're still one of the biggest employers out at the Brooklyn Navy Yard," Poppa continued. "But oh my God. I'm glad you weren't here last year during the blackout. That was really something. Half the downtown burned!"

"I don't feel at home here any more," Stephen said. "I just don't know what's happening."

They drove through the huge stone arches of the ancient Brooklyn Bridge toward the skyscraper-filled island. "When they first built the bridge, people weren't sure it could hold the weight of all the people and vehicles," said Poppa. "But then P.T. Barnum sent a parade of elephants across it. I would like to have seen that!"

The car went around the bottom edge of Manhattan to Battery Park, a dusty piece of land with a few trees on it, bounded on the north by skyscrapers. "They've been trying to get a big housing project going here for quite a while," said Poppa. Near the water, the air was fresher, the breezes blowing. Trash and homeless people ruled the park benches. The lady of liberty looked out across the water from her high perch. Line could see tiny people walking on the island below the statue.

Poppa bought ferry tickets and their little group climbed the stairway to an upper deck. Line carried Ivy at her waist and held firmly onto Heather's hand. Stephen hung onto 4-year-old Fern, but Christopher was way ahead of them as usual.

Catching up to Christy at the ferry railing Line grabbed him by the hand. As sharply as she could she said, "You must not run off. There are so many people in New York. You could end up getting kidnapped, or in a police station. I swear to you, Christopher Cohen, that if you don't stay with us, we will go straight home and never go out again!" Christopher looked solemn as Line dragged him by the hand and demanded Poppa's complicity. "Poppa, can he stay with you? I won't worry if I know he's with you."

At they neared the island, Line looked up at the massive statue. The eyes of the lady, under huge eyebrows, were looking up, as if focused on higher thoughts. Large lips were set not in a smile, but in a thoughtful complement to her eyes. She had big bare toes. By the time they had debarked, it was almost impossible to see her. She was too close and too high.

"Climb up inside?" asked Poppa. "I often take my clients out here. I've climbed those 377 steps many times."

"Me too," said Stephen ruefully. "I don't think I need to go today!"

"Christopher?" asked Poppa. "You can look out of the windows of her crown. That'd be something to tell your friends at school."

Christopher looked thrilled and the two of them went off to the entrance. "Be careful Poppa!" said Line. He was certainly spry, but he was in his sixties.

Line and Stephen were content to wander around the pedestal and look in at the immigration museum.

Emma Lazarus' poem was embossed in bronze. Reading it, the melody Line had sung it to in high school chorus returned to her. A majestic melody, simple and sure, like a hymn. "Give me your tired, your poor, your wretched masses yearning to breathe free." She thought of her own ancestors who had arrived, poor and sick on ships coming from Norway and Denmark a hundred years ago. Probably the statue, which was 92 years old, was not yet there when their ships pulled into New York harbor.

Line and Stephen sat waiting for Poppa and Christy, the little girls around them, the breezes whipping through their hair. "Do you wish you were back here?" asked Line.

"No," said Stephen. "There's a lot of innovation and cultural movement going on where we are in California. I'm perfectly happy in Santa Cruz."

"I'm glad to hear that!" Line said. "Visiting is fine, but I don't want to move anywhere." She nuzzled Ivy's little neck with her nose.

When they got back to the Brooklyn townhouse, Poppa brought out his photograph albums. Line sat on a big leather sofa in the waiting room of his office, turning the pages with Heather, the little girls looking on. They were all sleepy in the heat. During the day, the room overflowed with people, but now the evening sun sneaked in through the blinds, lighting up the rows of dusty law books, some of them very old.

Stephen sat on the coffee table in front of them, watching. There was Poppa and Sima at their wedding under a little velvet canopy. Sima wore a white coat and high heels. Her dark brows and deep-set eyes were lovely in a long face. Jacob, who had come to New York as a baby with his parents, wore a suit.

"Your mother was lovely," said Line. She had only met her once, when Jacob and Sima had come to Iowa for Line's wedding, the blessing of Line and Stephen's union. Line looked up, but Poppa was in the office, looking through the notes Ashik had left him from the afternoon. Always, work pushed up through the cracks of Poppa's life, no matter what he did. Line exchanged a look with Stephen. "Like father, like son," she said. Stephen also usually had work on his mind.

There were snapshots of Stephen, taken on the stoop of this very house, and one of Jacob and Sima in the office. Stephen's school pictures. "See," Line pointed to Heather. "Dad was once a little boy!"

"He looks like Christy!" said Heather.

Line turned the page. There was a clipping of a news photograph, with Stephen's face in a crowd of demonstrators. And then, there was Line's own wedding photograph. Line in a printed dress, carrying tulips. "See Heather," Line pointed to it, "Mom and Dad got married at Grandpa and Grandma Mikkelsons' church in Iowa." She remembered Poppa crushing a wineglass under his feet, shouting "It's bitter, make it sweet!" There had been some bitterness, Line reflected. But also lots of sweet.

"Are they still there?" asked Heather. "Can we go?"

"Someday," said Line. "We should really get all our photographs together in an album. That would be a good summer project for you Heather," she said. She felt sleepy and lazy in the heat which didn't seem to dissipate.

"So Dad," said Stephen, moving into the office, which was cluttered with big desks and tables piled with file folders. Bookcases lined the walls. "I'd really like to get in touch with Bayard Rustin while I'm here.

While I was working on my A.J. Muste book, I wanted to learn more about Rustin. Do you know him?"

"Sure," said Poppa. "He's been working with the International Rescue Committee. Also Freedom House in Washington. But I know him through the IRC, through Leo Cherne. If he's in town, I bet he would meet with you."

"Do you know how to get in touch with him?" asked Stephen. "I'm thinking about my next book."

"I can check with Leo," said Poppa. "He's sure to have Rustin's number. I think Rustin lives somewhere in Manhattan."

Rustin was in town, between humanitarian missions. During the week, Stephen followed him around. Rustin was about to leave for the Philippines where refugee camps were beginning to fill with Cambodians, Vietnamese and Laotians. Poppa did not have many Indochinese clients. His clients were largely dissident Russians, Jews and Armenians who were pouring out of the USSR at a rate of 50,000 a year.

Line spent some of the time in the kitchen with Sadia, but she also tried to occupy the kids. While she was chopping vegetables or talking to Sadia, the kids drew and colored on the dining table. Line felt marooned. It was just like being at home, without the resources. The old Brooklyn brownstone was like a ship, sailing in choppy waters. Inside it was serene, a big old house party going on. Outside it could storm or bluster, but if you had food and things to do, you were fine.

Poppa helped. He took Line and the kids to a Brooklyn library, and they brought home a load of books. The long flights of stairs in the house were a novelty to Christy, almost a room in themselves. He sat on the stairs, reading *Hardy Boys* mysteries.

One day they went to Prospect Park, which had a playground but was also dirty and scary. It wasn't kept up any better than Battery Park. "There's just no funds," said Poppa. Another day he took Christy to the Metropolitan Museum of Art, which Christy had read about.

Fern and Ivy made one corner of the guest room into a "hospital." Line ripped up a sheet into bandages and showed Fern how to make splints and dressings, how to make a sling for a broken arm. Thereafter, the dolls, and sometimes Ivy, often appeared with bandages wrapped around their heads or arms. A goulish red crayon marked the blood from the injury. "What happened to you?" asked Poppa. Big eyes looked up at him. "Car accident," was the answer. Or "Fell out the window."

Line and Sadia took Heather and Christy to the Indian Market. The little girls were left in Poppa and Ashik's care. "Don't worry, Line," said Poppa, holding up the little bandaged Ivy, laughing. "What can go wrong?"

Sadia wore an attractive flowered scarf over her head, which she pinned to reach around and cover her neck and her front. "Hijab" she called it. They took two buses crammed with people of all kinds, sweating in the heat. Line held firmly to a beltloop on Christopher's jeans and Heather's hand.

The market was full of barrels of spices and huge bags of unusual items Line had never seen before and could not imagine needing. It smelled wonderful. Coriander, turmeric, cumin, black mustard seeds. Sesame, fenugreek and saffron. There were also soaps and ayurvedic remedies, colorful saris and dishes. Part of it was a deli and produce market piled with unusual vegetables.

Line hovered over the ayurvedic remedies. Sadia came up to her. "We use these too," she said. "Except it is a little different. We call it Unani. It is based on balancing the humors, the elements in people, like Ayurvedic medicine."

Line looked at Sadia, rather plump like herself, but at least ten years older than Line. Sadia looked a little sallow to Line, but she was also far from her natural environment. Line used a person's skin as a gauge of health. "Is your daughter studying Unani?" asked Line.

"We are very lucky," said Sadia. "She got a scholarship into a university. So she is studying Western medicine. But we must go back to Bangladesh. Things are very disorganized there, and education is poor. They need us. But things are getting better."

"Do you miss it?" asked Line.

"Every day," said Sadia. "Like an ache." She collected big bags of rice, lentils and peas and measured out quantities of spices, as well as coconut oil and nuts. "We must take a cab home," she said. When she asked the man behind the counter to call her a cab, Line noticed she used English. "I am happy your father-in-law likes our food," she told Line on the way home. "We agree we do not want to eat pork!"

"Poppa is lucky to have found you," said Line. "He was lonely before you came." She saw though, that Poppa was the most rooted person she had ever known. He was connected everywhere. The Mikkelsons were transients by comparison, always moving to new small towns in which everyone else had settled long before. Line herself had picked up stakes and moved to California without a backward glance. By this time, Santa Cruz was home. Many of the people Line knew in California had come recently. They were like each other.

What would it be like to live in the same old house for 50 years Line wondered. To watch things come and go, and change around you. She was also thinking of her own ancestors, who had come by ship to New York and kept on going until they got to the farm land available in the Midwest. How hard it must have been to uproot themselves. None of them could go back. No one did it unless it was necessary. It was necessary for me, thought Line.

At last the week was over and Line found herself in sandals in her own garden in Santa Cruz in the evening, watering after supper on a hot, dry day. She moved from shrub to shrub, picking off brown leaves and opening up space where one plant shaded another. The rosemary was thriving. Sage, oregano and mint had all been given sunny spots. The water from Line's hose brought out the smell of the herbs and soil in the heat.

Heather picked purple flowers off the fuzzy borage to make flower fairies for Ivy and Fern. "Don't take too many," said Line to Heather. "Borage seeds itself if we let some of the flowers dry." The little girls' shadows were long across the grass, already thin and browning.

The week in New York had felt long to Line, but now it was like a dream. Had they really done that? Had she been cooking in Poppa's basement kitchen with bars on its windows only two days ago? Quick changes in environment made you see things more clearly, thought Line.

The Cohen's own house in the northern part of Santa Cruz, between a freeway and a woods, felt open and fresh after the hot, muggy East. We live in a desert, Line realized. No rain during the summer. Her plants had to dig down deep to find water, or store it for themselves. Line watered the potatoes and onions, beans and carrots, squash and tomatoes she had planted. The timing of their return was just right. The vegetables were just beginning to push up and beg for water.

The girls in the garden, Christopher visiting his friends nearby. Line had never appreciated her home so much. In the middle of the back lawn, the fruit on the apricot tree was ripening. Line reached up and felt some of the apricots to see whether they were ready. Pink blush was developing on some. One of the apricots came off in her hand.

"Fern, Ivy, Heather," Line said, holding it out to them. "Try the first apricot?"

Line felt around in the tree for ripe fruit, wondering whether there might be enough for an apricot pie. Probably not that day, she thought, but soon. Soon there would apricots everywhere. Line thought about her drying system, a series of screens set up in the garage. She had not had good luck with it last season, but this was another year! She hoped for enough fruit that some of the dried ones would turn out well.

A few days later, when apricots had begun crowding onto the surfaces of the kitchen counters, Line announced, "Okay, today we make pies!" She and Stephen were having coffee and toast. Heather was awake, putting peanut butter on her toast. In the summer Line let the kids straggle in as they pleased in the morning.

"I'll bet you could make a pie, Heather," said Stephen. "Will you make one for me?"

"We'll make some tarts," said Line. "And I want to try some with the pits in them. I've heard they change the taste of the pie. I want to see for myself."

"Are you thinking about laetrile?" asked Stephen. "I've been reading that it's all a hoax." Laetrile was a manmade substance said to stop cancer cell growth, similar to what was found in apricot pits. It had not been approved in the United States, but people went down to Mexico to clinics to ingest it.

Line made a wry face. She was more open to alternative cures than Stephen, but she was also practical and believed in her own observations. "I'm not going to crack the pits," said Line. "I just want to see what they taste like baked in with the apricots."

"Cyanide in them," said Stephen darkly.

"Don't worry!" said Line. "The Hunza people and other mountain cultures where apricots grow hardly ever have cancer."

"Yes," said Stephen, "but they also don't eat processed food and get a lot of exercise!" He stood up and began making himself a peanut butter sandwich to take to the university library where he would spend the day.

"Take some apricots," begged Line, watching him put his lunch together.

Stephen put a few apricots in his paper sack, put on his backpack and strapped a little band around his trouser leg so it wouldn't get into the gears of his bicycle. "Have a fine day, my darlings," he said as he kissed first Line and then the top of Heather's reddish-blonde head.

Line stood up and began to clear one end of the table. She measured flour, salt, butter and oil together and began cutting it with two knives to make a pastry. Since Ivy was now big enough to play with her sisters, Line didn't feel a need for any help that summer. She let Christy roam, as long as he came home for meals. The little girls were easy. All Line had to do was shop for food and keep things reasonably clean. The water situation was much better now, and she worried about it less.

Christy looked sleepy, but sweet when he arrived in the sunny kitchen. He put granola in a bowl and poured milk on top of it. "Have an apricot!" Line said, smiling. "You could take some to your friends today. Everyone doesn't have an apricot tree."

Christy nodded sleepily. Line wasn't sure what the boys were doing. There were three of them that she knew of. Probably making forts of one kind or another now that it was nice enough to be outside all the time. She was pretty sure the well-off Summerwoods were traveling during summer, which left the field of Christy's friends more level.

"So Heather," said Line. "Do you want to try this?" She showed Heather how to hold the knives and cut the flour into the butter and oil. Heather tried, but wasn't as energetic as Line. "I'll finish this one, and start another one for you," Line said. "We should make one pie that is all yours."

By evening, Line and Heather had made two large pies and several small ones in tart pans. Some were seasoned with nutmeg, some with cinnamon and one had cream in it. The pie that had pits in it was marked with a 'P' which Heather had pricked into the pastry with a fork.

After dinner Line cut slices of pie. "Please get the ice cream," she requested. Christopher took a tub of vanilla ice cream out of the freezer. Line dished out pieces of pie, making sure Ivy and Fern didn't get any pits. Line and Stephen, Christy and Heather tried thin pieces of each kind of pie.

"The one with the pits in it is definitely darker tasting," said Stephen. "I think I prefer it."

"Me too," said Line. "The other one tastes high and insipid beside it." She beamed at Stephen.

Heather fastidiously ate one spoonful at a time, tasting. "I can taste it," she said.

"I can't," said Christy, spooning big heaps of ice cream and pie into his mouth.

Line looked at them indulgently. "I wish we could send Poppa a plate of pie," she said. "I don't think he gets very much fresh fruit. You kids should count yourselves lucky." There were also few fresh vegetables in the dishes Sadia served.

"California kids," said Stephen. "'Course, now that we have Proposition 13, they won't be so lucky," he said sardonically. "It's going to cut all the money out of the schools up and down the state."

"At the university level too?" asked Line. Proposition 13 had loomed on the political horizon for quite a while and had just been passed.

"Absolutely," said Stephen. "Taxpayers revenge. Schools are financed by property taxes, and Proposition 13 severely limits them."

Line sighed. "There's always a worm in the apple," she said. "But our taxes will be less too," she said reasonably. "We'll just have to put our savings into our own educations."

"If they still teach history after all the cuts, and I still have a job," Stephen said bitterly.

Line looked at him. Having seen his Bedford-Stuyvesant home, she felt she now knew a lot more about his ominous worldview. "Well we'll cross that bridge when we come to it," she said firmly.

Stephen stood up and put his arms around Line's neck. "You are absolutely incorrigible," he said. "Incorrigibly optimistic!" He looked around at his four kids who gawped at them. "I guess that makes you kids lucky," he smiled.

"We know Dad," said Christy, with a hint of sarcasm.

Line laughed at him. She was so glad to be home!

28

Paul and Marie parked their little pickup near the side of a sandy road and walked out into the woods, looking at the low bushes under the pines. "This looks like the place," said Paul. The undergrowth wasn't very dense, as if it had been cleared out by fire or logging not so long ago. Tiny, wild blueberries were not hard to find on every bush.

Paul leaned down and picked a couple. "They like acidic soil," he said. He took the top off the plastic ice cream bucket he had brought and began to pick.

"They're so delicate," said Marie. "They've got a frosted look."

Paul looked up at her against the blue of the sky, the tall pines, holding a blueberry out to him. "You look like the perfect northern girl," he said. Marie was tanned and dark, in a red gingham shirt and shorts, hiking boots on her feet.

"It's a lot like Quebec here," Marie said. "Without the judgment!" She had many older brothers and sisters, and parents, spread through the farming country along the St. Lawrence River. Paul hadn't met any of them yet, but he and Marie hoped to go to Quebec in the fall.

The air was dry and fresh-smelling. Paul moved through the light shade, the sun giving just the right amount of heat. It was mid-July and the mosquito population had subsided. Paul picked as he went, blueberries falling with a satisfying thud into his plastic bucket. Marie headed in the other direction. Have I ever been happier, Paul wondered. He doubted it.

It was Mother's idea, as usual. She had heard about a wild blueberry patch on a road about five miles from the cabin on Lake Michigami. There were always a few at the edge of the bog near the cabin, but not exactly enough. Mother was hoping to make a pie, or two pies! The Californians were about to arrive.

Paul and Marie had been living in the beach house below the cabin for two weeks already. They had driven the little pickup with its camper shell on top across Canada, stuffed with their few possessions. Paul had set his heart on moving to Ely, Minnesota, perhaps working for a canoe outfitter. But neither of them was worried. Paul had some savings and Marie could get work anywhere.

For the last few weeks it had been just Mother, Paul and Marie at the cabin. But tomorrow the California Mikkelsons would come with their families, and Kristen, Hanna and Dad would arrive soon. The only one of Paul's immediate family who would not be there was Ellie. She and her husband and two girls were in Chile. They would likely come in August. Aunt Rose, from whom Mother and Dad had bought the cabin, would not come until later either. She was 73 and now felt the rigors of life in the woods, Mother said.

"What do you think?" asked Marie, coming up to Paul and showing him her mostly full ice cream tub.

"Looks like a pie to me," said Paul. He lifted his, which had about the same amount of berries. "I think we can call it a morning."

"We should leave a few for the bears," said Marie, smiling.

"I have seen black bear here," said Paul. "On the other side of the lake. Deep in the woods once, with Dad. A mother and two gamboling cubs."

"I know," said Marie. "You've told me." She put an arm around Paul's waist as they walked back to the pickup. "Is it surprising I never saw bear in Alaska?" she asked.

"You have to be out in the woods," said Paul. "We had a big guy worrying that construction site I worked on in Tetlin, but that was the summer you left me, and all I could think about was you." He stopped and gave Marie a full frontal hug. "Can't believe we've made it this far. That you've been willin'."

"'I've been from Tucson to Tucumcari, Tehachapi to Tonopa,'" sang Marie softly. "Don't think Ely, Minnesota's gonna stop me." She kissed Paul's lips with her soft ones.

Back at the cabin, Mother stood up from the little loom where she was weaving textured cottons and said, "Great! Do you want to make the pies, Marie? I've got Betty Crocker pie crust mix. It's pretty easy."

"Sure," said Marie. "I can do that."

Paul had been impressed at how well Marie got along with Mother. But everyone got along with Mother. She enjoyed new people. Marie warmed to Mother's generosity and liveliness. Marie's own mother was reported to be dour and exhausted.

"The Californians' plane lands around 5 p.m.," said Mother. "Which puts them here maybe around 8 or 9 p.m. Unless they stop for dinner." Paul could see how excited Mother was. She did not see her grandchildren every year. Paul had not even met his new nieces. "Tomorrow we'll shop for food," she said.

The summer had been relaxed. The craft barn which Dad and Paul had put up a few years ago had not progressed much past their initial work, because Dad was now working on winterizing the cabin. There was never much extra money and he was actively planning for retirement. He wanted to put an extra room on the cabin, enlarging the family's living space. When he finally retired and was at the lake full time, he would finish the barn.

Dad and Mother were thrilled that Paul and Marie had moved back to Minnesota and would be more available. No big project was planned this summer, except that Dad was building a stairway from the lower level up into the interior of the cabin. Previously one could only go up and down by entering from the outside. "Won't work in the snow," Dad told Paul, smiling. Wood for the Ben Franklin stove, the water pump, some of Dad's library was now in the basement of the cabin. There was also a tiled and finished room which was dehumidified and used as a bedroom during the damp summers.

By the next evening, Paul could tell that anticipation was getting to Mother. After their light supper, she didn't even try to weave. She sat reading in a rocking chair, looking up hurriedly any time Paul walked by. The shadows were long and the evening breeze came sweetly in through the screened windows. Mother's like me, thought Paul. A calm exterior might mask seething excitement!

Paul and Marie went down to the dock and stood watching the sun, which set into puffy golden clouds on the western side of the lake. Pink and purple colors took over the sky and turned the gently rolling surface of the water opalescent. A loon fished about 100 yards off shore. Disappearing while he swam under, he came up to warble his eerie song. Paul's ears were cocked for cars crunching on the gravel up above, or voices and slamming screen doors. But nothing happened.

Paul and Marie went up to the quiet, lamp-lit cabin. Something about being so far out in the woods amplified experiences. In normal life, people came and went and the quick pulse of life didn't hang very heavy on anyone. But here, in the damp, fecund forest, in an outpost cabin along the shores of a lake, time could elongate, or compress. It didn't have the force it did during the school year. Paul was grateful. It had been a long time since he had let time have its way.

"Tea, Mother?" asked Marie as Paul put out the chess pieces. She poured hot water over tea bags in ceramic mugs and passed them around.

Marie was a competent chess player. Neither of them took much time for it in the past. Paul made no attempt at strategy and just enjoyed the game.

"Check," said Marie, looking up at him teasingly as she moved her queen into position.

Paul was flustered. He did not like it when Marie beat him, which she sometimes did when his mind wandered. But he was also pleased with her. Marie's queen was far down the board. Paul couldn't do much without jeopardy.

"Where are those guys?" asked Mother, standing up and going to the screen door. The clock above the refrigerator reported 11 p.m.

The plan had been for Hanna to meet the Californians at the airport in her car and take Line and some of the kids, while Erik rented a car and brought the others. "Do you think they're having trouble?" Mother asked.

Paul tried to look at it from their point of view. "More people make things harder," he said. "Luggage; kids are hungry; they don't know where they're going."

"I know," said Mother, gently. "But I did think they would be here by now."

Marie poured more hot water into the tea mugs. Paul yawned. He was more relaxed than he had been in many years, he realized. Soon he would have to swing into action, find a place to live, work, a new life. But not just yet.

"Nine people I don't know," said Marie. "Paul has told me stories about Line and Marty, and Hanna," she said. "But then Line has all those kids! And they have husbands!"

"I don't think you'll have much trouble keeping them apart," said Mother. "I haven't seen the little kids for a couple of years. Kids change so much as they grow."

"The kids will all be asleep when they get here!" said Marie.

Just then Paul heard a car crunch on the gravel outdoors.

Mother, Marie and Paul went out into the dark to look. The porch lamp threw a pool of light which got dimmer close to the woods. It was Hanna, driving the impossibly long Plymouth with a cargo of little kids who stumbled out into the light, prodded by Line and Hanna.

"Oh my goodness," said Line, getting out of the car. "It smells just like it did when we were little. Piney, wet forest humus. Do you smell it Christy? Come on Heather," she said.

Mother was counting. "I'm missing one of the girls," she said.

"Fern," said Line. "Fern is coming with Stephen." She carried a sleepy Ivy. "I'm so excited to meet you Marie," she said. "This is your aunt Marie," she held out each kid's hand as she said their names. "Ivy. Heather. Christopher."

"Come on in!" said Marie holding the door open. "We want to see you in the light!"

"Hurry! Don't let the mosquitoes in!" said Hanna banging the door shut.

Paul watched as Hanna and Marie took each other in. Both of them were the youngest kid, both singers and performers. Marie was dark and full of latent energy, but Hanna's skin was as pale, as ethereal as Paul remembered, her face beaming. Hanna lived in Minneapolis, was going to a

Lutheran college right in the center of town and working at a theater that summer.

"Why are you so late?" asked Mother, hugging Line. "Did Hanna get lost?"

"A little," said Hanna. "Things look different at night. And we stopped to eat."

"I hope the others aren't far behind," said Mother. "Should we wait for them, or do you want to get these kids to bed?"

"It's a special day," said Line. "Let's not rush anyone. We'll wait for Stephen and Fern, and Marty and Erik. It doesn't matter how late it is."

"We made wild blueberry pies for you," said Mother. "They've been sitting here waiting!"

As everyone stood about talking, another car pulled in, headlights moving slowly up the two-lane track. Paul went out to greet the newcomers.

"We're so late," said Marty hurriedly. "I'll just run in and say hello. The resort people will be mad at us."

"Oh, come on in," said Paul. "They've probably put out a key for you by this time. Don't worry. Let Erik come in and say hello!"

"Quite a place you've got here," said Erik, getting out of the driver's seat. Tousled curls fell over his forehead and he smiled as he held out a hand. A foolish grin came over Paul's face as he greeted Erik.

Stephen lifted his lanky legs out of the back seat. Paul had met him in Alaska, years ago. Stephen was a sandy-haired academic, a grown-up version of Christopher. He carried Fern, who looked shyly out from his arms. When Stephen set her down, Paul could see she was tall, with spindly legs, looking to be about five.

Everyone talked at once, standing around in the dim midnight light in the cabin. Mother would have served blueberry pie with ice cream right then and there. But Line wanted to put the kids to bed and Marty and Erik needed to get settled in the resort cabin at Point of Pines Erik had insisted on renting. Paul helped collect the Cohen's luggage from the trunk, Christopher at his elbow.

"We'll see you tomorrow," Marty waved goodbye, looking wistful. Point of Pines was just down the road.

At last everyone was salted away, and Paul and Marie went down to the beach house which jutted out almost over the lake. The windows on all three sides of the tiny house, just one square room, were open, screening out mosquitoes, but not the wind in the soughing branches, the waves gently lapping the pebbled shore beneath them. The effect was like living in a tree house.

The graceful web of an orb-weaving spider under the eaves shown delicately when Paul turned on the light. The spider hung, head down in the center of the wheel-shaped web. Marie had named her. "Shall I leave the light on?" asked Paul. "Do you want to watch Charlotte?" The spider's abdomen was puffy. She must be getting enough to eat.

"No, thanks," said Marie, who was already under the covers. "I'm too tired." She smiled, turning her head on the pillow. "So many people!"

Paul turned off the light and lay listening to the night noises, the lapping water, stirring wind and birds stumbling about in the undergrowth.

That week there was lots of coming and going, greetings, talk, and cooking. Christopher took to following Paul around. No one tried to get much done besides taking care of kids and meals.

Kristen brought her husband Scott Michael, and Frodo, the black Labrador who had gone to live with her on her farm in northwest Iowa. Kristen was visibly pregnant, a little wan and weary, but obviously thriving. Her husband was young and not very talkative. Scott smiled genially, his face dark from the sun while the white skin on the dome of his head shone. From his farmer tan, it was easy to imagine him spending days, weeks on tractors.

Dad drove up from Iowa where he had been attending to pastoral duties, his little green Volkswagen Rabbit stuffed with things Mother had asked him to bring. His energy was contagious. He brought a heavy mill for grinding wheat and other grains to make bread. Kristen and Line lost no time in using it.

Paul planned an all-day canoe trip for Christy and Marie. Hanna and Marty would take the other canoe. "It's probably my only chance," said Marty. Her husband Erik was often out exploring the surrounding area, only intermittently turning up to be with the family.

The two canoes left early on a calm morning, paddling the mile and a half across the lake into the eastern sun. Paul took the helmsman's position in the stern. Marie was happy in the bow, paddling energetically, letting Paul steer.

"You'll get to paddle when we get across the lake," Paul told Christy, who sat in the middle in a little padded life jacket. "You don't want to get dumped in the lake," Paul told Christy. "Trust me!" Paul paddled powerfully, keeping the canoe perpendicular to the gentle troughs. Paul was proud of Marie's strong strokes. He needed her help to cross the deep part of the lake, where the fetch of the wind was stronger.

Paul felt responsible for the other canoe too. He noted that Hanna took the steering position. Marty was older, but Hanna was more experienced. The canoes were very close to the water, but Paul was comfortable. Dad's light canoes were just his size, making his body wilderness-capable. These canoes could carry a pack, Paul thought, but could also be portaged.

They headed toward the reeds which hid the channel flowing between Lake Michigami and the Bucket lakes. Beyond them, water spilled into a marshy bay before ending up in the huge Leech Lake which dominated north-central Minnesota.

The lakes were all high that year, and so was the channel. Thick reeds left a wide and welcoming path. Leaving the big lake the two canoes, one after the other, entered a narrow peaceful stream where the water was so transparent they could see everything down to the golden sandy bottom. Pine trees stood on the sand banks. Sand this fine was rare. When picking rocks around their dock, Dad had built a jetty, but it hadn't made much of a beach.

"Let's pull up," said Marie, looking at Paul. "I want to lie in the sun a minute." She took off the cotton shirt she was wearing, revealing a halter top.

"I can't do that," said Marty ruefully. "I'd be red as a beet in about five minutes!"

"Me too," said Hanna. "But I really want some sun." Hanna jumped into the water, pulling their canoe up onto the bank.

Paul did the same, the hot sand squinching under his bare feet.

"This is surely the life," said Marie, lying down on the clean golden silt and smiling at Hanna who lay down beside her.

Paul and Christy waded at the edge of the water, watching the thin green perch, their backs striped with black, swimmng around a submerged log covered in algae. "One year I saw a lot of turtles here," said Paul.

"I'd like to see a turtle," said Christopher.

A school of tiny blue minnows slid past. Paul hadn't seen many this year. Lake Michigami was definitely less clear than it used to be, he thought, affected by acid rain from the East. It was full of soupy green algae now, but still noted to be among the clearest lakes in Minnesota.

Paul coached as they put the canoes back in the water, Marie in the middle and Christy paddling. Christy was thin and tall for his age, but had a powerful little arm. Paul could feel the pull of his paddle. "Good work!" Paul told him.

They pushed on into the Little Bucket lake, a round pond. The log pile of a beaver dam rose out of it. "You can't see the door in a beaver's house," Paul explained. "He swims under water into his lodge, but inside there's a dry den above water where he can breathe and sleep."

Paul steered over to the edge of the lake, showing Christy where a beaver had chewed off young poplars. "Their faces look like they are all teeth!" said Paul.

"Can I see one?" asked Christy.

"They are mostly nocturnal," said Paul. "This lodge looks like it's old. I'm not sure how many years." Farther over, on a log at the edge of the water, in the sun, however, Paul noted a big, black turtle. "Hey!" he pointed it out. "Somebody's taking a nap!" It looked like a rock.

"Can I touch it?" asked Christopher.

But Paul was inclined to leave the turtle alone. "Animals are for observation," he said. "We don't want to bother them. They have fewer and fewer places they can get away from us. This is an old grandpa, I think. We shouldn't disturb him."

Little Bucket was less protected from the wind than the sunny, warm channel. The sky grew overcast as they paddled back into the calm stream with its pine trees on either side. Once again the two canoes pulled up on the sandy bank and Marty and Marie unpacked the sandwiches, fruit and thermos they had brought. The sand was still warm, but the sky was heavy, the air oppressive and wet.

"Looks like rain," said Paul. It was not good to be out on the lake in the rain. You did not want to be the tallest thing on the lake, a human conductor. Luckily the canoes were mostly fiberglass. "We'd better not waste time getting home."

Everyone packed up and got back in their canoes. "Hug the shore when you go back," Paul told Hanna. "Less chance of lightning." Christy looked at Paul with big solemn eyes. "Don't worry," said Paul smiling as he directed Christy to the middle of the canoe. "We'll be fine. You are a great paddler, but I think Marie should finish the trip."

It was hard going as they emerged from the protected channel onto the windy lake. Paul could see that the wind was whipping up white-capped waves. He angled the canoe against the waves, which were not as rough at the shore. Taking the long way, Paul steered along the shore on the northern side, rounding Preacher's Point. Paul looked around to see how Hanna was doing, but she and Marty were not even in sight!

"Marie!" yelled Paul. "Do you see Hanna and Marty?"

Marie looked around too, but the other canoe was nowhere to be seen.

"I think they went the other way," said Christy. "I saw the wind blowing them by the reeds."

Paul froze. There was no other way except across the lake. If they had gotten blown along the northern shore in the other direction they would not get home. Surely Marty knew that, even if Hanna didn't. Paul felt instantly responsible. He should have waited, should have followed Hanna. He could not see anything up and down the lake that looked like a canoe. His best bet was to high tail it for home and send out the motorboat, he thought.

"Heave ho, me hearties," said Paul. "Let's get home as fast as we can and alert the others." Paul paddled hard and so did Marie. They wended their way along the shore, past the iron creek, past the pine-covered hillside where new cabins had sprung up. When they got close enough, they could see someone on their dock. It was Line with a pair of binoculars, watching for them. Two of the little girls were down on the dock with her. The air was thick and wet, but not quite raining.

"Line," yelled Paul across the water when they were a little distance away. "We lost Marty and Hanna. Can you ask Dad to go out and look for them?"

"Okay," said Line, training the glasses on the far horizon. "I haven't seen them either." She turned to go up the hill, taking the little girls with her.

Paul brought the canoe masterfully in toward the dock and held it for Christopher to get out. Christy ran up the hill after Line. As they were tying up, Paul heard Hanna's voice. And there she was, meeting Line on the path half way.

Tension slid off Paul. "What happened to you guys?" he yelled. "Is Marty okay too? How did you get here so fast?"

"We got blown back by the wind," said Hanna, with some nonchalance. "I didn't think we could make it, so we pulled up at a dock on the other side and the people there drove us home."

Paul looked at Marie and laughed. "Well that just shows you!" he said. "There's more than one way to skin a cat!"

"We were so worried when we realized you weren't with us any more," said Marie as she and Paul dragged the canoe far up on shore and turned it over out of the coming rain.

"What did Dad say?" Paul asked. He did not usually try to solve his problems by asking other people's help. And neither would Dad.

"He said we could go over and get the canoe tomorrow," said Hanna placidly. "Kristen's making chocolate chip cookies! Come on up!"

Paul looked at Marie significantly. "She's a different generation than you," Marie said, linking an arm around Paul's back. They followed Hanna, who raced up to the cabin on her thin, pale legs.

"Not really," said Paul. "She's twelve years younger than I am. But she's almost from a different family. There are three families of Mikkelsons," he said. "The first was Ellie and Mom and Dad. And then there was Line, Marty and me. Sparky and the gang, Dad called us. And then there is Kristen and Hanna."

"It's like that in my family too," said Marie. "I was the tail end of the donkey, coming after everyone else was up on their hind legs. The not-very-welcome surprise."

"Hanna was very welcome," said Paul. "Mother dotes on her. But her world is different."

Fifteen people drank coffee and ate cookies in the cozy, warm cabin which smelled like baked brown sugar and butter. Even Erik had shown up and Marty hung on to him possessively. Paul asked Marty quietly how she felt about being led around by her youngest sister.

Marty laughed and shook her head. "I love Hanna," she said. "But, if I were in charge, I think I would have managed to get home under my own steam. Hanna's method worked. The people were perfectly happy to help us. We were a long way from home, straight across the lake!"

"Wonders never cease," said Paul softly.

In the failing light Mother turned on the lamps and sat down at the little organ. She could never bear to part with it, so it came up to the lake on a trailer in the spring, and went back to the parsonage in Iowa at the end of summer. She pulled song books out and began to play, Hanna coaching her on what she wanted to sing. There were hymns and old favorites, spirituals and folk songs. Paul joined in with his clear tenor and so did Marie.

"I'm not sure this is going to happen when you come to Quebec," Marie whispered to Paul. "It feels a little too good to be true."

"It won't last," said Paul, deprecatingly, though he did feel proud. "It's all due to them," he indicated Mother and Dad. "There's room for all of us in their big, spacious hearts," he said. He felt tears welling up. None of us kids make it easy for them, he thought. But somehow, Mother and Dad find the space.

Connie Kronlokken

296

ACKNOWLEDGEMENTS

The author would like to thank her siblings, cousins and friends who have shared in the experiences of which this is a fictionalized account. She thanks Raven Lang and Paul Lee, of Santa Cruz, who allowed her to use their real names. She would also like to thank Susan Korn, who took the cover photo, and Don Starnes for his cover design. For his support throughout the project, she deeply thanks Don.

Connie Kronlokken

ABOUT THE AUTHOR

Connie Kronlokken grew up in a large Norwegian/Danish Lutheran family. She spent her childhood in small towns across Minnesota, North Dakota and Iowa. In 1969 she moved to the San Francisco Bay Area and now lives in Los Angeles with her husband Don Starnes. Connie studied filmmaking in Denmark and has been a student of yang style tai chi for 25 years. She loves being with her family, the march of the seasons, cooking and gardening. She's been parsing romance from reality for most of her life.